NIKI
UNLEASHED

NIKI UNLEASHED

A Niki Undercover Thriller

James M. Jackson

First Edition
Trade Paperback Edition: November 2025

Wolf's Echo Press
PO Box 54
Amasa, MI 49903
www.WolfsEchoPress.com

This is a work of fiction. Any references to real places, real people, real organizations, or historical events are used fictitiously. Other names, characters, organizations, places, or events are the product of the author's imagination.

ISBN-13 Trade Paperback: 978-1-943166-50-3
ISBN-13 e-book: 978-1-943166-51-0
Library of Congress Control Number: 2026932124

Printed in the United States of America
10 9 8 7 6 5 4 3 2 1

For Jan, alpha, omega, and all the letters in between.

ONE

HOLDING A CLANDESTINE MEETING AT a venue with 40,000 screaming fans was not the craziest thing Niki had done in her undercover work. It wasn't standard protocol, either. FBI Deputy Director Ambrose had insisted only three other people know of their ultra-secret relationship. Yet the ticket he'd sent her was for a suite that, according to the Washington Nationals website, held nineteen people.

If he planned on double-crossing her, this was the kind of venue the Bureau might choose. But if this was her first sub-rosa assignment under their agreement, she wanted to set him straight on a few rules. Either way, fun and games.

She showed her ticket to a gate agent.

"This is for a Jefferson Suite on the first-base side. We're Center Field. You can use the Media and Suites entrance."

"Oh gosh." Niki touched the older woman's arm and rolled her eyes. "Silly me. It's my first time in one of those Fancy Dan suites. I'm more a bleachers girl myself. Well, I'm already here." *Which I did intentionally to make sure no one was following me.*

The woman returned her ticket and motioned her toward the next person, who searched her cross-body bag, missing the thin ceramic knife hidden in its false bottom. A third person wanded her body for metal, not that she could hide anything in her little black cocktail dress that showed a glimpse of cleavage and a lot of leg. The guy didn't check her head, where she could have hidden contraband under the blond wig with the French braid she'd chosen for tonight, and he didn't bend down to check her black trainers.

Amateurs.

Waved through the gate, Niki took two steps and stopped. To the world, she might appear confused or disorganized. She memorized faces of the nearby crowd while she fumbled with the clasp on her bag before storing her ticket.

The air was festive with merry voices, upbeat organ music, and the smell of grilled food. She matched the pace of those around her, scanning for threats: familiar faces or anyone acting strangely. Once she reached the vicinity of the suites on level three, she kicked her threat detection into a higher gear. She stopped, reversed direction, apologized to the couple she nearly bowled over, and memorized the nearby faces, then reversed direction again to join a long concession line. No one hung around during the ten minutes it took her to purchase a Nationals ball cap.

Snugging the cap on her head, she followed signs to her assigned suite, the next to the last on the first-base side. A placard outside the door welcomed her to the AHI Executive Committee. What, she wondered, is AHI? She engaged the recording app on her phone, slipped it into her bag, and pulled out her ticket.

Inside, the waiter, a six-footer fit enough to be on the playing field, rearranged the sparkling glasses next to the hot buffet. "I wondered if anyone was gonna show."

That struck her as a strange first comment. She acted the dumb blonde. "This is suite seventy-two, right?" She held up her ticket.

"It surely is. Can I get you a beer? Wine? Help yourself to the food. First come, first served. You want the TV on or are you a purist?"

She followed his pointing finger past a polished table for six to the TV fixed to one wall, screen on, volume barely audible. Tucked in the corner near the food and refrigerator were another table and chairs. Outside the suite were two empty rows of padded blue seats overlooking first base. Her gaze automatically drifted to the second baseman finishing his warmups.

"I'll wait for the others before I have anything." She wandered toward the outside seats and second-guessed her decision. The suites on either side were active, with more than half of their outside seats occupied. Sitting alone would draw attention. She shook off the shiver that ran up her spine. What the hell was going on here? Where was Ambrose? She retreated from the windows. "This a regular gig for you?" she asked.

His eyes flicked up, and he fiddled with the glasses again. Something was odd. She gave him a closer look. His haircut looked fresh. Solid face, clean-shaven, late-twenties or early thirties. Moving, his buffed body rippled beneath the Washington Nationals polo shirt. Pressed khakis led her eye down to polished oxfords.

"I work wherever I'm assigned. It's my first time in this suite."

"Oh yeah? What's your day job?"

He laughed. "Studying at Georgetown Law School. What about you?"

She amused herself speculating what his reaction would be if she said, Former FBI Special Agent—now nominally a U.S. Marshal being paid off the books to work undercover. "Restrooms?" She'd seen them but had no problem acting like a typical ditz to buy time.

He motioned in their general direction and appeared relieved that she'd broken off the conversation. She retreated to the sanctuary of the ladies' room. Sure, she was on edge. It had been more than ten weeks since she and Ambrose had made their agreement. Thus far, they had paid her for sitting on her ass and doing nothing. She'd become more and more convinced her new "assignment" was only a bribe to shut her up. Now she'd find out. Maybe.

Like a lightning bolt, she realized the guy was FBI, working undercover for Ambrose. She checked her image in the mirror. She'd hidden her Midwest pallor under makeup to give the impression of an aging party-girl with a great tan. Contact lenses brightened her eyes from hazel to pale blue. Shadow and eyeliner made them look bigger. The sunbaked crinkles at the corners of her eyes combined with the anxiety shadows she had created under them added a decade to her thirty-six years.

Unless someone knew her well and saw her up close, they'd never recognize her. That was one of her superpowers, not the waiter's.

Through the walls came the sounds of a soprano belting out the National Anthem. Niki removed her cap and stood at attention until the singer finished to a roar from the crowd. Why had she ever thought this relationship would work? Because she wanted to—no, had a fierce drive to—bring bad guys down, and Ambrose had offered her a path after her former boss torpedoed her FBI career. That, she reminded herself, was the goal.

Get off your fucking high horse, Ashley, and play the hand they dealt you.

She straightened her shoulders and pushed through the door. "When did you attend Quantico?"

A deer in headlights couldn't have looked more startled than this guy. Not undercover material. Where had they found him? She followed his look and discovered Ambrose had arrived while she was in the head.

Two

Ambrose's chuckle broke the tension. "Busted, Steve. Thanks for holding down the fort until I could get here." He pulled a ticket from a shirt pocket. "Consolation prize. Box seat right behind the visitor's dugout. Enjoy the game."

Niki read confusion in Steve's eyes. Not what he was expecting, but he accepted the ticket with a cheerful, "Thank you, sir," and left without a look back.

Ambrose said, "I learned I would be late and asked Steve to make sure you didn't leave. He's safe. He went through Quantico a few years after you, and I checked that your paths had never crossed. Have you eaten? I'm starved."

His idea of safe and her idea of safe did not have a lot in common. "I'd rather you explained why I'm here."

He lifted the covers of the serving dishes, releasing scrumptious smells that triggered her mouth to fill with saliva. "Looks good. You were a four-year starter at UCLA. Second base. Three national championships. You look fit enough to still play. I thought you would enjoy a ballgame. I know it's not softball, but—"

He was clueless. "That's not what I meant. Has something happened at Patriots For Freedom? Did Colonel Pete reappear?"

Telling the truth wouldn't require him to stall, but he did. While he pulled a domestic beer from the refrigerator and filled a plate with a sampling of the items, she studied his appearance. He had swapped his nondescript suit for nondescript khakis—similar to Steve's—and a pressed oxford shirt open at the neck. He stood a few inches taller than her five-six. Wedding band on his left hand; the right devoid of ornaments.

The guy was not a gym rat and had gone a little fleshy around the neck. Sharp eyes hid under bushy eyebrows and missed little. In his mid-fifties, he was the kind of guy you'd walk by without a second glance. If you weren't careful, he could suck you in with his good-ol'-boy honey-sweet drawl.

She reminded herself to keep that in mind.

He stepped aside, inviting her to take some food. She shook her head and motioned him toward the tables. "Suit yourself," he said. "Patriots For Freedom shut down your old unit, and the other units have gone silent.

Your Colonel Pete is deep underground—one way or the other. No clues who burned down his country estate or trashed his in-town house."

Meaning tonight didn't relate to PFF. Alright, time to lay down the ground rules. "Have you ever run an undercover agent?"

"At least join me at the table. We can catch some of the game. I promise to answer every question you ask."

Niki's eyebrows rose in disbelief. With a moment's reflection, she realized he had deftly deflected her question. The honey trap of "truth."

He smiled at her expression. "I know. It's D.C. Promises are cheap, but I keep mine." His smile grew wider. "Promise."

He sat at a table, his back to her, leaving her the seat across from him with a view of the entryway. She pulled the chair away from the table, sat on its edge, ready to spring at any trap, and waited for his next move.

Ambrose washed down a couple of bites and broke the silence. "I couldn't have you come to my office. Since you no longer have an FBI badge, you'd have to sign in. And we don't want your N. Iki Marshals Service badge recorded on the official register. By the way, your friend Rick never told me what you thought of the name he picked. He seemed immensely proud to figure out that play on words."

Pain in her heart blossomed at being reminded of the day Ambrose had forced her to resign from the Bureau, swept her badge into a desk drawer, and offered her a secret deal to work directly for him and Assistant Director of National Security Park. A few days later, Special Agent Rick Kaska had shown up with a Marshal's badge, which allowed her concealed carry and the ability to arrest people. She didn't plan to tell Ambrose that Rick's off-the-wall recommendation to use her favorite undercover name, Niki, and convert it from a first name into an initial and last name, had pleased her.

She walled off the pain to deal with later. "It's a fine placeholder . . . until we have a specific assignment, at which time we'll create a whole new identity. What is this about?"

"During the seventh-inning stretch, you'll meet a friend of mine who's in the next suite. I'll brief you before he arrives. But first, the food's good, we have the game to watch. I was sorry to hear about your father and brother. How are—"

He was changing the topic, but his first pitch was out of the strike zone. "The deaths of Robert and Bradlee Pendergast do not concern us. What should concern us is you breaching our security setup. We agreed to have Rick act as a cut-out between us. You contact him. He contacts me. If you can't contact Rick, you go through his backup, my friend Seamus McCree. That protects my identity. I won't be successful if everybody and his brother knows I'm working for you. Having Agent Steve here introduces an exposure point. I almost didn't come. Damn good thing I wore a disguise."

"But you did come."

And that may have been a mistake. "Because you need to hear directly from me how important this is. And frankly, I'm bored out of my skull." She blew out a long breath of air. "Right now, you are treating me more like a source than an undercover asset. Maybe you don't know the difference. You can squeeze a source because you hold something over their head. You can tell sources when and where and what, and they have to comply because otherwise something bad happens to them. You can write things like 'dress appropriately' and a source has to swallow the insult. A UC operative is a member of a team dedicated to a common cause. You may not like all your team members, but you treat them with respect. I am *nobody's* source."

Well, crap, Ashley. Tell him how you *really* feel.

He set his knife and fork on the plate. "I'm sorry. I screwed up. Will you accept my apology?" He offered his hand across the table.

Regardless of the final outcome, she must appear to accept his apology. She grasped his hand and gave it a single firm pump. "Did your file," she gestured toward his attaché case, "mention that I tend to be direct?"

His smile crinkled his eyes. "I seem to recall something concerning an abrasive personality, lack of decorum, refusal to follow guidelines and procedures. Of course, that was just your fitness report for your first UC assignment. The one that got you transferred to the backwaters of Mississippi. Despite that, with your talents and hard work, you forced your return into good graces. Look, Ashley, if I wanted a smooth politician, I could find plenty to kiss my ass. Your history describes an agent dedicated to taking down bad guys, a woman with a terrific record of success who was being chewed up and spit out by a grinding bureaucracy. And, I might add, whose bosses tended to step on their dicks because you showed them up. I want us to succeed. As a team."

A roar from the crowd drew their attention to the field. The Nationals led 1-0.

His drawl thickened. "It was not my intention to treat you as a source. Tell me how I can change that."

Niki eased farther back in the chair, two feet still on the ground ready to move. "Where to begin?" she mumbled to herself. "First, you can't use my real name. If you do, you'll slip around other people. In any communications between you, ADNI Park, Rick, Seamus McCree, and me, I should be referred to by my file codename, Beorn. Here's a secret about great UC operators. We don't role-play, we *become* the person from our deep background, the details of which have to be comprehensive and bulletproof. That takes time. If we have to meet, you *must* think of me by whatever undercover persona I have adopted. For today, we'll use Niki."

"All right, Niki. Points taken. But for what I am proposing, we don't have time to develop a deep background."

THREE

IT'S LIKE HE DIDN'T HEAR a thing I said. "If we don't have time," Niki enunciated each word to control her temper, "it's a disaster waiting to happen. I'm not the Secret Service sworn to throw my body in front of a target and take a bullet, and this isn't some novel where magic occurs off stage during a scene break and everything is designed for the hero to succeed—after overcoming a shit-ton of unforeseen obstacles."

"Niki, we're on the same side. You won't do the country any good if you're dead. May I tell you about the situation? It involves a radical group that splintered from Greenpeace. Call themselves Greenwar. They espouse violent means to achieve their objectives. Their Midwest group publishes the *Blame and Shame* blog." Ambrose removed a yellow folder from his attaché and placed it and five red files before her. "Each of the five victims was featured twice in the blog, once before and once after their deaths."

Following Ambrose's presentation, Niki summarized the material spread on the table in front of her. "Someone is killing senior executives who retired from some of the biggest polluters in the United States. The President's donors are running scared, and the President is pissing all over the FBI because you haven't solved the crimes. These people have nothing in common with the militias I've infiltrated. There's nothing I can leverage from any previous assignments. I can see no reason you even thought to come to me. What am I missing?"

"Terrorism is your thing and these people are domestic terrorists. The Alcohol, Tobacco, Firearms, and Explosives Bureau has an undercover agent who can introduce you to them."

"If ATF has a guy in place, why do you need me?"

"He's there because of the explosives they've used for their ecoterrorism. He's not trained in murder investigations. Secondly, women run Greenwar, and he's a he and you're a she." He leaned back in his chair as though that sealed the deal.

"And what? You want me to join them in the restroom because they trade secrets in the stalls?" *Back off, Niki.* "This—"

"Look, it's not just the president who's interested in solving this. Greenwar's blog called out my best friend from high school. He's exactly the kind of target they've killed. This is personal for me. Jim and I have an idea about how you can gain entry. I'll let him tell you when he gets here.

You're trained. You're experienced. You have the time. And you are creative and adaptive. For example, why did you choose that particular outfit?"

Another diversion. "Why did you write dress appropriately on the ticket?"

"Your training taught you that you learn more by asking subjects open-ended questions. Same thing." He cocked his head.

"You used it like an open-ended suggestion to let me fill in the blanks. What did you discover?" She shimmered her hands down her body.

"That you're not answering my question."

Talk about black pots and kettles. She could play this game. He who speaks first loses. To occupy her mouth, she nibbled on a gourmet brownie. Her knees went weak with the pleasure of its rich chocolate taste. She might take a doggie bag. On the second brownie, she won.

"Okay," he said. "Tell me if I get this right. You researched the Jefferson Suites and found pictures of business types and wore your little black dress to fit in with whatever gathering I had planned. You bought a new ball cap, which you could use to dress down or throw away if no one else was in fan wear. Sneakers are comfortable, and you're too smart to wear heels if you don't have to. Your wig and makeup disguise you, make you hard to recognize. How am I doing?"

"Close. Working undercover, you look for escape hatches in every situation. This dress has the added advantage that it won't slow me down if I have to run, and the trainers give me good stability."

His body language suggested this was not the answer he expected. "Why would you think you might need to escape?"

"If you were reneging on the deal we made and double-crossing me, this would be a perfect place to take me into custody. A place you thought I must be unarmed. Your agent Steve could have a few friends ready to appear at your call."

His face fell and he blinked several times. "That never crossed my mind. I understand why you might not trust the Bureau, but I see you don't trust me either. I asked and now I know." At a crack of the bat, he swiveled to catch the action on the field. "Let's watch a little baseball." He waved toward the field. "We're down a run with two men on and one out. Do you sacrifice? Bunt, I mean."

Sacrifice was an interesting choice of words. Despite his assurance that she wouldn't do him any good dead, she wondered if it was a Freudian slip.

Four

WITH THE SCORE TIED 3-3 going into the bottom of the seventh, Niki stretched, sucking in the energy from the packed stadium butchering A-ha's "Take On Me." A knock sounded at the door, and an older gentleman dressed in a cashmere sports jacket entered.

She recognized the face, the mane of gray hair, couldn't come up with the name. Chairman, CEO, something of one of the big international oil companies. He and Ambrose hugged. The guy indicated her with a tilt of his head. "This your agent?" Like she was a slab of corned beef or something.

With hand stretched out, she interrupted the bromance. "I'm Niki. Or if you don't like first names, you can call me ma'am."

"Jim Ford," he said. "Thank you for your work."

Whatever the hell that meant. She'd give him credit. He gave her a firm handshake, didn't hold on too long or do the power move of touching her arm with his other hand.

Ambrose ushered them to the table away from the windows. "We've talked, but you need to sell her on the cover we planned for her."

"Oh," he said. He fiddled with the American flag pin on his lapel, gears recalibrating behind his deep-set eyes.

"Let me be perfectly frank. Even though the blogger mentioned my name, I'm here because it's our civic duty to help in any way we can."

In other words, you're scared shitless that you're next. "My cover?"

"Right. I'm the chairman of American Hydrocarbons Institute. AHI is the world's largest—"

"Jim," Ambrose said, "you're not recruiting a new member."

The gears behind his eyes clicked again. "So, Niki, what we thought . . . " His arm sweep included Ambrose in the we, "was we make you my special assistant at AHI, give you access to files that Greenwar would find interesting. With that currency, we thought you—"

"Jim. I get it. You're worried you have a target on your back. AHI special assistant won't do. Too many loose ends. Can you hire me, or must it pass through HR? Whose noses will be out of joint when you show up with a special assistant? Desk or cubicle? My own extension? Are there employee lists I need to be on?"

Ambrose cleared his throat. "You know that if we follow regular FBI procedures, we can't get any operation up and running for at least three months. The embedded ATF agent will be arrested later this month along with several of Greenwar's activists *before* they blow up a pipeline. AHI is a small organization. We can make it work."

"I'm not saying I'll do it, but the only way this *might* work is for Jim to personally hire me to become his assistant. You worked for a multinational. I'm fluent in Mandarin and Spanish. How can you use those skills and provide me with information I can take to Greenwar?"

Niki wondered if Jim's furrowed brow was because he was trying to figure out a workable cover or he was worried about the personal expense.

He said, "What does it matter if it gives you an excuse to possess the documents?"

She blew out a long breath. "So, Niki," she drawled to sound like Ambrose while mirroring Ford's language, "tell me how you spend your day working for Jim Ford. What do you do when he travels? How did you come across this document? Where does he keep files like this? Is there a way we can raid his office and get them all? So on and so forth."

Understanding sparked in Jim's eyes. "Personal assistant it is. I'll set you up in the AHI conference room next to my office. That allows you to match real names to real people and learn their real reactions to you. Half of them will be annoyed that I didn't ask them, and the other half will think I hired you to cover up an affair. How about researcher for an autobiography? I had projects in South America. The environmental reports and official government correspondence will be in Spanish."

Niki offered a smile. "Stick with translator." To Ambrose she asked, "What's the status of my current assignments with Benedict Arnold and Sonic Boom?" She hoped he remembered the code names she had insisted he use for her assignment infiltrating the Patriots for Freedom militia and her work with the Chinese arms dealer.

"They are both in limbo. We think this is a more urgent need."

Of course, "we" did. Oil and gas and coal bought elections. Militias mostly loved the current President, to the extent they loved any government. She ignored Jim and lasered her glare at Ambrose. "If this jeopardizes continuing my earlier work, I can't accept the assignment." She rose. "I'll show myself out."

Ambrose stayed seated and laid a hand on Jim's arm, preempting his rising. "I thought your life's purpose was broader than one militia. I didn't select you because we wanted a source. You have the skills for this opportunity and one thing no one else in the world has. Availability right now. Maybe we'll be lucky, and they won't kill anyone before we can install another agent. Did you notice the murdered individuals have been past CEOs or board chairmen? Jim's both. And the interval between blog publication and the subject being murdered is getting shorter. Can you live with Jim's death if you do nothing?"

The bastard didn't get to be Deputy Director of the FBI without learning how to push people's buttons. It wasn't that she was limiting herself to one militia, but she was the only one who had an in with that particular militia and with their Chinese weapons supplier. It might take years for the Bureau to develop another UC with equivalent intel.

If she were still in the FBI, she wouldn't have a choice. Now she did and with choice came consequences. She was unwilling to give up her work with PFF, but she could only do that work if she stayed in Ambrose's good graces, and that meant making this abomination of an assignment work.

She let silence be her answer.

Ambrose said. "Greenwar has several cells spread across the U.S. We hope you can use material Jim provides to develop an in-person meeting. As Jim said, we can find reasons for his assistant," he finger-quoted assistant, "to be anywhere. If you need to be in St. Paul to take care of your fath—take care of that personal business, we can arrange that too."

The weight of that personal business pressed hard on her shoulders. *Focus on the issue at hand.* She returned to her seat. "Do I have your word that if Benedict Arnold revives, we will pursue that if at all possible?"

"Yes." Ambrose offered to shake her hand.

"And the same if Sonic Boom makes contact?"

"Even more so." Ambrose extended his hand a little farther.

"And I can pull out if I think this assignment's cover isn't adequate to protect me without it negatively affecting our other . . . um . . . agreements."

"I'm sure the cover will work," Ambrose said.

She had already conceded that her Patriots for Freedom infiltration was on hold, but on this point she wasn't yielding an inch. She gave him her best hairy eyeball.

"Yes."

She took his hand. "So we're clear. If you lied to me. I will destroy you regardless of what damage it causes me. You still want to shake?"

He pumped her hand. "Has anyone ever told you that you negotiate like a porcupine?"

Jim Ford pushed his chair away from the table. "I should get back to the gathering next door before the game ends. Here is my personal cell number." He placed a card on the table between them. "May I add your phone number to my contacts list? What name shall I use?"

With no time to create a detailed backstory, she had to choose one of her current undercover roles. The Niki persona used for the Patriots For Freedom involved someone who thought both political parties were out to line their pockets and those of their big business friends, like Jim, at the expense of regular folks. She could see that morphing into radical environmentalism after she "discovered" evidence of corporations hiding the truth about the harm they caused ordinary people.

She gave Jim Niki's cellphone number. "Label it Niki Foster. N-I-K-I. Call me now and I can grab yours." Seconds later, a technobeat sounded from her bag. She retrieved the phone, rejected the call, and entered his number under "Boss."

"I'm in D.C. the rest of the week," Jim said. "When can I expect to hear from you?"

"The deputy director and I have a few issues to work out," she said. "I'll call tomorrow."

"Thank you, Niki," Jim said. "I look forward to working with you." With a last glance at his watch, he hurried from the room.

"What's that ringtone?" Ambrose asked.

"It's from the trailer for Wonder Woman 1984."

"Naturally," Ambrose drawled. His face brightened. "I have an operation code name picked out for this assignment: Svalinn. What do you think?"

"That you have the cart before the horse. But I'll bite. Who or what is a Svalinn?"

"From Norse mythology, it's a shield that protects the earth from the sun burning it up. You are all that stands in the way of people dying."

FIVE

AT TEN-THIRTY THE NEXT MORNING, an elevator delivered Niki to the entrance of American Hydrocarbons Institute's lobby on the sixth floor of a K Street building. The left glass door proclaimed the institute's name in black script. A chemical representation decorated the right door, a hydrocarbon, Niki assumed. Inside, a middle-aged receptionist, who was so made up she looked plastic, welcomed her. Niki wondered if her own all-natural wool go-to-FBI-headquarters pantsuit was a fashion faux pas in a place that promoted polymers and other unnatural creations. At least her American flag lapel pin matched the twin flags flanking the woman's monitor. "Please tell Jim Ford that Niki is here."

"Oh yes, he told me to expect you." She gave Niki the once-over. "I'll have his assistant collect you. Excuse me, I didn't catch what firm you work for."

"I work directly *under* Jim." She waggled her eyebrows. The receptionist's eyes widened at the double entendre. Niki offered her a knowing smile and was amused by the blush tingeing the receptionist's neck and face, its heat releasing a whiff of citrus from her perfume.

Mission accomplished: if anyone asked the receptionist if she had ever met Niki, they'd get an earful.

While she waited for someone to collect her, Niki inspected the stunning wall decorations. "Acrylics," the receptionist said. "Everyone thinks they're glass."

Nothing, Niki thought with irony, in this room is what it seems.

Mrs. Dover, Jim Ford's assistant, introduced herself. She ushered Niki into his office and asked with a glacial tone if Niki wanted coffee, tea, or a soda. Niki declined and Mrs. Dover hovered at the door. Jim waved Niki to a seat and asked his assistant to please shut the door.

This office was a quarter the size of the one at Pendergast Holdings she had inherited in June from Robert Pendergast. Ford's was furnished in what she thought of as Scandinavian: light wood, walls a light beige. The desk was a minimalist affair with a polished surface and curved legs. An eight-foot-long credenza under the window made up for the lack of desk drawers. On her right, floor-to-ceiling built-in cabinets covered the entire wall.

She appreciated the ten-by-twelve Persian rug patterned with blues and golds with a swath of deep red that brought the only color into the room. It delineated the relaxed sitting area to the left of the door.

"A gift from the Saudis. Beautiful work, isn't it?" Jim Ford said.

"Spectacular." She settled into the chair and crossed her ankles. "Your assistant seemed frosty. What did you tell her?"

He fiddled with the American flag on his lapel before answering. He'd done that at the ball game, too. A nervous tell?

"She's known me more than twenty years. I could tell she wasn't buying that you were helping me with my personal investments, translating documents and the like for a possible South American opportunity. I switched and said I was writing a memoir. You are my ghost writer."

Great, now she'd have a suspicious assistant watching her every move. She tuned back in to Jim saying that he had granted her unlimited access to AHI's files.

"Having unlimited access is fine. The rest of your idea sucks. Why would a ghost writer require AHI documents, especially those Greenwar would find interesting? Now she'll watch me like a hawk. Not to mention, it will take her two seconds of questioning me to realize I know nothing about ghost writing your autobiography. Once you set me up for today's work, you will inform her you were pulling her leg. You really do want help translating Spanish documents for your personal finances. If you can't do that, we have nothing further to discuss."

His eyes widened in shock, then narrowed in annoyance. Arms rigid, he glared down his nose at her. She framed her expression to be neutral and brought up an image of sunrise in Glacier National Park to settle her racing heart. This was on him, not her, but she needed him to come to that conclusion himself.

After what seemed like an hour, but was fifteen seconds tops, he said, "I think you negotiate more like a grizzly bear than a porcupine. Top predator who goes about her business but will roar when necessary. I screwed up. I'll fix it." He slid a pile of folders from a corner of his desk toward her. "I found six documents you can use for bait. They're in English and cover different areas of the country and different environmental aspects. I'm sure one of these will be . . . I should say, I hope one or more of these will work. Let me grab some documents written in Spanish to fit our story."

He searched through files stored in the credenza and added three to her pile. "These are harmless, but they're in Spanish to meet your cover."

She offered a single nod to show she appreciated his move from boss mode to a more cooperative approach. "Early this afternoon, I meet the ATF agent our mutual friend mentioned to learn what makes Greenwar tick. I'll evaluate these given what I learn and let you know if I require something different." Preferring to sound more collegial and less grizzly bear, she added, "Sound like a plan?"

Six

THE ATF AGENT WHO WAS to be her introduction to Greenwar had specified a spot in the rear of a Starbucks, and the damn table was right under the air duct. She'd arrived fifteen minutes before the scheduled meet, her clothes tacky from August's heat. Now her perspiration had frozen from the arctic blast blowing on her neck. To stave off hypothermia she had already downed a hot drink. Now her fingers tapped an urgent beat on her thighs. The ATF guy was late. Niki hated late. It was disrespectful. He'd better have a damn good reason because in two minutes she would have to order something else to justify her presence. And not a damn thing on the menu that tasted good had fewer than 48,000 calories.

She checked to make sure she hadn't hidden the paperback copy of *Cowboys are my Weakness*—the token to let him know she was his contact. She counted down from 120.

At seventeen, a fit-looking guy, square jaw, goatee, moseyed in her direction, steel eyes scanning the tables. At hers, he pointed to the book. "I could be a cowboy." His fifty-if-he-was-a-day eyes crinkled in assured invitation. "Or," sounding like John Wayne, "a gunslinger."

She narrowed her eyes and folded her arms across her chest. "And I could be Wonder Woman. But I'm not. I'm waiting for a friend."

"I could be your friend."

Was the asshole blind or testosterone stupid?

"It's Niki, right? Sorry I'm late. I'm Mike." Without waiting for her reply, he placed a to-go cup on the table, settled onto the opposite seat, and leaned in, speaking in a low voice. "I wish bosses would talk to us peons before they make promises they can't keep. We have two days for me to introduce you before the playbook calls for me to be arrested."

Niki closed her eyes and shook her head. Ambrose had said later in the month, which she had taken to mean she had two or three weeks to prepare. She slow-tapped her thighs to bring her patience. "Why the rush?"

"To paraphrase Alfred Lord Tennyson: Someone has blundered. Ours not to make reply. Ours not to reason why. Ours but to do and die. What I hear is the Federal Bureau of Incompetence set up a big elaborate operation to get one of their agents to cozy up to Greenwar, but Greenwar rejected the guy. And now some genius decides to try using the Marshals Service." He pointed at her. "Looney Tunes, you ask me. If I were in your shoes, I'd run for the hills. Here's an offer, one UC to another: if you decide they've sent you on a suicide mission, I'll scuttle the meeting in such a manner they can't blame either of us."

Now Ambrose's urgency made sense. The Bureau had probably been overstating their progress in their reports to the president and with their UC operation blowing up, their privates were hanging out in the breeze. Given that, Mike's gesture was generous, but meaningless. Ambrose would blame her, pure and simple and might use it as an excuse to sideline her.

Given her life might depend on Mike, she wanted answers and fast. That meant open spaces where she could confirm no one was watching or listening in on their discussion. "Nice day to stroll the Mall." She gathered her items into her backpack, slung it over her shoulder, and walked out, holding the door until he caught up.

A breeze had kicked up bringing with it a bite of discomfort. They chatted about weather and tourists and everything and nothing until they were well into the Mall, where Niki stopped at a bench to retie a shoelace. Using the shoe to shield her pointing finger, she said, "We've got a tail. Blond woman with a camera she hasn't used."

He broke into a wide grin, jumped onto the bench, and signaled the woman like an umpire ejecting a player from the game. "You're good. If I thought you'd be a risk to me, I'd shut you down so fast you wouldn't know what hit you. Now that we have that out of the way, what did they tell you about Greenwar?"

His testing her showed a survival instinct she appreciated. Now she needed to suck him dry of information and for that she chose a vague truth. "I gather it's a loose collection of individuals who spun out of Greenpeace. My boss thinks one of them is killing people."

"We know of several cells. Not sure how much national coordination they do. It appears to be led by women but has members of both sexes. My contact is the daughter of the person who runs the Midwest. On Sunday, she's expecting to buy a shit-ton of explosives from a guy I introduced her to. We'll call him X. Other agents had X under tight surveillance and determined he's acting on his own. The plan called for picking up X and his explosives on his way to the meet. That would keep my undercover role intact to find out if the whispers I heard of another explosives source are accurate. Everything was going smooth as silk until X and the explosives disappeared."

Their stroll had brought them opposite the Smithsonian castle. Niki acted like a gawking tourist, stopping to take a picture with her cellphone. "Meaning they'll raid the meet, assuming it still takes place?"

"Exactly."

Niki let loose a long sigh, "This gets better and better. Have the Greenwar people mentioned the murders?"

"They've discussed the *Blame and Shame* blog in my presence and their plans to target those named individuals with protests and such. Killing them? Not a whisper. That's not exactly surprising, but given two different weapons have been used, there may be two killers."

Mike clapped his hands to scare off gathering pigeons. "The planned raid puts us in a bind. The only time before the raid we can meet the daughter, who is possibly one of the killers, is tomorrow. She and I are meeting in Minneapolis. From there, she's taking me to meet her mother at her camp in remote Northwest Wisconsin. I'm supposed to present my plan to disrupt a major pipeline without causing an environmental catastrophe. That's our only chance."

She was beginning to like Mike. "And all we have to do is figure out how I know you, why you know I have information that will be valuable to them, and why you would bring me to this meeting. Piece of cake. What motivates them?"

By the time they reached the Vietnam Memorial, they had a plan she could accept. Almost. "The only reason I'm agreeing to this is because you and I will be together. Something goes sideways, we have each other."

"Wouldn't do it any other way. See you tomorrow at noon."

SITTING IN THE AHI CONFERENCE room, Niki analyzed the six possible bait items Jim Ford had given her. Each one looked promising until a simple internet search showed the information was already public. By four o'clock she had verified that everything Ford had given her was useless.

She activated her phone's recording app and tucked the instrument into her front pocket. Carrying the files, she prepared to battle Ford's administrative assistant to break into whatever meeting he was in.

The administrative assistant was gone and her station in front of Ford's corner office looked like a cyclone had struck, papers helter-skelter covering its surface. Niki knocked on the door and stuck her head into the office. Ford was on the phone and held up a finger to signify he'd be a minute. She plunked down into one of the comfy chairs, closed her eyes and visualized standing on the shore of Iceberg Lake in Glacier. With each breath, tension released from her neck.

Ford got off the phone and joined her in the sitting area. "Is the meeting set?"

Niki breathed in the calm of Iceberg Lake. "I apologize for popping in. We didn't discuss office protocol. The good news, from your perspective, is I meet Greenwar tomorrow."

Ford beamed.

"But the bait you gave me is worthless crap. I found all the same material through internet searches and legally accessible court records. I need something nonpublic to bait the hook for tomorrow's meeting. This contact is especially interested in open-pit mines, toxic waste dumps, and the like. We, meaning you, have one and only one shot. Whatever I go in with must be so powerful they have no choice but to accept me on face value. I'm your new assistant. I'm shocked by the cover-up I discovered, and I want people to pay a price for illegal, immoral activities. You know where the bodies are buried. What have you got?"

He slumped in his chair and looked like he had swallowed a frog. "That's a problem. You need this exactly why?"

"To convince them I'm their Deep Throat," Niki said. "I'd prefer it was from the Midwest, but I'll take whatever I can get on short notice. Something like a groundwater pollution study that isn't public would work well." Ford's eyes widened. "Or a courtroom strategy concerning a pending suit." Ford shook his head. "A sealed settlement with a nondisclosure clause."

Ford adjusted his American flag pin. "What would that do?"

The flag pin fiddling gave it away. He has at least one of those. "*Bona fides,*" she said. "It shows I can get my hands on important inside information they can use in their campaigns against you."

Ford tilted his head. "How against us?"

Time to remind him of the stakes. "You can bait a hook with a plastic worm, but it never works like the real thing. I need a big fat juicy worm, or I'll never get close to them again. But," she offered an exaggerated shrug, "it's your life being threatened. You've got something. Give, or I call Ambrose and tell him I'm out."

SEVEN

ASHLEY CHOSE A WINDOW SEAT for the 9:45 pm flight out of D.C., which allowed her to pull down the window shade and avoid visual reminders that they were flying over water. She dry-swallowed a beta-blocker and prepared to perform a deep dive on the material she had extracted from Jim Ford.

Minutes before midnight the rideshare dropped her off in St. Paul at what she still thought of as Robert Pendergast's house, even though Robert was dead. Two months ago, her half-sister, Tabitha Maki, had inherited the stone mansion on River Road and had christened it "Legacy House." Tabitha had set aside a room for Ashley's use and given her an open invite to use the place whenever she was in town. The car turning into the driveway triggered the motion-sensor lights. She thanked the driver, slung her loaded backpack over her shoulder, and inhaled a deep breath. *You're not ten. He's not alive. You want to be here.*

She pushed open the hinged gate, marched up the path to the solarium, and punched in the security code on the outside pad. The pad sounded an angry beep and flashed a red light at her. She dug her cellphone from her knapsack and shook it to engage the flashlight. She carefully punched in the digits for the birth date of Robert's ex-wife. Error. She consulted her phone's address book—the code was what she thought she had entered. It was late, she was tired, the beta blocker was keeping her distress in check, letting her think through the options. She had one more chance to get this right before the alarm woke up the neighborhood. A shiver wracked her body. She'd forgotten how cold Minnesota could be on a clear summer night.

All right Ashley Pendergast Prescott, what will you do if this doesn't work because someone changed the passcode and didn't tell you? She scrolled down to find the "secret" phrase necessary to tell the security company to cancel the alarm and not call the police. Checking each digit as she punched it in, she sucked in her stomach until it pressed against her backbone and entered the eighth and final number.

A siren loud enough to wake the dead signaled her failure.

She dialed the emergency contact number on the keypad, wondering for the first time what would happen if they'd also changed the security phrase. She stuck her finger in one ear, held the phone tight against her other, and could barely hear the man who answered the phone.

From around the corner of the house, a hand appeared pointing a shaky Sig Sauer automatic pistol at her. "Hands up. Don't move," a female voice demanded.

Ashley raised her hands. Any sudden move might startle the woman into pulling the trigger. Above the alarm's whoops she heard the tinny voice of the security firm's agent, but had no idea what he was saying, and no way to respond. "Easy." Niki projected a steady voice over the alarm. "I belong here. Who are you?"

"Bullshit on that. We'll see what the cops have to say."

The only ones who should be living here were her sister, Tabitha, and her friend Seamus McCree who, like Ashley, had permission from Tabitha to stay whenever he was working on Pendergast Holdings problems. "Fine by me," Ashley said. "Can I talk to the security people and have them silence this damn alarm so we don't have to shout at each other?" She waved the phone.

The woman consented, and Ashley lowered the phone to her ear. "Are you still there?"

"Yes, ma'am. Police are responding."

"Can you please turn off the alarm? The security phrase is *profit margin*."

The alarm shut down, leaving a ringing in her ears through which she heard a dog barking from inside the house. "Thank you. Please stay on the line." She raised her hand back above her head. "I'm Ashley Pendergast Prescott. I have Tabitha Maki's permission to stay here. Who are you?"

The woman covered her mouth with one hand, lowered the pistol, and stepped into the light. From a photograph that had sat on Bradlee Pendergast's desk, Niki recognized his wife, Chloe—correction, widow. When Chloe's shock wore off, she might very well decide to shoot Ashley anyway. With the gun pointed toward the ground, Ashley could rush her. Risky. Instead, she focused on the Sig Sauer—a P365 model with a manual safety still in the locked position.

Ashley returned the phone to her ear. "I changed my mind. There's no reason for you to stay on the line. We can deal with the police when they arrive." Looking in the woman's direction she asked, "Do you agree, Chloe?"

That seemed to get through. "Oh my God. I am so sorry. Tabitha said you wouldn't . . . I thought . . . Well, you're here. You have the security word. You must be who you say you are. We changed the security pad code." She raised the gun. "We—"

"Both of us are shivering. Could we wait inside for the police? And maybe you could not point the gun at me?"

Chloe looked at the gun as if it were an alien form. "Oh shit." She lowered her arm. "I thought . . . Well, that . . . "

She's in shock. "Punch in the new code. I won't look." *And once I figure out what is going on, I can change the security.*

Chloe entered the numbers and led Ashley into a cacophony of a barking dog, two wailing little girls, and a boy holding a tissue to a bloody nose. Chloe rushed to the boy.

Ashley had never met the kids and dredged her memory for their names. The boy was Jacob; the girls were Jasmine and Jenny, but which was which she didn't know. The dog she had met, having taken care of him for a while. "Hey Max, how's my guy?"

Max's bark changed into a whine, his hackles lowered, and his lips relaxed from their curl. The brindled Plott hound plowed into Ashley, dumping her on the floor, and smothered her with sloppy, dog-breath kisses. "I missed you, too, big boy. Can you let me up now?"

EIGHT

THE ST. PAUL OFFICERS SHOWED more concern over Jacob's bloody nose than the false alarm. Chloe assured them her son had been suffering periodic nosebleeds for the last few weeks. The doctor said they'd either go away on their own, or he'd cauterize the blood vessel. Jacob supported her and the officers left.

Chloe escorted the kids upstairs to settle them in bed, promising to return to talk. Max trailed Ashley into the living room and stuck his head onto her lap once she settled in a wingback chair. She wondered what had happened that brought Chloe and her kids to live at Legacy House. It might just be they preferred not living in the house where their father/husband had hanged himself.

Chloe brought in a bottle of twenty-one-year-old Glengoyne Scotch Whiskey and two glasses. "Want some?"

Ashley held up her water bottle. "I'm good with water."

Chloe set the glasses on the table next to Ashley and poured four fingers into one. She pushed aside her phone and Sig Sauer and clunked the bottle down in the cleared space. She sank into the sofa opposite Ashley and sipped her drink. Bit her lip. "My pastor says I shouldn't hate you for ruining our lives. I agree Bradlee shouldn't have done what he did—dating women from the office." Her next sip was larger. "No one is perfect."

Niki controlled her urge to lash out at Chloe's use of the word dating— as if her husband hadn't been a serial philanderer using his position at Pendergast Holdings to bed employees, including the one responsible for the death of Robert Pendergast, her father-in-law, whose house she now lived in.

Chloe continued, "If it weren't for the kids, I would have left him. If you knew Bradlee would kill himself, would you still have fired him?"

A low blow that, but she had wondered the same thing and knew her answer. "Things were extremely confusing with Robert's death. As Interim CEO, I had to make a lot of tough decisions. Had I suspected he was suicidal, I'd have placed him on medical leave and made sure he got help." She left unsaid that she had planned to do whatever was necessary to assure Bradlee never stepped into Pendergast offices again.

Chloe finished her drink. "We were up to our eyeballs in debt but could manage with his job. Without that income, the bank was planning to foreclose. I could have dragged it out, but Tabitha offered to let us stay here."

Niki drank a glug glug of water to give her time to compose her response. That explained why they were here, but how you could be that deep in debt while making the kind of money Bradlee had made was beyond her ken. "I know they are hollow words, but I *am* sorry for your losses. How old are your kids?"

"Eleven, nine, and seven next month. Tabitha said she or Seamus would give you the new passcode and give me a heads up before you visited."

With a flash of guilt, Ashley remembered leaving unread an email from Seamus on the subject "Pendergast Resident Changes You Need To Know" or some such. "They probably did, but I didn't read it."

Chloe gave her a look that said, "See, it *is* all your fault." What she said, was, "I have to admit, it's a bitter pill to have you here. But it was part of our agreement, and my pastor is right about turning the other cheek."

Niki tensed at the attack, breathed through her nose, and reminded herself she, too, had blamed herself for Bradlee's death. Wiser voices had counseled her that her choice to remove Bradlee from Pendergast Holdings was legally and morally correct. The actions Bradlee had taken were on him, including his final decision to abandon his wife and children by taking his own life. There was nothing more she could say or do here to help Chloe with her grief. "Have you moved my stuff from the room I was using?"

"Seamus has it in his room. That's fine provided only one of you is here at a time, but my kids are too young to have you two sleeping together."

Not your house. Not your rules. Not a battle for today. Max bumped Ashley's hand, reminding her she was supposed to keep petting him. She had one issue to resolve before she prepared for tomorrow's meeting with Greenwar. "Why did you confront me with a gun?"

"I was upstairs and saw the rear security lights go on and stay on. That meant someone or something was still there. I thought it might be one of the assholes trying to collect our debts. You know, do some minor damage to harass me. I was angry that they had figured out I was here. I took my gun and slipped out the front door. It's perfectly legal to protect my children."

"Maybe if I was threatening them. Minnesota doesn't have a stand your ground law, except as a last resort. Have you practiced much with that gun?"

"Bradlee brought me to a range when he got it for me."

"Your model P365 is a sweet little weapon, but it has a manual safety. Because you didn't disengage the safety, your trigger couldn't pull to fire.

Had I been an actual threat, the only person who might have been killed with that gun was you. And then where would your children be?"

Blood drained from Chloe's face. She stared at the gun sitting next to her scotch bottle as if it were a cobra.

Good. "Promise that next time, you'll stay inside and call the police. You saw how quickly they got here. Consider what would have happened if the cops spotted you with a gun outside. Everyone would be at risk."

Chloe's long straight hair hid her bowed head. She mumbled into her lap. "I just don't know what I'm going to do."

"Right now, pour the rest of that scotch down the drain and go to bed. Your kids will be up in a few hours. I want to check email and catch some Z's. Don't know for sure how long I'll be here. A day or two, but I'll try to stay out of your way."

"I'm too wired to sleep."

"Once the adrenaline drains, you'll collapse. Do you have a gun safe or a lock for your Sig?" At her 'no,' Niki wanted to shake her. Three kids in the house, and she hid the damn thing in her underwear drawer? Just because mom didn't know how to disengage the safety didn't mean the kids couldn't accidentally do it. She snatched the gun off the table. "I'm storing this in Robert's basement gun safe until you install a gun safe in your bedroom and are fully trained to use that weapon."

Chloe sprang from the sofa. "You have no right."

Max scrambled to his feet, growling, his hackles raised.

Ashley shushed him and again got him to rest his head in her lap. "Until you know what the hell you're doing with this weapon, your children's safety—and yours and mine—are much more important than your legal rights. Go to bed, Chloe. We can talk in the morning. I have things to do."

NIKI STORED CHLOE'S WEAPON IN the basement walk-in gun safe that housed the one legacy from Robert Pendergast she chose to keep: his gun collection. No time to deal with it now. She locked the door on her guns and her conflicted feelings about Robert. *Focus on preparing for tomorrow.*

Upstairs in the kitchen, she washed the glasses and left them to dry in the drainer. She turned out the lights behind her, which left the first floor dark. Not remembering where the hall switch was, she toe-tapped her way past the ticking grandfather clock to the first-floor office, Max following at her heels. She opened the door and found the room stuffy, all sense of Robert's presence lost under the smell of lemon polish. She flicked on a light and sat at the desk, Max pushing past her legs to lie curled in the kneehole.

An email from Seamus dated ten days earlier gave her the new code and informed her Tabitha had agreed Chloe and her kids could stay here because, unbeknownst to Chloe, Bradlee had saddled their home with a second mortgage that he had not been paying.

Why the hell didn't Chloe understand the couple's finances? Or was she willfully ignorant, like calling Bradlee's behavior "dating?"

During Ashley's marriage, she'd made sure to know where their money was and what they were spending it on. When the bastard had cheated on her, she left, choosing to keep only his last name to avoid future comparisons with the fictitious FBI Agent Aloysius Xingu Leng Pendergast created by Douglas Preston and Lincoln Child. Ah man, all these years later and she could still get riled up over her ex's behavior.

She stretched to clear her mind before returning to the laptop. She recorded the new security code and scanned the other email subjects from Seamus. All related to Pendergast Holdings' projects on which she had requested his help.

She bullet-pointed the key items of the emails.

- Seamus was helping investigators track down the missing money stolen by Junior, who had disappeared after Robert's death and lived in a place without extradition treaties with the U.S.
- Unlikely to recover money—hidden behind a series of shell companies in countries without mutual legal assistance treaties with the U.S.
- Third brother—Garrett, helping root out bribery and kickbacks in his division.
- Seamus had finished recruiting an independent board of directors to implement her instructions to develop a long-term plan to stabilize the company and offer it for sale.

Relieved to have caught up with the emails, she pulled up her text-messaging app. *Seamus, thanks for all your work. Use my voting proxy to install the Board. I'm at the house. Chloe not happy I'm here.*

A response popped onto her screen. *My recommendation. YRU there?*

She checked the time. Three-fifteen. What the hell is he doing awake? *Beorn activated. YRU awake?*

Listening to the ululations of a wolf pack.

Ululations: that was the Seamus she knew and loved. Everyone else would have said howling—and slept through it. She felt a momentary flash of jealousy that he could be out in the wilds at his Upper Peninsula

Michigan home. Who am I kidding? I could do that, but tomorrow I'll be doing what I love. It's the family shit I don't need. *Give them a howl for me.*

Will do. Did they serve you papers today?

She typed three question marks.

Process servers looking for you and me today at Pendergast Holdings. Junior's lawyers want to depose us. They petitioned the court challenging provisions of Senior's estate plan disenfranchising him and Bradlee. Also objecting to your fiduciary decisions—including giving me your proxy.

She slumped in the chair, accidentally kicked Max, who grumbled in his sleep.

Seamus kept typing: *They have to find us first. Don't worry. Biggest issue is the waste of time.*

And, Niki thought, mental energy, of which she had none to spare if she was to survive environmental extremists who killed people.

NINE

ASHLEY WOKE TO THE HIGH-PITCHED shriek only a young girl can make. She reached for her weapon and stopped when she heard giggling and the galloping of kids' footsteps running past her room. The bedroom clock read 8:27. If she had Seamus's money, she'd definitely choose a quiet hotel. But she didn't—well, she did, actually way more than him. It was from Robert. She was trying to refuse it, and she'd be damned if she'd spend a penny of that money.

A steaming shower stung her back and flushed the cobwebs from her brain. Dressed, she padded downstairs barefoot to get breakfast. Her toes curled when the little girl again squealed. She'd been a tomboy and had never used her voice like that. Catching a glimpse of the two youngest kids chasing each other in the side yard with Max in the mix, she wondered what it would have been like to have grown up with a sister.

Chloe looked up from washing breakfast dishes in the kitchen sink. "I'm sorry. I asked them to be quiet. That worked about five minutes, so I sent them outside to try to let you sleep."

More cordial than last night. "I needed to be up anyway," Ashley lied. "They're cute as buttons, those two. From the pictures I saw, your son is going to turn into a looker, too." Embarrassment heated Ashley's cheeks. Bradlee had once been a looker, although he'd gone to fat. Joking about a son's attractiveness was probably bad form. What she *didn't* know about kids could fill encyclopedias. "Did you get back to sleep?"

"After worrying about the bill collectors for a while. There's still a cup of coffee left in the pot." Through clenched jaws Chloe asked, "Will you be joining us for lunch or dinner?"

"Chloe, please stop. I'll try to stay out of your family's way as much as possible. If I'm screwing something up, let me know, and I'll try to fix it. You don't need anything more to worry about. Are the bill collectors harassing you?"

"Before we moved. I stopped answering my phone. Then they started showing up at all times of the day and night."

Annoying phone calls were par for the course for debt collectors, but personal visits were unusual. "The ones who showed up, who are they representing?"

"Gambling debts—markers." She strangled the dish towel. "I sold Bradlee's car and paid them off. Still . . . " She rubbed her forehead with both hands. "I'm dumping on you. Sorry."

Time to eat and get out of her hair. "I'll make myself oatmeal if Seamus left any."

"You eat it with brown sugar like he does? Jacob, my son, loved it. If you don't mind, maybe I can use eating oatmeal with you to pry him out of bed?"

Before the five-minute oatmeal finished cooking, Jacob, still with bed-head and crusts in the corner of his eyes, was seated opposite Ashley, slapping his hand into a baseball glove. At least she had something to talk to him about. "You play baseball?"

"Yeah." His face fell. "I made the traveling team, but that was before."

She knew what the before was, but she wasn't sure what had happened with the team. "What's your position?"

"Third," he mumbled.

"Oh, the hot corner. Good reflexes and a cannon for an arm. My reflexes were good enough, but my arm was not strong enough for third."

He raised his head to look at her. "You played?"

"Second base. I started with hardball but switched to softball in high school."

"Oh." Disappointment dripped from that single word.

Chloe slammed a spoon on the counter. "Jacob, don't be so dismissive. Ms. Prescott earned a four-year athletic scholarship and won the national championship at UCLA. Here's your oatmeal, you two." Chloe placed steaming bowls in front of them.

That Chloe knew about her background was a surprise. That she had defended her was a bigger surprise. "Jacob, what's the strongest part of your game?"

"Defense. Coach says I have the fastest hands he's ever seen."

Ashley nodded to show she appreciated his comment. After she swallowed, she said, "That's a gift, but footwork is what makes the difference. What do you need to work on the most?"

Jacob shot her a look of suspicion. "I just need to get bigger. Hit more home runs."

Jacob's father hadn't been tall and his mother was small-boned. Jacob was not going to grow into a major power hitter. "Home runs aren't everything. Wade Boggs proved that. Hall of Famer with a lifetime three-twenty-eight batting average." She could tell he had no idea who she was talking about. "Look him up. If you end up six-three, then go for the power. But quick hands, good eye-hand coordination, and practice can get you to hit consistently." His look told her he didn't believe a bit of it. Why the hell did she bother? Because the kid just lost his father. Still . . . "You ever play slap hands?"

He pushed his empty bowl away from him. "Never heard of it."

Ashley held her hands out, palms up. "Place your hands lightly on mine. Then when—"

"You mean 'Red Hands.' No one plays with me anymore because they all lose."

Ashley smiled. She never lost at this game, and the only person who could play her to a draw was, surprisingly, Seamus McCree. "A little bet then." She grimaced and shot Chloe a look, but she didn't seem to react. "I win and you have to learn all about Wade Boggs and download and watch the final game of this year's NCAA national softball championship game. If you beat me, what do I have to do?"

Chloe had stopped fussing with the dishes and leaned against the counter with an amused smile. "We're talking consequences, Jacob. Ms. Prescott has told you the consequences of choosing to compete against her and losing. You don't have to compete. That's your choice and nothing bad comes of saying no. But if you decide to take up the challenge, what are the consequences for Ms. Prescott if you win?"

He stuck out his lip. "You mean *when* I win." No one took his bait. He tucked his lip back in and chewed on one corner. "She has to take me to see the Twins, and she has to play video games with me after dinner."

A fleeting narrowing of Chloe's eyes suggested to Ashley that Jacob's mom was not thrilled with his choices. "Well—"

"I accept," Ashley said. "I may have to work this evening, but I'll spend—shall we say three hours—playing your favorite video games whenever I have the free time. And if your mom is worried about you going to the ballpark with a stranger, I'll take the whole family. Fair?"

"Okay, whoever quits loses."

Ashley gave Jacob a wry smile. "I'm not a quitter and I doubt you are either. How about we count touches for three minutes? That should be long enough to declare a winner."

"Deal. Who goes first?"

Ashley liked that he didn't assume he should go first. "You first. Let's give ourselves some room."

They set up away from the table. Ashley held her hands out straight and lowered them to adjust for their height difference. Jacob placed hands palms up under hers and had no sooner made contact then he made his first strike with his right hand. She purposefully didn't move until the very last and let him smack her a good one. She wanted to beat him, not humiliate him, and to do that she needed to judge his speed.

Ashley settled her hands over his. "One for Jacob."

He tried again with his right hand, and this time she let him catch her fingertips. "Two." Jacob tried a third time with his right and came up empty. "My turn." Ashley turned her hands palms up and waited until Jacob settled his hands lightly on hers. "Well, Jacob. Now we get to see whether I can get back those two strikes you have against—" She flipped her left hand over his and caught his entire hand. "—me. Oh, I guess that's one."

"That's not fair. You were talking."

"Is that what you say to the catcher who's trying to distract you from concentrating on the pitcher? No such rule. But since you feel that's taking advantage of you, I won't talk."

They lined up again. This time her left hand caught half his fingers. He was good. If she kept doing the same thing, he'd get better at anticipating. The third time, she used her right hand and caught most of his left. She was up. Time for a miss. She telegraphed a left-hand swipe and came up empty.

Jacob squinted in determination and waited for her to place her hands on his. She watched his eyes, letting her hands sense his movement. A microsecond before he swung, his eyes narrowed. She let him nick her fingertips. Tied up. She stared into his eyes. Again, his eyes narrowed before his hand moved.

"Miss. We're even." Ashley extended her hands. "No talking, right?"

"Right," he said and placed his hands on hers, twitched them back, and settled them once more.

She got him with her right hand and just as he settled his hands on hers, she twisted her left around and got him again.

"Is that fair?" Chloe asked.

Ashley waited for Jacob to answer. "Yeah, Mom. She got me."

Time to up her game. She waited until he had settled, and continued to wait, and waited until she felt his hands grow a little heavier, and then she flipped hers over, catching both of his hands halfway. "That just counts as one. Jacob, you're fast. Not the fastest I've ever played against, but faster than most and that includes pro ball players. But you telegraph your moves. Your eyes tighten a little before you start your move."

If it were possible to look down his nose at her while looking up because she was taller, that was the look he gave her. "Okay. I'm ahead," Ashley said. "You don't believe me. I forfeit my turn until you slap me." She held out her hands. "Go ahead."

He tried and missed. Tried again and missed. Missed a third time.

"Humor me? Try this again, except I'll close my eyes. All I can use is my sense of touch. Fair?"

She lowered her hands, closed her eyes, and concentrated on feeling his hands. She jerked away at his movement, but he caught her two longest fingers. "Good. Try it again, but this time don't think about what you are going to do, just do it."

She lowered her hands, closed her eyes, and he caught a bit more of her hand.

"Again."

He came up empty. "You thought about it that time. I sensed a tightening of your hand before it actually moved." His face gave away the lie he was forming. "Tell the truth. It's the only way to get better."

"Yeah," he dragged it out. "You felt it?"

"When you play third base, you catch the ball and throw from wherever you happen to catch it. You don't think about it, and you don't have time to wind up. Right?"

"Sure. That's what Coach says."

"Reflexes are the same. You do it without thinking about it. Training is about creating muscle memory, so our muscles do what we want without our brains having to get in the way. I have the championship game on my laptop."

"I really have to watch the stupid softball game?"

"Yes you do," Chloe said. "And tell her all about Wade Boggs. Go brush your teeth."

Jacob slunk from the room as only a preteen boy can do.

Ashley cleared the table and washed the dishes in the sink. After Jacob's footsteps sounded on the stairs, Chloe said, "That's the most animated he's been since we moved. He loves baseball, and I hated pulling him off the traveling team, but without the nanny to take him—well, I couldn't justify the cost, given our situation. Anyway, that's not what I wanted to say. I wanted to thank you for going out of your way to be nice to him."

"Jacob's a good kid going through a tough time. He's at the 'I-know-it-all stage.' It will do him good to watch the championship game and see not all girls play like sissies."

The front doorbell rang a four-tome chime. Max barked up a storm. Chloe's smile disappeared. "This can't be good news."

Ashley quieted Max with a pat on the head and slid into the solarium out of sight before Chloe opened the front door.

"Ashley Prescott?" a male voice said.

"No. Can I help you?"

"The kids said she was here. We just need to speak with her for a moment."

Ah crap, the process servers. Ashley slipped out the back door, paid the price of having bare feet when she ran into the alley behind the house to wait until she was sure they had left.

TEN

A COOL BREEZE AND LIGHT drizzle that had soaked her made her as stiff as the Leif Erikson statue in St. Paul, where she had rendezvoused with Mike. In her rush to get on the last plane from D.C. the night before, she hadn't thought to pack a raincoat, and now she shivered under Mike's too-small umbrella.

Mike pointed to a woman on the opposite sidewalk on the far side of the Christ Lutheran Church. "Olivia Jorgensen. Let's meet her at the corner."

Niki stepped away from Mike's umbrella to observe the girl without having to match Mike's stride. Covered by a blue poncho, Olivia walked head down, thumbing her phone. At the opposite corner, she checked the traffic light, saw Mike, and waved for him to cross to her.

Olivia finished a flurry of thumb-typing and shoved her phone in her pocket. Closer to her, details became clear. Unlike Niki's own sharp angles, Olivia was rounded in the places men liked. She encased her legs in skinny jeans with ripped knees. Multicolored socks poked out of well-worn hiking boots with rainbow-colored laces. Auburn hair framed a face with full eyebrows, gold stud in one nostril, red lip gloss and closed lips that made a slashed underline below the upturn of her slender nose. Her dark eyes had the thousand-yard stare of a druggie. Or aggravated teenager. Or psychopath.

Mike and Olivia fist-bumped. "Niki, I assume," Olivia said. "You're older than I expected. We've got a long drive. You can fill me in on the way." She spun on her heel and walked away.

Niki shuddered from a chill she did not think came because of the rain. Olivia didn't sound or act like a teenager or druggie.

AT HER RAV-4, OLIVIA PULLED the poncho over her head and shook it out. She pushed her auburn curls behind her ears. Niki glimpsed a tattoo on Olivia's wrist of an upraised fist, a green version of the Black Power symbol.

"I'll take the back." Niki hopped in before anyone could object and dropped her knapsack on the seat next to her. While undercover, she never wanted to be in the position of having someone sitting behind her. It was too easy for them to pull a weapon or slip a garrote over her head. She had no reason not to trust Mike, but it was a safety measure she did not plan to abandon.

Olivia tossed her poncho into the back seat, told everyone to buckle up. Glancing over her shoulder at Niki as she reversed from the spot, she said, "I tried looking you up online and couldn't find you."

Mike stiffened. "No surprise," Niki said. "I'm not on any social media. Too much negative energy. I bet you found the woman running for Congress, right?" At Olivia's nod, Niki continued. "She spells it with two Ks. My mother used only one. N-I-K-I." The folks at the FBI who had created her backstory had worked hard creating search engine de-optimization that pushed inquiries away from Niki and toward those with the more traditional double-k spelling. Niki was pleased it was still performing well.

Olivia paid the parking fee, exited the garage, and was soon on I-94 heading east. Following Mike's lead, Niki kept her eyes forward and didn't speak. Wet wool scented the air. Not unpleasant, unless you didn't like sheep.

Once Olivia made it through the downtown curves, she shot a look over her shoulder at Niki. "Remind me how you two know each other."

And the interrogation begins. "Pure happenstance. We use the same shooting range. A buddy of his egged him into challenging me to a contest. I managed to edge Mike. Since then, whenever we're both there, we have a little friendly competition." She punched Mike's headrest to let him know he should jump in with their prepared story.

"Usually it's close, but this last time I cleaned her clock. She was erratic, and I asked if something was wrong."

"It was like he opened a floodgate," Niki said. "I mentioned that I'd found documents that need to see the light of day, and I was considering mailing them to a news station."

Mike said, "But I thought your *Blame and Shame* blog would have better results, and here we are."

"We'll see," Olivia said. "Mom asked me to decide if this is worth her time, especially since we have this other thing going. What *do* you have?"

Hurdle one passed. Olivia accepted the premise. "Proof heavy metals from a Wisconsin sulfide mine are leaching into the underlying aquifer pumped for drinking water and used by farmers for irrigation. From what I read, they are neurotoxic, nephrotoxic, and carcinogenic. I have the original and doctored tests from a monitoring well."

Olivia shook her head. "You can fake that shit. Corporations would like nothing better than for us to show up with fake news. They could sue our asses and totally discredit us."

"And you think what? I'm a plant?"

"All I'm saying is until we scrutinize them, all you've got are two supposed reports. Either could be fake."

Exactly the point Niki had used to force Jim Ford to cough up a series of emails that confirmed the cover-up. "I copied emails that back them up. Remember, I'm the one who stole them. It's me they'll go after. Your mother will have to reassure me how she'll use this information, and how I'm protected. Mike, I thought I made that clear."

"Hey." He held his hands up in a surrender gesture. "All I promised was to make introductions. Sounds to me that this is the toxic stew that creates cancer clusters. Totally despicable. But what you and Christine do is up to you two. Just like Olivia and I are working on this other thing that's got nothing to do with you."

Mike was good. With this little improv, he had both supported her position and distanced himself from her. Olivia used the rearview mirror to study her. Time to act offended and add a fat grub to the wiggling worm on her offered hook.

"This isn't some one-time thing, Olivia. I have access to American Hydrocarbons Institute's files. More reports like what I have today, sure, but I can also access donor records and tell you whose pockets they're lining. If you think that's a waste of your time, take me back now."

BY THE TIME OLIVIA EXITED I-94, they were forty-five miles into Wisconsin, the rain had stopped, and the sun looked like it might poke out. She drove a lettered road—Wisconsin was the only state Niki could think of that used no numbers, only letters, to label county roads—past a Walmart, small municipal airport, made a right turn, and pulled into the parking lot of the Menomonie Public Shooting Range.

A second test. There were so many ways this could go sideways. In concocting the story of how they had met, Niki and Mike hadn't discussed how good a shot each was. The problem was they had told Olivia that they were closely matched. If they didn't pull that off, it jeopardized both of their assignments.

"Do we have time for this?" Niki asked. "I need to catch a plane home tonight. I've got work tomorrow."

"Not a problem," Olivia said.

Given Olivia's tone, Niki wasn't certain if it wasn't a problem because they'd have plenty of time or not a problem as in Niki had something worse to worry about. She tried catching Mike's eye, but he was staring out the window at the facility.

"What length range do they have?" he asked.

"One, two, and three-hundred yards," Olivia said. "And pistol."

Niki took heart that Olivia mentioned the rifle range first. With a pistol, Niki was fine, but not top-notch, and that could have been an issue. With a rifle, she'd been a state youth champion and had taken first in her class at Quantico. Provided she went last, she could beat Mike by a point or two. To try to shade things in that direction, she asked, "Do they rent rifles?"

"I have my favorite deer rifle in the trunk. We have time before Mom expects us. I thought we'd do a little qualifying round. What's your usual wager?"

"Loser has to pick up the brass and clear the targets," Niki said. "Last winner goes first. Mike's up." When no one objected, Niki's nerves dropped one notch.

"Yep," Mike agreed. "Or do you want to go first, Olivia?"

"I'll defer." Olivia pulled a rifle case out of the trunk and handed Mike three boxes of .260 Hornady Superperformance.

The supervisor was a pleasant gent, happy to lend them ear protectors and placed them at the end of the range. They walked past the one other person shooting: his target, set at 100 yards, looked like a colander with holes peppered around the untouched bullseye. He'd been at it awhile, the surrounding air tinged blue, the scent of spent gunpowder heavy in the air. She breathed in through her nose and felt herself settle at the familiar smell.

At their station, Olivia removed a Savage 11/111 Trophy Hunter XP from its case. Nice gun and serviceable with its Nikon scope. "You've already got this sighted in for yourself, Olivia. Sure you don't want first up?"

"Sighted-in is sighted-in," Olivia said.

"Only if it's clamped to a bench," Niki said. "Different head shapes lead to different positioning. Our eyes aren't spaced the same. We grip the stock a little differently. It may be close, but it won't be the same."

Olivia snorted. "Sounds like a bunch of bullshit to me. But fine, I'm not giving you any excuses. Since you're so persnickety, I'll even let you choose the distance."

"One hundred," Mike said at the same time Niki said, "three hundred."

Olivia looked from one to the other. "Is it always like this with you two?

Mike, set the target for two hundred." He reeled a target out 200 yards. Niki adjusted the ear protectors on her head. They were top-notch, doing a great job of deadening the pop each time Olivia pulled the trigger. She didn't rush and scored seventy-seven for her ten shots. Not bad, but not expert. Her pull could be smoother.

Olivia handed the rifle to Mike. "You need to change the scope?"

Niki dipped her head to encourage him to say yes. "Keep track of the adjustments, Mike, that way we can return it to the original settings for her."

Mike used five practice shots to zero in. His pull was smooth, breathing steady, he avoided shooting when the wind picked up. The guy knew what he was doing. While Mike took his shots, she performed a deep breathing exercise, filling her lungs, expanding her ribcage, bringing calm into her core. He scored a decent eighty-nine.

"Left me an opening." Niki checked the rifle's action, getting a little gun oil on her fingers. Olivia kept it in good condition. Her first practice shot hit at ten o'clock at the eight-ring. She overcompensated and hit the eight at four o'clock. Her third shot nicked the bulls-eye also at four o'clock. With a minor adjustment, she declared herself ready and totaled ninety-one. That should pass Olivia's second test. Were there more?

She popped off her ear protectors and gave Mike a big grin. "You're on cleanup."

ELEVEN

THE THREE OF THEM SPENT another hour in the car before Olivia pulled off the main highway onto a dirt road that wove through a mixed forest. "How far from here?" Niki asked.

"A ways," Olivia responded.

Not exactly helpful. Niki activated her phone's OnX app and engaged the tracker function. Her time training PFF members on orienteering skills deep in national forests had taught her that, despite phone company claims, there were plenty of spots with spotty or no cell coverage. They drove into one of them. She added a pin to the OnX track at the point she lost coverage.

From there, it was another seven miles before they crossed a bridge spanning a trickling river. Christmas trees dotted the hill beyond the river. At the top of the hill, the road narrowed and passed through a slough before climbing a fern-covered slope to a bluff.

Rounding a bend, they came to a wildflower meadow of several acres carved from a mixed hardwood forest that continued up the hill. A log cabin with an American flag attached to the front porch sat on a rise overlooking a reedy marsh with the river wiggling through it. Two cars were parked in front of a woodshed filled with split hardwood. Beyond the woodshed was a monster vegetable garden surrounded by eight-foot fencing to keep the deer out.

"Nice," Niki said. "Solar power works good?" Below the nine-panel solar array was a board and batten shed. If this setup was like the one Seamus had at his U.P. camp, the shed housed a backup generator and huge battery bank. It nagged her that something felt different, but she couldn't place her finger on it.

Olivia parked next to an F-150 that was more rust than metal. "It's a work in progress. I need to talk with my mother. Mike, you can wait in the house. Niki, why don't you stretch your legs? Outhouse is on the other side of those buildings."

Olivia was playing this close to her chest. Nice move, separating her from Mike—a technique police used to check for inconsistencies in witnesses' stories. She and Mike had kept their story simple to prevent screw-ups. Nothing she could do now.

Outside the car, she tucked her phone into a pocket and slipped on her knapsack. The wildflower meadow glistened from the morning's rain. The air buzzed with the sound of hardworking bees. Butterflies were everywhere. The place smelled clean, healthy. Her clothes had mostly dried, but the breeze had a bite to it. The sun was out now, but the western sky boiled with ominous clouds.

Since Olivia had given her free run of the place, she used the time to find the back road OnX showed led to the property. She followed a worn path through the yard. On the other side of the cabin, she came to an unobstructed view of the marsh. She'd been on the wrong side of the car and didn't realize that this spot provided a clear view of the bridge they had crossed. Had to be a half-mile away. No one could sneak up using the road.

At the edge of the hill, a half-dozen chairs circled a firepit. A lean-to woodshed held a neat stack of split wood and a wooden box with kindling. If only the firepit could talk. With no trees to deaden coverage, she tried sending a text. No go. At times like this, she wished the technical wizards could make a satellite phone that looked like a regular cell phone. Maybe some day.

The sun ducked behind a dark cloud, and the unfettered breeze off the meadow brought goosebumps to her arms. Enough lollygagging, she had more to explore and moving would warm her.

She followed a two-track beyond the fenced-in garden bursting with early-summer produce and into the woods. The majority were maples, the mature trees showed scarring from syrup taps. Did the mother live out here year around? In another hundred yards, the two-track petered out in a thicket of tag alders growing on the built-up road crossing between the marsh on the right and a swamp on the left. OnX showed a road up ahead, but given the amount of growth here, not even an ATV or snow machine had been through this tangle in years.

A mosquito's drone disturbed her reverie, and soon she was waving them away with one hand and swatting her neck with her other. No wind here. She retreated to the more open woods exposed to the air currents and worked sideways up the hill overlooking the camp. A grove of mature hemlocks dominated the top of the hill with a magnificent view of the camp, marsh, the distant river, the rolling hills in the distance, and the gathering storm. Again, the text message failed to transmit.

She returned to the two-track and followed it to the firepit where she found a middle-aged woman kneeling, blowing into a pile of kindling. Each puff produced a growing flame. She looked up and waved Niki over.

This is it. Niki used several deep breaths to calm herself. *You are in control. You are Niki Undercover.*

"I'm Christine," the woman said. "That storm won't get here for another couple of hours. It's too nice to stay inside and a bit chilly for sitting around. You good with a fire? Not asthmatic or anything?"

"Perfect." Niki offered an appreciative smile. The similarities between Olivia and her mother were apparent, although Olivia had a bigger frame. Christine's weathered face spoke of much time outdoors. Her boots were well-worn, but clean. She wore a plaid wool shirt over a cotton turtleneck. A Minnesota Twins cap topped a helmet of graying hair.

Christine pointed to a chair. "Take a pew. Tell me something, Niki. Why did you choose us?"

To get more information, Niki deflected. "I'm sorry. Choose us?"

"With the information. Why us and not one of the big environmental outfits with hot and cold lawyers on call?" She added several larger sticks to her nascent blaze. "Let me put it another way. What's your motivation? What do you want to accomplish?"

This was make it or break it time. "I am sick and tired of corporations getting away with murder. Literally killing people and getting away with it. Their executives and owners extract billions, trillions from folks like us, and it's never enough for them. By the time they get caught and get slapped with a fine, it's too late. They've already sucked that company dry. All that's left is a husk that declares bankruptcy. No one is ever held accountable. No executive goes to prison. I want people to pay for their crimes against humanity. Is that so wrong?"

"You think your stolen files can change the system?"

"Of course not." Niki glared at Christine, letting her anger shine. "The same old same old doesn't accomplish shit. It's why you split from Greenpeace, right? Because the only thing that gets attention is direct action. Only if we make it no longer profitable for corporations and their owners to pollute our air, our water, our bodies will they stop. They've got the system rigged. Legal action, suits, the traditional approach, doesn't work. It takes forever and accomplishes nothing. The people who make the decisions have to pay a personal price."

Christine added a tepee of split logs to the fire. "And?"

"And when Mike mentioned Greenwar, I thought, huh, this is different. You—the organization, I don't know who is responsible—you don't pull punches in the *Blame and Shame* blog. You lay it right out there. People you name feel the heat. Stuff happens. You take protests to them at their homes, their wives' charities, their kids' schools. Because it's personal, it costs them. You know?"

Niki would not be the one to mention the equipment they destroyed, the operations they shut down, and that someone had killed several of the people named in their blog. Keep it simple. Keep it focused. People who killed polluting executives would have no problem killing undercover agents.

Christine's eyes seemed like they were plumbing for Niki's soul. Niki raised her eyebrows and held her gaze. If she read this situation correctly, this was one tough broad. Showing weakness was a mistake. Movement in the driveway caught her attention. Olivia and Mike got into her car and drove off. *WTF?*

Mike had said they'd stay together, have each other's back. Even if it was only to go into town for sugar, wouldn't it be normal to let the person you brought with you know you were leaving? What just happened?

Christine busied herself with the fire. She leveled the flaming tepee with a log and laid a crosshatch pattern of eight logs across the resulting base. Rocking on her heels, she rose in a fluid motion and brushed off her hands. "That will do us for a while. I think you should show me what you brought."

Standing, Christine acted like a chimney and pulled the smoke toward her. She accepted Niki's folder, hooked a chair with her toe, and settled at a ninety-degree angle to Niki, giving herself a view of both the marsh and the house. The smoke followed her until she sat, and then, like magic, drifted away with the breeze.

Niki warmed her hands with the fire, watched anger darken Christine's face, and wondered where the hell Mike was.

Twelve

WHILE CHRISTINE SCRUTINIZED THE DOCUMENTS, the sun disappeared and the wind strengthened. Any time Niki moved closer to the fire, she drew the smoke to her, burning her eyes. Instead, she alternately warmed one side and froze the other. She was one layer shy and considered more than once asking to borrow a jacket. She resisted on the theory that Christine keeping her uncomfortable might also be a test.

Christine finished the last page and tapped the pile on her legs, straightening the edges. "Do you want these back, or . . . ?"

"Yours, if you'll use them."

"This is powerful stuff. The reports and internal company emails show an intent to defraud the public and pose a health threat. Drawing and quartering is too good for them." She sharpened her focus on Niki's face. "Or for you, if these are fake. I don't suppose you have any outside sources that can corroborate this?"

A suspect with an airtight alibi for a specific date and time was more suspicious than a suspect with no alibi. Niki couldn't remember what she had for breakfast—actually, it was Seamus-style oatmeal shared with Jacob—let alone where she was at 1415 six days ago. Never oversell, one of her trainers had pounded into her head. She formed her face into a disappointed frown. Shook her head. "Outside source? Can't you get someone to test the water?"

"Not legally."

Niki sprang to her feet and shot out her hand, demanding the file. "Apparently, I misunderstood your dedication."

Christine did not flinch. "We must pick our spots. What time's your flight? Do you have time to share dinner with us before we get you to the airport? Zed would like to meet you."

Had Mike mentioned her timetable? Was this another test? "I'd love to. I purchased an unrestricted ticket. The last flight won't be full. Where did Mike and Olivia go?"

Christine rose without effort. The woman had a strong core. "We keep plans on a need-to-know basis."

THE LATE AFTERNOON SUN POKED through a slot in the clouds and painted golden the knotty pine paneling inside the cabin. They passed a silent refrigerator in the corner next to a sink with a stove on the other side. Christine gave the bubbling soup a quick stir. The steam tickled Niki's nose with a mixture of onion and herbs she couldn't identify. "Smells good."

Christine smiled in appreciation and led the way to the dining area. A vase of cut flowers graced the center of the plank table, above which hung a four-light propane lamp. She pointed to one of the eight cane-seated chairs. "The best view is there. Zed will be with us shortly."

Niki strolled past the table and sitting area to the woodstove in the far corner and made a production of warming her hands. Something about the camp's layout had bothered her, and now she knew what it was. They used propane, but she had seen no evidence of a propane pig, like the 1,000-gallon tank Seamus had at his camp to run his refrigerator, stove, and generator when his solar required backup to charge the batteries. Unlike oil tanks, she didn't think people buried propane. "This feels good. Can it keep the cabin warm in the winter?"

The door opened and a man filled the entrance, blocking the light from outside. He stomped his boots on the threshold, shaking the house, stepped in and closed the door behind himself. Walking past Christine in the kitchen, he gave her arm a pat. "They're off. No one followed them to the ninety-four. I kept on them for a couple of exits to make sure."

She hadn't seen a second car leave. Where, Niki wondered, had Zed been to follow Olivia and Mike onto Interstate 94?

"Let's eat," Christine said.

Zed sat at the head of the table. Niki chose the seat with the best view. Christine settled opposite her. Niki unfolded the cloth napkin and laid it on her lap. She reached for her spoon and realized the other two were watching her.

"Would you lead us in grace?" Christine asked.

Niki's thoughts flew to a summer camp where she had chanted, "Rub-a-dub-dub. Thanks for the grub. Yay, God." That would not work.

"Our tradition," Zed added, "is to hold hands and express our thanks for being alive today. It doesn't matter whether you deliver that thanks to a deity, or Mother Earth, or toward self." He held his hands out to the women.

Niki grasped their offered hands: Christine's calloused with work, Zed's smooth but strong. "All right. Thank you for the food we are about to eat. Food that will strengthen our bodies and feed our resolve to bring justice into the world." Was she supposed to say amen to signal she was done? No, wasn't that what others said in response? She burned with embarrassment at not knowing how to end this ritual.

After a moment's pause, she felt her tablemates squeeze her hands. Zed let go, leaving her hand tingling with warmth. "Well said," Christine squeezed it again. "Strong words. Thank you. The bread's fresh baked this morning. Butter, not margarine, in case you're dairy intolerant."

Niki used eating to avoid being first to break the silence. No hardship there. She wafted the earthy aroma to her, couldn't identify the spices. The taste was rich, with a touch of hot pepper that left a tingle in her mouth.

Christine spoke first. "Where do we send our well water sample for testing?"

"County, why?" Zed took a bread slice.

"Didn't we use an outfit to test an aquifer for pollution? A couple years ago?"

"Oh sure, at the—" Zed shot a look at Niki. "Uh, yeah. Whitewater Associates up in Amasa in the U.P. What are you thinking?"

Niki's heart jumped at the mention of Amasa. That was the village nearest to where Seamus McCree had his camp. Was the Whitewater group mixed up with Greenwar?

During the meal, Christine summarized the material Niki had provided and her concerns that although Niki presented herself as a nice, motivated woman, she could be setting them up or was a dupe herself.

Zed placed his spoon in his empty bowl. "Whitewater did the sampling for us at a monitoring well. There's refresh rates and other stuff I don't understand, but the point is you need professionals. Professionals require permission. Which we had because it was part of a court order at the—you know."

Christine said, "You're saying we can't verify this?"

"Not through a legitimate lab like Whitewater without the property owner's permission."

That gave Niki an idea. "What if Whitewater believed they had permission because they thought the company that owns that monitoring well ordered the test? But . . . " She swept her arm in an arc to include the three of them. ". . . we get the results."

"You can do that?" Skepticism clouded Christine's face.

"Not me. But the material I brought has copies of the corporate letterhead. And signatures of several of its officers. Kids have software to cut and paste and make fakes look perfect. Set up a post office box somewhere to receive the results."

"Even if you could pull that off," Zed said, "you'd still need access to the wellhead."

Niki didn't like his distancing use of "you." She had to return them to "we" or they'd cut her loose. "We'd know when they planned to collect their sample, right? The mine's in the middle of flipping nowhere. What's guarding it? A chain-link fence and a five-dollar lock? Those haven't stopped Greenwar before. Provided we have the gate open, no one has to be there for them to gather the sample, right?"

Unspoken words passed between the two of them. She'd made her pitch. To prevent herself from overselling, she concentrated on her soup, dinging the bowl with her spoon chasing the last drop. "That was delicious. Thank you."

"I was prepared to turn you down," Christine said. "But you've given us much to evaluate. I'm sure you want an immediate answer, but I can't do that. Zed'll drive you to the airport and see you off. How can we contact you?"

Niki allowed a disappointed expression to play on her face. She gave them Niki's cellphone number. "Regardless of what you decide," Niki said, "I'll search for more stuff. If Greenwar can't or won't use it, I'll find someone else to work with—before AHI catches me. Thank you for listening."

Christine said, "You'll hear from us soon."

THIRTEEN

WITH ONLY TWO PEOPLE, NIKI'S objective was to avoid sitting in the passenger seat. She wanted to drive and control the vehicle or be in the back seat, where she had a tactical advantage over the driver. While they walked to Zed's truck, a middle-aged GMC Sierra, she explained her "problem" with car sickness. "I hate to be antisocial," she concluded, "but if you don't want me puking on your dash, I should sit in the back, or if it's okay with you, I can drive."

"It's stick."

A few weeks ago, she had borrowed her sister's car, which was the first time she'd driven a manual transmission in years. "I'm a little rusty. They're getting to be scarcer than hens' teeth."

Zed tossed her the keys. "Good catch. Now, don't you go changing the radio dial."

She raised her hands in mock surrender. "Let's see. With a reaction like that, it wouldn't be rock or country. Probably not classical. Jazz?" She slid into the driver's seat and adjusted it to her legs. Fiddled with the mirrors and clicked her seatbelt.

Zed cranked his seat to allow maximum leg room. "Country. Christine can't stand it."

"So much for my ESP." Niki engaged the clutch and moved the gear lever through its positions before starting the engine. It pleased her to see Zed's smiled approval of her preparations. She had more than an hour to pump him for information before they got to the Minneapolis-St. Paul airport. The more she got him talking, the less she had to talk herself. She waited until she'd navigated the driveway and was past the bridge before she started what she hoped would be an informal interrogation. "How did you and Christine meet?"

He decreased the radio's volume to become background. "Through our kids. They both got arrested protesting the Keystone pipeline. Christine didn't have the money to bail out Olivia, and Timothy, my eldest, convinced me to front the money. The kids are still friends, but they stopped being a couple not long after that. It worked okay for me."

"You guys live there or . . . ?"

"Pretty isolated in the winter. What about you? Where do you live?"

Back and forth the conversation went, guarded on both sides. Niki picked up bits and pieces of his biography, enough to allow her to determine his name if she couldn't get it from the cabin's property tax records. "Curiosity question, were your parents big into religion. With a name like Zedekiah . . ."

His knee slap sounded like a gunshot, and he burst into laughter. "They were, but that's not it. Zed is Christine's nickname for me—the letter Z. With Greenwar, she's like the alpha and I'm the omega because I came so late to the movement. Since omega has negative connotations, she tagged me 'Zed,' the British way of referring to the last letter in the alphabet. It stuck, and I kinda like it now. But I remind her to watch out. You know, 'So the last shall be first, and the first last: for many be called, but few chosen,' as the Bible verse goes."

Sometime later, Niki focused the conversation on Greenwar. "I read a year's worth of the *Blame and Shame* blogs. They're detailed and specific. Who writes them?"

"Christine decides who to target and writes most of them. Olivia and my son plan the protests. Organizing them is a young person's game, what with flash mobs and such. They're great at figuring out venues where the targets or their wives will be that will generate the most publicity."

Niki expressed interest in how they did that, but Zed claimed ignorance. If the two youngsters had a way to anticipate where to find their targets would be, were they using that to target them for assassination too? Niki debated how to bring up the five deaths.

"I'd like to get on their distribution list," Niki said. "Weekdays don't work, but if there's something during the evening or on the weekend, I could help. I have to admit that after I read that some CEOs named in the blogs had been killed, I debated coming today. But I realized my exposing misdeeds didn't mean I was responsible for their deaths, you know? They brought that on themselves—not that I'm condoning killing people. You know what I mean. I'm sorry, I'm kind of running off at the mouth."

Zed's voice became darker. "It wasn't just CEOs. One guy was a division head, but regardless, it's something I pray on. I believe capital punishment is wrong. Any killing is wrong, even evil people. But I haven't lost sleep over any of those deaths. I pray for understanding." He pointed at the sign ahead. "Airport's coming up. Pull into parking. I'll make sure you get off okay before I leave."

It sounded gentlemanly, but her body went to five-alarm fire stressed. "That's kind, but it's not necessary."

"What would my mother think if I didn't?"

And what would he think if she pulled up at the departures area and got out? She could skedaddle before he parked and returned to the area. And kill her chance of their ever contacting her. Nope. She'd have to ditch him without his knowing it. *Put on your thinking cap, Niki.*

With her jittery left leg. She pressed the clutch to downshift around the curve. Not engaging the gear, the engine whined in protest. "Sorry," she said automatically. "Now you've got me worried about my flight. What *would* your mother think?" *Mine would think I'm in deep shit and short shoes.*

WALKING FROM THE PARKING GARAGE to the terminal with Zed at her side, Niki sensed he planned to stick with her all the way to security. She focused her imagination away from her growing concern to enjoying a solo hike up to Nauma Lookout in Glacier. That made her feel lighter, less weighted down by worry. "First thing we get inside," she said, "I want to use the facilities."

She didn't, but it would buy her five minutes to switch her flight from tomorrow to tonight. Scanning the departure board they walked past, she found the last evening Delta flight to D.C. In the privacy of a stall, she pulled up Delta's app and what the hell? The flight was full. She pressed her fingers into her closed eyes, producing shooting stars. *Shit.*

Where else was Delta flying tonight? Chicago in an hour. She booked the ticket. *This will be a bitch to explain on her expense report. Ambrose had damn well better approve it.* She flushed the toilet, waited until the whoosh had ended, and exited to find Zed waiting for her. The promised rain had begun, and she suggested he should leave before it got any worse.

No go. He accompanied her until she reached the TSA checkpoint. She thanked Zed for the ride, walked to the agent who checked her Delta app boarding pass and subjected her to the standard questions. She waved Zed a goodbye and passed through the scanner, retrieved her x-rayed knapsack. Zed was still watching her.

What was going on? She gave him a last wave and walked toward the gate. Given his level of distrust, she'd be prudent and get on the flight. Hopefully, there was a later flight she could catch from O'Hare to D.C.

She plunked onto a seat in the waiting area and checked for Chicago to Washington flights. Nothing available. *Just great. If she couldn't find a hotel, she'd be sleeping in the terminal.* Using a secure browser, she scanned her emails, nothing important. In the transcriptions of her personal cell phone messages, she found one from Chloe Pendergast dated ten past six.

JACOB GONE!! BIKE GONE!!! WHAT DID YOU DO??? CALL ASAP!!!

Using Niki's phone could create an operational catastrophe. Her personal one remained locked in the gun safe. The airport kiosk that sold phones was closed. She scanned the crowd for a kind soul likely to lend her a phone. The overhead speakers erupted with the announcement that her flight was pre-boarding, causing the entire waiting area to queue up. She couldn't do shit for anyone in Chicago, and she couldn't get to D.C. to report to Ambrose. No reason to fly there.

She informed the gate agent she had learned of an emergency and would not be boarding. She hadn't checked any baggage, and she wanted to let the agent know to minimize staff, crew, and passenger inconvenience. The agent thanked her and suggested she stop by the service desk to see if she could rebook later. No time for that. She pulled up the MSP airport map to see how to get to St. Paul while avoiding Zed—if he was still around. If she were him, she'd watch the taxi stand nearest to Delta. The train symbol caught her eye. She could take the light rail into the city and catch a rideshare or walk to Legacy House.

She bought a rain jacket and ball cap from the PGA store, stored her wig in her knapsack, and donned the new gear. Instead of slinging the knapsack over her shoulder, as she had done all day, she carried it in one hand. It wasn't much of a disguise, but better than nothing.

FOURTEEN

ASHLEY ARRIVED AT LEGACY HOUSE to find a friend of Chloe's babysitting. Following introductions, the woman said, "Chloe told me you might show up. She said you work for the FBI. Can they help?"

Ashley didn't bother to correct who she worked for; instead, she quizzed the woman on what Chloe had done.

"Called everyone she could think of. The police took her report, but there's not much they can do, right? Chloe's driving around looking for his bicycle. Look, it's getting late and Chloe might need my help tomorrow, which will be tougher if I don't get home at a decent hour tonight. Can you watch the girls?" She put on her coat. "You should wake Jasmine and have her use the bathroom before you go to bed. With all that's gone on, she's backslid and sometimes wets her bed. Chloe didn't say when she'd get home, but it's been three hours. I expect her soon, unless she stopped at a bar."

"She'd do that?"

The woman's eyes became cagey. "If everything that's happened to her happened to me, I'd self-medicate."

Ashley showed the woman out. The house felt like a tomb, the only sounds her breathing and the donk, donk, donk of the grandfather clock in the hallway. She tiptoed upstairs, keeping to the outer edge of the steps to avoid the squeaky spots, and deposited everything in her room. She cracked the door to Jenny's room. Max scrambled to his feet. "Just me, big boy," she whispered.

Jasmine sucked her thumb. Her other hand clutched a worn teddy bear tight to her chest. Jenny's head popped up from the other side. "Mommy?"

"No, it's . . . " What did she call herself with these kids? "Ms. Prescott. We met this morning."

"Is Mommy back? Did she find Jacob?"

"Not yet, honey."

"I don't really hate him. And I didn't mean it when I told him to go away." She sniffed back tears. "Is he going to be okay?"

Ashley walked around the bed, sat on its edge, and rubbed Jenny's back. Ashley remembered a time she had believed her thoughts could make things happen before she had learned better. "Tell me what happened, kiddo."

Jenny rolled over and balled tears from her eyes. Between deep breaths and sniffles, she got the story out. She was playing a game on the tablet. Jacob stole it because he had "something important to do." When she grabbed it, he held on and pushed her away. That triggered her outburst that she hated him, and nobody wanted him living with them, and he should go away and never come back.

"What did he do?"

"He laughed at me."

"Big brothers can be real meanies. Let me ask this, Jenny. When's the last time you yelled at Jacob and he did what you wanted? Like never, right? Everyone knows you didn't mean it. Jacob included. I am one hundred percent, positively, absolutely, without a shadow of a doubt, cross-my-heart-hope-to-die sure it wasn't because you told him to."

Ashley's over-the-top response got a single giggle from Jenny, which was better than she expected. "Okay, you should get some sleep to be bright-eyed and bushy-tailed in the morning."

"Will you be here when I wake up?"

"That's the plan."

She woke Jasmine, carried her to the bathroom, then tucked her into Jenny's bed. Jenny was already asleep. She left the door open a crack to hear the kids if they stirred.

Exhaustion dragged at every part of Ashley's body except her brain. She should compose her report on the day's activities. Instead, she checked Jacob's room, not expecting to find anything useful, but hoping she might spot something his mother had missed. Max followed her in and curled up on the floor at the foot of Jacob's bed.

Either the kid was a neatnik or his mother had compulsively cleaned his room. Ashley opened the closet and stepped back in surprise. The rod sagged from the tightly packed clothes on hangers. Power Ranger PJs hung from a hook on the door. Boxes covered the floor, all unopened except one that had Jacob's baseball glove on top.

Something felt off. She squatted and peered under and around the baseball glove to discover the cause of her concern. A glance at her hands offered the solution: no gloves, and she was acting like an investigator. "You're not a crime scene," she declared to the box. "Let's see whatcha got."

She set the glove, with a baseball in its web, next to the sleeping Max. Underneath was an autograph album. Judging by the date of the first entry, he had received it two Christmases ago. All athletes, no friends or family. Several Vikings football players, Timberwolves and Lynx basketball players. A half-dozen hockey players from the Wild. At least twenty from the

Minnesota Wind Chill, whatever they were. She found only two autographs from the baseball Twins and wondered why, since the kid was a baseball fan.

Next came a notebook filled with baseball cards separated into sleeved compartments. She'd pinned hers to the spokes of her bike to make it sound like a Harley. Next, programs from Twins games. He'd done a nice job of completing the scorecards inside, showing each at bat. Huh? He'd gone to games but didn't have autographs. Weird. Next were several programs from basketball and hockey games. A Frisbee with the Minnesota Wind Chill logo—must be an ultimate pro team.

The final item was a shoebox. One corner, crushed like someone had stepped on it, had snagged a tuft of pink insulation. She lifted it and caught its top on the packing box's edge, spilling a three-by-five ringed notebook onto her lap. Her yelp startled Max, and he scrambled to his feet, scattering the box contents into the room. She collected and counted thirty-two one-hundred-dollar bills.

What the hell was Jacob doing with more than three thousand dollars cash?

Ashley flipped through the notebook. Each line had a date, monetary amounts—more negative than positive—and various symbols. No key she could see. The downstairs grandfather clock chimed eleven. Where the hell was Chloe? If she was drunk somewhere, Ashley would ream her out but good. She replaced everything other than the notebook and the shoebox into the packing box and closed the closet door.

She looked in on the girls, both asleep. Depositing the notebook in Robert's office, she continued to the basement, Max padding along behind her. She locked the money in the gun safe, retrieved her gun and personal cell phone, and noted in passing that Chloe's gun was still there.

On the way up to the first floor, she heard the doorbell ring. She hushed Max, took the stairs two at a time, and raced to the front door. At the door, she shoved the phone in her front pocket and tucked the pistol into the small of her back. She flicked on all the light switches, not remembering which one was for the outside. On the stoop she saw two guys, one her age, the other older, both looking like detectives. She disarmed the alarm and pulled open the solid wood door. "Did you find Jacob?"

"Ma'am?" the taller of the two said.

His voice sounded vaguely familiar. Was he one of the St. Paul cops she'd hired a couple of months ago as security for various family members after Robert Pendergast had gone missing? Ashley opened the screen door and pulled closed the wood door to restrain Max. "Jacob Pendergast. Have you news?"

"We'd like you to look at this." The older one offered a sheet of paper. "It might help."

Confused, Ashley accepted the folded material.

The older guy said, "Ashley Pendergast Prescott, you've been served. Have a pleasant evening."

She'd heard him speaking with Chloe this morning. A little late for that memory to help her. "Fuck me."

"Regrettably," the young one said, "that would be a breach of our duty as officers of the court. Good night."

ASHLEY'S EYES WERE DROOPING BY the time she finished her report documenting her meeting with Greenwar. She emailed Rick Kaska a few minutes after midnight. He would deliver it to Deputy Director Ambrose in the morning. She sent a blind copy to Seamus and followed it with a second email to him.

Family crap here. Jacob missing since yesterday afternoon. Now Chloe gone, too. Searching Jacob's room for clues, I found $3,200 cash and a notebook with weird symbols. PLUS I just got served papers to appear for a deposition this Friday to justify my actions regarding Pendergast Holdings. We need to talk. When are you coming to St. Paul?

Hugs and kisses, Niki

The floodlights in the back kicked on. She hadn't heard any cars. A raccoon or stray dog? Remembering she had forgotten to rearm the system after dealing with the process servers, she grabbed her pistol and shut the door on Max. Keeping close to a wall, she eased down the hallway to the kitchen. Someone was opening the door from the solarium. She assumed the Chapman stance, two hands on the gun, right arm extended, cheek touching her bicep.

A shadow thrown by the outside lights showed an extended arm, hand holding something solid, pointed away from Ashley. She inhaled a deep abdominal breath to steady herself and waited. The door swung open and the shadow's arm rotated toward her.

"Drop your weapon," she yelled in her FBI command voice, "or I'll shoot."

"Don't shoot," a woman shrieked. Keys jangled striking the floor. The woman collapsed to her knees in a puddle of sobs.

"Chloe?" Ashley flicked on a light. She looked past Chloe, finding no one and no car in the driveway. She closed the door and engaged the alarm. "Sorry to scare the piss out of you. What happened? Where's your car?"

Max, trapped in the study, began whining. Ashley didn't want him to wake the girls. "Hold that thought."

She returned with the dog to find Chloe gripping a glass of scotch. Under questioning, Chloe said she had driven everywhere Jacob might have gone. No sign of him. While parked in a church parking lot considering where else to look, she had turned off the car to save gas. Pressing the start button, nothing had happened. It had fuel, although less than an eighth of a tank. She called AAA and discovered their membership had expired months ago. Before she came up with an alternative, a guy with a tow truck showed up.

"Triple A changed their minds?" Ashley was incredulous.

"Hardly." Chloe downed the rest of the scotch. "He repossessed the car. When we financed it, the firm installed a kill switch and GPS tracker. I had to walk the four miles home." She cast a covetous glance at the scotch bottle.

Ashley washed Chloe's glass and placed it on the shelf. "Why didn't you call someone?"

"I'd drained the phone's battery using the map app and forgot to bring the charger. A sympathetic lady lent me her phone to call AAA. I didn't have enough money for a cab."

That scenario struck Ashley as incomplete. Instinct suggested it wasn't the right time to tell Chloe about the $3,200. "Get some rest. The girls will be up in a few hours. May I search Jacob's room to look for anything that will help us figure out where he went?"

"There's not much to see. He's hardly unpacked." She waved a hand toward Jacob's room. "Sure."

No way Chloe would give her permission if she was the one who had hidden the money. Where had it come from?

FIFTEEN

Ashley reached the bottom of the last box of Jacob's possessions without finding anything she recognized as a clue. She rested against a wall. Beyond tired, she was on her third wind. Unless she could shut down her busy-brain, she wouldn't be able to sleep.

She had run away once. Her best friend had joined the other girls laughing at her because Ashley was wearing clothes one of the girl's older sisters had donated to Goodwill. Her mother was totally unsympathetic. She was working two or three jobs to keep them housed and give her three squares a day, but that didn't mean anything to Ashley at the time. What mattered was her mother gave her some bromide about clothes not making the woman, and that maybe Ashley should find better friends. Ashley wrote a note to Robert, who had more money than God, asking him to buy her new clothes. Her mother discovered it—as she discovered *everything* Ashley wanted to keep secret at that age—and shredded the letter. "You want those clothes, start earning your own money. Go babysit."

Ashley's experience with babies was they crapped their diapers, which was disgusting, and they cried a lot. Besides, she was only ten. Her mother was totally unreasonable. It was late spring, the days were getting warm, the nights not too cool. Her bike could take her wherever she chose. She could make campfires and brush shelters. In the small town, she knew who had gardens from which she could filch food and which mothers hung clothes outside if she needed extra layers.

She'd stay away long enough to make her mother sorry she'd been so mean. Real sorry. On the second night camping in the nearby state park, thunderheads raced across the plains, throwing lightning around like it was the Fourth of July. Long cannonades of thunder rolled across the sky. She loved that. What she didn't love was the downpour that followed.

Ashley shivered at the thought. The rain soaked her clothes. Extinguished her fire. Drenched her collected wood. Melted the iodine tablets she used to purify water. Even once the rain stopped, she couldn't light a new fire. Faced with the prospect of a paltry dinner of pilfered soggy lettuce and snow peas, and with no way to get dry or stay warm, she decided her mother had suffered enough and rode her bike home.

Her mom greeted her with a hug and no questions. She made Ashley soak in the tub until she stopped shivering and sent her to bed. Hungry. The next morning, her mom called in sick and cooked Ashley a big pancake breakfast. She made Ashley wash and iron the clothes she had stolen and deliver them to the house she had swiped them from. Only then did her mother ask Ashley what she had learned.

Ashley didn't remember what she had said that day, but she remembered what she *hadn't* said, which was that the next time she left she'd have a better plan. She smiled at that thought, because the next time she left was with her full-ride softball scholarship to UCLA.

She had gone to the state park because she had camped there with the scouts and felt safe in its wilderness. Jacob was a city kid. Where would he seek safety?

THE TECHNOBEAT FROM NIKI'S PHONE blasted Ashley awake. Sunshine flooded an unfamiliar room. After the cobwebs cleared, she realized she had fallen asleep on the floor of Jacob's bedroom in Legacy House. The cellphone claimed it was 0830. The house was mausoleum quiet—if the crypt had a ticking grandfather clock. Even Max had deserted her.

The two-sentence voicemail said, "This is Christine. We need to talk."

Ashley closed her eyes, breathed deeply through her nose, and pictured herself as Niki. Exhaling, she said, "I am Niki, and I am mightily pissed at environmental polluters." She pressed the callback symbol and listened to the buzz of the phone.

"That was quick." Christine clipped her words, like she was in a hurry. "The only way to confirm your information is to test the well. We have legal approaches to get that information. Unfortunately, they require court action and take years. We like your suggestion of using a qualified independent lab to secure the sample and we want you to be the one to let them in to the mine site."

"Me?" Niki didn't have to fake her surprise.

"Not alone. We'll have someone with you to help with stuff like cutting the chain and determining the exact location of the wellhead."

Time for Niki to become pissed and a bit paranoid. "You don't trust me, do you? You think I'm—I don't even know what you think I am— working for the industry? Trying to get you arrested? Or are you setting me up to get arrested, make a splash in the newspapers—free publicity—and then you do that courtroom stuff you mentioned?"

"That's actually an interesting idea, but it's much simpler than that. We want you leading the action because if you *are* some kind of cop, that's entrapment. Right?"

"I don't know what that is, but I'm telling you, I want to see these people brought to justice."

"The lab sends people only during regular weekday work hours. You'll cut the gate's lock before they arrive at the mine site, escort the tech to the wellhead, and close the gate after he's gone. As I said, we'll have someone help, but you'll be the one to cut the lock. Open the gate. Close the gate."

Her idea, her leading the way, entrapment indeed:. The plan wasn't to arrest Greenwar members on a trespassing or minor destruction of property charge. It was to stop a killer. If she were Ambrose, she wouldn't have a problem with this, but it was virgin territory in their relationship. What would happen if Greenwar was setting her up, and she was arrested? Time for another heart-to-heart with her new boss.

"This is so different from what I expected," she said. "I'm just not—I need to think—Maybe I could call in sick or something. I've got to check my boss's schedule. I'll need time for the round trip."

Christine's voice lightened. "I like the way you think on your feet. This Friday would be perfect."

Oh crap. The only day in the next two weeks she had something she couldn't miss—unless she could postpone the recently served deposition. "This Friday? I'm not sure I can get free. Can I let you know Monday, Tuesday at the latest?"

"Tuesday works. If I don't hear from you, I'll assume it's a no."

"That's—" Niki didn't bother finishing her sentence because Christine had ended the call. This group did not screw around. Under other circumstances, she could find herself liking Christine. Problem was, the woman might be a killer—or know one.

Still using Niki's phone, she called Rick and related Christine's demands.

Rick's response was typical Bureau thinking. "That's a darned brief window for us to set this up. Contact the property owner to get permission. Maybe we can get the water testing company to allow us to add an agent to their run to give you some back-up. That—"

"Risks the entire operation. Sure, the testing company is totally legit, but why couldn't a Greenwar sympathizer work for them? I want Ambrose to give me his written directive permitting me to break the law to complete my assignment."

"He won't do that."

Niki chuckled. "I expect not. But we need to record him telling us it's okay. If it goes south, he'll intervene on my behalf if his own ass is on the line. And we don't have much time. Remember, Mike thinks they'll arrest Christine's daughter tomorrow. I want to reach Christine today before she's distracted by that. I'll tell her I checked Jim Ford's calendar, and the only days I can do it in the next two weeks are this Wednesday or Thursday. That applies a lot of pressure. First thing Monday morning, before they can contact Whitewater, they have to set up a mail drop to receive the invoice and results."

"No way. I can't possibly see Ambrose until Monday. Besides, won't Greenwar just push it back another week?"

"If so, it gives us time to do this right. I'm working. You're working. No reason Ambrose can't work on the weekend, too. If he's unwilling to meet you in the office, invite him for lunch, or go visit him at his house. As you've reminded me more than once, he's known you your whole life."

"Has anyone ever told you how impossible you are?"

"Thank you for the compliment, Rick. Let me know what he says. Did you ever run away?"

"Nah-uh. Too risky. Why?"

Safe and steady Rick, she should have known. "Because a ten-year-old is missing and I need to find him."

Sixteen

Ashley came downstairs to find a note from Chloe on the kitchen table. The girls and Max had a play date at a friend's house for the day. Chloe had borrowed a friend's car and was looking for Jacob. Ashley's original plan had been to get from Chloe a list of Jacob's friends and where they lived. Without Chloe, her only option was to determine if Jacob had gone to his old home, which she had decided was what she would do if she were him. With a key or a "secret" way to break in, he might camp at the empty house.

Breakfast could wait. She installed her ankle holster, stuck her personal phone, license, and credit cards in her front pockets. She snagged the keys to Robert's Mercedes from the key rack by the solarium door, punched in the code to the garage—fortunately, that hadn't changed—and powered on the beast. Its engine purred like a contented kitten.

She'd only been to Jacob's house one time, but finding his father hanging in the basement had burned the location into her memory. A wooden For Sale sign planted in the front yard had a placard slotted at the top proclaiming Open House 10-2. She had time for a quick explore. Neighbors would think the Mercedes parked in the driveway meant a realtor was visiting.

She didn't bother checking the lock box hung on the front doorknob. The double-wide garage door, windows too high to see in, didn't budge from her tug. A wooden fence with a gate protected the back yard from prying eyes. The latch released with a click and the gate opened a crack before an eye-hook latch stopped it. Failing to pry the hook up with a credit card, she clambered over the fence. The house windows were locked. He wasn't hiding in the doghouse. The storm door protecting the back door to the house was unlocked, but the door itself had a deadbolt in addition to a doorknob lock.

The back people door to the garage provided her best chance. A simple push-button mechanism was all that stood between her and making sure Jacob was not in the house. That, and criminal trespass laws. Her former roommate, Liya, had lock picks and the skill to open anything in seconds. She smiled at herself—she was more of a crowbar kind of gal.

Using the most flexible of her credit cards, she wiggled a corner into the space next to the latch and eased it against the sloping edge. With firm pressure, she released the latch and scanned the empty garage before walking in.

No bicycle. Not a good sign, but the kid could have brought it inside. The finished walls provided no crannies for a key on a nail. Dim oil spots ghosted where two cars had once parked. Otherwise, the floor was clean and showed no footprints or bicycle tracks. A pull rope dangled from the ceiling, too high for Jacob to have grabbed it to pull down the folding stairs.

A deadbolt secured the door into the house. No key above the door transom, and her finger found only dust along its upper molding. But, if Jacob had used a hidden key, he'd have it inside with him. She pounded on the door. "Jacob. If you're in there, open up. This is Ashley Prescott."

The swish of tires on the road indicated an approaching car. She held her breath until it passed—not people coming to set up for the open house. She pounded on the door and called again. Frustrated, she stared at her feet and spotted a tuft of pink fluff stuck to the doormat. Pinching it between her fingers, she jabbed a sliver of insulation under her skin.

Huh. Movers would have brought anything from the above-garage storage down the driveway to their truck.

Ashley jumped and grabbed the pull rope, her weight extending the stairs with a creak that could raise the dead. She unfolded the stairs and scurried up. Pulling a light chain from a bare LED attached to the sloped ceiling provided illumination. Plywood covered half of the open space showing skid marks from dusty boxes pulled from storage and several sets of shoe prints. Beyond the plywood, batts of pink insulation filled the spaces between the joists, except in one spot, where someone had disturbed the insulation.

She crossed the plywood, knowing any slip would punch a foot through the garage ceiling, duckwalked the joists to the disturbed area. On closer inspection, the batt's paper backing had ripped and pulled away from the joist, as though someone had shoved something the size of a shoe box under the insulation.

She poked the batting, found nothing. Assuming this had been the box's hiding place, who had removed it, and how had it come into Jacob's possession?

Trusses separated the garage from the main house and light from a house vent patterned an area with plywood flooring. If it was another storage area, it must have access from the house.

She crawled through the trusses, pricked her head on a roofing nail, ducked past air ducts, and reached the plywood flooring with no further pokes. She circled her hands above her head and connected with a pull cord. Her sharp tug resulted in a satisfying click but no light. Must be a switch, and she had probably turned off the light. She pulled the cord again and inched toward the interior wall where her fingers flicked on a light switch. Success.

She eased open the door connecting the storage area to an empty bedroom, its clean carpet showing tracks of a vacuum cleaner. She willed the house to speak to her. No sound. No scent. Not a living thing, not even a fly buzzing at a window.

Jacob's father hung before her in the basement, his unseeing eyes stared bloodshot, his tongue protruding from purple lips, the stench of piss and shit and desperation. Magma welled in her stomach, burned up her throat, choked off her breath. Would she find son like father?

She ran into the house, yelling his name. Flew down the stairs, burst into the kitchen, and flung open the basement door. The basement lights were on. "Jacob," she yowled. She took the stairs three at a time, misjudged the landing and smacked her crown into the header. Her tailbone smashed down on the last step. Tears blurred her eyes.

She rose on shaky legs, blinking to clear her tears, believing she would see Jacob hanging from the same beam his father had used to hang himself. No body. Nothing amiss. She steadied herself with a long slow breath.

Returning to the main level, she pushed the stairs back into the ceiling and unlocked the door between the garage and kitchen to extend her plausible deniability in case anyone saw her enter or leave. She wandered the main floor looking for any sign Jacob had been there. In the kitchen, the refrigerator hummed but proved to be empty, as was the dishwasher. The kitchen sink felt damp to her touch, but that meant nothing. A potential buyer or agent could have tested the faucet.

The kitchen clock said nine-thirty. Almost time for the open house. She resumed her search upstairs for evidence of Jacob. The first two bedrooms were clean and empty. In the third, she found traces of dirt in the carpet. Prints remained from where the legs of a single bed had pressed into the rug. Between the four marks was an area slightly smoother than the rest of the carpet. Like someone had lain there?

On closer inspection, she confirmed the carpet pile had been smooshed. At the edge of the disturbed area, she found the hint of a dark red stain. She ran a credit card over the surface of the rug and confirmed the stain had seeped down through the pile. Blood? It wasn't much, whatever it was, but it had gotten there after the carpet had been cleaned.

She entered the bathroom and her stomach clenched. Pink tinged the sink bowl, and on the floor beneath the sink were three drops of blood.

Blood-soaked wads of toilet paper filled the wastebasket placed between the sink and toilet. Someone had bled. A lot.

From downstairs came a call. "Hello? Is anyone in here?"

Ashley judged the voice to be from a middle-aged male. Ex-smoker, maybe.

"A neighbor parking in the driveway, do you think?" Female. Younger. Eager.

"We've blocked it in. If they haven't returned, we'll leave a note on the windshield when we leave. I'll bring in the stuff. You turn on all the lights and make sure everything is shipshape."

Real estate agents. If she could get outside, she could claim she parked in the driveway while searching the neighborhood for Jacob. Could they please move their car? Footsteps on the wood floors downstairs echoed in the empty rooms. Niki tiptoed to the storage area door, silently passed through, and extinguished the light, only to realize she had left the light on above the stairs into the garage.

The open house lasted five hours. Too long, she'd pee her pants. If it got busy, could she slip into the spare bedroom and pretend to be another prospective buyer? Not the way she was dressed. Bluff her exit with her Marshals badge—no she'd left that in the Legacy House safe.

Better to wait until the open house was busy and the two agents occupied inside. She'd sneak down the stairs into the garage, leave by its rear door, come to the front, and do her poor-me-blocked-in-while-looking-for-Jacob routine.

She inched along the rafters and breathed a sigh of relief on reaching the plywood flooring. At the shallow compartment that held the folded staircase, she examined its mechanism. It looked straightforward—if she could lower the stairs from this position. Lying on the plywood she placed her hands on both sides of the stairs and pushed, gently at first, then harder and harder until her arms trembled at the exertion. The stairs hardly moved.

Did pulling the cord from below unlock the mechanism somehow? She couldn't find any obstruction. She'd have to use leg strength to force the stairs down but didn't dare try until the open house was well under way.

"Criminy!" The guy's voice came from below. "Did they not turn any lights off in this house? And who checks a storage space anyway? One more trip to the car to get the step stool. What next?"

Get out now! Lying on the plywood, she grabbed a two-by-six framing with both hands. Bending at the waist, she lowered her feet onto the far edge of the stairs and pressed. The stairs moved a few inches, the hinge protesting its lack of lubrication. She thrust her legs down, pushing the stairs. With maximum effort, the top had partially opened, but not enough for gravity to release the bottom half of the stair system.

The garage door motor kicked on, and the door rattled open. She dropped into the opening, forced the gap wider by pressing with her ass, and using her core, straightened her body until it was perpendicular. She let go, dropping to the garage floor.

"Hey!" The guy carrying a metal step stool yelled at her from the driveway.

Ashley sprinted to the rear garage door, pulled it open, and raced through the backyard. She hurdled the fence like a pommel horse and ran toward a fifth-wheel RV with extended slideouts occupying the end of a driveway on her left. Perfect to screen her from searching eyes. Reaching it, she ducked down to catch her breath and determine if anyone was following her.

Under the camper was a bike with a license plate proclaiming "Jacob."

Seventeen

AN ELECTRICAL CORD CONNECTED THE trailer to an outdoor socket on the house. No noise from inside. Door unlocked. She eased it open. To her right were steps up to a closed door that barred her way. To her left was a spacious kitchen. An empty pop bottle and an open peanut butter jar with a knife sticking out of it sat on the center island.

"I win." An excited child's voice—not Jacob's—came through the closed door.

She tiptoed up the two steps, past the bathroom on her left and slid the bedroom door open. Jacob and another boy, both wearing headphones, lay on the bed playing a video game. They had supplemented their peanut butter meal with microwaved popcorn. Saliva filled her mouth at the smell. Her stomach gurgled, reminding her she had not had breakfast.

She waited for them to notice her. When that didn't happen, she walked into the room, blocking their view of the TV. The kids were a hoot. They dropped their controllers and pushed themselves against the pillows at the head of the bed. Eyes saucers, mouths open like an alien had come to abduct them. Headphones lying next to them, pumping out loud, suspenseful music.

They found their voices, words tumbling out without benefit of coherent sentence structure. Ashley perched a hip on the near corner of the bed and said, "Jacob, do you want to introduce me to your friend?"

"He's Austin Rathsburton. It's not his fault. How did you find me?"

She held her hands up to show she wasn't a threat. "Hi, Austin. I work for the United States Marshals Service. Finding people is what we do. Your Mom's been super worried about you. I'll take you to her, but first, let's have a little chat. Austin, your parents don't know Jacob is staying here, right?"

He shook his head, which she guessed meant they didn't know, and he preferred to keep it that way.

"Okay. Last night, Jacob's mom called all his friends' parents, and when she finds out where he's been—and she will—she'll call your parents again. I don't know whether you lied to them or they don't know. And I don't care. I suggest you get ahead of that."

Jacob's eyes glistened. "Can't you leave Austin out of it? He was just being my friend, the only one who stuck with me after—" The dam broke and tears streaked down his cheeks and dripped off his chin. "I knew they kept their RV unlocked. You don't have to—"

"Look, guys, when I was your age, I sometimes lied to my mother. Mostly because I'd done something she wouldn't approve of, and I didn't want her to find out because I knew she'd punish me. Later, I realized that if I fessed up before she found out on her own or from nosy neighbors, it went better for me than when she caught me in the lie. I'm not telling either of you what to do. But the truth will come out. Jacob, I've got a car parked in your old driveway. I'll take you and your bike to your mother."

"She doesn't want me." More tears rolled down his cheeks.

"That's where you're wrong. She's been frantic looking for you. Are there tissues in the bathroom? I think Jacob would like to blow his nose before we head home."

"I don't *have* a home."

Stepped in that one, and it wasn't time for one of those adult bromides about home being where you made it.

ASHLEY DIDN'T WANT JACOB TAKING off on his bike and insisted he walk his bicycle around the block to the car. To allow him to feel less like a prisoner, she walked on the other side of the bike. A thousand things she wanted to say or ask went through her mind, but best she keep her own counsel.

They turned the corner at the end of the block. Jacob said, "Can I ask you something? What did you do to your hair?"

He'd only ever seen her in a wig. "This is the real me, not pretending to be someone I'm not."

He cleared his throat. "I didn't plan to run away, you know."

She responded with a casual, "Oh?"

"I read about Wade Boggs like you said. He's some weird dude, you know? He ate chicken before every game. Every game! And he had a certain path he'd take to get to and from third base. That's totally weird. And he ran sprints at 7:17 every night. Why did he do that?"

Ashley chortled. "I had forgotten how superstitious he was. Every day he'd visualize getting four base hits. Not one, four. Positive imaging." Jacob's eyes glazed and she mentally kicked herself. It was his story. She should let him tell it.

"I asked mom to take me to the store and buy me his book on hitting. She told me she couldn't go to the store, she had to watch my sisters, and besides, we didn't have any money. She told me I might find it at the library. My library card was in one of those boxes I threw everything in when Mom made me pack my stuff. It's so unfair. She helped my sisters, but I had to pack all by myself. Dad would have helped me, but *she* doesn't care."

He sniffed and swiped his nose with the back of a hand, the bike wobbling until he got two hands on it. "I peddled to Bobby Hiestermann's house. I know he has a library card. But Bobby's at baseball practice. I don't know why, but I started bawling like a little kid. I got out of there, and I couldn't think of what to do. I pedaled to my old house. It looked so lonely. And I saw the 'Open House' Sign. You know?"

As Jacob talked, his pace got slower and slower, until he stopped and leaned on his bike for support. Ashley wanted to give the kid a hug and tell him it would all be okay. But he was at the age where girls had cooties, and it might *not* be okay. She could be there to listen though and gave him time to collect his thoughts.

"We kept a spare key under the rock by the fence. I hid my bike in the backyard and let myself into the kitchen. It was the first time I saw the house empty. I couldn't go into the basement. That's where dad . . . I went to my bedroom. It was bigger than I remembered. I tried rubbing out the spots on the carpet from where my bed and dresser were, but they were too deep. I laid down on the floor where my bed should be and it all hit me, you know?"

Tears again streamed down his cheek. He raised the bike on its kickstand and used his free hands to heel his eyes. She gave him a minute of silent weeping before prompting, "What hit you, Jacob?"

"It's my fault Dad killed himself. He used to pick me up at practice, and he'd yell and cheer even though he never really liked baseball. My friends were all over me about it, and I told him I didn't want to see him at practice anymore. I didn't mean to hurt him. If I—" His sobs grew into choking gasps.

Despite her earlier reluctance, she hugged him. He curled into her, tears soaking her sweatshirt. She wished she had a magic wand to take Jacob's troubles away. "Your father was very proud of you. He had a picture of the two of you on his desk where he could look at it every day." To get Jacob away from thinking he had hurt his dad, she returned to his story and asked how he ended up in the RV.

"I fell asleep in my bedroom. When I woke up, it was dark, and I felt a nosebleed starting. I ran to the bathroom and got it to stop. Don't tell Mom. I don't want them to burn the inside of my nose."

Ashley assured him she would not tell and encouraged him to continue his story.

"It was so late, Mom was going to kill me. I wanted to stay there, but my stomach was starved, and I remembered Austin's parents never locked their RV, and he and I had stolen cookies from the kitchen. I ate the peanut butter and crackers I found and fell asleep, and Austin found me in the morning, and I swore him not to tell, and he brought me cereal from the house, and we cooked popcorn, and we played some games, and then you found me. Mommy's going to ground me, isn't she? I'll never get to do anything."

Ashley recognized his regression as he moved from Mom to Mommy. She held him at arms length. "I think she'll be relieved to see you. You've given her a big scare. Tell her what you told me. Other than the nosebleed. I think it will be okay. Shall we?" She motioned forward.

He surprised her and grabbed her hand. She released the kickstand and controlled the bicycle with her other hand. Some people say they wish they could be kids again. No way did she want to go back. To change the subject she said, "I saw you have a lot of athlete's autographs."

"Uncle Robert got them for me. He knows everybody. But Mom says he's gone for good. And he promised this year we'd get more Twins autographs. I only have a couple from games Dad took me to." His bottom lip quivered. He blinked away tears. "Nothing's ever going to be like it was."

Ashley had no words to take away that hurt. She gave his hand a squeeze.

When they made the turn onto the street with Jacob's old house, they got their first sight of two cop cars blocking the driveway, flashers on. Neighbors gathered across the street in animated groups of twos and threes.

"Am I going to jail?" Jacob's voice trembled.

"You're not in trouble, Jacob. I am."

Eighteen

"That's her." The guy who had spotted her in the garage pointed in her direction. "That's the woman I saw." The police officer, a blond six-footer, spun, his hand moving to his weapon.

Ashley lowered her voice so only Jacob could hear. "The police officer will ask you questions, Jacob. Tell him the truth and everything will be fine." Her hand steering the bicycle was visible to the cop, and she swung Jacob's hand, allowing him to see her other one was weapon-free.

Her ploy had the desired effect and the cop's posture relaxed. She waited until she was within hailing distance. "Morning, officer. This young man is Jacob Pendergast. Your morning briefing may have alerted you that he's been missing. My name is Ashley Pendergast Prescott. I have an ankle concealed carry."

The officer's eyebrows rose with interest. "Yo, Alex," he called in a loud voice. "Need you out front."

"She was inside the house," the male real estate agent screeched. "That's breaking and entering."

"And," added his female associate, "She's armed and dangerous."

Ashley brought Jacob to a halt and released his hand to assure the officer that she was not restraining him. "If you two will kindly shut up, I'd like to speak to the officer, who knows no breaking and entering statutes exist under the Minnesota penal code. Burglary requires an intent to commit a crime, which is not the case."

A female police officer jogged around the far end of the house, saw the confab and shifted to a fast walk.

"I was driving around looking for Jacob." She gave his trembling hand a supportive squeeze and dropped it again. "I wondered if he might have returned to his former home, and I parked in the driveway. I found an unlocked entry. Thinking that was suspicious and not seeing any no-trespassing signs, I checked the premises and found lights on. I was upstairs and heard two individuals enter the premises. They were scouting the place. I thought they might be methheads stealing copper and anything else they could lift from abandoned houses. Rather than confront them, I escaped through the garage. I spotted this gentleman carrying a metal step stool, making me think I was right. I ran out the rear door rather than risk a confrontation.

"Good thing I did, too, because that's what led me to find Jacob. I know one of you will want to talk to the boy and confirm my story. Jacob, may I store your bike in the car so I can bring it to you? After the officers finish talking with you, one of them will take you home because I have no guardian authority. They'll want to talk with your Mom, too. Help you explain things. It's all good."

"Jacob," the male officer said, "can you do me a big favor and talk with Officer Alex?"

The female officer squatted and held out her hand. "Ever been in a police car before? Let's go to mine and you can tell me what happened."

Jacob looked to Ashley for assurance. "Go ahead. It's fine." She gave his shoulder an encouraging pat.

The male cop told the two real estate agents they could proceed with their open house and waited until they were out of hearing before asking. "You a lawyer or something?"

Something. "Former FBI special agent."

"Let me see your ID and permit card."

"And current U.S. Marshal, which is why I have the weapon and don't have a Minnesota concealed carry permit." *Oh man, I don't have the badge with me and it's the N Iki name anyway, and I don't live in the Virginia apartment anymore.* She handed him her Virginia driver's license.

He copied the information into his notebook and returned the license. "Marshal's ID?"

"That's at the house Jacob's family is staying in."

"House address?"

"It's on Mississippi River Boulevard. I know this sounds suspicious, but I don't know the number. I can drive there, but . . ." She shrugged.

"Who owns the car?" He indicated the Mercedes.

"My sister, Tabitha Maki. She owns the house."

The officer's nod told her he had already run the plates. Ashley related how she found Jacob in the RV with his friend Austin Rathsburton. From the corner of her eye she observed Jacob, accompanied by Officer Alex, go behind the house and soon return. Probably showing her the hidden key. Jacob and Officer Alex joined her.

Alex said, "The agents found no damage to the premises. I've informed them that entering an unlocked building not posted against trespassing to look for Jacob is not a crime. They weren't happy."

"You take Jacob home and talk to his mother. I'll take Prescott and verify her story."

Officer Alex let Jacob ride in the front seat. The male cop led Ashley to his vehicle, secured her weapon in the trunk, and ducked her into the rear. Before he cranked the ignition, she said, "I was hoping I wouldn't have to tell you this, but it's clear I do. You've already verified my story with Jacob. Otherwise we'd be heading to booking. Jacob's mom will verify the rest. The problem will be confirming the U.S. Marshal's information."

His look said he knew she had been bullshitting him all along.

"I work undercover. My badge is in an assumed name. I have it locked in a gun safe in the basement. No one in the Twin Cities is privy to that information. In fact, only . . . " Ashley counted on her fingers, "five people including me know both my real name and my assumed name. I'll go to jail before letting you become number six, which will be a huge hassle for everyone."

"This is way above my pay grade."

"I hear you. I'll open the gun safe and show you the Marshals ID but cover up the name with my fingers. Remember, I didn't have to tell you I wore an ankle rig. I did it to avoid any accidents and keep us all safe. Everything I've told you is true. Do you really think anyone could make up this shit? I suggest you do everyone, including yourself, a huge favor, and ignore the issue of me not carrying my concealed-carry ID."

"As I said, that's not my decision to make."

Nineteen

IN THE END, A BABY shower saved Ashley from spending the weekend dealing with the criminal justice system. Officer Alex was hosting the event for her sister-in-law and convinced her partner that if Ashley came up with an official badge from a gun safe, they would walk away. She did, and Alex drove Ashley to pick up the Mercedes. On her return, Ashley stopped for fast food. She garaged the car and slipped into her room without disturbing the mother-son conversation in the living room.

She expected to see a message from Rick reporting on his meeting with Ambrose. Nothing. She left a message on his cell phone asking him to call, then texted him the same message. Her body wanted her to grab a nap while she waited. She lay on the bed and suffered from busy brain. What a waste of time. Up and pacing the room, her eye caught sight of the papers requiring her deposition on Friday. She read them for the umpteenth time, like how her tongue kept worrying a sore tooth. Her usual cure was to take a run and clear her head. She hadn't expected to still be here and didn't have her running clothes. Besides, it was pouring again—and what the hell was up with Rick?

"Okay, Prescott," she said to her reflection. "Pity party is done. Live in the present, not the past or the future."

She found her yoga mat tucked into a corner of the closet and laid it on the oriental rug. She kicked off her shoes, peeled off her pants and began her standard routine. No sooner had she rolled into a shoulder stand than her cellphone rang.

She pressed into a handstand and flipped to standing. Racing to catch the call, she caught her thigh on the edge of a table. "Dang. Dang. Dang." She pressed the spot to deaden the pain.

"Dang what?" Rick asked.

"Just abusing myself. What—"

"Sounds like fun. But we've got a big problem."

Rick could blow things out of proportion, but Ashley sensed this wasn't one of those times. "Talk." She engaged the speaker, dropped the phone on the bed, and pulled on her trousers.

"I'm feeling sorry for myself, right? I mean, what a fool I am, barging in on a deputy director of the FBI on a Saturday morning and asking for a written get-out-of-jail-free card for you. And the fan belt on my car recently started squealing. It's only got a hundred thousand miles, but I haven't done the timing belt yet. Anyway, I turned down Ambrose's street and spotted an open parking space. It's the better part of a block away, but I'm figuring better to take that than get shut out. I have to lock the Honda with the key because the battery in the fob is shot.

"If Clara—that's his wife—answered, I'd apologize for disrupting her weekend and tell her I urgently needed her husband's advice on a personal matter. She might tell my father, but we'd deal with that if it came up. I was looking both ways, considering my best line if Ambrose opened the door, and—"

"Rick, can you get to the big problem?"

"Sure. I stopped to engage the recording app. Had to shield the screen from the sun. Got 'er done and hid the app from the screen. And nearly shit myself. The vanity Virginia plates on the Lexus SUV in front of me said GEX."

Wait, what? Gex, her former FBI boss, the guy who, to secure an appointment to head Quantico, had fucked her over by leaking her undercover information to Robert Pendergast and then used the leak to torpedo her career, was meeting with Ambrose? She had brought proof of GEX's betrayal to Ambrose. Gex had quit the FBI rather than have his "indiscretion" exposed and made it clear to anyone who would listen that Ashley had screwed him.

Given that history, what earthly reason did Ambrose have to meet with him on a Saturday afternoon?

"Sorry, Rick. My brain froze. The last thing I heard was the license plates said GEX."

"He didn't leave for an hour. I waited in the car, thinking about the last time I had seen him. He had promised he wouldn't get mad at me for disobeying him and supporting you to keep the operation alive. No, he planned to stay cool and get revenge. I'll be honest, Ashley. The longer he was there, the more I wondered if this was him getting revenge, and the more pissed I got. When he finally left, I toggled the recording app, hid the phone, and marched up to Ambrose's door, not caring what he thought. Ambrose was standing there, scratching his head. Soon as he saw me, he asked if something had happened to you.

"Caught me off guard. I said no, then yes, then asked why Gex was there. He grabbed my arm and hustled me into the house and up to his study. He claimed the hush-hush was to prevent Clara from realizing I was there and insisting on entertaining me. The place looked like the last time I was there, except that time I'd worn an elf's hat and sipped cognac. He shut the study door, and he's like, 'What happened to Niki? She okay?' At that point, all my anger turned onto myself because I had let him gain the upper hand, let him use his wife to get me to tiptoe up the stairs and everything. Hell, I never saw her or heard boo from her. She might not have even been there."

"He's a master, Rick. Don't beat yourself up."

"I briefed him on your activities, the demand from Greenwar that you be involved in the illegal entry into the mine site, and your request for written approval. He's like all excited that you had already progressed to Greenwar testing you. I pointed out they might be setting you up to learn what happens when you're arrested for trespassing and destruction of property. He says you shouldn't let yourself get caught. There's no way the Bureau could help because it's not official. You might have to spend a few nights in jail and deal with a public defender, although it would never come to trial because the Feds wouldn't want your actions disclosed in open court. I countered, reminding him that you're worthless on Svalinn if you're sitting in jail."

Maybe this is how Ambrose stabs me in the back.

"Then he gets up like everything is decided. I didn't let him bulldoze me and reminded him that you don't have a lot of reasons to trust FBI leadership. Since he was unwilling to give you written authorization, I threatened to talk with ADNI Park and see what *he* would do."

"Good thinking, Rick."

"Yeah, well, first he got grumpy. Reminding me how he rescued you from that mess in St. Paul, and that you were wise to ask for guidance, but you either trust him or walk away. I said trust is a two-way street, and you *would* walk away unless you knew why he met Gex. I could tell he had never considered that possibility. Ambrose claimed someone had told Gex your personnel file had been stripped of anything beyond the barest facts of your postings. Gex somehow learned that Ambrose had met a female undercover agent at the ballpark, put two and two together, and smelled a rat."

"Dammit, I knew that meeting was a bad idea."

"Ambrose claims he gave Gex a cock-and-bull story implying the meeting regarded a white-collar crime. Seems Ambrose *is* involved in such an operation, and it uses several undercover agents, including two women. I asked if Gex believed him. He laughed at me. 'Of course not,' he said. 'Gex is a bitter man and has nothing better to do than dig.' Ambrose then used that to kick me aside! He claimed one of Gex's Bureau friends might figure out our connection. His solution is to use Seamus McCree as the conduit between you and him.

"That pissed me off. Ambrose screwed up and now he's covering his tail by shunting me aside. I should stay involved, not him. He's the one compromised. He should transfer operation Svalinn to ADNI Park."

Ashley's head was spinning. "You said that?"

"Yeah, and we came to an agreement. I get to brief Seamus and keep my job."

His bitter tone hit her like a punch to the gut. "Rick, I'm sorry for screwing things up for you. That was never my intention. You're safe though. You've got the whole conversation recorded. He can't touch you."

"Not exactly." Rick sounded even more depressed.

"He had a jammer in place?"

"Not hardly. When I saw Gex and retreated to my car to wait for him to leave, I forgot to stop the recorder, so when I turned it back on again—"

Ashley's stomach dropped with disappointment. "You actually turned it off. Crap." Nothing she could do to change it. "Could have happened to anyone." She hit her head on the bed half a dozen times. Yelling at Rick wouldn't change a damn thing, and it wasn't like he did it on purpose. "No biggie, Rick. After you pass your instructions to Seamus, I'll talk with Seamus and ask him to record Ambrose confirming those instructions."

"I've already talked with Seamus and brought him up to speed. I'm really sorry. I—"

"Got it, Rick. Can you tap the grapevine and learn what lies Gex and his henchmen are spreading? Not directly. Tiny might be a source for you. My old roommate, Liya, could work. I'll make sure Seamus keeps you in the loop. Okay, let me see how Christine reacts."

"No, wait. There's one more thing. Ambrose promised he would try to contain Gex. He claims he reminded Gex of the saying that 'he who seeks revenge should dig two graves.' Ambrose told me he wasn't sure Gex was rational enough to be contained, and that you were unleashed. Whatever it takes to protect yourself from that self-serving asshole—his words—is fine in his book."

"He said that?"

"God's truth, but I don't have it recorded because—"

"Rick, please stop beating yourself up. If you hadn't agreed to go to Ambrose's house, we would never have known about Gex. We are much better off knowing."

She spent fifteen minutes reassuring Rick and convincing him his most important role was to be Special Agent Rick Kaska. He must pretend he was unaware of anything happening and do his work extraordinarily well. It was mission impossible, but she counted on him to pull it off. He sounded positive by the time they ended the call.

She was fighting a two-front war: keeping herself in Ambrose's good graces and eliminating Gex's ability to undermine her. Good thing he wasn't standing in front of her, because she'd castrate the bastard and—and that was not productive.

She flopped onto the bed and gazed at the ceiling. Gex was a long-term problem. Greenwar was the immediate concern. Should she call Christine back immediately or strategically allow time to pass? What reason could she use that only this Wednesday or Thursday would work for her to take two days off from her "job" at AHI? If Ford had an aide, she'd have online access to his calendar, and it wouldn't take long to determine his schedule once she checked. Meaning, the sooner Niki called Christine, the better.

Hopping off the bed, she pulled her shoulders back, stared at the mirror and in that forced tension became Niki. Using Niki's phone, she pulled up the recent call log and pressed redial for Christine.

"I didn't expect to hear from you so soon."

"Me neither, but I thought to access his online calendar. I can't do it—"

"Uh-huh. That's—"

"No, no, wait. I want to. But the only time I can is this coming Wednesday or Thursday. After that, it doesn't work with his schedule for at least two weeks." She rushed ahead to prevent objections. "I could claim a stomach bug or something Wednesday. First thing Thursday, we get the sample. That gives me time to return to work Friday morning. Can Thursday work?"

"Are you in Washington this week or traveling?"

"D.C. After that, we're pretty much all over the place, which is the problem."

"I'll see what we can do and let you know Monday."

Twenty

A **COMBINATION OF BETA BLOCKERS,** one whiskey sour, and a late-afternoon Delta flight returned Ashley to D.C. She ordered delivery pizza from her favorite takeout place and spent Saturday evening doing laundry, cleaning the apartment, worrying what would happen with the ATF raid on Sunday at which Mike expected Olivia's arrest for attempting to purchase explosives.

Sunday morning arrived gray and dreary and slightly hungover. Before she woke up enough to make excuses, she changed into her running attire and stuffed several sports gels into the pocket of her water belt. In the kitchen, she rolled the die to determine which of the six exits that didn't trigger an alarm she should use—a strategy she had devised to make it harder for anyone to anticipate her moves and follow her while she was working undercover. Seeing a four, she used the stairway to the first floor, departed through the rear exit, and walked a path that led down the hill to the Klingle Valley Trail.

Fifteen miles and two and a half hours later, she returned to the apartment, her legs pleasantly fatigued, and with a fresh to-do list. While cooling down and drinking her post-run energy drink, she tackled the first thing on her agenda. She left a message for Seamus to contact Deputy Director Ambrose and ask him to provide her access to all the information the Bureau had regarding Greenwar. Their attempted infiltration had failed, but they must have collected some intel. Just because Ambrose didn't mention identified suspects didn't mean they didn't have any. Were there court-ordered wiretaps on anyone's phone? Had they found suspicious vehicles on CCTV feeds near the five murder sites? Probably not because they weren't close to making an arrest, but whatever information they had, she wanted.

Her second call was to her sister, Tabitha Maki. Ashley didn't know her well—three months ago, she hadn't even known the girl existed—but she thought the kid had a caring soul.

"It's Ashley," she said. "I think it's a wonderful thing you've done to let Chloe and her family stay in your house. I've got a favor to ask."

She updated Tabitha on the situation with Jacob, her encounter with the cops, and Chloe's car being repossessed. "Would you be willing to let Chloe drive the Mercedes?"

"Oh gosh. What else can go wrong? Of course you can tell her she can use it."

"I'm not her favorite person, and I'm in D.C. Probably works better if you make the offer and don't mention me. I can't imagine being in her position. A news station exposes her philandering husband to the world. He kills himself, and she discovers everything is mortgaged to the hilt. They've been living on easy street and—" She snapped her fingers. "It's all gone."

"And her being an accountant too?"

"Really?"

"Before she had Jacob, she was a CPA at one of those big-name firms. Bradlee convinced her to become a stay-at-home mom."

Not just a pretty face. That gave Ashley another idea, but she needed to talk with Seamus. "Call her but leave my name out of it. Did you get a subpoena?"

"For what?"

"Junior is contesting Robert's trust provisions. I wondered if they were roping you into this, too."

"I thought Junior was hiding in some country where he can't be extradited."

"Yep. But he can still hire lawyers and make my life miserable. I suspect this is round one."

Twenty-One

NIKI ROLLED THE DIE MONDAY morning before leaving the apartment to spend the day at American Hydrocarbons Institute. Drat, three pips. Taking the elevator to the garage and walking up to street level was the slowest of all her exits. The flipped nickel showed heads, meaning today she'd use the Woodley Park Metro station.

She had dressed for the office in a gray pantsuit and a prim and proper blouse. Her pack weighed a ton, what with her laptop, a ream of documents she was supposed to translate from Mandarin, and low-heeled pumps the color of her pantsuit. Whoever was the first woman to wear sneakers on her commute should receive the Presidential Medal of Freedom. She double-checked that the cellphone and ID were Niki's. The external pouch still contained her quick-change kit comprising a kerchief, two ball caps, and a reversible windbreaker—black on one side, maroon on the other.

Before leaving the apartment, she checked images from the three spy cameras she had installed to cover her floor. All clear. As she walked from the garage, a guy and girl chatting together across the street stiffened. Rookie tell. During her time assigned to the D.C. area, Quantico had used her to train recruits because she had a sixth sense about being followed—the hairs on her neck tingled—and had excellent skills at ditching her followers. They never forewarned her they were running an exercise; it was up to her to spot them. That they were waiting for her at this exit suggested they were part of a large group assigned to track her.

Except she no longer worked for the Bureau, and how the hell did they even know she was in D.C.? She did nothing to give away that she had spotted them, but mentally she morphed into full Niki mode, changing plans before she reached Connecticut Avenue. She strolled past the main entrance of her apartment building and spotted a second pair—males, one white, one black—waiting at the bus stop. Dressed preppy, but with cop shoes. Given their incompetence, this must be their first outing. Typically, they'd have two at each of the six exits and stage more near each of her possible Metro stations.

Okay kiddies, here's lesson number one. She placed herself in the bus line behind the preppies. They did a good job appearing to ignore her until she pulled her SmartTrip card from her pocket and held it between her teeth while she extracted her cellphone and engaged the camera. White guy gave black guy a panicked look and pulled out his wallet. The black guy jammed a hand into his pocket—hopefully, he was searching for quarters. She snapped their picture.

The bus arrived with a screech of brakes. Its doors opened. Niki waited for the guys to commit. If they both got on, she'd follow them up the steps until they had paid their fares and moved past the driver, then she'd back away and wave goodbye.

They got that part right. The one who had extracted money from his wallet got on. The other one stepped aside, like he was waiting for the next bus. She delayed getting on, making the driver impatient. "Coming. Sorry." The driver closed the door behind her. *And then there was one.*

She tapped her SmartTrip card on the reader. Her follower had taken a seat halfway between the entrance and exit and was busy tapping on his phone. She sat down next to him, forcing him to scoot over. "What story did they tell you about me?"

The kid dropped his phone. She picked it up, read the text he'd sent: *Subject is on L2 bus heading north on Connecticut.* She typed another message. *Subject now interrogating me.* Hit send, noted it went to nineteen contacts. She showed him the message and returned his phone. "I asked you a question."

"Nothing," he stammered.

She had only a minute before the Cleveland Park stop, where reinforcements would surely arrive. Giving his shoulder a reassuring squeeze. "Don't feel bad. I also made the couple across the street from the garage entrance. In the future, if you're at a bus stop, have the fare ready in your pocket. Will there be one or two of your buddies joining us at this stop or the next? Doesn't matter. I'll spot them too. But I'm curious. They always give you a scenario for these exercises. What was it this time? Foreign national suspected of spying? Domestic terrorist? Girlfriend of a most-wanted subject? What happens if I spot you?"

Her patter was working. The tightness in his shoulders eased, and he found the courage to look up from his lap and at her face. "Diplomat suspected of spying. We're to stay with you. They don't care if you—the diplomat—know. They'd rather you left the country than have to deport you. It sounded kind of hokey." He offered a smile. "At least we got out of the classroom."

"It *is* hokey." And dissimilar to any surveillance training she had experienced either as a trainee or the target of Quantico training exercises. You never let the subject know you are following them. The training officers at Quantico certainly knew she was no longer part of the FBI. What the hell was going on? "Gonna be a hot one today, but you're outside. I loved going to Quantico's outdoor ranges for the same reason. I'm Ashley, by the way. You're—?"

"Alan."

"Great, two As, head of the class." She lowered her voice. "This is what will happen, Alan. See that big dude?" She tilted her head toward a tall, overweight man three rows behind them. "He's my protection. He looks like a teddy bear, but he's a martial arts pro. At the next stop, I'll wait 'til the last minute and dash out the back. If you follow, I'll punch you in the balls and scream that you groped me. The big dude will be all over you. Painful and embarrassing. I suggest you pretend to grab me, miss, and lose your balance, preventing you from following me. Embarrassing, but no pain. Either way, you won't be following me."

His mouth dropped open. In his eyes, she read confusion and then determination. His face broke into a smile. "This part of the game?"

"I play for real, Alan. You can text your team once I'm off the bus, but you'd better believe me that what I am telling you is true."

The bus slowed. Niki sent a prayer to the universe that the big guy wasn't getting off at this stop. "Now let's talk real world, Alan. I've made you. You're armed, but you have civilians present, inhibiting your options. You don't know if either my friend or I are armed. I have diplomatic immunity, so maybe civilian casualties don't bother me. How you gonna play it?"

She could tell he went into student mode, his brain juggling what he should do in her hypothetical situation and how he should act in the moment. As the bus stopped, a car pulled up, and two people hopped out. A male agent or trainee rushed to cover the rear exit, and shit! Bianca Jenoff, a great trainer and tight with Gex, covered the front. No one at Jenoff's level had ever been involved in a previous training exercise. What had been fun was now a serious problem.

The doors opened. Alan tensed. Wet circles had formed under his armpits, and his forehead shone with perspiration. "Don't get hurt, Alan. It's only a class assignment."

She flexed her toes to stay relaxed, fighting against the adrenaline rioting through her. Wait for them to make their move. She focused on Jenoff, who had a phone to her ear. Alan's phone buzzed with a text. Damn. Nothing she could do until Jenoff decided. If she boarded, Niki left; Jenoff remained off, Niki stayed on.

Jenoff stood on the first step, fumbling at the machine to scan her fare— biding time, not committing. Niki adjusted her feet for a quick exit, tightened her grip on her knapsack. A guy entered the bus behind Jenoff, forcing the issue.

Still, Jenoff delayed, first fiddling with counting change, then crumpling a dollar bill to make sure it wouldn't go through the machine—excellent technique. The driver told Jenoff to step aside and let the next guy through and try again. Jenoff sidled in, and the guy pressed behind her, blocking her exit.

Niki burst from her seat, raced down the steps, slammed her knapsack into the closing door. The outside trainee had positioned himself too close. She reached the curb at a run, nailing the guy's solar plexus with her elbow. "Sorry, tripped," she said to the doubled-over man. She hoisted the knapsack onto her shoulders and sprinted up Connecticut, past the Broadmoor, followed its driveway into the parking garage, raced through the lot, and hopped a low wall at the back. Only then did she stop and look behind her.

No one following. Yet. Pushing through the trees at a fast walk, she reached the Melvin C. Hazen Trail and ran it at a steady nine-minute-a-mile pace. Pulling up her mental map of the Rock Creek Park complex, she decided the Grove #2 parking area was a good place for a ride to meet her. Once past the Pierce Mill, where roving cars could no longer spot her, she stopped, caught her breath, and ordered the rideshare to arrive in fifteen minutes. She'd get there in ten.

Per Alan's briefing, they were happy to let her know they were following her, making harassment and disruption their likely objectives. This must relate to Gex's visit to Ambrose. She was confident no one had followed her around D.C., which meant either someone had wired Niki's apartment or had tapped her phone's GPS.

Ambrose had arranged for her to temporarily retain Niki's apartment—

paid through some black funding source—until they devised a more permanent arrangement. The Bureau had the standard keys, but would have to pick the extra locks she had installed—not a high barrier for pros.

The tapped phone might not be illegal since the FBI had paid for the number. In either case, Ambrose could order that. Or one of Gex's friends. She had turned the GPS off, but if they overrode her setting, they could know exactly where she was. She pulled off the phone's rubberized protective cover. Straightening a paperclip she'd attached to a document she planned to translate, she disengaged the SIM tray and removed the card.

Solving that problem created others. She must procure a new phone and give Christine the number ASAP. And give it to Seamus to allow him to tell her how to access the Greenwar files she'd requested from Ambrose. Definitely not Ambrose. Unfortunately, not Rick, either. She trusted him, but the FBI knew all his devices. Ambrose or rogue agents working with Gex might compromise his communications. She couldn't use the Beorn secure communications either because Ambrose got those.

Wait! If Ambrose was suspect, could she still trust ADNI Park?

If not, nothing could save her. But that did not mean sharing everything with Park. She needed a secure communication system for herself, Seamus, and Rick like what she used as Beorn. She knew the perfect guy to consult.

Twenty-Two

NIKI'S MORNING DISAPPEARED IN A flurry of activity: making nice to American Hydrocarbons Institute's receptionist; the awkward exchange when Jim Ford's administrative assistant thudded a stack of folders on the conference room table and rapid-fired instructions that "Mr. Ford thought these would prove useful before you and he talk tomorrow." Niki glanced at the documents, all in Spanish, dealing with some oilfield or the other.

At ten, she ducked away and bought a new phone and number for Niki. Back in the conference room, she used it to call Seamus's son, Patrick McCree. She left a message telling him to give his father this new number and to please return her call.

Patrick called Niki within a minute. "You okay?" he asked. "What trouble has my father gotten into this time?"

"Not him. Me. Let me give you a hypothetical and you tell me if you can solve it. Let's say the three musketeers wanted to communicate with utmost security among themselves. So secure that no one snooping, including a very rich and motivated uncle with unlimited resources and technology, could tell where any of the three are located."

"What type of communication are we talking about? Can it be text or must it be auditory?"

Niki would love to speak with Seamus and Rick, but it wasn't safe. The Feds had amazing technology to conjure voices from vibrations on windows and ripples in water glasses. "Text."

"Good. But here's the thing with that uncle. If he throws his bottomless resources at the task, eventually he can crack anything you set up. You remember how law enforcement took down Silk Road in 2013? That's kindergarten compared to what they can do now. Most people don't realize that the NSA has cracked TOR and most of the other anonymizing browsers. That's not divulging secrets from my contract work with them. It's common knowledge within the hacking community. That doesn't mean using a new, lesser-known one won't make it hard for them. So yeah, your three musketeers could create an encrypted chatroom, use a VPN to obscure their locations, and use a special browser to make identities nearly anonymous. With appropriate computer hygiene, you can limit the risk of exposure unless the uncle grabs one of the musketeer's computers during a session. Or one of the three turns traitor."

His last line knotted her stomach. She trusted Seamus, and Patrick for that matter, to the ends of the earth. Could she say the same about Rick? Not that long ago, she was leery of his intentions. He had demonstrated his loyalty, but he had limits. Her gut said to trust him. "Is it legal? I desperately need this, Patrick, but I won't ask you to help me if it's illegal."

"Nothing illegal in setting up the communication structure. What someone uses it for is another issue. What's this all about?"

Patrick knew she worked undercover. Without disclosing any confidential details, she explained she was working to expose rogue federal agents who, she believed, were illegally hacking her communications. "What would it take—money, material, time—to set this up?"

"Two hours and access to the three people's computers. Access can be physical or remote. They'll have to trust me to control their computer to download the required files and show them how to use the setup. But—thinking out loud here—if you're working undercover, you might not have access to your computer. Give me a day or two, and I can design a secure communications structure you can use with any computer or phone. That'll avoid people having to let me muck around with their computers. The trick is structuring a secure randomized blockchain—never mind, you don't want the details."

"Cost?"

"You kidding? This will be a blast, and I don't have any urgent consulting assignments. I assume you needed this yesterday."

"I can give you access to my computer whenever. Your dad is one of the other two people. The third may not want you to know who he-she is. Can you show your father how to install it on the third person's hardware? You're right, I'll need remote access, and your dad forgets to charge his computer."

Patrick laughed. "Yep, I can see why you want him to have it. The long-term solution will take time, but I'll create the easy part this afternoon and install that on your computer and Dad's."

"Can you tell your dad about all this? I don't want to call him because—"

"Got it. This number good for me to reach you?"

"Yep. If I were there, I'd give you a big hug. You're a lifesaver."

"I hope you mean that figuratively."

So did she.

Niki ended her phone call with Patrick, cranked that she had figured out a way to communicate securely with Seamus and Rick. Well, Patrick had found the way, but she had thought of Patrick. Inspiration had to count for something. Her eyes were glazing from reading deadly dull Spanish documents when the buzz-buzz of the conference room phone brought her blinking to the present. "This is Niki."

"There's a Mr. Gentle here to see you."

The name rang no bells. "Be right out." Other than AHI employees, the only people who knew she was at AHI were Seamus, Rick, and maybe Ambrose. Had Ambrose sent someone?

Fighting the tension of facing an unknown disaster, she staged the room to look like she'd been interrupted and hid anything important from prying eyes. She stuck her hands in her pockets and moseyed to the receptionist. Mr. Gentle, a stranger to her, was a thirtyish Caucasian with receding brown hair, whose lively hazel eyes watched her approach. She said, "How may I assist you?"

"I hoped I might catch you for an early lunch. My treat." He offered a flirty smile, which Niki noticed the receptionist ate up.

Niki bit her bottom lip, a picture in evaluating his offer. "I've got a ton of work, but a quickie sounds good." The receptionist unsuccessfully hid her surprise. Niki gave the guy a smile. The double entendre would give the AHI rumor mill more grist. "Let me get my things. Be right back."

"I'd love to see where you work."

The guy did not give her a federal-agent vibe. Either he was exceptionally good, or—or what? Niki framed her face into a question for the receptionist. "Is that permitted? I don't want to break any rules."

"Please sign your guest in." The receptionist unearthed a sign-in sheet and handed the clipboard and a pen to him. With a flourish, he signed Timothy Gentle.

They passed Jim Ford's office, and she said, "Here's where the big boss lives. I'd introduce you, but he's meeting with a bunch of lobbyists."

At the conference room door, Niki swept her arm, "Ta da. Let me grab my bag." Gentle followed her in, head swiveling like a bobblehead, looking for what she did not know. He picked up one of the Spanish documents she was "reviewing." If he understood Spanish, he might fall asleep reading about viscosity of oil from test wells drilled in Ecuador.

She pulled a black cross-body bag that contained Niki's wallet and new cellphone from her pack and slung it on her shoulder. Motioning toward the exit. "Seen enough?"

"Very impressive." He dropped the papers on the desk. "Let's grab a bite and then I'll let you get back to collecting useful documents."

Collecting useful documents. Greenwar? His hint of a drawl led her to conclude he hailed from Northern Virginia or Maryland, not the Midwest.

She closed the conference room door and let him lead the way back to the receptionist. Her tingle of anticipation grew as they held their silence on the elevator ride, through the lobby, until they were outside.

He turned right. She followed, scanning pedestrians, doorways, and windows for anything that twitched her antennae. At Franklin Square, he slowed and pulled a phone from inside his jacket. He shielded it with his body, not allowing her to see the number he dialed. Holding it to his ear, a faint ring escaped followed by an indistinct voice.

"No issues," he said. He steered her to an empty bench, where they sat, and offered her the phone, "Christine."

Greenwar! She showed Gentle big, startled eyes, and let surprise sound in her voice. "This is Niki."

"If we set it up for Thursday morning, how would you get there?"

As though recovering from her surprise, she paused and used the time to craft an answer she hoped demonstrated a certain level of competence combined with a naiveté. "I checked flights. I might not even have to fake being sick in the office, although that still might be better if I like threw up or something. Make it more convincing. I can fly to Minneapolis-St. Paul and rent a car. I'd have to get a hotel and find a Home Depot or someplace to get bolt cutters. Do they come in different sizes? Do you know what kind of lock or chain is there? I guess I get the biggest, right? This will set me back a lot of bucks, do you guys have funding, a way to reimburse me, 'cause I really don't make that kind of money."

Christine wasn't interrupting, so Niki blasted forward like a nervous woman would. "I mean, I just bought a new phone with a new number on my way to work this morning. I didn't think we wanted to use my regular phone. My credit cards have enough room to charge everything—well maybe I want to pay for the bolt cutters with cash, 'cause if you believe those TV shows, the cops check for recent purchases and stuff. Anyway, this whole thing makes me kind of nervous. I think throwing up on Wednesday may be pretty easy. I—"

"Have you gotten your hands on any more documents?"

"Not yet. I can only snoop when both Mr. Ford and his battle-ax assistant are gone. That doesn't happen all that often. Mr. Ford is having me review a bunch of material in Spanish concerning test wells in Ecuador. I can get copies of those, but I don't think they're worth anything. Let me give you my new number."

Christine's sigh came down the line before confirming the number with

Niki. "We'll reimburse you. Assume it's a go. I'll call Wednesday with the exact time and who and where to meet one of us. Please give the phone to Timothy."

That went well, Niki thought. Too well?

TWENTY-THREE

THAT EVENING, ASHLEY WALKED UP Connecticut Avenue toward Niki's apartment carrying Thai carryout for dinner by the top of the bag because she'd burned her hand on the hot bottom. She walked through the archway to the complex and twigged to the young woman wearing sweats sitting with one haunch on the rock wall surrounding the front fountain—a place in the shade hardly ever used by the residents. Ashley modified her approach to keep the woman in her peripheral vision. Noticing the woman's lips moving, Ashley made a beeline toward her, waving to draw her attention. "Excuse me?" Ashley said using a voice that turns every statement into a question.

The woman tapped her phone twice and looked up, pointed to herself.

"Have you been here long? My boyfriend was supposed to meet me? He's like six-feet? Looks like an FBI agent? Clean-cut, polished shoes, preppy in an older good sorta way?" Until the woman heard 'FBI,' she had done a good job of looking perplexed. That word triggered six or seven eye blinks. *Gotcha. Now twist the hook.* "I'm a little late, and he and some friends had a big surprise for me this morning, and I kinda ran away from them? I know, TMI? You haven't seen him?"

The woman didn't stare at her or get up and walk away as a normal person would. "Sorry. Can't help you."

"Huh, I thought sure you might have worked for him." Ashley skipped up the stairs, waved her way past the doorman. She got off the elevator on the third floor and walked to the end of the hall to a window that overlooked the fountain. The woman was gone.

Time to remain ice-cool and focus on tactics. She could get pissed later. The FBI had probably compromised Niki's apartment—she'd be a fool to think otherwise. Her new cellphone was clean, but was Rick's? She'd have to risk calling him before Patrick created the secure communication link. Rick answered, and she filled him in on her recent run-ins with the FBI.

"You sure know how to beard the beast," he said. "Rumor mill had it that Bianca Jenoff was to be Gex's number two after his appointment to run Quantico. Don't know what's going to happen to her now that Gex is out of the picture, but I'd give a billion to one odds that she's pissed at you for spoiling Gex's promotion. Look, I didn't mention this earlier because I had nothing solid. Tiny recently told me several random people have asked him what made Gex decide to retire. And Liya told me that people have been asking her what you're up to. I'll eat my boots if there's not something big going on with Gex."

She released a puff of air. "With operation Svalinn heating up, I don't have time to wait for this to resolve itself. I need to disappear from their radar. That requires securing a new ID that I can use to fly on Wednesday. I'll shake my current tail and hide until I get them. We don't have to create a background, just the IDs. Passport, driver's license, couple of credit cards with decent credit limits."

Rick cleared his throat. "Ambrose will shit a brick."

Ashley smiled to herself. "Ambrose won't know a thing."

"Black market stuff is a terrible idea."

"No kidding. Bring your car and meet me at the pedestrian entrance to the zoo at oh-two-thirty hours tomorrow morning. Make sure you're not tailed. We're going to make a house call."

ASHLEY WAS AWAKE FROM A restless nap before her alarm went off at 0200 hours. She painted her face and hands commando-style, put her phone into the Faraday portion of her knapsack, rendering it untraceable, and left the apartment fifteen minutes before Rick was to pick her up. Arriving before him, she crouched in bushes beside the pedestrian entrance to the zoo. He pulled up right at 0230, his fan belt squealing like a tortured banshee. She waited until the street was empty of traffic, then dashed to his Honda Accord and hopped in. Snapping the seatbelt in place, she told him to drive.

He pulled onto the street. "What the hell do you have planned? And what's in your belly band?"

"If you don't know, you won't have to lie. You should get that fan belt fixed, Rick."

His hands tightened on the steering wheel. "Give me the five Ws."

She pointed for the next turn and outlined her plan.

He slammed the brakes and parked at the curb. "That is the worst idea

I have ever heard. Who cares if ADNI Park's not married? He could have a girlfriend with him. A hooker."

"You don't have to yell. I'm wearing paint, not ear plugs. If someone's there, she or he will get a surprise. We're wasting time. If you won't help me, then drive as close as you dare, and I'll walk. I'll walk from here if I have to."

"Fine."

As in, *not fine,* but he resumed driving. She was glad she hadn't asked him if Patrick could load software onto his computer. Better to see how he reacted to everything before committing to include him.

TWENTY-FOUR

RICK SAID NOTHING DURING THE rest of the ride. He let her off in the Sibley Hospital outdoor parking lot, far away from eyes in the hospital and guarded from the street by a row of tall bushes. She switched off the dome light, got out, and disappeared between the bushes. In a few minutes she'd learn how bad her plan was.

She shifted into Niki mode and crossed the street, projecting the thought to the world that despite how she had dressed, she belonged there. She entered the woods and navigated by general feel and occasional glimpses of the rocking-chair moon high in the sky. Temps had dropped into the sixties, and a modest breeze gave her some noise cover. Fingers crossed, Spring Valley was the kind of neighborhood where dogs slept soundly inside houses.

She left the woods, raced across a lawn to the nearest shrub, and triggered security lights from the houses. Dropping to the ground, she waited until the lights extinguished before crawling the hundred feet to the street. Positioned in front of Assistant Director of National Intelligence Park's house was a dark sedan sporting two whip antennae. Squatting next to its front panel was someone scanning in her direction with binoculars. *The damn security lights alerted him.* Standard procedures called for the guy in the car to monitor their electronic surveillance while a second guy patrolled outside.

Rick was right: she *was* fucking crazy to think this would work. Well, one way or the other, she would have a private tête-à-tête with ADNI Park in a few minutes.

Keeping to the shadows, she slipped through a backyard, scaled a wire-mesh fence, and squatted in a fragrant rose garden in the next backyard. From there, she spotted her target house and verified that the massive tree she had seen on the satellite view of the neighborhood gave her access to its garage roof.

Peripheral movement jacked her heart rate into the red zone. The partner? She held her breath to the point of fainting, and a whitetail deer ambled into view, stretching for a bite here and a nibble there, triggering the next motion sensors as it reached the target's yard. It walked to a circular flowerbed and chowed down, ignoring the multiple lights.

The deer had habituated to the lights, which meant the security forces had become accustomed to deer triggering the lights. No shadows appeared at the windows. No one came to check on foot. Nothing spooked the deer.

She followed a deer trail carved into the dirt to a storage shed at the rear edge of the target's property. Kneeling, her legs brushed together, denim on denim. The deer's head swung toward her, a green leaf hanging from the corner of its mouth. She and the deer froze, a living Norman Rockwell painting.

The world held its breath.

Thirty feet of open ground separated her from the climbing tree, a sturdy maple. The deer returned to grazing. She sprinted to the tree and jumped, caught the limb with both hands, and swung herself up like she was mounting uneven parallel bars. While the deer made a racket running through the brush, she scrambled up the tree and shimmied out a limb above the roof. She lowered herself and dropped the last eighteen inches onto the roof with a too-loud thump, scrambled to the darkest spot, and plastered herself to the shingles. The kettle drum of her heartbeat pounded in her ears. She breathed through her nose and waited.

A beep from a walkie-talkie announced the presence of a security officer. "I wish we could shoot the damn deer. Out."

The guy was below her. If he stepped away from the building and shined a flashlight up, her only recourse was to smile, wave with both hands, and hope he didn't shoot her.

A garbled male voice said, "Copy that. It was almost time for the perimeter walk, anyway. Complete the circuit. See you in a couple. Out."

"Roger. Out."

Her ears followed his progress up the cement walk, the rattle of a door handle, return steps. A flash of light bounced off a window. Retreating steps. Then nothing.

Still there?

She counted seconds. At one hundred and eighty, the lights clicked off, leaving her in the dark and quiet.

She climbed from the garage roof to the attached house and shuffle-stepped along that roof to the nearest dormer. The dormer's alcove blocked her view of most of the room, but the dim glow from a clock on top of a bureau painted what she could see in soft red light. Nothing else on the bureau. Carpeted floor. Quilt precisely folded at the foot of the bed. No shoes, slippers, socks on the floor. It had all the trappings of a spare bedroom.

A full-window screen covered a six-over-six vinyl window inset four inches from the outside edge. Probably double hung, upgraded from the original, which required storm windows during the winter. Centering herself on the window, she found no visible sign of security. With her luck, it was one of those systems built into the window frame.

She pulled a utility knife from her bellyband and ran the blade along the edge of the screen in short cuts. She rolled the screen and tucked it under the flashing. Pressing hard on the sash of the lower window, she pushed it back and forth into the casing. Up close the noise was like a hurricane rattling the window. She hoped her body blocked most of the noise as she rocked it a dozen times until the lock loosened enough for her to disengage the mechanism.

She raised the bottom sash and climbed in. White noise from warm air flowing through metal ducts masked any other house noises. No sooner did she have that thought than the furnace rattled to quiet. The high nose-whistle of someone sleeping nearby replaced the white noise.

If security included an inside guard, she was at most risk of dying the moment she stepped from the room into the hall. She gathered her nerves at the doorway and strode past the threshold.

No one there.

She followed the nose-whistle down the hall and found ADNI Averell Harrington Park sleeping on his back diagonally across a king-sized bed. At six-nine, that was the only way he'd fit the bed. Despite the heat being on in the house, a breeze rustled curtains secured to let in the air and brought in a hint of his neighbor's rose garden. The nightstand next to his bed held no weapons. Folded glasses lay on an electronic reading device in front of a lamp. The drawer might hold a gun, but she could prevent him from getting to that. No panic buttons she could see.

She snapped her fingers to wake him. The whistle continued without modification. She reached down and squeezed one of his feet. Park's eyes blinked open, and she stepped into his view. Using a calm, though forceful tone she said, "Director Park, we need to talk. Please don't yell, I have no reason to hurt you, but I'll silence you if I must."

He squinted at her. Guessing his glasses were more than for reading, she unfolded them and tossed them on the bed, keeping her distance from his long arms.

"Is my security detail dead?" He looped the glasses over his ears.

A rush of positive feelings that he thought of his men first warmed her. "No sir. Not injured either. If you know me at all, you know me by my code name—Beorn."

His eyes widened in surprise. "I know the name, although in this light you could be anyone."

"I'm in disguise. Even if I were stupid enough to turn on a light and alert your security, you wouldn't recognize me. Deputy Director Ambrose gave me that code name because he thought when cornered, I rear-up and fight like a bear. Given my sex and size, he figured it would throw off anyone who stumbled across the name. Has Ambrose made you aware of Operation Svalinn?"

"No."

"I should backtrack. Did you and Ambrose agree Beorn should work for the two of you on special sub rosa assignments without affiliation with any official federal agency?"

"What assurance do I have that you are not recording this conversation?"

Smarter than Ambrose on that account. "My word. I'm here because I require help to complete an assignment. Lives are at risk, and I cannot trust anyone at the FBI." Saying it made her realize that wasn't an accurate statement. She *was* trusting Rick. "Either talk with me or call security." She sat on a corner of the bed and folded her hands in her lap.

"Tell me everything."

She didn't do that, but she included her meeting with Ambrose and Jim Ford, the status of the assignment, Gex visiting Ambrose early Saturday morning, the FBI "training" operation run against her Monday morning, and the FBI presence at Niki's place Monday evening.

"If I am to complete this assignment, I can't have FBI interference—well-intentioned or otherwise." She gave him a few seconds to respond. He did not. She continued. "I need a new identity—enhanced driver's license or passport—that allows me to travel. And two credit cards to purchase plane tickets, rental car, motel, meals, cell phones. It has to happen today."

"That's a tall order."

"But not impossible. All due respect sir, I can get black market fake IDs in an hour." *If I had cash, which I don't.* "This isn't about what I want. This is what I need if you want me to work the Svalinn assignment."

He cocked his head. "If you were me, what would you do?"

"Personally take me to the lab to create my identity."

"And explain your presence here how?"

"Summon your limo. When it arrives, we leave together. Tell your bozos you hired me to test their security. They failed. I get in the limo's rear seat with you and off we go. You badge us into whatever NSA facility does the work on your authority."

TWENTY-FIVE

THE LIMO AND ITS SUPPORT vehicles arrived with fresh security. At Niki's appearance with Park at his front door, the looks on the faces of his security guards were perfect to illustrate a Wikipedia entry for *mortified*. Park ripped them both new assholes and sent them home.

Park's limo brought them to an underground garage. From there, Park escorted her through underground passages, badged them through a security station, more underground passages, an elevator taking them further below ground, two more sets of security stations including a full-body scanner, another elevator up (at least she thought it was a different one), and into a warren of rooms. There, Niki changed from ninja to civilian, donning provided clothes that fit, applying proper make-up, and choosing from the hundred available wigs which to use for her photo shoot.

While she waited for them to produce her new IDs, Park had her review photographs of FBI staff and trainees currently assigned to Quantico. The only fully trained FBI employees were Bianca Jenoff and the woman Niki had accosted the previous night, another special agent assigned to Quantico. She identified Alan and several of his classmates. "I do not want anything negative to happen to those kids. They thought it was a routine training exercise."

Park disagreed. "What if they chose those individuals because Jenoff could influence them?"

She shook her head to indicate her dismay. "I suppose the Bureau's Internal Investigations Section should look at them." She caught the tightening around his eyes. "Maybe not them, because they could be involved, too. However you do it, do it gently. Gex shouldn't ruin any more lives."

"Any more *innocent* lives," Park said. "Where do you want my people to take you?"

"Any Metro station tworks. I'll grab stuff from Niki's apartment. From there, I'll shake any followers, grab a Zipcar, and drive to a distant airport to catch a flight to Minneapolis-St. Paul using one of my new IDs."

"And if they're waiting for you in the apartment?"

"Then it's going to get ugly."

He subjected her to an analyzing stare. "That would be unfortunate. Give me an hour. We'll electronically surveil Niki's apartment from a distance. If anyone is in there, a SWAT team will remove them. Shall I also detain any external watchers?"

"That would tip my hand. I'm confident I can shake them." She offered a self-deprecating smile. "It's what I do. Here's a wild thought. Can you legally bug that apartment if I give permission? I'd love to know who is doing what in my absence."

"I'll take it under advisement. Ah, here we are."

An older woman, open-toed sandals, sequined top over crisp jeans handed Niki a brown paper bag. "Six sets of IDs, each containing a Virginia enhanced drivers license and two credit cards with limits of twenty grand. I assume I don't need to tell you that if you get caught with more than one ID on you, the jig's up. Give us until ten this morning to update all the computer files before you use any of them. You'll also find a money clip with $500 in used twenties."

Twenty-Six

ASHLEY GATHERED THE NECESSITIES FROM Niki's apartment and spent much of the rest of Tuesday making sure no one was following her. Convinced she was unaccompanied, she traveled to a lower-tier motel near the Richmond airport. Wednesday morning, she flew to Minneapolis-St. Paul and picked up a rental car.

She stopped after entering Wisconsin at a restaurant with public Wi-Fi and had Patrick McCree, who had already installed the software on his father's computer, do the same for her. That locked down her communications with Seamus. Patrick would install it on Rick's computer once Seamus convinced Rick it was okay. Patrick also instructed her how to access the communication structure from any device with an internet connection.

"Remember," Patrick said, "use a VPN to obscure your location. You'll see the password screen asks for a fingerprint or a password. If anyone tries to use the fingerprint sensor, the computer automatically wipes itself. No way to stop it. If someone inputs an incorrect password, you have ten seconds to give it the correct password, otherwise it's toast."

"So no one can force me to unlock the machine. Nice."

"You're welcome. Using other devices to access the network is not as secure, and the more times you use them, the less secure they become."

"Got it," she said. "I don't need to hear technical stuff I won't understand. Thank you and hugs to your family."

Yesterday, the two male McCrees had ganged up on her, Patrick acting as intermediary between her and Seamus. They had insisted Seamus be her backup for the break-in to the mine site to let in the tech guy taking the water sample. If nothing else, he could report to Park if the plan went sideways.

"You betcha," Patrick said. "Try this system with Dad once you learn the details of your meeting. Last I heard, he will be a birdwatcher exploring the area—which is a role he can play well."

She still had to learn the final details from Christine. That call interrupted Niki's dinner in an A&W restaurant outside Minong,

Wisconsin. Niki let it ring twice while she chewed fast and choked down a mouthful of burger. She stuck a finger in her ear to block the background noise of the busy restaurant, and answered with, "This is Niki."

"Where are you?"

"Holed up in the lovely megalopolis of Minong, Wisconsin. What's the plan?"

"Meet your contact at the Nelson Lake boat landing at eight tomorrow morning. That's pretty much due west of you. Plenty of parking for your car and our man will bring you to the site. The well sample collection is scheduled for ten, give or take. That gives you plenty of time to cut the chain and verify the exact location of the well head."

"I'd rather we meet at the gate."

"That's not the plan."

"Christine. I'm not comfortable getting into a vehicle with someone I have never met. You trust the guy, but that's something I don't do. I want my own wheels. We can meet at the gate. If you only want one car there, I can follow your man down and one of us can park nearby."

"Donnie is trustworthy. He's committed to the cause."

Niki let silence make her argument and again counted seconds in her head. Christine caved at twenty-three. Niki and Donnie would meet at the boat landing and drive in separate cars to the mine site.

Niki bolted the rest of her food and hurried to her motel room. Using the new protocol, she notified Seamus that he should be there by eight to make sure he arrived before them.

Seamus responded, *Any birdwatcher would be there by dawn. You want me to hang near the gate area or by the wellhead?*

Wellhead, she responded, and remember the only reason you're there is to let Donnie know someone else is in the vicinity. Something goes sideways, stay down. Anything else?

Ambrose called this afternoon. He sounded nervous and asked if I knew where you were. I said I hadn't heard a peep from you. Which is true, you haven't peeped in any of our conversations. He gave me a link and password to information you requested.

Excellent. She'd be able to review that information tonight. Maybe learn about this Donnie she was meeting.

He gave her the login information and added, *Bad news on the home front: Chloe joined Junior's suit to challenge Robert's estate provisions.*

Niki signed off. That was Ashley crap. Until she survived tomorrow's games with Greenwar, she required Niki's full vigilance and concentration.

The FBI's files revealed an investigation in disarray. It wasn't until the third executive murder that local law enforcement had made the link to the *Blame and Shame* blog and contacted the FBI. After the fourth, the Bureau initiated the long process to infiltrate Greenwar. Not until the last few weeks had they formed a joint task force with ATF. Assuming Ambrose had provided everything from that task force, neither side trusted the other: the ATF had shared overview information with the Bureau, protecting its sources, and the Bureau had shared no specific details from the murder investigations.

And on the murder investigations, the Bureau had diddly-squat. The shooter profiles were useless crap based on nothing more than who the targets had been and the ammunition used. One interesting tidbit was a statistical analysis the Bureau had run on the five victims. The link with the highest correlation was each had management responsibility overseeing a project that had polluted drinking water and led to alleged cancer hot spots. Was that why Ambrose had said Jim Ford met the profile of those targeted?

A judge had approved tapping Christine's phone because the Bureau convinced him she was responsible for the *Blame and Shame* articles. But the judge had labeled monitoring anyone else a fishing expedition, unjustified by facts.

Scanning transcripts of Christine's calls, the major conclusion she drew was Christine was circumspect—as she had been in her conversations with Niki. Thinking over those conversations, they'd used Niki's first name, but not her last name. She had to make sure it stayed that way.

The files had no mention of Donnie. All that work, and she was still going in blind.

NIKI FOLLOWED DONNIE'S ANCIENT FORD Ranger on a direct route from the Nelson Lake boat launch to the mine site. She knew they were getting close when she spotted signs nailed to trees on the west side of the road proclaiming, "Private Property No Trespassing," with the mine owner's name. They slowed to a crawl passing the entrance. She recognized Seamus's Subaru Outback parked in front of one half of the gate.

A quarter mile later, Donnie pulled into the remnant of an old logging road, its route blocked by a rusty wire cable so long in place the trees had grown around it. She idled next to him, powered down her window, caught a whiff of leaf mold. Donnie yelled for her to turn around while he got his stuff.

She found a place where the road was marginally wider, did a seven-point turn. She applied mosquito dope to fend off the buzzing bloodsuckers. "Stuff" meant a blue aluminum thermos clipped to his belt, a hand-drawn map to the well head, and a set of wrenches. He hopped in and Niki drove to the gate, parking next to the Outback.

Donnie circled the Outback, looking in the windows. Niki followed, spotted McDonald's wrappers behind the driver's seat, a bunch of field guides—birds, butterflies, amphibians—scattered on the back seat. The passenger seat held an empty binocular case partially obscuring a folded Wisconsin map marked up with several routes. "Looks like some kind of naturalist," she offered.

Donnie grunted something unintelligible and moved to the gate. "Better open this thing before our guy shows up."

Niki popped her trunk and retrieved her new bolt cutters. A chain double-wrapped the two sections of the gate together; a keyed lock secured the chain. She pulled the chain.

"Just cut the darn lock."

"Chains are easier. I hoped to cut it in a place that allows us to rearrange it and make it to look like it's locked. Chain's too short, though." The chain snapped with a twang.

Donnie pushed on the gate sections. The half in front of the Subaru swung open. The other half did not budge.

Niki knelt and brushed leaves and dirt from the bottom of the gate. "Someone cemented this half in place. Why the hell would they do that?"

"Didn't want oversized trucks driving in. That's rebar into the concrete. Your bolt cutter's useless on that. Unless the Subaru's owner moves his car, we are royally screwed. Honk your horn."

Niki remembered Seamus had once used three toots to signal for help. Hadn't worked then; didn't work now. While she was in the car, Donnie couldn't see her hands in her lap. It was risky, but she texted Seamus to get his ass to the gate and move his car. *Message not sent.* "You got tow straps or a heavy chain?"

Donnie scratched his beard. "Nope. Guess this proves it was a shitty idea."

All it proved was Seamus had parked in the wrong place. She picked up a softball-sized rock and rifled it through the driver's window, smashing the glass into hundreds of pieces. *Thank you safety glass.*

"The hell? Listen lady, cars don't work that way. You can't shift it into neutral without a key."

Mansplaining at its worst. With a screwdriver they didn't have they could have accessed the shift lock release. "Ninety percent of people keep the valet key either in their glove compartment or center console."

"Huh. Really?"

No, asshole, I made it up, but I know Seamus keeps his in the center console. "Donnie, if this is more than you bargained for, then give me the damn map and tools and get the hell out of here." She pulled her sleeves past her fingers to avoid leaving prints and cleared the remaining glass. Wiggling far enough in to reach the center console, she opened it and retrieved the valet key. "Bingo." She slithered out, reached in to retrieve the rock, and heaved it far across the road into the woods.

"What you gonna say if the guy shows up?"

"Cross that bridge if we come to it. No prints. No proof."

"Yeah, but if he goes for the cops, we're toast."

The key opened the door. She tossed her keys to Donnie, which he caught one-handed. "After I back his out, pull mine through. I'll tuck this thing close to those bushes where, with a little luck, the water guys won't notice the broken window. Then I'll take care of him going for the cops."

Maneuvers complete, she pushed aside bushes to reach the Subaru's far side rear tire. Using the key, she deflated both tires on that side of the car. "Spare won't help him, and I have no cell service. It'll take him time to get somewhere he can contact the cops. We'll be long gone."

"What if he sees us?"

She replaced the valet key where she had found it. "Same bridge we didn't cross before."

THE TECHNICIAN ARRIVED ON TIME and completed his sampling in four minutes. He could find his way out. Donnie reattached the wellhead cap, nattering away while he tightened the bolts with the wrenches. With the mission accomplished, Niki had no reason to think Donnie would do her harm, but she wouldn't let her guard down either, which is why she stood next to another fist-sized rock. She listened with one ear in case his nervous patter revealed anything worthwhile. The only hitch in the assignment had been Seamus parking in front of the wrong half of the gate. She didn't have a solution for fixing his flats, but they'd figure out something.

With the last bolt tightened, Donnie finally got around to asking a question. "What's gonna happen if the Subaru guy is there when the technician leaves?"

"You sure worry a lot. Maybe they'll both be gone. Maybe you'll offer to drive the guy to the cops. If I wasn't willing to drive here with you, even with Christine's assurances, I sure as hell won't drive with a complete stranger. Particularly one who's likely pissed off about his car. Maybe he pulls a gun and shoots us dead. Maybe he's a she and she pulls a gun and kills us. Maybe. Maybe. Maybe."

Donnie raised his hands in surrender.

"Get in and let's find out."

Twenty-Seven

AT THE GATE, NO ONE was around, and the Subaru was where Niki had parked it. They hauled the gate shut and Donnie followed Niki's car to the main road. She stopped at a gas station to pee, then drove past the turnoff for Nelson Lake. He stayed on her like a burr on a dog's tail all the way to Minong. She pulled into the cafe opposite the motel, where she still had to check out. He joined her at her table.

Speaking in a low voice that wouldn't carry above the generalized din but also wouldn't attract attention like whispering might, she said, "Do you think it's a good idea to be seen having lunch together?"

"Now who's the worrywart?"

"Being careful. The fewer people who see us together, the better."

Donnie caught the server's attention and ordered.

Be that way. Niki decided against asking the thousand questions she had to understand Donnie's background and his engagement with Greenwar. Too many ears. They finished their meal without further conversation.

Niki was glad she had reserved the motel room for two nights because it gave her the ability to return to the room and execute her plan to ditch Donnie. She pulled across the highway with Donnie still dogging her. Fortunately, he didn't try following her to her room. She changed into running clothes. If going for a run convinced Donnie to leave her in peace, she'd find a hardware store and buy a couple of those cans to inflate tires and get Seamus on the road. If that didn't work, she'd have to call a tow truck to save Seamus, lose Donnie, and drive to the Twin Cities to sit for the deposition the next day.

She loaded her fanny pack with Niki's phone, cash, the fake ID and credit cards she had been using, and the rental's key. She locked the room behind her and tucked that key in with the rest of the stuff.

Donnie got out of his truck. "What's up?"

"Does Christine know you're acting like a stalker creep? I didn't get my morning run in, so I'm doing it now. Have a safe drive home." Without waiting for a response, she jogged off at a good clip, using a cutoff that led her onto the Wild Rivers Trail. She figured since it was next to Railroad Street, it was one of those rails-to-trails deals.

She covered two miles running through the woods in sixteen minutes and decided that was far enough. Kneeling to retighten her left shoelace, a mosquito swarm, accompanied by their annoying whine, descended with sex and blood lust on their minds. She finished the double-knot and took off at a sprint. What a sight she must have looked, waving her hands and slapping herself, smearing her blood over every square inch of bare skin.

With the added incentive provided by the mosquitoes, she returned to the motel averaging 7:24-minute miles. She cut through the tree line in its rear and used the gap between the two buildings to surreptitiously observe the parking lot. Donnie had moved across the street and backed his Ford Ranger into a spot in the diner parking lot, giving him a clear view of her rental car and her room.

She wanted to be rid of him but do it in a manner that he didn't think she was ditching him. The annoying noise of a vacuum drew her attention to a cleaning cart parked a few doors away from her room. That gave her an idea. She retreated, staying close to the side of the building until she reached a spot out front hidden from Donnie's view. Keeping low, she crept to the nearby cart and ducked behind it. Using several stacked towels to hide her face, she rose and wheeled the cart four rooms to her door. She knocked. "Room service." Mimicking a maid's behavior, she waited a few seconds before letting herself in.

Using the room phone, she called in a suspicious vehicle report: guy in a truck's been there for a while, Michigan plates, she's afraid it might be her ex. She's got a protection order against Billy—William O'Keefe is his full name, officer. Her name? Charlotte Abel—took back her maiden name. Promise not to tell Billy she was the one who called. God, he'll kill her for that. Could the officer make it look like it was routine questioning? Oh yes, she would appreciate him keeping her name quiet.

If the officer mentioned Charlotte Abel's name, the jig was up if Donnie determined she had registered under that name. She threw clothes on over the running stuff—maybe if she sprayed on enough mosquito dope, it would cover up the body odor that was sure to come. With everything packed and waiting by the door, she poked the curtain away from the wall to view the diner.

She waited until an officer engaged Donnie in his truck, before hustling everything to her rental and dropping off the key at the motel office. She drove five blocks to the Do It Best Hardware store she'd spotted while running and paid cash for bug spray and two cans to inflate Seamus's tires.

"Can't say I've ever sold that exact combination before," the geezer manning the checkout said.

"Longer story than I have time to tell." *And hope to hell no one ever asks you about me.*

Exiting the store, she glimpsed a dirty white truck turning the corner and her heart kicked up a notch. Spotting its red GMC on the grill, she breathed easier knowing it wasn't Donnie. She chose side roads to bypass the diner, caught a flash of red and blue rotating lights, suggesting the police were still interviewing Donnie. Once she got on Highway 77 and engaged cruise control, she called Christine. "Thought you should know, I saw Donnie parked at a diner in Minong talking to a cop."

If it weren't for Christine's breathing, Niki wouldn't have been sure she was on the line. Following a too long pause, she continued. "Everything went fine except we had to move a car that was parked in our way. Donnie and I grabbed a bite, after which I went for a long run on one of those rails-to-trails deals. I was dropping off my key at the hotel and flashing lights across the street caught my attention. I couldn't believe Donnie was talking to the police. Anyway, I thought you should know."

In an assured voice Christine said, "Thank you. We've received an email from Whitewater Associates. They have the sample in the lab and expect to provide us results tomorrow afternoon."

"Excellent. Then what happens?"

"Depends on what the tests show. Are you working in D.C. tomorrow?"

Niki had told Christine she was unavailable on Friday, but had she said why or where she'd be? Couldn't remember. After Donnie's acting like a limpet, was Christine planning to send Mr. Gentle to check up on her? *Quick, say something.*

"That's a negative. Remember, that's why we did this today not tomorrow."

"Yes. Yes. You told me that. Since you had time for a run, I'm guessing you must have a later flight. When do you get back?"

Niki's eyes ached. Christine was probing. To have Mr. Gentle meet her at the D.C. airport? Follow her home? What was this lady's agenda? Maybe calling had been a mistake. Although in retrospect, it might have been a blessing.

"You're right. It's real late. I thought I'd visit the Mall of America. Never been. Oh geez. My battery's at two percent. You'll let me know what Whitewater Associates finds, right? Okay, then. Bye."

She had planned for the off chance whoever she met might demand to see her ticket and had purchased a round-trip. Now, thinking like a skeptical Christine, she might order someone to buy a cheap ticket from MSP that allowed them to clear security and check for Niki at the gate of every flight heading to the greater D.C. area. And, after Christine talked to Donnie, she might send him to verify that Niki wasn't meeting up with that disabled Subaru.

Niki pounded her fist on the steering wheel. *Sorry Seamus. Surviving undercover meant minimizing risks.* She called the tow-truck company and, using a different credit card, sent them to assist Seamus. Nothing for it but to drive to the MSP airport, let watchers see her grab the Delta direct flight to Richmond. There she would rent a car, lose any followers, crash at a motel for what remained of the night, and take a return flight to MSP in time to prep with the lawyer for her deposition later that day.

All assuming everything went as planned.

TWENTY-EIGHT

ASHLEY TREATED HERSELF TO A long dinner at a place that knew how to stretch a multiple-course meal over two hours. Sitting alone at her table in the rear, she sipped wine that cost more per glass than the official government per diem allowance for travel—hey, the sommelier said it was the perfect pairing for her smoked duck with potatoes and frisée—and transacted Pendergast Holdings business. By the time she licked the last of the yummy tiramisu from the dessert fork, she had responded to every business email and had a clean inbox.

She arrived at the airport early enough to stroll past all Delta's gates and did not recognize anyone. She silenced the voice that said no one was watching, she was being paranoid, she should save herself hours of anxious flight time and stay in Minnesota. *Easy can get you killed.*

She medicated with beta blockers, flew to Richmond, found a motel near the airport, and after a few hours of sleep was on the same plane first thing in the morning, arriving at the same MSP gate she had departed from the night before.

Traffic into the city was terrible. She felt her body grow increasingly tense, worrying whether she would be late for her deposition regarding Junior's suit. She was representing Pendergast Holdings and did not want to show up wearing clothing more suited to the Boundary Waters. That meant a quick stop at Legacy House to manifest corporate Ashley.

With the cab waiting for her, she ran up the walk to the front door and pressed the doorbell. The Winchester chime announced her presence. Max barked from the other side of the door. Chloe shushed the dog and opened the door. Surprise covered her face. She unlatched and opened the storm door. "Why are you here?"

"I'm running late and have to change costumes. I'll be gone for the day. Hey Max."

Chloe stepped back. "Why did you ring the bell?"

"Because you and your family are living here, Chloe. I didn't think it was right to barge in. Now excuse me." She brushed past her, gave Max a passing pat, and took the stairs two at a time. She found the door to her room closed. Was Seamus in there? He was an early riser, she assumed he'd already left. She tapped the door, heard nothing, and stepped in. No Seamus.

She found her clothes in the closet, but Seamus's were gone. No time to worry what that meant. She executed a quick change, brushed her teeth, and was soon in the taxi and again worrying whether she'd get to the deposition on time.

She did, but her mouth was dry and the back of her neck ached. She'd rather face an armed bank robber than lawyers looking to eviscerate her.

Twenty-Nine

ASHLEY'S FIRST REACTION AT SEEING her lawyer, Daren Gottkind, pacing the reception area was to snicker. He looked more like the Pillsbury Doughboy than a Doberman Pinscher. His handshake was firm, though. He brought her into a small conference room.

"This is like defense counsel cross-examining you at a trial. Give me a second to object before you answer. If you know the answer, give basic facts. Don't elaborate. If you might have known the answer once, but you're not sure now, say, 'I don't recall at the present time.' Should you recall later, we can amend the deposition. If you never knew the answer, then you say, 'I don't know.' And remember to answer questions only, not statements by counsel. If he says, 'So, your name is Ashley Prescott,' he hasn't asked a question and you don't respond. You didn't review old notes or anything did you?"

"You told me not to."

"Good. They can't hang you for what you don't remember."

A blond twig collected them and ushered them into a larger conference room. Surrounded by lawyers, Ashley's gut reaction was to curl into a fetal position. She brought up a picture of Wonder Woman, feet wide, hands on hips. She didn't assume that position, but she stiffened her spine and kept her head up. The room contained big dark furniture, chairs too big for comfort, glaring-old-men portraits on the wall. All designed to intimidate. She caught a hint of lemon cleaner, and that destroyed the room's power.

Gottkind introduced her to Junior's lawyers—one male, one female—and a court reporter, who swore her in. The female lawyer faked a sip from her coffee cup, deliberately set it down and asked, "Can you tell us your name for the record?"

Ashley saw no reason to pause for this question. "Yes." She waited for the next question.

The woman gave her a belittling smile. "Please do so."

Ashley glanced at Gottkind, whose eyes crinkled with interest. Ashley waited for him to object. When he didn't, she said, "I'm sorry. I didn't hear a question."

The woman released a dramatic sigh and asked the court reporter to reread her original question, which he did. Everyone looked expectantly at Ashley who had formed her face into a picture of helpfulness. Gottkind hid his smile with a throat-clear. "Asked and answered. Counsel should rephrase the question if she wants a different answer."

"Are you kidding me?" The woman screeched. "Is it going to be like that? Fine. What name is on your driver's license."

Technically, Ashley had nine driver's licenses with different names, but having made her point, she answered, "Ashley Pendergast Prescott."

"And. Ashley Pendergast Prescott, what is your official address?"

"Excuse me, I need to speak with my counsel."

"You need to speak to your counsel to know where you live?"

Ashley was sure the woman had taken acting lessons to effortlessly drip sarcasm. Gottkind motioned her to the corner of the room. "My stuff's in storage because I haven't found a place to live after I moved from a shared apartment. And the place I've stayed in most recently is part of an undercover operation, which I can't talk about."

"Alright, this will be interesting. Remember to pause after each question for me to object, and if you want me to object, raise your right pinky finger. Tell her you are between residences."

Ashley did, and when asked, provided the address of the apartment she and Liya had rented together.

"What is your occupation?"

"I am an independent contractor."

"Doing what?"

Ashley raised her right pinky.

Gottkind cleared his throat. "The exact nature of Ms. Prescott's work is confidential. Should this case come to trial, we are prepared to discuss this matter with the presiding judge *in camera*. I will object for the record on questions that infringe on this area and will not allow my client to answer them."

The opposing counsel huddled, the court reporter flexed his fingers, and Ashley envisioned herself taking in the views from Glacier's Going-to-the-Sun Road. *Be calm. This has nothing to do with you.*

"Please let the record show," the male lawyer said, "we think your objections are overly broad, but in the interest of getting to the truth, we will press on. Ms. Prescott, what education do you have that qualifies you to be the Chief Executive Officer of a billion-dollar company?"

Hearing no objection, she answered, "I don't know."

"You don't know what education you have?

"I know what schools I attended, but I don't know what qualifies someone to be a CEO. Bill Gates never graduated from college. He seemed to do okay."

"Please just answer my questions. Did you take any business courses?"

"No."

"None?"

"Asked and answered," Gottkind said.

"No MBA. No marketing courses. No organic chemistry. You must have an innate talent. My question, Ms. Prescott, is why on God's green earth, given your total unpreparedness to operate a multi-national company, did you agree to be the Interim CEO of Pendergast Holdings?"

Gottkind burst from his chair, crashing it to the thick carpet that muffled the thump. "Counsel, one more instance of badgering the deposed, and I'll file a formal complaint with the court.

The stares were worthy of a Clint Eastwood western. The court clerk called a time out to use the facilities. Once everyone returned, the female lawyer questioned Ashley.

"Please tell us why you accepted the Interim CEO position?"

"Robert Pendergast, Senior left communications asking that I do it to protect the company's forty thousand employees."

"What were your thoughts when you first read the note?"

That he was out of his gourd. "I don't recall."

"Were you surprised?"

"Very."

"Were you pleased?"

"No."

"Why were you not pleased?"

"Because I had no desire to be involved with the company."

The lawyer placed her hands on her hips, stared down her nose. "Then why did you? Strike that. What did you hope to accomplish by accepting the Interim CEO position?"

"I hoped Robert would reappear, and I could step away. Anton Hack,

Robert's personal attorney, told me that if I did not accept this responsibility, a lot of lawyers would get rich litigating a rudderless company. A rudderless company would endanger the jobs of the forty-thousand employees."

"Do I understand you to say you steered the company?"

"I don't know what you understand, but that is not what I said."

"Did you have any other motivations for taking the position? If so, what were they?"

Ashley had been anxious to learn who had given Robert her FBI undercover contact information. Hack had suggested the best way to find out was to be in charge. *That* she could not tell them because it exposed her undercover work. "I hoped it would help law enforcement discover what had happened to Robert."

The lawyer looked incredibly pleased with herself. Had that answer dug a hole? Ashley asked for a break to use the ladies'. Gottkind accompanied her through the lobby. Seamus was waiting there and handed her a key to a hotel room. "I moved out of Legacy House to give Chloe and the kids space. I got you a room, too, and I arranged dinner with a few Pendergast folks. Details are in your room."

Another curveball to worry about later. She tucked the key into her pocket. "Fine. See you after I finish with the Inquisition."

THIRTY

ON HER RETURN, SHE NOTED how stuffy and claustrophobic the conference room now felt. She settled into her seat, tried bringing up a pleasant image from Glacier. Couldn't do it. Well, at least she should be halfway through this nonsense.

The female lawyer ticked off something on her pad of paper and said, "Please describe for us the actions you took on your first day as Interim CEO of Pendergast Holdings LLC. That was a Monday."

"I do not recall."

"Is it true you hired Seamus McCree to work at the company?"

"No."

"No? If you didn't bring him into the organization, who did?"

"I did, but I did not hire him. He consulted with officers of the company without compensation. Well, the company covered his expenses, but that was it."

"And why did Mr. McCree do that?"

Gottkind raised his hand. "Calls for speculation."

"Fine. Are you and Mr. McCree friends? Lovers?"

Had the receptionist seen Seamus give her the hotel room key and tipped off the lawyers? "We have been lovers."

That elicited another tick on the lawyer's pad. "When was the last time you were sexually intimate?"

Ashley considered the room key and the night's possibilities and felt a warm glow spread from her chest to her face. She wanted to say that whenever it had been, it had been too long. Instead, she said, "I do not recall," and fended off attempts to pin her down, other than to agree it had been sometime earlier in that calendar year.

"Have you and he discussed this deposition?"

"Yes."

That elicited an eye roll and exasperated sigh. "What did you discuss? Please be specific and leave nothing out."

"He informed me of Junior's suit and that you were deposing us. He said—and I'm paraphrasing here—that the suit was total bullshit, and the biggest problem was that it would waste a ton of our time and money while a bunch of lawyers ran up their hourly fees."

The attorney used her answer to shift tacks and ask a raft of questions concerning Seamus's qualifications. Most she answered with "I don't know" or "I don't remember."

After beating that dead horse, the male attorney took the lead. "Thinking back to your first day on the job, is it true that you only worked a partial day?"

"I do not recall how many hours I worked that day."

"Is it true you commandeered the company's jet that afternoon and flew to Washington, D.C.?"

"I flew on the corporate jet to Washington that afternoon."

"How did that assist in stabilizing the company, acting as its rudder?"

For five hours, the lawyers traded off picking apart her every action, framing their questions to highlight her incompetence. Perhaps figuring they had worn her down, the male lawyer shifted his focus and asked, "What compensation have you received from Pendergast Holdings?"

"My contract calls for no salary. The board can approve a bonus."

"Which was how much?"

Ashley struggled to anticipate where this questioning was going. "I am unaware of the board approving any bonus."

"Maybe they're waiting to see the outcome of these proceedings." Before Gottkind could object, the opposing lawyer moved to his next question. "So, is it true you have not received any money, goods, or services from Pendergast Holdings, LLC or any of its subsidiaries?"

The question's wording made the trap clear. "I used the Pendergast plane for personal travel and understand that is considered personal income." She admitted she did not remember the number of times, and she did not know the amount of income, but yes, it was substantial. For the first time in the proceedings, she worried her antiperspirant might not be up to the task.

"Did you or did you not receive anything of benefit from any of Pendergast Holdings international subsidiaries?"

She screwed up her face in genuine confusion. "What?"

"Oh please. It's not that difficult. I didn't ask how much you took or how often. You either did or didn't receive benefit from the international subsidiaries."

The lawyer's use of the word "took" suggested the lawyer was up to something with this line of questioning. Not seeing a trap, and hearing no objections from Gottkind, she answered that she was unaware of anything.

He flipped a page on his pad while nodding his head. Next came a series of questions regarding her relationships with Robert's sons. All routine stuff until he asked, "The last time you saw Robert Pendergast, Junior did you offer him a bribe?"

"No."

"Did you threaten to provide evidence of his alleged criminal acts to the police and press if he did not comply to a request you made?"

"That is not how I recall the conversation."

When the logical follow-up question asked what her recollection of the conversation was, she tamped down anger caused by remembering the events two months earlier. "Someone had kidnapped Seamus McCree. I met with the three Pendergast brothers and told them if Seamus did not appear in two hours, I would provide evidence of their *alleged* crimes to the police and the press. It didn't matter to me who had done it. I was leveraging the threat to expose their misdeeds to get Seamus released."

"How is that not a threat?"

"It *was* a threat, but not a bribe, and not directed specifically at Junior and his actions. I didn't know who had taken Seamus, and my threat was to expose all three of them if Seamus did not reappear."

"How did you obtain this information?"

"From material developed from investigations I instigated at Pendergast Holdings."

"So you used corporate information based on confidential sources, not to benefit the company, but to benefit your friend Seamus McCree. Isn't that true? And isn't it also true that prior to you using these company secrets for your own purpose, that at no time did you discuss how you planned to use this information with any officer or employee of Pendergast Holdings?"

Gottkind was up and snarling. "Counselor, refrain from putting words in my client's mouth and thoughts in her head. You know full well she won't answer multiple questions. This deposition has gone on far longer than you led us to expect. In the interest of truth, I have allowed this proceeding to continue. You have already delayed by several hours a scheduled deposition of Seamus McCree, who I also represent. I'm calling a break and telling him to leave. We will set a mutually agreeable time to reschedule. Then, Ms. Prescott and I will continue this deposition until you finish. We will not allow you to drag this out and make her appear for a continuance. Are we clear?"

Break concluded, the female lawyer resumed the lead on questions. "Please explain why, as you testified, you used information gathered from corporate investigations to threaten Robert Pendergast, Junior."

Ashley waited to see if Gottkind would object. He did not. "I believed it might save Seamus McCree's life."

"In retrospect, do you think what you did was a good idea?"

She had had good intentions. Justice, not revenge had motivated her. The results had been a disaster. Junior and his family had escaped to a country without extradition to avoid prosecution. Bradlee had committed suicide, and his family was emotionally and financially devastated. The threat hadn't been effective in releasing Seamus. She could have avoided all that trauma and rescued Seamus sooner if she had more quickly understood the evidence in front of her. What the lawyer was really asking was whether Ashley would do it again if faced with the same circumstances.

"I don't know."

"Well, isn't that a sorry situation?"

THIRTY-ONE

ASHLEY ACCEPTED GOTTKIND'S OFFER TO drop her off at her hotel. Saying yes, no, I don't recall, and responding with details to six hours of the lawyers' tag-teaming was a lot more tiring than she had expected. Once they were in the car, safe from prying ears, she asked Gottkind how he thought it had gone.

"You did fine. More than fine. To overturn the legal documents Robert Pendergast, Senior crafted—asking you to take the job, giving you proxy for his shares, the way he designed his living trust to disinherit his sons if they didn't meet certain criteria—they must show Senior was legally unfit to make those decisions. Making unorthodox or unwise decisions are not grounds to declare someone unfit. Entrepreneurs do that all the time."

Ashley pointed to the hotel on the next block. "Does that mean you think we don't have anything to worry about?"

"They have two strategies. The first is to convince a judge that Senior was legally incompetent. They'll hire shrinks to cherry-pick things Robert did in the last few months to show he was mentally unstable. But with the testimony from you, Anton Hack, and Seamus, it's a real long shot. Seamus predicted their other strategy. They drag it out and force you to spend time and money. Worse case, they get a court order prohibiting you from making any decisions that would disadvantage them should they prevail in their suit. Opposing counsel earns thirty percent of whatever they get for Junior. Even if you settle their claim for ten cents on the dollar, they make tens of millions. They'll rake you over the coals until you cry uncle."

Great. More family distractions to fuck up her life. "Then they don't know me very well."

SEAMUS DID NOT ANSWER HER tap on his hotel room door. In hers, he had deposited suitcases containing everything she had at Legacy House and left three notes in the center of the bed. One informed her the secure link with Rick was active but that she should call Rick at a number she did not recognize. The second said he'd made reservations at a nearby restaurant. She was to meet him there. Her sister Tabitha and brother Garrett were coming, as were Gabriella Linz, Pendergast Holdings' CEO, and Malachi Cluff, Pendergast's new VP of sales. Terrific. More dealing with the damn company when all she wanted was a quiet meal, a good fuck, and a full-night's sleep before she caught Amtrak's morning train to Chicago with connection to D.C.

The third was the copy of the bill for replacing his broken driver's side window. Right. Not an expense Christine would reimburse. Would Ambrose? Park?

She used the hotel phone to dial the number Rick had left.

"'Lo?" A male voice she did not recognize.

She asked for Rick Kaska. He yelled Rick's name, a faint reply came down the line, followed by the clunking of the phone hitting wood.

"This is Rick."

"Seamus said to call. Where are you?"

"Tom Sawyer party at a friend's house. Seemed a safe place for you to call. I figured you were dead when you didn't return to the Sibley Hospital lot where I was waiting. Thank God, Seamus knew you were okay. Why didn't you let me know? Don't do that to me again. That wasn't why I wanted to talk to you. Today a guy stops at my cube, introduces himself. His name rings a vague bell, but I can't remember seeing him before. Anyway, he wants some help on a case he's working on. He says he understands you and I did some work together and asks if I'm still friendly with you.

I tell him I'm not sure you could characterize our relationship as friendly. We worked together on an assignment. He asks which assignment, and I tell him a joint task force with Homeland, ATF, couple of other interested parties. He asks who else from the Bureau was involved?

"I was getting a hinky feeling and tell him he needs to get that info from personnel, and I ask what's going on.

"He gives me this hang-dawg look—same one I use to let a suspect know how sad their last answer made me. Next, he tries for my sympathy. He's trying to unravel his own little SNAFU and hopes to avoid dealing with that bureaucracy. One tiny corner of his situation might loop in with a case you worked on a few years before you arrived in D.C. He hopes to pick your brain, but no one can tell him where to find you. He's having trouble sleeping at night. Have I seen you recently?

"I admit to seeing you a couple of times since you left the job, but I didn't know where you were. All true. He wants me to speculate where you might be, which I refused. He gives me a card and tells me to contact him if I hear from you. When I see his name in print, I realize how I know it. He's the number three guy in the Bureau's Office of Professional Responsibility. Ambrose say anything to you?"

Ashley wondered if Ambrose had instigated the investigation or whether this was more Gex interference. "Bupkis. Even with the secure communication structure Patrick McCree set up for us, we should be super careful. No direct contact between us. Go through Seamus. That way, you don't have to lie to anyone. Lies are what they hang you for. Go back to whitewashing the fence."

"I know that. It's why I called Seamus. And I'm painting the walls."

That was Rick, the literalist. She wasn't one who automatically disliked those who investigated agents for alleged violations, even if they were too rule-bound for her taste. One thing she would say in their defense is they were relentless. They'd worry whatever bone they unearthed until they gnawed it to a nub or realized it was plastic.

Three hours to herself before she had to act like a grown-up. A bubble bath would help restore her balance: chamomile-laced bubbles to treat her dry skin, water hot enough to last for a long soak, lavender-scented candles, the sound of ocean waves from the hotel's mp3-player clock radio. She eased into the tub and kept her eyes open, but unfocused. Her muscles relaxed, and she realized how much stress they were carrying.

Worries arrived like a whack-a-mole. No sooner had she pushed one to the back of her mind and regained her sense of calm, than another appeared. She needed an apartment. Had to bait the next hook for Christine and Greenwar. Wanted to learn why Gex was meeting with Ambrose. What were the Bureau's internal investigators digging for, and why? Had Park set up electronic surveillance of Niki's apartment? What was going on at Pendergast Holdings that Seamus invited that particular mix of people to dinner? She rubbed her head, added getting a haircut to her list. And she needed to shave her legs.

Sometimes, you are your own worst enemy. Make a damn list and start checking things off. First thing, shave your legs.

Halfway through the first leg, the room phone sounded. *Brleep, brleep.* A pause. *Brleep, brleep.* She refused to drip her way to get the phone because Seamus thought he had to check up on her. He could leave a message.

She finished her legs, drained the bath, and stepped into the shower. Moments later, a heavy pounding sounded at her door.

THIRTY-TWO

ASHLEY READ THE NOTE SLIPPED under her door. "The Mississippi is about to drown you. Meet me in ten minutes with your bags at my rental car parked on LL3. I have to use the executive bathroom.—SM"

Seamus had picked up that "Mississippi" was code for "I'm in trouble, come quick with guns drawn." But his usage implied she was in trouble, not him. She had no clue what the bathroom reference was and no time to figure it out. It had been at least five minutes since the room phone rang, giving her less than that to reach Seamus's rental. Fortunately, she'd parked hers on the same level.

She threw on clothes, donned a brown wig with purple highlights from one of the suitcases, and swept her toiletries, make-up, and her beta-blocker pills into it. She counted cellphone and chargers, IDs, and credit cards, and dumped everything into her knapsack.

Before opening the door to the hallway, she inhaled and released a long breath that moved her from tornado mode to outward calm. No one was in the hallway, and nobody joined her in the elevator. The roller-bags thumped in unison on the tiled lobby floor between the room elevators and the one to the underground garage.

Seamus stood by the open hatch. She threw the bags in, slammed the hatch, and tossed the knapsack at her feet. Before she had buckled in, he had the car rolling. She kept her curiosity in check until he had exited the garage. "What the hell is going on?"

"Based on your instructions, Pendergast Holdings opened its books to the FBI to help them track the money Junior skimmed from his division. Given my experience investigating financial crimes, Gabriella asked me to coordinate with them. She has Garrett assisting them on the bribery issues related to getting approval for the new pesticide. Everything had been going well on both fronts until two weeks ago they stopped communicating. Do you remember Harlan, the newspaper reporter? He still feels like he owes us. I just heard from him."

"Don't be such a fucking drama queen, Seamus. Cut to the chase."

"Harlan sent me a blue-line version of an article his paper plans to publish. It's an exposé on Pendergast Holdings. It says the FBI will charge you with shaking down Junior. They followed a few million bucks of recent activities and discovered a new shell company whose beneficial owner is Ashley Pendergast Prescott. The article suggests you have slipped FBI surveillance, and they consider you a flight risk. They're running a picture of you provided by the Bureau. Harlan thinks the national syndicates will pick it up."

She felt as though the Washington Monument had collapsed on her. The pressure crushed her lungs, stopped her heart, severed her spine. Her brain spun like a lopsided top. Her picture in the paper was like getting the black spot in *Treasure Island.* Now she understood why Junior's lawyers had asked some of their questions. They were setting her up and someone in the Bureau was making it worse by releasing her photograph, knowing it would destroy any current or future undercover work. She'd be exposed to Greenwar, but worse, Patriots For Freedom would put a price on her head.

"Knock, knock. Anyone home?"

"You're aiding and abetting a fugitive, Seamus. Cut me loose."

"Not happening. Whatever spiderweb Junior wove, I can tear apart. You need sanctuary. I'm taking you to my camp. They won't find you there. Then I'm picking up Paddy in Chicago and bringing him here. Between his computer skills and my forensic accounting skills, we'll expose the fraud for what it is."

"Seamus, don't think I'm not grateful for what you and your son are offering. And I'm sure I'll need that help. That's defense. If I am ever to work undercover again, I need a knockout counterpunch right now. Pull over. I want you to make two phone calls."

"To avoid alerting anyone I was leaving, I escaped Pendergast Holdings through the hidden exit in Robert's bathroom. In my rush I forgot my cellphone."

The bathroom reference made sense now. "Plan B. Drive me to the airport." She extracted her newest Niki undercover cellphone and punched in the emergency number Park had given her.

"I'm sorry," a recorded voice said. "The number you dialed is no longer in service." She carefully entered 23676, the number equivalent of Beorn. "Connecting, please hold." Silence, no canned music to distract her.

Seamus was buzzing down I-35W, keeping dead on the speed limit when Park's voice came on the line. "This better be a true emergency."

She explained the situation. "If you want me to work undercover, you need to squash the picture."

"Not the story?"

"Tell them it's to protect ongoing investigations involving national security on which I worked while at the Bureau. It's a fine compromise since they don't mention any of my undercover roles or aliases. The picture is the only thing that could tip anyone off. They'll take it. Second thing, contact Ambrose. Tell him I learned of the arrest warrant and will turn myself in first thing tomorrow morning at a place of his choosing in the D.C. Metro area. He can let Rick or Seamus know, and they'll contact me. If we don't go through the hoops, people will know something suspicious is going on. I'm not saying this is part of some larger conspiracy against me, but if they're behind getting my picture in the news, we can't let them think we're onto them. That said, I have to be released on my own recognizance or Operation Svalinn is down the tubes."

"You do remember that tomorrow is a Saturday. If you're right, they'll hold you for the weekend and say you're a flight risk because you have access to money."

"Monday morning, Greenwar will check that I'm with Jim Ford. You better get a judicial officer lined up during the weekend to secure my release. I'll turn in my Ashley Prescott passport, but I can't wear a tracker, and despite what everyone believes, I have no money."

Park let loose a massive belly laugh. "You don't ask for much, do you? Before I forget, write down this URL." He gave it to her. "That's where you can view the footage from the three cameras a private firm installed at Niki's apartment. They verified someone had installed audio bugs—confirming your suspicion. They disabled them prior to their work and switched them back on after they were done. So far, no one has been there. Fly safe, you hear?"

The thought of flying filled her stomach with acid. *If it kills you, your troubles are over.* She booked Delta's evening direct flight using her phone's app. She should have asked Park to get her another beta blocker prescription.

THIRTY-THREE

ASHLEY SURVIVED THE FLIGHT AND while waiting for her bags to appear, used her phone to check the secure communication setup for messages. Not a damn one. Bags in hand, she used Uber to take her to the storage facility where she had stored all her stuff from the apartment she had shared with Liya.

Given D.C.'s heat and humidity, she had chosen a climate-controlled facility. She entered her code to get into the building. Inside, the temperature was warmer, but the humidity was less. As she rolled her bags to her individual unit, lights flipped on ahead of her and turned off behind her. She dialed in the code for her lock and rattled the door up. She tapped on her phone's light and pulled the door down. The ribbon of light under the door vanished. Good. The exterior lights were her early warning system.

She stored the clothes and electronics from her bags, keeping out only the Ashley Pendergast passport and driver's license, and some cash. She changed into comfortable clothes, rearranged boxes to free the love seat, and set an alarm to wake her from what would be a too-brief sleep.

The phone's buzz woke her at six. She found a series of secure communications from Seamus. Park had contacted Ambrose, who discovered the Minneapolis field office had initiated the original investigation after Ashley had given the Bureau unfettered access to Pendergast Holdings' physical and electronic records. They started with Junior's money laundering and the EPA bribes but discovered Ashley's name linked to an overseas account through which money laundering was occurring.

At that point, the Bureau's Internal Investigations Section pulled rank and grabbed responsibility for that part of the investigation. They forced the communications blackout from the Minneapolis office to Pendergast Holdings.

When IIS agents went to a DOJ prosecutor for an arrest warrant, the Minneapolis office strongly objected that the case was not yet ripe and charging Ashley now would jeopardize their work. Ambrose said this inter-

Bureau disagreement can happen—however, the person leading the IIS charge was a Gex protégé.

Answering the question whether Gex was behind it.

IIS told the prosecutor that Ashley's ability to use disguises and shake tails, combined with her multiple identities, made her an extreme flight risk. The prosecutor planned to argue for no bail because of the high flight risk.

Hard to argue against that.

Ambrose had arranged for her to turn herself in at nine o'clock at the safe house her team had used for meetings during her undercover work on Patriots For Freedom. Two agents would take her to a nearby facility for processing with no one else knowing. The prosecutor and a magistrate judge, who Park knew, would meet there at ten for the bail hearing, at which Park claimed the magistrate *would* allow cash bail, and Park had arranged for someone to be there to provide it. She should be free by noon.

THIRTY-FOUR

ASHLEY ARRIVED FIFTEEN MINUTES EARLY. Two male agents, twins except for the color of their skin, greeted her at the door of the suburban house in which she had spent many hours planning and debriefing her PFF mission. They introduced themselves, showed IDs—she recognized one of the names—and ushered her in.

The Bureau had stripped the place of its furnishings, leaving no trace of its former use. Although the walls had been repainted, her nose twitched at the still present hint of mold.

They formally arrested her and agreed that cuffs were unnecessary. After inventorying and bagging her personal possessions, they carefully labeled the bag with her name, the date, and the arresting agent's name.

"Been a last-minute change in plans. Your magistrate is from Fredericksburg. To save his Honor traveling time, we're doing this all at Quantico. We gotta hurry. You want to use the facilities before we leave?"

Ashley wondered if that might have been part of the deal Park cut to assure she got bail. If so, why hadn't Seamus known and called her? "Can I have my phone or borrow one of yours to let my counsel know of the change in plans?"

"I'm sure the powers that be already informed him. Bathroom or are you good?"

"Thanks, appreciate it." It was fifty minutes to Quantico. The nine o'clock timing still worked, but the "powers that be" hadn't told her counsel anything because she didn't have counsel—unless that was the individual Park had arranged to cover the bail? Didn't matter. It might be a normal administrative cock-up. *Yeah, and she could be Mother Theresa.*

The only window in the bathroom was too small for any adult to fit through, and the only exits were the front door or through the garage. Either meant physically disabling the two agents. Assaulting federal officers was a felony—and *that* charge would stick.

She found nothing in the bathroom suitable for leaving a message. The idea of tearing toilet paper into letters to spell something coherent brought a grim smile to her face. The best she could do was decorate the bathroom with her prints to prove she had been there. She added a full handprint to the left rear panel of their car before she got into the standard issue sedan.

They offered to let her sit in the passenger seat if she preferred. She chose the back because that gave her a tactical advantage. They knew that, and knowing they were fine with her having the upper hand eased her concerns. The black guy even made a joke about not having to sit at the back of the bus.

The conversation between the two agents was of barbecues and kids' soccer and whether it made sense to save money by sending the older ones to community college for the first two years and then on to university.

Early in the ride, the sun slipped in and out of scattered clouds. The closer they got to Quantico, the denser the clouds and the less she caught any ray of sunshine. By the time they reached the facility, the brooding gray sky hung not far above their heads.

Ashley felt a mixture of nostalgia and nerves as they passed the Hogan's Alley welcome sign, which she read to herself.

"Welcome to Hogan's Alley City Limits. CAUTION: Law enforcement training exercises in progress. Display of weapons firing blank ammunition and arrests may occur. If challenged please follow instructions. HAVE A NICE DAY."

All that was missing was a smiley face—and better punctuation. She had spent hours training in this ten-acre facility. It had everything, including facilities to interrogate prisoners. What Hogan's Alley didn't have was free access to the public. She supposed the Bureau would make exceptions for a magistrate, but what about the person Park was sending with her bail?

On an early Saturday morning the place felt deserted. Even the Subway, the one real business in the town, hadn't yet opened. They passed no agents, no actors, no instructors.

They parked in front of the Biograph Theater. In her day, it had housed a real FBI office. They escorted her from the car, opened the door—it still looked like a functioning office—and led her down the hall to an interior room. "We'll leave you here. There's a john in the back if you need it. Everyone should be here in ten or fifteen minutes." They closed the door behind themselves, leaving Ashley to a silent room and her dark thoughts.

Thirty-Five

SEVEN MINUTES LATER THE DOOR opened to reveal two men dressed in black tactical gear and wrap-around sunglasses, the only color on them from face masks depicting grinning skulls. She rose from the chair and moved to the center of the room.

She assessed them and their approach. Not the guys who had brought her here; these men were each at least six-two, two-hundred-plus pounds. Their clothing looked reinforced to soften kicks and punches. Kevlar vests protected their vitals. Lug-sole boots protected their insteps and ankles. Knees, elbows, the backs of their heads and necks, and their eyes—if she could remove their glasses—were their only vulnerable spots.

With no protective gear, fighting was losing. She had to escape.

They angled in, giving away their plan to force her into a corner. There, one would grab her and pull her far enough from the corner and the second could pile on.

She flexed her knees, shifting her weight to her toes. "What do you want?" Her voice sounded deadly calm to her, even though adrenaline flooded her system.

Using hand signals, the two split apart, daring her to try a sucker's dash between them.

Instead, Niki feinted left toward the larger of the two men and pivoted hard right. The smaller attacker lunged to intercept her, and she dropped low, sweeping his legs with everything she had. His boots caught, and he went down hard, the back of his skull cracking against the floor. The thud reverberated through the room.

One down. But not for long.

The remaining man cursed behind his skull mask and rushed her. She rolled away into a crouch, but he was faster than his size suggested. His gloved hand nailed her shoulder, spinning her around. She twisted, driving her elbow toward his exposed throat. He jerked back, and she caught only air.

His partner had rolled over and was already pushing himself up on his elbows.

The standing attacker's arm snaked around Niki's neck from behind, cutting off her air. She clawed at his forearm, but the reinforced fabric gave her nothing to grip. Stars danced at the edges of her vision.

His partner staggered to his feet, one hand pressed to the back of his head. The man holding her shifted his grip, pinning her arms while loosening his forearm enough to let her breathe. She kicked backward but had no leverage to cause damage.

"Told you she'd be trouble," the injured man muttered, his words slurred. He lumbered toward her. "This one's for screwing Alex."

Her right kidney exploded with pain. She arched her back, pulling hard against the restraining arm, but had no air to scream.

"And this is for not screwing Martin."

The blow to her left kidney caused her bladder to release.

"I thought she was supposed to be tough," the injured one said. "Look at that, she pissed herself."

Niki's legs crumpled and darkness crept in from all sides.

THIRTY-SIX

ASHLEY OPENED HER EYES TO pain beyond anything she had ever experienced. She tried to inventory the sources of the agony and failed. Either brain fog from having been unconscious dulled her thinking, or the pain was overwhelming and had no individual parts. Using the light leaking under the door, she determined she lay on her stomach on the tiled floor of what must be a private bathroom, there being only a single toilet and pedestal sink. Her left arm was free, but they'd cuffed her right wrist to a sweating copper pipe running into the toilet.

Look on the bright side, Ashley. The beating didn't leave you deaf or blind. And pain meant her nerves still worked. Quit feeling sorry for yourself and plan how to survive the better part of two days until the office opens Monday.

She tested the cuffs. They bit her wrist and rattled against the pipe and weren't coming off without a key. Unless she broke the pipe—something to keep her occupied. Feeling her brain fog lift, she accomplished a physical inventory. Pain was still everywhere, but other than ribs and the one tooth her tongue kept checking, nothing seemed broken. Her mouth tasted of stale vomit. She needed to pee.

She marshaled her energy to push up onto her knees.

One. Two. Three.

She pressed up on her elbow. Lightning bolts of pain skewered her kidneys. Her back spasmed, a blowtorch of agony. She collapsed to the floor, bit her tongue to stop her scream.

Stupid. Scream—someone other than the two guys might hear.

She tried taking light breaths, but the pain won. Fuck it. I know how to do this. She pressed her forearm against the floor and pushed, letting loose a scream loud enough to make a banshee blush.

No one came.

* * *

Over several hours, Ashley determined several critical points. It took bloody forever to wiggle down her trousers and undies to pee and twice as long to get them up; her piss was more blood than urine; she could drink water by scooping it with her unshackled hand; no one responded to her calls for help.

Oh, and she hurt like a sumbitch.

And the copper pipe would not break in her lifetime.

Hours of thinking left her no closer to understanding why this had happened. The two agents who met her at the U/C house hadn't disguised themselves. Even if the names and IDs were fake, with a sketch artist, she'd have their faces memorialized in a couple hours' time. If they had wanted to kill her, she'd be dead. And why use Quantico? Quantico trainees led by Gex fan Bianca Jenoff had followed her. Was this Jenoff's doing? The first blow had been for screwing Alexander Gex. She got that part, lots of people were pissed at her because Gex had proclaimed she had lied to save her job and ruin him. But the second had been for not screwing her ex, Martin. He was still in the Boston office, and she didn't know of any connection between him and Gex. She had only come to D.C. after her divorce. The whole thing might be a bunch of frat boys making a painful point that they didn't like her.

At every assignment there had been at least one guy who had to tell dirty jokes or commit petty acts of vandalism or whatever other childish thing they thought made them strong. Nothing like this, though. Her policy was to give as good as she got, but verbally. And she never admitted defeat.

She pushed hard against the copper pipe. Let go. Pushed hard.

Thirty-Seven

Hours later, Ashley heard a noise over the whoosh of the air-conditioned air. The light under the bathroom door grew brighter. Someone had turned on the lights. "Hey," she yelled. "Help. I'm in the bathroom." The effort sent her back into spasm again. She groaned and laid her head on her arm, willing her muscles to relax.

The door rattled.

"Help," she drew it out into a scream.

"Can you unlock the door?"

The hairs on her neck tingled. She recognized the voice but couldn't place it. "No. Kick the fucker open."

"Just a sec. Be right back."

She rested her head on her arm and laughed at herself. In what world did she think someone would kick in a door at a federal facility? She could be here for hours before the guy found a key or maintenance. And she had to pee. Again.

She waited a minute to see if her rescuer—if that was what he was—was coming back before undertaking the laborious process of pushing down her pants. She was halfway there when the door flung open and the lights popped on. Standing in the doorway gaping at her was Special Agent Clyde Barton.

She reflexively covered her crotch. It was the first time she had ever witnessed him speechless.

He faced away. "Pendergast, what the hell have you done? Real cuffs? Now I got to find a key."

"Barton, wait. I need—"

The man who had been the lead range instructor when she trained to be an agent was as bullheaded and arrogant a bastard as ever, walking away before she could tell him to call Ambrose. She got her pants pulled up and a back twinge let her know those muscles were threatening to spasm again. She rested her head on her arm and waited for his return.

Her relief morphed to anger when he remained in the doorway and snapped pictures with his cellphone. Pass around to the good-ol'-boys network? No, she realized with embarrassment that he was documenting a crime scene. She used the camera flashes to check the condition of the copper pipes. Her pushing and pulling had hardly dented them.

He placed a hand on her back and reached to undo the cuff around her wrist. A moan escaped her lips. To remove the cuffs without leaning on her, he scooted around to her other side. "What the hell did they do to you, Pendergast?" The cuff clicked open. "I'll help you up in a minute, but I need to bag these cuffs."

She raised her head and watched his glove-covered hands unlock the other half of the cuffs and slip them into an evidence bag. Without touching her, he backed away. "How badly are you hurt?"

"I've had better days. Can you give me some space? I gotta pee and you need to call—"

"Already called it in. I don't know what the hell is going on here, Pendergast, but I know a crime scene when I see one. You can use the restrooms down the hall to the left. You need a hand?"

She pushed to her knees. Breathing in fast through her nose to fight the pain and nausea. She got halfway to standing and her back spasmed again. A groan escaped her. She held onto the toilet for support.

"Don't you go all faint-y on me." He squatted next to her and slipped one arm under her knees. "Steady. Put an arm around my neck and lean in. I know you hate my guts, but right now I'm what you've got, so suck it up, Pendergast."

She clamped her arm around his shoulders. "It's Prescott."

He lifted her like she was a bag of potato chips and carried her through the room and into the hallway, whose lights shone brightly. "I heard you married and divorced that douchebag. Kept his name, huh? You should have asked me. I'd have told you he'd cheat on you." He kicked open the ladies' room door, flipped on the lights. "You gonna be okay if I leave you to your business?"

"Thanks." She gave him a weak smile.

His eyes narrowed. "Broken tooth, black eye. Someone worked you over pretty good. You should have a doctor."

"Barton, if you don't leave, I'm going to pee my pants." *Again.*

He wagged a finger at her. "You're not finished in five minutes, I'm coming in."

The five minutes rushed by and Barton was banging on the door. She flushed the bloody urine and yelled she was coming. Her back let her shuffle-step like a bent old lady. To open the door, she had to turn the handle and shuffle backwards. Backwards hurt more than forward. Retreating always did.

Barton stuck his head in the door while she was gimping out. "Smells like you're pissing blood."

He had a good nose, or he already knew they'd punched her kidneys. "A little. No biggie. Who sent you to find me?"

"Shit, Pendergast, you are the toughest bitch who's ever been through this place. You know that? I say that with complete admiration. Might have been a couple of guys tougher. Maybe. That pinned a target on you from day one. You didn't need my help on the range, but you sure as hell needed someone to help you navigate the Bureau. I tried my damnedest to break down your prejudices. To teach you to go along to get along, unless it truly, truly mattered. That just because someone acts like an asshole doesn't mean they aren't sometimes right. And here we are: proof I failed you."

He pointed her down the hallway past the doorway to the room in which they'd beaten her, now marked off with crime scene tape. "I'm giving you this great big speech because I know you think I'm the biggest asshole down here. This time, I'm right. This is clearly an inside job. It pisses me off something fierce to say it, but, Pendergast, for once you're right not to trust anyone. For the love of God, keep your damn mouth shut until you have a witness you trust, and that's not anyone connected with the Bureau."

Barton could be in this thick as thieves, and yet, somehow, she trusted his advice. "How did you find me?"

"Trust no one, remember. That said, like it or no, I'm taking you to the hospital. Kidney damage can be fatal."

"On two conditions. You let me call a friend and tell him where I am and where we're going."

"Now you're hearing me. Second?"

"You arrest me." She barked a laugh that sent a stab of pain up her spine. "I agreed to turn myself in and thought they'd arrested me. But maybe not. I want to prove I followed my half of the bargain."

"I'm not comfortable having my name attached to the record of this . . . Whatever this is."

"Special Agent Barton, I am officially turning myself in to your custody, stating I am a fugitive wanted by the FBI. Arrest me or I walk to the nearest police station or you're kidnapping me."

"It's never easy with you, is it? You want cuffs with that charge? And what *is* the charge?"

Thirty-Eight

ASHLEY'S FIRST VISITOR IN THE hospital room—other than nurses checking to make sure her IV drip was doing its thing and Barton, who sat outside the door—was Keenan Thigpen, the prosecutor she was supposed to have met earlier that morning. He looked like he was fourteen, except for great gray owl eyes that spoke of having seen many bad things. Accompanying him were two federal marshals, male and female. The female marshal was six feet tall; the male six feet wide. Thigpen took one look at Ashley and ordered the marshals to relieve Barton of his guard duty, but to keep him around to answer questions.

"I've heard second hand from . . . um . . . sources . . . that you've had an eventful day. I'd like to hear the details from you." He sat in the visitor's chair, pulled a legal pad from an attaché, and clicked a cheap ballpoint pen.

She gave him facts and zero speculation. He didn't interrupt. She concluded with, "and here we are," and he returned to the beginning and pinned down the specifics. "You thought the men who picked you up at the safe house and brought you to Quantico were FBI agents?"

"Clearly, or I wouldn't have gotten in the car with them. Get me a sketch artist."

"The names you provided belong to two Special Agents. We're bringing them here for you to identify. If they're not the ones, we can go the artist route. What about the guys who beat you up? Think you could ID voices?"

"One was growl-y, like he was disguising his voice. The one I hurt? Maybe, but I wouldn't bet on it. I don't suppose I'll get a bail hearing today."

"Doesn't matter. The doctors aren't releasing you until your kidneys work right. Besides, with the marshals stationed on the other side of your door, this is the safest place for you. What do you think of Barton's story?"

"He kept changing the subject when I asked him how he found me. Otherwise, he was straight-up. He let me use his cellphone to call a friend and kept the line open until we got here." She did not think the prosecutor needed to know her "friend" was ADNI Park.

"You're sure Barton didn't help beat you up? Buyer's remorse?"

"Wrong size. If you won't allow me bail, what is your plan?"

"Well, that's a problem, isn't it? On one hand, you are under arrest for some serious shit. On the other hand, nothing about the investigation of your alleged crimes has been normal, topped off by everything that's happened today. Week-old dead fish smell better than this. Now, if I get my way—and I usually do—after I talk to my boss, he'll talk to his boss, who is the Attorney General. And the Attorney General will order the Office of Inspector General to search under every rock—hell, every pebble—until they get to the bottom of this."

Ambrose would not be pleased with this direction. Park might be, though. Hard to tell with him. Thigpen's baby fat covered a mean mountain lion ready to jump on the Bureau's neck and shake it until it coughed up the answers.

Ashley yawned her boredom. "Yeah, and in two years someone's wrist might get slapped."

Thigpen relaxed in his chair and breathed deeply. "After the previous director pissed off both the right and left, the Bureau is short on high-powered friends to sweep this under a rug. Getting back to your question: On my way here, I informed the magistrate of the reason for your not showing up. To say he'd been ticked at you for your no-show would be an understatement. He's now directing his ire at the government. My guess? He'll grab your passport, stick a monitor on your leg, and let you go. I won't fight that. But for now, Uncle Sam is paying for your hospital stay and your protection. Anything you think I should ask Barton other than how he found you?"

"He took a bunch of pictures with his phone and bagged the cuffs. Where are they?"

Thirty-Nine

ASHLEY LAY PROPPED UP IN the hospital bed finishing a not-half-bad dinner when Thigpen returned.

"I want to see if you can identify the two men who brought you to Quantico. I can stick them in an operating theater, and you can view them from a place they can't see you."

"No reason for secrecy. They know who I am. Bring them here. Let them see what happened to me. It might make them more cooperative."

"They seem to be cooperating, but I like your thinking. One at a time or both together?"

"Let's have a party." Remembering Barton's advice, she added, "Make sure the marshals are here as extra witnesses."

The two FBI agents acted shocked at Ashley's appearance. They each claimed they had received a text message that morning from the Washington SAC notifying them of the change in plans. They showed Thigpen the messages on their phones. Thigpen set his cellphone to speaker and dialed the number the texts had come from. The greeting was the voice of the Special Agent in Charge of the D.C. office.

Ashley wanted one more piece of information before she'd agree these two were pawns. "Why didn't you guys let me call my lawyer?"

Thigpen answered: "The text message said that for security purposes you could not contact anyone. Ms. Prescott, do you want to press charges for unlawful imprisonment?"

"Hell no. The SAC is way too smart to send that message from his phone. You'll find someone spoofed the text messages to sucker these two into doing the dirty work. Send them home to their wives and kids. But, if these guys *are* lying, throw the unabridged dictionary at 'em."

ON SUNDAY MORNING, THE DOCTOR praised Ashley for her fluid intake that had her urinating at least once an hour. He ordered the IV removed and gave her permission to get out of bed. He informed her and the attending marshals—a new set she had not seen before—that he would not sign her release until she no longer showed blood in her urine, which, given her progress, he guessed would occur that afternoon or evening.

She found her clothes in a sealed plastic bag tucked onto the shelf in the room's closet. She cracked the seal, and the room filled with the acrid stench of dried urine. Using the antibacterial soap, she scrubbed her panties and jeans in the sink, discovered the smell had permeated her bra, shirt, socks, and even her shoes. She scrubbed them all the best she could and left the clothing strewn across the bathroom fixtures to dry.

She rang the nurse, explained the problem. The best the nurse could offer was to bring a second hospital gown for Ashley to wear backwards to cover her tush and help hide her boobs. "Hey guys," she yelled through the door. "Can I call someone to bring me clothes?" Who could she call to visit her storage locker? Liya would do it for her.

"No can do," the woman marshal said. "Give me the person's name and number, and I can relay the information."

Which meant the marshals would learn of her storage facility, and the FBI could execute a search warrant and discover Niki's undercover documents and fake IDs and credit cards. That was a no go. "My bad. No one has the key. Can you relay my sizes to a friend, and she can buy me some duds?"

"Okay, but don't go crazy. Once the doc releases you, we'll be giving you a nice set of orange coveralls."

"Orange is not my color, but I'd rather wear an orange onesie than hospital halfsies. You have the coveralls with you? Can I have them?"

"Do and can't. Not until you are officially released to us."

"Bureaucracy. Let me write down my sizes and you can give my friend a call."

"Not so fast," the male marshal said. "This gives the person your location and the sizes could be some kind of code to set up an escape attempt."

Heat boiled into Ashley's face. "Unfuckingbelievable."

"Now calm down, I'm not saying it is, I'm just saying it could be."

Her next urine test was clear of blood, which meant she could soon be traveling. She paced the room. Anticipation grew to concern. Concern to worry. Worry to despair. In the twenty-four hours since she had arrived at the safe house and met the two agents, she had heard nothing from Park or

Ambrose or Seamus. Even the prosecutor, Thigpen, who had seemed outraged at what had happened to her, had disappeared. It felt like the authorities, whoever the hell they were on this deal, were keeping her on ice.

Was she a pawn in an interagency power game within the DOJ? If Thigpen got his way, the DOJ's Office of Inspector General would crawl up the FBI's ass. But that was unlikely to happen until Monday, which meant a lot of people, including Ambrose, were spending the weekend covering their butts. She figured Park was the least likely to hold her back. He could have shut her down earlier and hadn't. Seamus must be wondering what had happened, but even if he were jumping up and down making a nuisance of himself, he had no pull with the Feds.

She gave it four-to-one odds that if she wasn't available to Christine and Greenwar on Monday, Svalinn would fall apart. That *should* motivate Ambrose to help her—it was his friend Jim Ford in jeopardy.

The male marshal stuck his head in the room. "Want to read the Sunday Post? We're done with it."

Trying to make amends. "Thanks." She eased onto the visitor chair and flipped through the pages to check the headlines. Two-thirds down an inside page in the second section, a headline stopped her.

CLOSED MINE LEACHES DEADLY CHEMICALS INTO AQUIFER

In the article's six column-inches, they packed in the mine's name, the forged tests, the current results, their inability to reach anyone at the mine's owner of record, and a no comment from a spokesperson for the American Hydrocarbons Institute, which the article implied was the origin of the forged documents.

Not having internet access sucked. She had no way to learn if this was a *Post* exclusive or other news sources had picked it up. She'd bet Greenwar had posted a blog with copies of the documents she had provided them. Had Christine called to warn her this was coming? If so, Niki would need a damn good excuse for not calling her back.

Here she sat: not dressed up and with nowhere to go. She asked herself, "Why does Svalinn's fate worry you when nobody else seemed to give a flying fuck?" Because you care.

Voices outside her door grabbed her attention. She crept to the door to pick up the conversation.

Voice 1: ". . . sign here and here."

Male marshal: "Why didn't we hear about this?"

Voice 1: "All I know is JPATS has a plane leaving, and she's supposed to be on it. If I had to guess, they want her in Minneapolis for questioning on Monday."

Niki recognized the voice of her former arms instructor and most recent "savior," Special Agent Clyde Barton. Was he rescuing her a second time or was he one of Gex's schemers?

Female marshal: "You got the hospital discharge papers?"

Barton: "Took damn near an hour to process this crap. You want to look at it, be my guest."

Female marshal: "Just dotting i's and crossing t's."

Male marshal: "Any idea what she did to get all this attention?"

Barton: "Beyond me. My job is to bag 'em and drag 'em. You think we need the leg chains or are cuffs and belly chain enough?"

Male marshal: "She's been cooperative—"

Female marshal: "And she's beat up. Belly chain's enough."

Voice 4: "That plane won't wait on us."

Ashley backpedaled from the door in surprise and collapsed in the chair, an arrow of pain stabbing her kidneys. If that last voice wasn't Seamus McCree's, he had a vocal twin.

FORTY

ASHLEY CHANGED INTO THE ORANGE jumpsuit, and Barton shackled her and led her from the hospital to an unmarked SUV. U.S. Government plates, two whip antennae and brush guards front and rear marked it an official ride. But not *whose* official ride. Seamus tucked her into the rear seat; a metal grate separated her from the front. He whispered, "Keep your head down, your mouth shut, and your thoughts to yourself."

"Thank you, marshal," she said.

Fifty minutes of silence later, they passed a sign proclaiming, Alexandria Virginia Established 1749 Welcome. Soon the three of them were walking in the back door and up a darkened staircase of the Albert V. Vickers U.S. District Court, Eastern District of Virginia. Each step brought a mournful clank of metal chains. This building was a hundred years younger than the slave trade, but the sound made her wonder if the spirits heard and trembled. They led her into a judge's chambers, where a single lamp on his desk cast the room into shadows. The judge motioned for them to sit. "Name?"

Everyone looked at her, so Ashley decided she could break the head down, mouth shut routine. "Ashley Prescott, Your Honor."

"You know why you're here?"

"Not exactly, sir."

"I have before me a bail application that calls for your release without conditions pending future court actions. The prosecutor has tied himself into knots to agree." He laid the papers down and looked at her over his tortoiseshell half-glasses.

Thank you, Director Park, for whatever strings you pulled.

"Normally, you'd have a lawyer to advise you. Of course, normally, this would happen in open court, and I wouldn't have to give up my golf game to be here on a fine Sunday. Do you have anything you wish to say?"

She shook her head rather than trust her voice.

"If the charges against you are true, you have the wherewithal to disappear. I shall attach two conditions to your release. You will relinquish your passport to me and agree to remain within the lower forty-eight states and the District of Columbia. Your face suggests you have a problem with that."

"I had my passport when I was taken into custody, but—"

Seamus deposited a passport in front of the judge.

"No objections, your Honor."

"You will wear a GPS device on your ankle. If you plan to travel outside a fifty-mile radius from this building, you will inform the court ahead of time of your expected destination and the duration of the travel. You will be charged a two-hundred-dollar setup fee plus twenty-five dollars a day for the monitoring."

Yikes. Probably not an expense Ambrose would approve. "I do a fair amount of traveling."

The magistrate's eyebrows arched. "Then I suggest you add my clerk to your speed dial. You gentlemen will accompany Ms. Prescott to the firm that does our monitoring and make sure they outfit her with a monitor before you release her." He dropped his glasses on his desk and rubbed his eyes. "Understand, Ms. Prescott, that this proceeding is most unusual. I'm sure the government has its reasons, but if you violate the conditions we've agreed on today, I won't care how much pressure they apply. You will not pass go and get your two hundred dollars back. You will go directly to jail and sit there for a long time. Are we clear?"

Ashley clinked and jangled from the magistrate's office a semi-free and confused woman. She had no idea how she was supposed to work with a tracker on her ankle, but she kept Seamus's warning in mind and kept her thoughts to herself. The three of them, her still shackled with a belly chain, drove to the offices of the GPS tracking company where a pimply tech guy, who might have still been in high school, fitted her device, showed her how to charge it, warned her of all the things that would trigger an alarm, and told her to "have a great day!"

SPECIAL AGENT CLYDE BARTON UNSHACKLED her and raised a finger to his lips. Seamus walked three cars down and beeped open a gray Toyota Corolla. Barton whispered in her ear. "You're McCree's problem now. Your tracker allows them to listen whenever they want. Should anyone ever ask, I'd appreciate it if you say you never caught the names of the two marshals who collected you from the hospital. I hear tell there was some kind of mix-up. Whatever the hell you got yourself into, Pendergast, I hope it works out, and we send some misguided assholes to prison. In the meantime, do me a big favor. Next time you get kidnapped, don't let them take you to Quantico."

She cupped her hands around his ear. "One question, Barton. Why do you keep calling me Pendergast?"

"Because that's the name of the lady who smoked my ass on the range. And your ex is probably one of the aforementioned assholes."

Forty-One

Ashley used the backseat of Seamus's rented Toyota Corolla to change from the orange jumpsuit into a set of clothes she'd never seen. They fit, and the blond wig matched the set of documents she found tucked into the pocket of her new jeans. Park's work, she assumed, but given her monitor could hear, she kept her supposition to herself.

She slid into the passenger seat, and Seamus passed her a note. "One more stop. Keep your ID handy." Seamus tuned the radio to an all-news station. She'd missed nothing important, and the *Washington Post* story about a Wisconsin mine leaching toxic chemicals was not part of the rotation. Seamus pulled into the same underground garage ADNI Park had used five days earlier when they created her fake IDs.

She wondered if the ankle monitor's GPS worked this far underground. And if not, how long before someone tried to call her on a phone she didn't have with her. Seamus presented their credentials at the security station. A uniformed guard escorted them through underground tunnels to a room filled with electronics. Behind a table waited a black male, mid-forties, wearing a pressed white lab coat. Park stood to the side, arms crossed, frowning.

"Let's see what you got?" the technician said.

Park interpreted. "Roll up your pant leg. He'll remove your monitor."

She lifted her foot to rest on the table and exposed the device. "This thing can hear."

"Not in this room," the tech said. "This sucker's gonna be a bitch." He rummaged through bins on the shelves behind him, selecting several tools and bits of wire. In less than two minutes, he installed a bypass to prevent the bracelet from realizing he was tampering with the fiber optics, unlocked the device, and slipped it off her leg.

"She's in 22F," Park said.

Ashley had a thousand questions but restrained herself until the technician left with the bracelet and Seamus shut the door. Park elaborated. "The person in 22F will wear your monitor while you continue your

Greenwar work. A lot has happened since we last talked. I hope you don't feel as bad as you look."

How she felt was not worth discussing. "I saw the *Post* article about the mine."

Park said, "Christine accepted your story, which is good because we have a big problem."

"You betcha. She blew my AHI cover. Doesn't take a genius to see who showed up at their offices just before the leak."

"That's not the problem I meant. Remember Michael Yoncey, the ATF agent, told you about a bust that didn't happen because the guy selling the explosives disappeared? Well, ATF used the guy's cellphone tracking data and found him decomposing in a shed, bullet to the brain. The sniffer dogs swear on their kibble the explosives had been in the shed. ATF used warrants to backtrack a bunch of suspects. The only one who had been in the vicinity was Christine's daughter, Olivia."

She checked Seamus for his reaction. Nothing. He'd heard it all. "Arrest her. What am I missing?"

Park said, "Her. Olivia didn't show up for her meeting with ATF's Mike. Ashley, enough C-4 is missing to destroy twenty miles of pipeline infrastructure or one good-sized office building. Mike is working his end to find her, but we need you at Christine's compound."

"Which is why someone else is wearing my monitor. I get it, but Christine burned me with that story. Why would she let me anywhere near her?"

"Because," Park said, "Ambrose is right now convincing Jim Ford to meet you at his offices first thing tomorrow morning to provide you with a new powerful allegation. That, by the way, is the limit of Ambrose's continued involvement in Svalinn. We require your eyes and ears. You have questions, and I want to provide answers."

Niki had lots of questions, with one top of mind. "Who told Special Agent Clyde Barton to look for me at Quantico?"

Park tilted his head, cracked the ghost of a smile. "You deserve an answer. Seamus, would you do us the favor of stepping out of the room?"

He did, and Park said, "I contacted the president. He made it happen." Park held up a hand to stop her from responding. "I don't know how, and I did not ask. I have heard, however, that the Attorney General is using your arrest debacle to have the Office of the Inspector General perform a colonoscopy on the FBI. Without anesthesia. The director, the deputy and assistant directors, Internal Investigation Section, Undercover Operations, and Quantico Training are all scrambling. That puts you at substantial risk.

"Suppose the FBI convinced others that you're crooked. They might make a big enough splash with their right hand to sweep their sins under the carpet with their left hand. Given the stakes, the affected parties might use surveillance techniques on you that we normally apply to organized crime or Mexican drug lords. Not legal, but that might not stop some people. We must assume they'll know if you use any of your personal credentials or Niki's."

"I've only used two of the IDs you gave me."

Park opened the door and motioned Seamus back in. "Destroy your unused ones. They should be fine, but some smart, motivated people with lots of resources want to find you. I have created six more sets of IDs and credit cards. Use cash and burner phones whenever you can. IDs and credit cards only if required. We'll get you more cash before you leave. I also have several sets of IDs and credit cards for you, Seamus. In theory, only Ambrose, Special Agent Rick Kaska, and we three know of your involvement with Svalinn. But nothing has been straightforward with this entire operation. Hell, if I were in your situation, I'd take the money, tell me to fuck myself, and go hide."

Ashley could not hide her grin. "Well, isn't it a good thing that I don't think like you?"

"And don't I know it? I understand you and Seamus are using some form of secure communication. That's good, but for me, we require something better. NSA learned a new trick from the Chinese that the Bureau does not yet know. It requires a cell phone. You dial a number I'll give you, and it installs an encrypted messenger app. Only the three of us will know that number."

She didn't believe that for a second.

Park wagged a finger at her. "Not even the techs. Once the app installs, you have five minutes to read or compose messages. After five minutes, the app disappears along with any messages. You do anything else with your phone, the app knows and vanishes."

Seamus, who Niki realized had remained silent since he had re-entered the room, said, "And if we're still reading a message?"

Park said, "Read fast. The next time you download the app, you'll see only new messages. I'd prefer you two use this to communicate, but I recognize right now you may not fully trust *anyone* in the government. I don't need or want status reports. Contact me if I can help. I *will* read your communications."

The worse Park made it sound, the more Ashley wanted to catch that monster wave and ride it into the shore. But her thrill of living on the edge didn't mean she should suck Seamus into the dangers of her world. She jabbed Seamus in the ribs. "This should scare the crap out of you. Park and I can do this. You've done more than enough."

His blue eyes burned into hers with the intensity of a Himalayan sun. "You two believe this is what's needed to stop Greenwar, I'm in. I hate what those executives have done, but killing people is not the answer." He shook his head. "Growing up, my mother insisted that I should assume everything I did or said would become public knowledge. If she only knew."

Ashley wondered again at the universe that had dumped her at Seamus's camp all those years ago. Was there a master plan, as some insisted, or was she just one lucky woman? "I don't want to know the details, but am I correct in assuming no one tracking my ankle monitor can learn I am not wearing it?"

Park said, "The woman will wear your monitor in a safe and quiet location. You being taken into custody without the monitor is the real risk."

Niki accepted that as gospel. "Here's what that means, Seamus. We must assume people at the FBI know you and I are working together. When they can't find me, they'll likely monitor you. That means no one can see us together anywhere in the D.C. area. So, go do tourist-y things and get some rest. You and I have a few errands to run starting at two in the morning."

Park crossed his arms. "That sounds ominous. You aren't planning on testing my home security again, are you?"

Ashley was beginning to appreciate Park's way of easing tension. "Not this time. Since I can never use Niki's apartment again, I have things to remove. The audio bugs will catch us, but I'll be in and out in minutes. And I have other items to pick up around town. I can use a second set of eyes, and I doubt anyone will be tailing Seamus at that time of night. I'd like to walk out of here. Can your folks provide me a disguise?"

They could.

"Great," she said. "I plan to recuperate in a hotel close to the American Hydrocarbons Institute headquarters. Tomorrow I meet Jim Ford to retrieve whatever juicy thing Ambrose convinced him to cough up to justify my dropping in on Christine. AHI offices are another pinch point the Bureau might know about. I'll meet Ford in a nearby coffee shop, one whose location allows me to verify no one is tailing him from his office. That work for everyone?"

Park offered a single nod. Seamus provided the last word. "It *sounds* like it should work."

FORTY-TWO

ON A DREARY MONDAY MORNING, Niki adopted a homeless-person persona, seeking donations on a street corner with views covering both the building that housed American Hydrocarbons Institute and the coffee shop where Jim Ford was to meet her. Her gig had netted no donations. Her wig of disgusting dreadlocks and green trash bags to ward off the coming rain were probably off-putting, but she suspected the thing that repulsed people and encouraged them not to make eye contact was her fake cough and the medical face mask that covered her nose and mouth. All the better to see and not be seen.

While waiting for Ford, she used Park's newfangled app and confirmed which flight Seamus was taking to MSP and that he was bringing everything the two of them had retrieved in the wee hours of the morning from Niki's apartment and Ashley's storage unit. He reminded her he had rescheduled the dinner canceled from Friday when he'd had to spirit Ashley from Minnesota. He'd booked a private dining room at the hotel where they were staying for seven o'clock that night under Pendergast Holdings' name.

That sounded less attractive than going to the dentist for a cleaning, where you never knew what bad things might happen.

Two minutes before the time of their scheduled rendezvous, Ford exited his office building with a slow step, labored even. He focused on the sidewalk, paying little attention to anything around him. No one followed him, and no one on the street seemed to pay him any attention. The question was, would anyone show after Ford turned off K Street?

Not immediately. She waited another two minutes to make sure no one appeared interested in him before briskly walking into the coffee shop. Lots of noise and lots of people—perfect for a quiet conversation, but first she needed to make a quick change. She ducked into the restroom and shed her homeless-person clothes to reveal casual attire underneath. Tucking her outer garments, wig, and mask into the shopping bag she carried, she donned a different wig, one he would recognize. She placed her order for a fruit smoothie—breakfast—and walked to his table.

"You look worse than I feel," he said. His gaze jittered around the room like he'd been mainlining caffeine. He leaned across the table. In a stage whisper he said, "You didn't tell me the story was going to end up in the *Post*."

Thanks for asking why I look like I do. "We convinced Greenwar the material was legit. That's great. Our mutual friend says you have something else I can bring them."

He closed his eyes, his head twitching like he suffered from Parkinson's. He opened his mouth, but before he spoke, a barista yelled, "Niki!" She collected her smoothie and returned to the table and waved for him to continue.

"AHI's board is demanding an explanation for how the *Post* got that material. My assistant, Mrs. Dover, has their ear and is accusing you of being the source. She's made the not-unreasonable observation that you are the first new face there in five years and have been rooting through old files."

Niki raised her hands in frustration. "Wasn't the plan, but it's spilt milk. What have you got for me?"

He rubbed his temples hard with both hands. "You're not hearing me. Your services are no longer desired here."

Niki leaned back and blew air toward the ceiling, returned her gaze to a still nervous Jim Ford. She took a long pull of the smoothie, deciding what approach to take. "I understand you don't want me at AHI. We can create a story for Greenwar to explain how I still have access to material. It is critical that I have another piece of intelligence to legitimately contact them again. And for various reasons, I must meet with them tomorrow." Not true but adding time pressure might get him to act.

He stiffened, and for the first time, looked her in the eye. "There *is* no next time. I expected you to discreetly use the material to infiltrate Greenwar and arrest the killers. You failed at both parts of that. Since you cannot control how information will be used, I cannot do it."

Oh, now it's all her fault. Talk about unreasonable expectations. What the hell had Ambrose told him? She choked down a snarky comment to remind him he fit the profile of executives killed, not because he was a CEO, but because he had allegedly hidden company pollution that had led to a cancer hot spot. Instead, she said, "Right now, this is the best way to prevent future murders."

His mouth thinned to a knife's edge. With difficulty, his Adam's apple bobbed once. He leaned away from her and said so softly she almost didn't catch it, "I have nothing for you. After I attend a board meeting next Monday, I'll be leaving for my place in Mexico."

"You can run away. Maybe that will save you. Before you ghost, *you* need to let your good friend Ambrose know you refused to help." *Because then he'll know exactly what a chickenshit you are.*

Ford slid from the chair, gave her a condescending nod, and weaved through the tables toward the front door. Niki bussed the table and caught up with him on the street side of the door. She snagged his arm, stopping his progress. "It's not too late to—"

Ford tried to wrench away, but she held on. A green-dot speckle appeared on the image of a cup painted onto the coffee shop's window behind them and moved to Ford's chest. She jerked him toward her and registered the sharp crack of a rifle firing and the shattering of the coffee shop glass window. She shoved Ford into the coffee shop's entrance, yelled for him to get inside and not leave except with the police, and sprinted across the street in the direction the shot had come from.

WITHOUT CONSCIOUS THOUGHT, NIKI HAD processed the scene. The image on the window was lower than Ford's chest, meaning the laser scope was at considerable height—an upper story or roof of a building on K Street. She had instinctively run toward the building to make it harder for the shooter to hit her with his next shot. A shot that never came.

It was a fool's errand to guess the exact location where the shot had come from and apprehend the shooter. Instead, she headed for the Metro. By the time she reached the station, the skies delivered their promised rain. The first downpour distracted other pedestrians from paying attention to her standing under an awning, reprising her homeless-person outfit. In her undercover work, she had memorized the metro station security camera locations. Between the mask and turning her head away from the cameras, she was fairly certain no one could identify her.

Waiting for the train, she replayed the events. Only two things made sense. Ninety-nine percent chance, Greenwar was moving fast following the Post article and had attempted to kill Ford. One percent, she was the target, not Ford, and someone at the Bureau was willing to kill her. One of Gex's fans exacting extreme revenge? Or Ambrose guaranteeing she couldn't testify to his actions?

The train whistled its approach and rumbled into the station. She was the only one to get on the last car. That allowed her to use the app to inform Park what had happened and to ask if he could secure and eliminate any CCTV footage that captured her image. She'd tried to keep herself hidden, but . . .

Park: *Acknowledged. Next steps?*

She replied: *Use a new ID. Book a different flight to MSP than Seamus is on. Have idea how to get accepted at Christine's compound.*

Park: *Stay safe*

That, she thought, was easier said than done.

Forty-Three

ASHLEY CHECKED IN AT THE Minneapolis hotel using a different ID than the one she had used to book her flight. She had enough time to shower, change into her corporate duds, and check online to determine what the press was saying about the attempted assassination in D.C. The *Post* reported that an unnamed disgruntled ex-employee of the coffee shop was a person of interest in what was being called a malicious revenge event. No mention of Jim Ford. No mention of anyone like her. No mention of a panhandling homeless person.

Sounded to her like Park's troops had done excellent work. Thinking about Park triggered her to check the URL he had given her to view video of Niki's apartment. She zipped through the fifteen minutes she and Seamus had been there retrieving her belongings and was surprised to find more video. The cameras had caught Gex, dressed in an FBI jacket, badge folded over his belt, a ring of keys in hand, entering her apartment midafternoon. He had removed the four audio bugs and left, turning at the door to give the apartment the finger. She found a frame, zoomed in, and snapped a screenshot of the device's make and serial number.

That and the video were all she needed to nail Gex—assuming she could use the evidence. Feeling ecstatic, she jogged down the stairs to the second level, where the restaurant was. The server showed her to their assigned room. She slipped inside unnoticed and surveyed the gathering. Her half-brother, Garrett Pendergast, was chatting with two Pendergast Holdings employees, Gabriella Linz, the CEO, and Malachi Cluff, now head of sales. Her half-sister, Tabitha Maki, had Seamus pinned in a corner and was emphasizing a point with theatrical gesticulations. Ashley had never seen Tabitha really pissed but guessed she was now. Better learn what was going on.

"Here she is," Seamus said. "You can ask her yourself."

Tabitha spun around and skewered Ashley with a look that threatened bare knuckles and knives. *What the hell did I do wrong?* "Ask me what?"

"Is it true Chloe joined Junior's suit against you and Seamus? After all we've done for her? That's despicable."

Ah. Ashley's jaws clenched, her body remembering how she had felt when she first heard. She forced calmness into her voice. "She's broke and homeless and desperate. Bradlee's suicide cost her family twenty-five million they stood to inherit had he lived another month. Her kids lost their father and their upper-middle-class lifestyle. I bet Junior convinced her they could use her plight to sway the judge—or at least public opinion. We should cut her some slack."

As Ashley reasoned with her, Tabitha continued shaking her head. "That may all be true, but her behavior sucks. I delayed my plans for Legacy House to help her."

This was the first Ashley had heard that Tabitha had plans for the house, and she asked her to elaborate.

"I created a nonprofit to use Legacy House to provide temporary shelter to battered women with families. I'll hire staff to be present and assist women to transition to a new life."

Which, Ashley realized, was what Tabitha had done with Chloe and her kids. "That is commendable," she said. "And I'm sure it's much needed. I understand your anger. I really do. But I am begging you to reconsider, more for the kids' sake than Chloe's."

Seamus herded everyone to the table. Ashley sat between Garrett and Tabitha. Gabriella was opposite her, flanked by Malachi and Seamus.

Time for one of her fake-it-until-she-made-it moments. Ashley tapped her water glass with her knife, creating a pure tone only good crystal could make. The conversation stopped, and all eyes turned toward her. She stood. "I want to thank you all for coming tonight after I blew you off Friday night. I decided getting arrested had priority." That elicited nervous chuckles.

"Junior framed me. It's one front in his battle to discredit his father's wishes and gain control of Pendergast Holdings, a battle with many collateral damages, including to each of you and to our stock value. Later this week, we're installing our new, independent board. I'll strongly encourage them not to entertain any offers to buy us. My preference is to focus on strengthening our business, which will allow us to go public and fulfill Robert's ambition to have Pendergast Holdings grow through acquisition."

She sipped water and checked their expressions, reading neutral to positive around the table. "Seamus has informed me of the tremendous work you have already done. Thank you collectively and individually. Thank you, Tabitha, for having faith in my decisions. Gabriella, please know I have your back as you mold Pendergast Holdings from a family-run business. Garrett, I know the work you have done with Seamus has been painful for you—to learn of the hidden corruption in your division. Sadly, I have one more favor to ask of you before you pursue photography full-time. Malachi, tonight I'd like you to temporarily return to your Pendergast Holdings' Head Conscience Guru role. Because—"

"It was Chief Conscience Officer, and Gabriella has already impressed on employees that every one of us is the firm's conscience."

Ah Malachi, the thing is, I know you will tell the truth. "Even so, you've had more experience than the rest of us. You all know I worked undercover for the FBI. I ask you to please not share with anyone that I am *still* working undercover. My current assignment involves national security and many lives are at stake. Why, you wonder, have I gathered you here?"

Five pairs of eyes focused on her. "Well, I didn't, Seamus did, but I've hijacked his meeting. Despite our contacting them and providing them the information we gathered, the Feds are dragging their feet investigating the bribes Pendergast Holdings paid to EPA regulators. With your permission, I want to leak that information. Perhaps the leak will stir the Feds to speed up their work, but to be honest, that's not my reason for asking.

With your permission, I would leak it to the domestic terrorist organization I am trying to infiltrate. I can't say who or why. If this works, I believe it will save lives. But it comes with costs, which is why I will only proceed with your unanimous agreement.

"Garrett, if everyone at the table approves my request, it's important for Pendergast employees that you remain in charge of your division to assure everyone of the company's commitment to legal actions. I promised you could leave once you had helped Seamus. If that's your choice, we'll make sure it's clear that you were not responsible, and the company is not making you its sacrificial lamb."

She faced Gabriella. "The information being leaked this way probably makes your job harder. Unanimous means you have veto power. Malachi, I want you to share your thoughts on whether it is proper for me to even make this request and whether it is proper for the company to comply with it."

"And me?" Tabitha asked.

"As a beneficiary of the Sisters Trust with its investments tied up in Pendergast Holdings, you have a significant stake in the company's future. As an outsider, you may have a perspective the others do not. Shall I stay while you discuss this, or shall I walk around the block?"

Tabitha still looked like she wanted to spit nails. "Now that I know why I'm here, I'll speak my mind. You and Seamus should leave."

Forty-Four

FOURTEEN MINUTES LATER—NOT THAT Ashley was watching the clock or anything—Malachi told her the others had questions for her. He was to keep Seamus company.

"Relax, Ashley," Seamus said. "Be yourself."

She found Gabriella now seated between Tabitha and Garrett, reminding her of a panel of three judges. In her absence, salads had been served and partially eaten. The click of the door closing sounded to her more like the clang of a prison door slamming shut. She recognized adrenaline had heightened all her senses, bringing her to what she thought of as Niki mode. She read their faces. Gabriella wore the hint of amusement she often had when dealing with Ashley. Tabitha looked like she had swallowed a frog. Garrett was the Cheshire Cat.

Gabriella motioned to the chairs opposite them. "Have a seat. The waiter will soon bring the main course. This won't take but a minute. Garrett and Tabitha have a proposition. Malachi spoke at great length regarding how important it is to view on its own merits your request to release information about Pendergast's government bribes. The three of us chose a broader view. We considered the entire transaction, not a single component.

"Malachi agrees you consistently and clearly have presented a vision of Pendergast Holdings' future. It's a vision we all agree will make the company a strong business we are proud to be associated with. That's why I agree with Garrett and Tabitha to support your request for Garrett to provide you with whatever material you need for your undercover assignment with one proviso: in return, you agree to be the Chairperson of the Board of Directors."

"Are you nuts?" She supposed that wasn't quite what Seamus meant when he told her to be herself.

Gabriella's smile broadened. "Malachi made the point, which seemed obvious once he did, that you have insisted the company must transition from being a family-run business to one professionally run. That's why we're expanding the board to include a majority of outside directors. Seamus and Garrett have prepared a presentation to the board regarding the past bribes and kickbacks they have uncovered, the steps they have taken to clean house, and their work with various police agencies. We all support you, but at tomorrow's board meeting, you must convince enough outside directors to form a majority."

Ashley heard all the words and understood their meaning yet felt like she was walking in a heavy fog that obscured anything beyond the vaguest form of the beasts threatening to devour her. "If this was Malachi's idea, why isn't he here?"

Garrett cleared his throat. "The four of us represent the family and insider board members. Malachi is a valued employee."

Ashley blurted her frustration, "I don't understand what that has to do with the price of eggs."

Gabriella gave her an appraising look. "Has Seamus discussed the structure of the board with you?"

"He has my proxy. Why would he?"

Garrett hooted. "She doesn't know. Here's the deal, Ashley. Seamus structured the board to have nine members. He's engaged five excellent outsiders who will bring terrific experience and great contacts. Gabriella, as CEO, is also a member. That leaves three slots to represent the family. After we take the company public, we'll give up some or all of those seats."

Seamus *had* outlined something like that a while back, and she had told him to do whatever made sense; she'd vote to support his decisions.

Garrett continued. "I agreed to remain a director because I could help Gabriella with continuity issues. Tabitha reluctantly agreed because the Sisters Trust is such a substantial stockholder."

That was nice of Tabitha. "Who's representing the shares Junior and Bradlee owned outright?"

Garrett pointed at her. "When will the lightbulb go on, Sis? You control more shares than anyone. Seamus added you to the board. We're just insisting that you be the Chair."

A polite knock sounded at the door. A waiter stuck his head in. "May I serve you now?"

Everyone was looking at her. Time to make her first executive decision. "Yes, that'd be lovely."

Now she knew why Seamus had waited until they were with a bunch of other people before springing this crap of making her a director: he knew she wouldn't kill him in front of witnesses.

Forty-Five

ASHLEY THREW UP FIFTEEN MINUTES before the board meeting. Last night's confrontation with Seamus replayed in her mind—following him to his hotel room, reaming him out for keeping her in the dark until it was too late to stop him. He'd been completely unapologetic. The anger had led to excellent sex.

While Seamus was sawing logs, she had researched the five outside directors he'd recruited: the CEO and chairman of a national bank, the CEO of a huge agribusiness, a former female state governor, a management guru from Wharton, and the COO of a Minneapolis top Fortune 100 company.

Fake-it-until-you-make-it assumes you have *some* idea how to fake it. Since she did not, she was wrapped around the porcelain pot, spewing up her stomach lining instead of mingling with the rest of the board members over coffee and pastries. She flushed the stench, washed her mouth at the sink, and checked her appearance in the mirror.

That morning, Seamus had surprised her with an outfit that reeked of power. A pale blue silk blouse and a blue pantsuit looked bespoke, its white pinstripes outlined with a hint of red. A Pendergast Holdings logo pin, a pH stylized like the chemical symbol crafted in University of Minnesota colors, maroon and gold, decorated her left lapel. The mule sandals with short block heels he had purchased were from Neiman Marcus, for crying out loud, but she had to admit they fit perfectly. A simple pearl choker graced her neck. He had even purchased a new wig. Must have cost more than the rest of the ensemble: dirty blonde, even length, hand-tied with feathered bangs. Professional and good-looking.

Seamus had remembered that Ashley had borrowed clothes from Tabitha that fit well and used her for sizing. "Did you pay for this?" she had asked him.

"Oh hell no, the Sisters Trust forked over the money. Tabitha has a new outfit too."

She had to admit, she looked the part, even if she felt like throwing up again.

The morning portion of the meeting brought the new directors current on Pendergast Holdings' financial position, several legal issues—including the embarrassing fact that their chairperson had been arrested for embezzlement. Seamus must have already greased the wheels on that because no one asked questions. She picked at her lunch, not wanting to give her stomach more to reject. After lunch, Garrett presented his findings about the bribery and kickback schemes he and Seamus had uncovered, finishing his presentation with, "Ashley has a few additional words to say on this topic."

She sipped water and licked her lips before standing. "I'll bet each of you Googled me or had an assistant do it for you. And you didn't find much post college graduation. There's a reason for that. I have spent most of that time working undercover for the federal government. Therefore, I cannot be the public face of Pendergast. Gabriella will be. Plus, I have no idea how to run a corporation. I rely on you and the employees for that. I believe I bring two things to this table. The first is the assurance that I'll support the collective decisions of this board, even if I do not agree with them."

She sipped water, licked her lips again, and relaxed. "Because we are not public and a charitable trust owns the vast majority of our shares, I want to encourage us to make decisions based on long-term goals. I don't know all the fancy business jargon, stakeholders and such, but I will hold you accountable for making sure Pendergast Holdings does well by doing good. What the heck does that mean? We shall prove to our customers that we are partners in solving their problems. That's doing good by our customers. And our employees must believe that we will not tolerate their exploitation for any reason. That's doing good by our employees. We are citizens in a connected web I think of as Mother Earth. I'm not asking anyone to buy my New Age philosophy, but Pendergast Holdings must do good by our environment and by the citizens of the communities where we work. I genuinely believe that if we focus on doing good for these others, we will do well by our shareholders.

"As you can tell, I'm passionate on this subject. I am even more passionate about bringing justice to those who have not received it. The primary goal of my governmental work is to prevent bad things from happening. When that fails, we bring perpetrators to justice.

"Pendergast Holdings has worked diligently to bring its past illegal actions to the attention of the proper authorities. Garrett and I wanted Pendergast to make a public confession of our misdeeds, but the Feds told us they don't want the information released until they've made their case against the others involved. They're dragging their heels for reasons that are not clear, but I suspect are political. We need to move on.

"Here's where you either agree or slap me down. In my current undercover assignment, I can use this information to gain access to a domestic terrorist group. Using that information places Pendergast Holdings in the position of reacting to reports of our bad behavior rather than appearing proactive, which had been our plan. What I am doing is secret stuff, and I can't give you details. Or promises. I can only tell you that I think in the end we will do well by doing good. I'm open for questions, and then I'll leave the room and you can decide."

The former state governor immediately spoke. "National security says our biggest threat is domestic terrorism. It was a huge issue for my state and from what I understand, the situation is worse now. Pendergast Holdings can have its response prepared and ready to release once the news pops. We're not running away from our past. We detail the steps we've taken, that we revealed our misdeeds to law enforcement and have remained silent at their request. The onus falls on them. You tell me this helps against domestic terror, and you have my vote."

Ashley sat stunned. In thirty seconds, she had her fifth vote. The other four fell in line after hearing Gabriella's support. With that settled, Ashley's attention drifted from the meeting to how she could best approach Christine and grab Greenwar's attention. Thursday was the day. Depending on how it went, it might be her last day.

Forty-Six

Chloe responded to Ashley's ringing the front doorbell and barred the way into Legacy House. "What are *you* doing here?"

"Jacob invited me to watch the NCAA championship softball game. You remember our bet? I promised I'd bring dinner." She held up the bags of food and drink. "He said he had cleared it with you."

"He told me a friend was coming."

Ashley broke into a wide grin. "And here I am. Are you planning to let me in or embarrass your son, who I hear racing down the stairs?"

"Hey, Mom," Jacob called from the end of the hall. "Is that Ashley?"

Chloe opened the door and said under her breath as Ashley passed, "We need to talk before you leave."

"Wouldn't have it any other way. Jacob, have you grown since I last saw you? I swear you look taller. I didn't know if you liked brats or footlongs, so I brought both." She held up the bag.

Jacob led Ashley to his room, where he had set up a tablet to watch the game. They chowed down on the junk food and devoured popcorn. During the game, Ashley challenged his assumption about softball being easier. She walked him through the math: yes, the pitches were slower, but the shorter distance from the mound to the plate gave batters the same split-second to react as in baseball.

"Whoa!" Jacob said "That is so dope."

Ashley was confused "Stupid?"

"Huh?" Jacob gave her a look of uncertainty.

"What does dope mean, Jacob?"

"Like, super awesome."

Ashley felt officially old. After the softball game, she let Jacob convince her to play some video games with him. "Okay, kiddo. This was a blast, but I have to talk to your mother."

"Can we do this again?"

"I'd like to, but I can't promise anything. I'm not sure how often I'll even be in the area." *And your mother may forbid it.*

"I'll even watch more softball."

She mussed his hair, feeling bad that an eleven-year-old was so desperate for companionship that he wanted to play with her.

Ashley found Chloe pacing the hallway at the bottom of the stairs. She gripped Ashley's arm with both hands and leaned close to hiss her message. Her breath smelled of alcohol. "I don't know what game you're playing, but it won't work."

Ashley tamped down her anger and resisted the urge to break Chloe's grip and dump her on the floor. In a quiet, firm tone she said, "Walk with me to the patio. You don't want your kids to hear this."

Chloe slit her eyes, cocked her head, must have decided Ashley was right, because she let go and yelled up to the kids that she'd be right outside if they needed her.

Ashley arranged two patio chairs and motioned Chloe to sit. "This way we can keep our voices down."

Chloe sat, sullen, spoiling for a fight.

"Chloe, I don't give a rat's ass what you think of me, but you should know several things. First, I don't give a shit that you joined Junior's suit. You're grasping at straws, and Junior's lawyers offered one. That suit doesn't stand a snowball's chance in hell, and I'll pay lawyers to fight it with whatever it takes. There will never be a settlement. You can believe that or not, but it's the truth. Here's another one: Tabitha is super pissed that you joined Junior's suit. I had to convince her not to throw you and your kids out of this house."

Chloe's eyes grew wide.

"You have two choices, Chloe. Do nothing, drink yourself stupid, and hope a miracle saves your ass, or get your act together and show your kids how to succeed in the face of adversity. To that end, I'm making you an offer. You're an accountant, and from what I hear, you were a good one. You have business skills even if they are rusty. Create a resume that highlights those skills, and I'll find you a job at Pendergast Holdings. Listen carefully, this isn't some make-work offer or me hoping you'll drop the suit. I told you, I don't give a shit about that suit. This is the Chairman of Pendergast Holdings' Board knowing the labor market is tight and seeing someone with the potential to make a positive difference for the company. It gives you a chance to regain your footing and earn money to put food on the table and clothes on your kids' backs."

Chloe's face was a picture of barely controlled anger. "Are you doing this to shove your superiority in my face?"

Ashley stood to leave before she said something she'd regret. "Jacob is a great kid. Let's say I'm doing it for him because if you don't get on the road to fixing yourself, you'll drown him and your girls with your self-destruction. Bradlee's benefits at Pendergast expire at the end of the month. With a job there, those would continue uninterrupted."

"I've got young kids at home."

"You and ten million other single moms. I'm not saying this is easy. You'll have to arrange for childcare, but right now you aren't paying any rent. With a job you can afford the extra expenses. But like I said, it's up to you. Tuck the kids in bed. Write a resume. It doesn't have to be polished. Get it to Morgan, Gabriella's admin. She's expecting it. One last thing. Jacob wants to see me again. I hope you'll say yes."

And that, Ashley thought while dialing for an Uber, was as much family and business stuff as she could stand for one day.

Forty-Seven

IT TOOK **G**ARRETT AND **HER** the better part of Wednesday to sort through the bribery information, cherry pick what they provided Greenwar, record it on a memory stick, and make printouts. To drive to Christine's remote camp, she needed a rental car. Thursday morning, she used a different credit card and driver's license to accomplish that task, choosing the cheapest model she could rent for a week. Uncle Sam might have unlimited pockets, but Niki wanted to look like an unemployed person pinching pennies.

She left the Minneapolis hotel, planned a stop to stretch and grab a fast-food lunch, and expected to arrive at Christine's around one in the afternoon. Approaching the camp, she caught a flash of reflected light on the bluff overlooking the marsh. She'd bet dinner someone was tracking her approach with binoculars. Good, she preferred to minimize the extent of the surprise. Christine surely would ask why Niki had not called—she was prepared for that—but she didn't want to appear like she was sneaking up.

On the final approach, Niki made another rueful discovery: she should have rented an SUV or at least something with higher ground clearance. To keep the car from bouncing and whacking the undercarriage, she had to creep the last half mile. She was probably violating the rental agreement by driving on these unpaved roads. If she busted something, it would cost a fortune to summon a wrecker. And with the road being less than two cars wide, they might push it into the marsh.

Such cheerful thoughts.

Despite her best efforts, she scraped bottom on the last hill climbing to the clearing. The grinding of metal on rock left her wondering what damage she'd done. If there had been room to pull off, she would have walked the rest of the way. She soldiered on and parked next to a vehicle that hadn't been there on her first visit. Beyond the unknown RAV4, clean and shiny with West Virginia plates, was Donnie's beat-up Ford Ranger. Zed's GMC Sierra was not in sight.

Maybe coming up unannounced was not such a good idea. She flexed her fingers to ease the tension from the drive. Once out of the car, she wanted to release the tightness in her neck and shoulders and shook herself like a dog leaving the water. No go. She dropped to her belly and shimmied under the car to confirm she wasn't dragging any parts or leaking fluids.

A male voice, not Donnie's, but one she'd heard before, said, "You're either brave or stupid bringing that car up here."

The hint of a drawl let her place him: Timothy Gentle, who had visited her at AHI's D.C. offices.

She tucked her hand into her sleeve and rattled the exhaust manifold. Solid. "Hello, Timothy. If you're placing a bet, go with stupid. I'm looking for Christine. She around?" She pushed out from under the car and used the remote to lock the doors with a confirming chirp. Standing, she faced him waving both hands to swat away the whining mosquito hordes that found her.

He held a single-barreled pump shotgun, pointed at the ground, but he remained far enough away that he could do her in if she charged him. A much-used Tilley hat, pulled low, covered his widow's peak and emphasized the straight line of his eyebrows. If she had a mind, she could consider his smile to be flirty. "Engine head attracts the bloodsucking varmints. That's why we park away from the cabin." He did a cartoon version of a second take. "What happened to you?"

"Got mugged and I don't want to talk about it. Okay?"

"Yeah, sure. Christine's not here. Something my dad or I can help you with?"

She walked toward him and caught a breeze. The mosquitoes thinned. "Your dad?"

"You might know him as Zed."

She pulled up her mental picture of Christine's husband, whose name she hadn't had time or resources to research, and supposed she could find enough similarities between Zed and Timothy to believe he was telling the truth. "She going to be back soon?"

He answered with a shrug. "Let's mosey to the firepit, and you can tell me what unexpected pleasure brought you here." He motioned with the shotgun, and although he did not point it at her, she figured she was more prisoner than guest.

Forty-Eight

THEY SIDETRACKED TO THE FRONT door of the cabin on the way to the firepit. Gentle kept his eye on her as he pounded on the door with his free hand. "Rise and shine. We've got company with news." He motioned Niki to keep walking.

Did his words mean someone was sleeping after being up all night, or was it an expression equivalent to get your butt out here?

Unseasoned wood produced a steady stream of smoke from the firepit and kept the mosquitoes at bay. A pair of binocs lay on one chair. A metal thermos sitting upright on the ground marked the chair Timothy had been using. She chose the one next to that, avoiding the direct smoke and giving herself a partial view of the entrance road through the marsh and a sideways view of the cabin. What or who was Timothy on the lookout for?

He sat down and laid the shotgun on the ground on the other side of the chair from the thermos. "We'll wait for the others to get here so you only have to give your news once."

"Who all is here?"

The cabin door opened and at least a partial answer walked toward them: Zed, followed by Donnie, who she had last seen a week ago explaining himself to the cops in Minong on the day they had broken into the abandoned mine site. Christine must have taken Zed's truck. She said, "Hey, Zed. Hello, Donnie. Good to see you guys again."

"You have a good memory to find this place," Zed said. "I wish you had called first. Christine isn't here."

Donnie picked up the binocs and glassed the road before sitting down. Zed sat with his back to the marsh. "Why are you here, Niki?" His face wasn't unfriendly, but his voice was strained.

"Things didn't go the way I'd thought they would." The day was hot, and she hoped the sweat pouring off her projected nervousness. She rubbed her hands to add to the impression. "I figured it would be a lot longer between Donnie and me helping collect the water sample and the news exploding in the papers. Like a month. Maybe more? And I thought Greenwar would write one of its *Blame and Shame* blogs or something, not an article in the *Washington Post.* And not that quickly." She smoothed her hands on her thighs.

"Anyway, the people at American Hydrocarbons Institute knew it was me who leaked the information. Jim Ford fired me. If I'd had more time, I would have gotten more stuff." She shook her hands like she was drying them off. "But as it happened, something super did come out of it."

Zed gestured for her to continue.

"I'm leaving the office and this older woman catches up to me. She jabbers up a storm. I stand there, being polite and nodding in the right places. Her mother died from cancer because the family farm's well became polluted. The mining company lied and hid their water contamination. That was a crime. She was all for extracting oil and gas and minerals but hiding toxic spills was wrong. Seemed to me she was justifying to herself that she'd been working for these big polluters. Anyway, she directly asks if I was the one. Her sister has been looking for someone to expose a company who's bribing the EPA and foreign officials and stuff. She has dynamite proof."

Niki made a big show of using her hands to rub both sides of her head. "I'm worried this might be a sting. You know, AHI is using her to set me up so they can sue me or something. But then she starts crying, and I figure maybe she *is* telling the truth. I asked if I *were* the one, what did she want from me? She says, meet her sister in Minneapolis to get the material. I'm figuring, no way will they ask me to schlep to Minneapolis just to set up a sting. Right?" Timothy and Zed both nodded, a good sign.

"I tell her even if I wanted to, I don't have money for that. This woman uses her phone and books me a round-trip ticket. You know that saying, one door closes and another one opens? I figure this is the universe telling me I got to do this. I have the stuff the sister gave me right here, in my car, not that I can make heads or tails of how they moved money around, and such. Anyway, I can't do anything with this myself. Who would listen to me? But Greenwar! You've got resources to verify these charges and media contacts to blow the cover-up wide open. It's not chemical spills, but bribing the EPA means whatever they're hiding must be bad. I figured you'd be upset because I lost my insider job at AHI and might not want to hear from me. So I drove here to beg you in person to please, please, look at this stuff."

She gave each one a pleading look, then slumped her shoulders and stared at the ground. It was *such* a shaggy dog story, holes a tank division could drive through. "Let me get it," she pleaded. If she could get them interested in the cover-up, they might not question how she got the info.

Timothy and Donnie both looked at Zed. Following an uncomfortably long silence, he said, "The timing is not good. But since you brought the stuff, you might as well leave it for Christine to review."

Niki wished he would give her some idea of why it was bad timing. Did they know the Feds were looking for Olivia? Was Christine with her? Was that why they'd been concerned who might come down the road? She'd played her hand. At least she could tell Park that Olivia was not at Christine's camp.

"I'm sorry, Zed. This was a lousy idea on my part. I should have called before I drove here, and I should have made copies. But I didn't. I owe it to those two sisters to make sure this story gets aired. Waiting to learn if you're interested is too risky. My money's running low. I need to go home and find a job. I guess I should head out."

"Someone's coming," Timothy pointed to a swirl of dust rising above the trees in the distance.

Forty-Nine

Zed grabbed the binocs and peered for a long minute at the approaching vehicle. "That's him," he said. "Seems to be alone, but someone could be hiding low. Donnie, take a position by the shed. Timothy, soon as he arrives, drive Donnie's truck down to the narrows and park. You," he pointed at Niki, "are with me. If anything goes sideways, follow that path ten miles until you hit a paved road."

Which was a weird thing to tell her. Everything was weird. Why would he have his son drive Donnie's truck when Donnie was right there? Zed took another hard look through the binoculars at the SUV heading toward the cabin. Timothy ran toward the parked vehicles. Donnie picked up the shotgun and ambled toward the shed. Niki waited until Zed lowered the binocs. "What's going on?" she asked.

Zed looked down at her. "That's the question, innit? I find it mighty curious that the first time you show up is on Mike's coattails, and here you both are again."

"That's Mike?"

"Supposed to be. You can understand my concern that you showed up today out of the blue. Come along." He brought her into the cabin, which hadn't changed since she was last there. "I changed my mind. It's best you stay inside until I make sure everything is copacetic. Tuck yourself low under the windows. You're hidden and can hear fine." He ducked into a bedroom and returned, racking the slide on a semiautomatic pistol. "I'll call for you if I want you outside, okay?"

"This is kinda scary," she said because that's what someone like her was supposed to say. If they thought she might be working with Mike, they should have searched her for weapons. And found the ankle holster. The scariest part was these guys didn't know jack about what they were doing and that could lead to accidents.

Zed waited until she curled tight to the far wall under the windows and gave him a thumbs up before closing the door behind himself. She followed the crunch of his footsteps on the gravel along the side of the cabin and into the driveway, where he stopped. She figured she'd hear Mike's SUV arrive regardless of where she was in the cabin.

Bending low, she scuttled across the room to the table and rifled through the papers covering it: crude maps with two lines running from Superior, Wisconsin, one southeast through Wisconsin, the other running across the Upper Peninsula of Michigan. The targeted pipelines? Underneath, pictures of an oil terminal. She flipped through them hoping to discover where it was and instead uncovered handwritten notes detailing Jim Ford's itinerary for this week and next. How the hell had they gotten that? This past Monday was circled and had a big red X scrawled through it. The attempt on Ford's life? A circle also surrounded this weekend and the following Monday. Monday's date had a checkmark. No X on any of the days. The itinerary indicated Ford was to be at his D.C. home. She hoped the attempt on his life caused him to change plans and depart early for Mexico. He'd shown a stubborn streak. He might still plan to attend his Monday board meeting.

The crunch of tires on gravel forced her to abandon that puzzle and resume her spot under the window. The car slowed to a stop. A door slammed. A car with a different engine sound moved away—Timothy plugging the pinch point at the narrows.

"He'll be back," Zed said. "You bring them?"

A response too soft for her to hear.

"We'll meet them later," Zed said. "Had a surprise visitor today. Any guesses who?"

"No clue, man," Mike said. "But that gun in your hand makes me nervous. What happened?"

"When did you last see Niki?"

"That day Olivia and I brought her here to talk with Christine. She's here?" Mike's voice projected incredulity. "I didn't tell anybody I was coming. What possible reason could I have to tell her squat or send her here? That's crazy, man."

"What's crazy, Mike, is the cops finding the supplier murdered and you filling the breach. And hours before this is supposed to go down, she shows up. Hard to believe, don't you think?"

"You can believe whatever the hell you want, man. I don't know anything about what happened to your supplier because Olivia made sure I didn't meet him, remember? It's not on me that your dealer shook you down for more money for the detonators. I told Olivia months ago I could get everything she wanted and show her how to use it. Why wouldn't I be able to supply you with the detonators? You're acting all hinky, man. Maybe I'll give this a pass."

Niki did not like the way this was going. Zed had shown Mike his gun, but she doubted Mike knew Donnie was lurking by the shed with a shotgun. How could she protect him?

"Easy, Mike. That's not what I said. I just wanted to hear from you what you knew about Niki."

"Like I told Olivia, Niki and I are gun-range buddies. I haven't seen or talked to her since that day."

Zed lowered his voice, but not so much she couldn't hear. "Thing is, now we have a problem. Niki's in the cabin, and you let slip information that can't leave here. How do we handle that?"

Right. Mike spoke about the detonators. She tapped her ankle confirming what she already knew: the gun was available.

Mike said something so low she couldn't hear.

"Good idea," Zed said.

Fifty

NIKI HAD SEEN **M**IKE OPERATE and felt confident he would find a way to warn her if she were in imminent peril. With both of them there, she liked the odds: two trained agents against three guys without a clue about security.

She ordered the portion of her mind worrying about the oil pipeline and the terminal to fire down. Ambrose and Park had been wrong. Mike and the ATF still maintained contact with Greenwar and could work that situation without her involvement. Her original task was to uncover who was killing people. The crossed-out circled date on the Monday of the attack at the coffee shop, the circles for the coming weekend, and the check on Monday were strong circumstantial evidence Greenwar planned to kill Jim Ford. She needed to alert Park and let him figure out how to involve law enforcement. She pulled up the secure app and remembered it only worked with cell service, of which she had zero.

Relying on the gravel to provide her early warning of anyone approaching the cabin, she resumed pawing through the material on the table. Under Jim Ford's itinerary with the circled dates, she found a draft Blame and Shame blog that was a follow-up to the *Post* article. Below that was a satellite photo of four houses lining a golf course fairway. Red ink circled the largest one—Ford's house?

Her best option was to leave and raise the alarm. If that seemed impossible, she had to slip Mike the information to pass along.

The crunch of gravel under multiple feet alerted her to their approach. It had been long enough she figured Zed wouldn't—well, shouldn't—expect her to have remained crouched against the wall. She raced to the kitchen and was hand-pumping water into a mug when Zed poked his head in.

"Time we talked."

Niki brought the mug of water and followed Zed to the firepit where Mike, Donnie, and Timothy all faced the marsh. Zed had tucked his pistol into his pants. She did not see the shotgun or the rifle in evidence. The three men turned at their approach. Timothy looked like he had lost an argument; she couldn't read Donnie; Mike blinked smoke from his eyes.

"The question we've been debating, Niki, " Zed said, "is the level of your commitment."

Niki took a long sip of water. Donnie and Timothy were watching Zed. Mike had edged a step backwards and was having trouble with his eyes, rubbing them with both fists. When she looked at him, he stopped rubbing and for a moment turned his fists into fingers pointing at his eyes. Strange and deliberate. She said, "I'm confused by your question, and I don't know how to respond."

"Well, we have a lot of things going on, and we want Christine to look at your new information. So—"

Mike closed his eyes and shook his head the slightest bit and started blinking again. She wanted to drag this out until she could understand what he was trying to communicate. "That's what I want, too." She sounded earnest.

"Yeah, that's where the commitment issue comes in. Donnie tells me you wouldn't drive with him in his vehicle that day you two got access to the mine site."

Mike had eased further back, waved a hand like he was shooing away a mosquito and blinked three short blinks, three long ones, three short ones.

Morse code for SOS. "Christine knows, I'm leery of riding with strangers." She gave a head bob, hoping Mike would take that as confirmation she had read his message. Not that she understood it. If it came to a fight, she was close enough to Zed to take out his knee and drop him to the ground. After that, things would get dicey.

"Yet you drove to the airport with me."

"That's different," she said. Mike waved away another mosquito—clearing the signal? "I had dinner with you and Christine. And I didn't really have a choice. It's a long walk." She offered a tentative smile. Mike had signaled three shorts, a long, a short-long. S—T—A. She couldn't watch any longer without looking suspicious. "I think I'm missing something." She directed her last statement toward Zed, but hoped Mike recognized it was also for him.

"You have a choice," Zed said. "We can send you home with no promises of whether we can use the material you brought. Or you can remain here with Donnie. Mike and I have to pick up Christine and Olivia. We'll be back late Monday. Tuesday, at the latest."

Niki's mind raced to understand the undercurrents. Leaving gave her a quadruple win: They'd consider it an obvious choice because she had already threatened that. She'd get out of the way of whatever Mike had going on. She could make sure Jim Ford had protection and pass on information about the planned raid and Olivia.

But Mike had signaled danger. Danger how? "I'm not understanding why those are the only two alternatives. I could go with you and Mike to fetch Christine. There's room in Mike's SUV for five of us."

Mentioning Mike's name allowed her to look at him and pick up T—A—Y and a mosquito swipe before she returned her attention to Zed.

"That won't work," Zed said. "They have a lot of gear. It's stay with Donnie or leave now."

At Zed's use of the word 'stay,' her brain clicked. Mike wanted her to stay. There was danger if she left. Because they wouldn't let her! She knew about the detonators and now of Olivia's planned return. "Alright," she said. "I really want Christine to see this new material. If that's the only way, I'm sure Donnie and I'll be okay. I might need to borrow a clean shirt and some toothpaste."

Mike bobbed his head once. "I can spare a shirt, and I might even have an extra toothbrush in my kit. Let's check. He walked past the fire toward the parked vehicles. Niki followed.

Zed said, "Donnie, help them carry the stuff."

Yep, she was a prisoner.

Fifty-One

IT WAS 1700 HOURS BEFORE they departed. Zed rode in Mike's SUV; Timothy took Donnie with him and followed in his RAV4. The four had been circumspect in their conversations while packing. At no time had they left Mike alone with her. That left warning Ford solely on her shoulders.

She didn't know whether the two vehicles were heading different places or traveling together. Donnie's role was clear. The others would follow Donnie's beat-up Ranger until the road was wide enough for them to pass. Then Donnie would turn the Ranger around and use it to block the road. Left unsaid was that would trap Niki's car.

She wished them safe journeys and returned to the firepit, where she could monitor the road. She needed to contact Park or Seamus to debrief, but unless a cellphone signal magically materialized, she'd have to be a long way from here before she could connect with a tower. Her OnX app showed the trail Zed had alluded to passed by several camps. But she had no reason to expect them to have cell coverage. And if Donnie discovered her missing, he could drive to coverage and alert the world before she had even cleared the woods. That would seriously screw whatever play Mike had going.

Should she subdue Donnie? That meant restraining him (wrongful arrest, wrongful imprisonment) and taking his truck (felony vehicle theft). And if something happened to him before she could get law enforcement up to Christine's cabin, wrongful death.

Let me count the ways that can go wrong.

Patience, Grasshopper. Use the time to explore. She was most interested in the large shed near the solar panels. The people door opened on well-oiled hinges, barely making a sound. No light switches by the door. Based on Seamus's solar power setup, she expected to find a battery bank, inverter, and back-up generator. And an electrical panel. Once her eyes adjusted to the dim light, she verified the shed contained none of those things. In the center was an orange Kubota tractor with a bucket on the front and massive backhoe on the back. Parked on the other side of the tractor were a riding mower and a couple of ATVs with brush guards. A workbench and tools lined the near wall, painted outlines showing where each tool belonged. Anal and none missing. Needing more light to explore and not knowing how long until Donnie returned, she didn't dare open the double-wide door.

A clock ticking in her head, Niki raced to the cabin, found a flashlight, and returned. The shed was surprisingly clean except for several dirt tracks near a rototiller parked on an oil-stained flattened cardboard box. On closer inspection, the cardboard was dry, no scent of oil, and under one edge that had curled up she found metal set in the concrete. The rototiller was a steel monstrosity that Niki muscled out of the way. Underneath the cardboard she found a metal plate with an inset handle.

She lifted the trap door and eased it onto the cardboard to avoid scratching the concrete. Her flashlight revealed a stainless-steel ladder descending into darkness. And a light switch. She flicked it on and illuminated a twenty-foot shaft. Across from the bottom of the ladder was a closed metal door. To what, and why did they have electricity here and not in the shed or cabin?

She wanted to explore, but her internal clock said Donnie would soon return. She snapped off the light, secured the trapdoor, dragged the cardboard over it, and rolled the rototiller into its spot. Poking her head from the shed, she heard Donnie's footsteps. She turned off the flashlight, rolled it into a corner, and closed the door behind her.

Her racing heart would give her away if she didn't control it. She couldn't afford to make Donnie suspicious—at least not any more than he already was. She visualized herself in Glacier. A smile crept onto her face.

FIFTY-TWO

WALKING UP THE ROAD, DONNIE played catch with his truck key. That gave her the idea to borrow—not steal—his truck during the night, drive it until she reached cell service, make her call, and return. Hopefully, Donnie slept soundly. Niki bird-dogged him into the cabin to see where he would leave the key.

Donnie stuffed it into his front pocket, dashing her hopes. He swept the papers on the table into a pile and stuck them on top of the cabinet that held dishes. He pulled a deck of cards from the cabinet drawer. "You play sheepshead?"

She had never heard of what Donnie claimed was the Wisconsin state card game. "We play with up to eight players," he said, "but two's an easy game to learn."

Niki had never been much of a card player, preferring to be outside. If she had to be inside, she'd read or engage in role-play games on the computer. "Is it like hearts?"

"Not exactly."

No truer words were ever spoken. Even after writing down the card ranking, she couldn't get through her head the idea that the four queens were the highest-ranking cards, that tens were higher than aces. But for scoring points, aces were the top.

And Donnie was a take-no-prisoners player, more interested in drinking beer than gabbing, quaffing three beers in the first half-hour. All it took to push him over the edge was to play "good little woman" and remove the dead soldiers and bring him fresh bottles. If she had drunk a quarter what he had, she'd have died of alcohol poisoning. And unlike her, he had a hollow leg. After her second beer, she refilled her bottles with water and still had to use the outhouse more frequently than Donnie.

By the eighth, or maybe the tenth—she gave up counting—he became chattier. He was the middle of nine children. His father had worked at a paper mill. Exposed to toxic chemicals, he had died at fifty-one. The company had lied, cheated, and paid high-priced lawyers to screw his mother out of a settlement. The stress had killed her. When Donnie ran into a Greenwar protest, he knew these were the people who could make his dreams of revenge come true.

He'd been a hunter all his life. It had helped feed his younger siblings after their parents had died. How much was fact or fiction was not clear to Niki, but his anger at powerful executives was deep, and he had the skills to hunt them down. Was he one of the two killers?

Donnie deflected most of her probes regarding the others in Christine's group. He expressed his aggravation that they'd left him to babysit her while the other four were up north "taking action." Niki at first assumed he meant Christine, Olivia, Zed, and Timothy, and realized she was wrong when Donnie let slip that Timothy was driving straight to the D.C. area to "take care of a nasty piece of business on Monday." He refused to elaborate and looked disconcerted that he had said that much.

That slip let her sort the puzzle pieces. Christine, Olivia, and Zed planned to blow up the pipeline with Mike's detonators and assistance. The ATF was on top of that situation, making it no longer her concern. Timothy Gentle was one of the shooters and planned to kill Jim Ford on Monday. Ford may be safe, but if authorities could detain Gentle and secure his gun for ballistic tests, that should secure a conviction.

After two and a half hours of getting her ass whooped by an increasingly drunk Donnie, she threw her cards on the table. "I give. Do you know any other games? While you're thinking, let me get you another beer."

Apparently "Go Fish" could be hilarious with enough beer. Donnie was at least a friendly drunk. While she was making herself a late dinner—he claimed to not need any more calories—he made a sloppy pass at her. It required damn near a full case of beer and six hours before he passed out.

Niki hauled him onto the linoleum of the kitchen floor and rolled him onto his side so he wouldn't choke to death when he puked. She emptied a wastepaper basket and placed it near his head. She removed his hunting boots and hid them in the bedroom closet to slow him down if he woke up.

It was a risk to leave, but this might be her only chance to discover what was at the bottom of that ladder in the shed.

Fifty-Three

Niki sprayed herself with mosquito dope, stinking up the cabin. Donnie wouldn't mind. She grabbed her knapsack, extinguished the gas lamps, and closed the door behind her. The wind had softened to a gentle breeze and carried the bzzt of nighthawks hunting above the marsh. It had been years since she'd seen those gorgeous birds, and she wished she could take time to watch them work: juking in the sky, white wing patches reflecting the quarter moon.

Before doing anything else, she wanted to clean up a loose end. She opened the car door to a beep that sounded like a trumpet blast. It and the dome light, bright as a lighthouse, set her heart to racing. *Come on, Niki. Donnie's out. No one else can see or hear.*

She pulled from the glove box the rental agreement that used a false name and shoved it, along with the papers "stolen" from Pendergast Holdings into her knapsack. With nothing else to hide, she left the car unlocked to allow them to search it without having to break a window. Now she would learn why whatever was under the shed had electricity when nothing else in the camp did.

She found the flashlight where she had rolled it and followed its beam to the rototiller—hauled it out of the way, opened the trapdoor, and descended the ladder. She easily opened the heavy steel door. A light switch inside turned on a panel of overhead LEDs. The room contained the battery bank, generator, and electrical panel she had expected in the shed. Passageways led to the right, left, and straight ahead.

To the left, more storage areas and living quarters comprising one bedroom with a king-sized bed and a bunkroom with a triple-decker-bunk, each bed dressed with flannel sheets and down comforters. A full bathroom featured a compost toilet. The bunker was twice the size of the cabin.

One supply room contained enough food and material to keep a half-dozen people alive for months. Jackets, snow pants, wool shirts, flannel-lined jeans, and the like crammed a second room. Behind a rack of clothes, she found an unlocked gun case containing two .223 AR-15s and a Remington Sendero, which had to weigh ten pounds. Too heavy for her to be accurate, but neither Zed nor Timothy should have an issue. Nearby were hundreds of boxes of ammo. Learning the Sendero used .300 slugs—the caliber that had killed two of the executives—her heart skipped a beat. Was Zed the second killer, a father and son team? Or was it Timothy using the heavy rifle and Olivia with her .260 Savage?

The opposite passage led to a great room that included a full kitchen, dining area with six chairs, and a section with a couch and several easy chairs. The kitchen island had a double sink with a hand pump on one side, a gas stove, and a built-in electrical heating coil. Below, she found pots and pans. An electric refrigerator and freezer hummed on one wall.

The passageway straight ahead from the battery room led to a room with a worktable. On one corner, a laptop rested next to a printer. The laptop was password protected. She rifled through the shelves, flipping through printouts of court cases, newspaper articles, and research reports. Working her way from the top, she had to squat for the lowest levels and fell on her ass when she opened the double doors in the center. An exhaust fan on wheels sat in a concrete tunnel cutting through the hill.

This must be how they got everything into the bunker.

She pulled the fan aside and shined light into the tunnel. With a flat floor and arched sides four feet tall at the center, it ran for maybe thirty feet before ending at a louvered grate, the kind that opened when the exhaust fan turned on. Partway down the tunnel, an intricate spiderweb had captured several insects and a moth.

Was it only used now as a conduit for exhaust air, or did it double as an escape exit and secret entrance? To avoid a splash of light outside if she removed the grate, she turned off the light in the room and shielded her flashlight beam, following fingers of light.

Four wing nuts held the grate in place. She spun those off, tucking the nuts and washers in a pocket, pulled the grate from the bolts, and discovered wing nuts with washers held the other side of the bolts in place. Once you removed the grate and went through the opening, you could push the bolts through their holes, reverse the direction, and reattach the grate. No matter which side you were on, you could get in or out. Genius.

The tunnel extended another three feet beyond the grate to a hinged screen door covered in camouflage cloth. She pushed open the door and discovered her instincts were correct: a footpath down the hill led to the marsh.

Seconds later, the first mosquito buzzed her. She couldn't allow them to follow her into the bunker for fear they would give away her snooping. She backed into the tunnel, snugged the screened door shut, replaced the louvered grate and exhaust fan, closed the double doors, and inspected the floor. The only evidence of her exploration was the torn spider web. She commanded the spider to get busy and make the repairs.

Time to check on Donnie. Without a search warrant, she couldn't take anything, but before she left, she wanted to finish a quick check of the rest of the cupboards. Good thing. She found a file box labeled "Termination Notices" containing six folders. In block print, Jim Ford's name labeled the top folder. The next five had the names of the murdered executives.

She spread Ford's material on the center table and snapped pictures: the *Blame and Shame* column with the paragraph exposing the purported cancer hot spot highlighted in yellow marker, his itinerary, the layout of his house taken from tax records, his daily routine those days he was home, surveillance pictures taken with a telephoto lens. She returned the material, replaced the Ford folder, and checked the next one. Same kinds of material with one extra page, a post-mortem closeup of the victim—a picture only the killer could have taken.

Mindful to not screw up evidence of murder, she replaced everything where she had found it. She scooted up the ladder and spotted a mechanism to allow someone to lock the trapdoor from the inside. Made sense for preppers. She dragged the cardboard and rototiller back into place. Poking her head past the shed's door, she heard and saw nothing and ran to the cabin. She cracked opened its door and the smell of puke and piss assaulted her. Afraid of what she would find, she rushed in.

And stopped three feet in front of the business end of the big-game rifle.

Fifty-Four

"Jeez, Donnie, point that thing somewhere else. It's me, Niki." Her eyes hadn't adjusted to the dark after using the lights in the bunker. He had pulled a chair close to the door. The rifle barrel wavered in circles, like it was heavy, or Donnie was struggling to focus. She couldn't tell for sure, but she thought his finger was inside the trigger guard. At this range, it wouldn't matter whether he pulled the trigger deliberately or accidentally, she'd be just as dead.

In slurred words Donnie demanded to know where Niki had been.

"Peeing." She waved her hands around, hoping he might swing the gun wide of her, allowing her to attack. It did not move from center mass.

"Nah-uh. I sh-shecked."

If true, he might have seen light escaping from the underground shelter.

A foot closer and she could knock the gun before he could react. That he could walk at all was incredible, but then again, he *had* found the rifle and his boots. "Did you check the firepit? After I used the outhouse, I went there and watched the nighthawks. They are amazing and it's a beautiful spot." She slid one foot forward six inches. "Wish I had a place like this." She motioned to the room and slid the second foot up. Six more inches. "You know when Christine and Zed got it?"

"Shay there." The barrel jerked up and down. "Waz on your back?"

Crap, her knapsack. "This is embarrassing, I started my period a day early. I thought I had some tampons in my knapsack. Turns out I didn't, but fortunately, I had them in the car." *Oh shit, that makes no sense, it's a rental.* "Put the damn gun down, Donnie. You're scaring me. It smells awful in here. Let me light a lamp, and we'll get you cleaned up You got the safety on?"

He looked down to check the safety. She kicked the rifle from his hand.

"Hey." He rose and swung a roundhouse hook that made him lose balance. She delivered a devastating head butt, toppling him like a fallen tree. She kicked the rifle away, grabbed her phone, and shook it to produce light.

Donnie lay face up, unmoving. She was relieved to feel his warm breath tickle her skin as she rifled through his pockets looking for the key to his truck. Nothing there. After again rolling him on his side, she checked the table, by the kitchen sink, the refrigerator next to the chilling beers. No keys.

She secured the rifle, engaged the trigger safety, and pulled back the bolt. A chill shook her. Donnie had a round in the chamber and four in the magazine. If he had pulled the trigger she'd be dead.

What she wouldn't give for a satellite phone right now. Maybe NSA had a small device she could conceal in a car to use in emergencies in places without cellphone service. But that wasn't a current option. She could tie Donnie up, do a thorough search to find the truck key, and drive his truck until she could make a call. That would blow her cover. It was only Friday, which gave her three days before everyone returned and discovered she had betrayed them. But if the circled dates indicated possible Jim Ford assassination days, she had only today to act.

Nothing was certain and no matter how unlikely, Ford's death would fall on her if she failed to sound the alarm. That meant finding the nearest cell signal, alerting authorities, and hoping Donnie didn't wake before she returned. Success would accomplish everything, including retaining her cover.

Good thing she was a runner.

Her quick search for energy bars and anything she could use to carry water proved fruitless. She grabbed the gun and the five rounds and shut the door behind her. The moon and stars gave her enough light to see the outline of the road, so she killed the phone's light to save the battery. She beeped open the rental's trunk, threw the rifle and rounds in, slammed the trunk closed. Should she deflate two of Donnie's tires? Better, she plugged his tail pipe, figuring he'd be in no condition to uncover the issue.

Choosing a pace between a jog and run she began what she guessed to be a sixish-mile trek—each way. At the top of each hill, she checked for a cellphone signal. She assessed her situation after an hour. With the frequent stops to check for coverage, she had covered only five miles, her jeans chafed, and sweat had stripped the mosquito dope from her skin. Another generation of Wisconsin mosquitoes owed their lives to the blood their mothers had siphoned from her face and neck. Despite the chafing, she still felt strong. The OnX pin indicated she had another mile before hitting strong reception. She continued her rhythm of swiping her face and neck free of mosquitoes every ten steps. The counting became a meditation.

At the top of a long incline, she caught the flare of light in the distance—headlights bouncing up the road. Over her breathing she noted the low hum of a truck engine.

She continued running until the truck's engine whine changed during a gear shift. Getting close. She hid in a patch of balsam firs at the side of the road that provided a narrow sight line and room to swat bugs. A truck rounded a corner and unmistakably downshifted in the manner of a manual transmission. Zed's truck with the bulk of Zed driving, blocking her view of passengers—if any. Were Christine and Olivia with him? Where was Mike?

She left her hiding spot, caught the hum of a second vehicle and dove behind a bush. Those headlights swept past her, and Niki used her best Obi-Wan Kenobi to tell the SUV to move along, move along. Its dashboard lights provided her a glimpse of the driver—maybe Mike—and a passenger.

What had caused their early return? One thing was for damn sure, unless she came up with a convincing story explaining why she had run away, she had no chance of regaining Greenwar's confidence.

The cold of the ground was settling into her bones. If she didn't get moving, her legs would soon cramp. The sound of the two vehicles had faded enough to convince her a third was not near.

Three hills later, she had two bars and 4G coverage.

Fifty-Five

RICK KASKA ANSWERED HIS PHONE with a groggy, "Hello."

"Rick, I need your help." She assured him she was okay and detailed the evidence she had found suggesting Greenwar was targeting Jim Ford this weekend or Monday. She gave him Timothy Gentle's name, the make and model of his RAV4, and its West Virginia license number.

"Why call me?"

"Because Ambrose must make a few things happen, and he'll listen to his godson. If Ford isn't already in Mexico, Ambrose can convince him to get his ass out of Washington. And you can suggest Ambrose assigns you to surveil Gentle or at least surveil Ford's home."

"I'll try."

"There's more. I need a warrant to search Christine Jorgenson's camp. I found a bunker under an outbuilding. Tons of Greenwar records, including material relating to the deaths we suspected they were involved with. There's a laptop that holds who knows what, but the fact it was in the bunker and not the cabin makes me think it's valuable. They're preppers, lots of guns. A couple of AR-15s, and in the cabin I found plans to sabotage a pipeline. There's an ATF agent with them, so we can't come blasting in to serve the warrant."

"They have a hostage?"

"No, the undercover guy who introduced me to Greenwar. Much as I'd love to talk, I'm deep in the woods with so many mosquitoes, I need a blood transfusion. Get Ambrose to act on all fronts. Talk to you later." She ended the call without waiting for his response.

She called up the app Park had given her; this time it loaded in a second. Must be the main app stays on her phone and this download acts like a key? Patrick would know, if she cared enough to ask. She punched in her unique number and saw a message from Park. *ATF raid in Superior, WI resulted in one agent dead, two wounded. Olivia Jorgensen person of interest. ATF & FBI planning joint raids at her Minneapolis apartment and Christine Jorgensen compound.*

The message had posted three hours earlier. She did the math and concluded Zed and Mike could have driven to Superior and back in that time. Her phone rang. Without thinking, she answered, and the message window closed.

Crap. "Who is this," she asked.

"Good work," Ambrose said. "Kaska filled me in and gave me this number. Jim Ford is gone from his house now. Kaska's on his way there to wait for Timothy Gentle. I'll have agents comb license plate reader databases to see if we can track him. We've deployed a joint ATF/FBI strike force coming your way. You need to meet them and provide your insider information. What's your position?"

She should have anticipated Ambrose would force Rick to give him her number. Clyde Barton had stated she should trust no one in the Bureau. She should have listened to him and contacted Park. Let him figure out how to solve her problems without breaking the law.

More spilt milk. "Does ATF know one of their agents is there? There's a truck blocking the road into Christine's camp. A back way in exists, but it's open only to foot traffic. Attacking will be a disaster. I'm doing my best to stop them from destroying the evidence. Are you working on getting that warrant I asked for?"

"Well . . . "

She disconnected, engaged Park's magic app, and punched in her code. No messages—she'd never know what else Park's text had said.

Her phone rang—Ambrose—she ignored it. She went online to the secure protocol Patrick McCree had designed for her, Seamus, and Rick. Using one hand to discourage the buzzing mosquitoes, she used the other to type the situational details and describe what she wanted Seamus to do. But only if he thought they could trust the person she had in mind.

To her surprise, Seamus was awake and responded, "I'll ask and let you know."

She smacked a mosquito, leaving a smear of blood on her neck and a sore jaw. Given Ambrose knew her number, keeping the cellphone was equivalent to stapling a GPS tracker to her forehead. She pulled the sim card and broke it under her heel. She threw the phone into the woods. Add littering to the list of charges against her.

No reason to run. Two hours walking would take her to the highway. From there, she'd head to town and borrow a phone to find out if Seamus was successful.

A perfect plan. Unless something else went wrong, like running into that joint ATF/FBI assault team.

FIFTY-SIX

HER FIRST COMPLICATION CAME AT a quarter of six. A deputy driving a county sheriff's car heading in the opposite direction spotted her walking toward town. He engaged his lights and executed a U-turn. Pulled up and asked if she was okay. Acting like she had been traumatized, she rambled a disjointed story: she'd gone into the woods with a couple of guys she thought were friends, but they had other ideas. No, she would not give names or press any charges. Her stupidity. Besides, they wouldn't be walking without pain for a while, but she regretted she hadn't grabbed her phone before running away.

He let her borrow his cellphone. She engaged Patrick's protocol and retrieved a message from Seamus. *On my way. Need location for rendezvous. Park working details. Use his app to keep him informed.*

Seamus had gone behind her back and contacted Park? She was sure he had reasons to suggest she keep Park in the loop. She pretended to text and then asked the deputy, "Where's a good place I can stay until my friend can come get me. It might be several hours. I don't exactly want to be visible, in case—you know."

"I'll contact the Fire Chief. He'll let you stay at the fire station."

"In Minong, right?" The deputy told her it was on the main drag. She typed that information into Park's app, hit send, touched the volume button, which triggered the message app to erase itself. She returned the phone. "Thanks. Can you recommend someplace I can grab a bite?"

"I'll take you there. Jeff Greenfield is the Chief's name. I'll have him meet you at the restaurant. You sure I can't convince you to file a report?"

"You're very kind. I've never ridden in a police car before. You sure you won't get in trouble for this?"

"I'd be in trouble if I didn't help."

THE DEPUTY DROPPED NIKI AT Wendy's Place, the same restaurant where she had sicced the police on Donnie eight days ago. No one could see inside from the road, making her safe, and she could eat a bear. Inside was warm and steamy. She broke into a sweat until she peeled her outer layer. The place was loud with the good-natured banter of regulars shouting across the room. Small towns.

She chose a stool at the counter and, instead of bear meat, ordered OJ, two pancakes, two eggs, a slice of ham, and a side order of hash browns with extra cheese.

The waitress arranged the plates in front of her. "How do you stay so skinny?"

Niki laughed. "Good genes and a lot of stress."

The food was excellent. Returning from the restroom, she found Jeff Greenfield, a weathered fencepost of a guy, waiting. She left enough money on the counter to pay for the meal and a generous tip and followed him to his truck. She hooted at the sticker on the bumper: a tree stump with the message, "I hugged it first."

"Teenage daughter got that for me. I'm supposed to convince you to file a complaint. I can see that ain't gonna happen, so I'll save my breath. Tell me you didn't kill them."

"I look that bad, huh? No, everyone lived and at least one of us is wiser. I sure appreciate you doing this."

She was thankful Jeff didn't want to talk. He unlocked the door of the fire station, showed her around the lounge: comfy chairs, adjacent bathroom that had a shower she could use if she wanted. "You'll be safe if you lock the door. Only thing I ask is don't press the red button. That's the fire alarm. I'll check around lunchtime to make sure your ride showed." He pulled the door shut behind him, mimed turning the lock, gave her a thumbs up after she complied.

It would take Seamus two-and-a-half hours to drive from Minneapolis. She settled into the plushest chair, listened to the rain pinging the metal roof, a sprinkle that grew into a downpour, and woke to a knock at the door.

Seamus greeted her with, "Holy shit, you look terrible. We should leave pronto. A posse of three unmarked cars with whip antennas passed me outside town. I presume they're Uncle Samuel's. Are they for you?"

Niki grabbed her knapsack. "Take a peek and make sure the coast is clear before I show my face."

FIFTY-SEVEN

SEAMUS, DRIVING HIS SUBARU WITH a new driver's side window, headed east on WI-77, which was what Niki had planned to suggest. She checked behind to make sure no one was following them. All seemed clear. "Okay, Seamus. Why did you talk to Park, and is there a plan?"

"Calling it a plan might be a stretch. I woke Paddy and had him use his computer skills to locate Clyde Barton's phone number. Thankfully, Barton remembered who I was. I made your request. He seemed sympathetic but decided he needed Ambrose or the FBI director to approve before he would act. I explained you were concerned who else had access to information that reached one or the other of their offices and asked him to stand down. I then asked Park if he could get the FBI director to approve Barton joining you without knowing the specifics. An hour later, Barton tells me he's on his way to Hayward Executive Airport using a private plane Park arranged."

Counting the growing circle who knew about Svalinn, Niki's stomach tightened: Seamus, Rick, Barton, Ambrose, Park and now the FBI director. Including her it was seven—a lucky number? "And . . . ?"

"He might have landed by the time we get there. You should check our secure communication app with Park and see if he's left any messages."

She borrowed Seamus's phone. "A burner?"

He gave her a thumbs up. "I left mine plugged in at Pendergast Holdings. Didn't want anyone using it to track me."

"Look at you, getting all sneaky." She dialed the magic number, entered her passcode. No messages.

Seamus offered his passcode, 66639. A message from Park stated Barton was bringing the warrant she had requested and tactical gear.

"Check it out." Seamus tapped her arm and pointed through the windshield.

Niki recognized the Oshkosh Alpha MRAP moving in the opposite direction. The side of the mine-resistant, ambush-protected vehicle proclaimed FBI SWAT. If she remembered correctly, the monster had a crew of six. This one featured the roof-mounted machine gun. Nothing subtle with that approach. Their car rocked from the vacuum created by the behemoth rushing past.

The Greenwar people would hear those guys long before they saw them. While the Feds did all the things the Feds would do before launching their assault, Zed and crew would have plenty of time to destroy the evidence stored in the bunker and escape by the back trail.

Using Seamus's phone and the secure app, she informed Park he had to pull whatever levers he had to make sure Greenwar didn't hear or see anything to warn them the Feds were coming. She needed time to secure the evidence.

The reply message read: *I'll try. No promises. Take care.*

FIFTY-EIGHT

THEY ARRIVED AT THE AIRPORT to find Clyde Barton waiting with three duffels at his feet. They each loaded one in Seamus's car. Niki chose the rear seat, her preference, and allowed Barton to ride up front. Seamus pulled away from the curb and asked where he was to drive.

Barton said, "Park at the end of the lot. I want to hear from Pendergast what the hell she's gotten me into."

Ashley ran down the assignment and the current situation. "We have four priorities. First, we must protect Mike, the undercover ATF agent. We can't do anything that risks his life. Second, we must secure the Greenwar evidence. There's some in the cabin, but the bunker holds the important documents. Fortunately, they have no clue I found the bunker. Once the Feds show up, Greenwar will assume I tipped them off, which puts the evidence at risk. That means we need the Feds to hold back until I can secure the evidence. Third, we need to eliminate Greenwar's escape route. Last, I'm not wearing the tracker and have to avoid running into anyone who might recognize me."

Barton squinted one eye at her. "We can get to details in a sec. I gotta know. Why the hell did you ask for me?"

She raised her first finger. "I wanted someone I could trust and—"

"You remember me telling you not to trust *anyone* in the Bureau?"

Like she had a choice. "And Seamus and I agreed the person we trusted most in the FBI right now is you. Let me ask *you* a question. Why are you here?"

"Because when Seamus made his pitch, I said I wouldn't do anything without *written* authorization from a superior command. I got it and obeyed."

She blew out a stream of air. Now even more people knew about this fiasco. "Who?"

"The president of the United States."

Her jaw dropped and she could hear her mother say, "You're catching flies." She checked Seamus's reaction. He appeared equally surprised. "The president signed an order?"

"He hauled my ass into the Oval Office and ordered me to do everything you asked. I don't want to know what you got yourself into, Pendergast."

"Call me Niki while we're working together. Makes it less likely someone can prove I was here. Plus, it retains the minuscule chance I can worm my way back into Greenwar."

"Yeah, well, you should ditch the Prescott name. Zero out that mistake you made with that loser. You don't like Pendergast, take your mother's maiden name or something."

Why he had such a hard-on for her ex was a mystery she would explore after this was over. "What's in the duffels?"

"Long guns, pistols, communication gear including secure sat phones, spotting scope, night vision gear, navigation gear, Kevlar vests, and Bureau windbreakers. For both of us. And a first aid kit. How does Seamus fit in?"

Niki said, "He doesn't. I'll rent a car here, we'll transfer stuff, and he's back to civilian life. Right, Seamus?"

"I respectfully disagree. Niki, you have to be a ghost, making Barton the face of this operation. He has to give the information to whoever is in charge of the raid to slow them down and make sure they don't do something that gets people killed. You, Niki, need to make sure no one escapes the back way out from Christine's. You two should have a communication cutout. I'll be Barton's driver and relay messages between you. If he has to introduce me, I'm McCree. Let people assume I'm with the Bureau or not."

"Seamus is right," Barton said. "You brief me, then I liaise with the assault team leader. Afterwards, I'll assist you to secure the evidence. I can locate you by your sat phone. We might be in the elements for some time. We need some extra supplies."

They found everything between a local Outdoor Store and the Walmart SuperCenter. They bought a knapsack for Barton and stuffed both of theirs with water, food, extra clothing, a water purifier, a skein of rope, and Mylar blankets. Seamus insisted Niki buy a Swiss Army knife. Niki covered her exposed skin with calamine lotion, and they bought the mosquito repellent claiming the highest DEET concentration. Enough supplies for four days, not that Niki thought it would take that long, but she didn't want to abandon position because they ran out of something.

One more thing, and they were ready to proceed. "I want to sight in my gun."

Barton gave her the squint eye again. "How accurate do you expect us to be?"

"Accurate enough that if someone has a gun to Mike's head, we can kill them from a distance. If things go wrong, it might be me, not Mike, with a gun to my head. That's the other reason I wanted you. Next to me, you're the best shot I know."

"One last civilized pit stop," Seamus said. Barton was fine, but Niki decided it was a good idea. Beyond Barton's hearing, she told Seamus to use Patrick's protocols whenever he contacted her.

"You don't trust Barton?"

"I do, but someone gave him this equipment. I want to minimize the chance of unknown parties listening in, including Park."

She returned to Seamus's car to find him stuffing a roll of toilet paper in her backpack. He shrugged. "Maple leaves are okay, but . . . "

While Seamus drove, she briefed Barton on Christine's camp and the people there. She drew one sketch of the general area including the bridge, where Donnie had left his truck, and the back trail into Christine's camp. Her second sketch detailed the buildings, including the underground bunker and its escape passage. "My initial target is the hill above the camp. From there, we can see everything. When Seamus lets me know you're coming, I'll meet you and lead you in."

Seamus parked his Subaru half a mile down a disintegrating two-track that OnX suggested had once gone all the way to Christine's place. Niki and Barton sprayed each other with mosquito dope. Niki donned her bullet-proof vest. With excellent equipment similar to weapons they'd used before, it took little time for them to sight in the guns.

Seamus had been wandering down the road to get away from the noise and met them at his car. "Two ORVs, I'm guessing side-by-sides, have traveled this road since it last rained. Heading in, nothing coming out."

Barton said, "But you can't tell how recently?"

Seamus shook his head. "I'm not that good, but I've seen enough tracks on the road by my place to tell them from cars or trucks or ATVs. Rain would blur them. These tracks are clear, so they appeared after this morning's rain."

"If we're lucky," Niki said, "it's Feds plugging the exit. If we're not, it's Greenwar reinforcements. I promise to stay alert and keep Seamus informed. You do the same. Now get out of here and stop that raid from being a disaster."

Fifty-Nine

FOR AN **A**UGUST DAY, **IT** wasn't bad for hiking. A light breeze kept the mosquitoes at bay while she walked. They found her each time she stopped to look at a track or check her OnX app to confirm her position. Their persistent whine drove her nuts until she dispatched the bloodsuckers. She kept to the edge of the road except at curves, where, to avoid walking into an ambush, she slipped into the woods until she confirmed the road was clear.

As time passed and she heard nothing more than the chatter of squirrels and a few birds calling from high in the trees, she wondered whether Barton was having success and what was happening at Christine's camp. Given her luck, this would be the first time the Feds were super-efficient, and Barton would arrive too late to prevent a bloodbath. She offered a prayer for ATF Agent Mike. What were the odds that the ORVs were Greenwar supporters? It wouldn't surprise her to learn the Feds had discovered the old road in and had sent a couple of agents to prevent that retreat, but could they have done that so quickly? Maybe, seeing the overwhelming force, Greenwar had surrendered peacefully. If they had, she could get the hell out of there and concentrate on her many personal problems.

She'd walked five miles when a distant engine broke the quiet of the woods. Cupping her hands behind her ears, she rotated her head like an owl. The noise was coming from the direction she had walked. She used the sat phone and found a single message from Seamus. He and Barton had reached the operations center for the assault on Christine's camp. Meaning whatever was heading her direction did not include Barton.

It was a Friday, late afternoon. Best case, it was locals coming in for the weekend to one of the camps she had passed. Otherwise, it was the Feds or Greenwar supporters, both of which were problems. She scanned the surrounding woods, satisfied she had evergreen clumps to hide behind if the engines came close.

The noise continued to grow. She kept moving, adjusting her escape plan to reflect the nearest hiding place. Like airline cabin crews said, your nearest exit might be behind you. Five minutes later, the single engine sound had become multiple engines reminding her of the ATVs Seamus had at his camp in the U.P. On this kind of two-track, those suckers could move darned fast. Better safe than sorry, she cut into the woods toward a group of young balsam or spruce, she couldn't tell which at a distance of two football fields.

She made good time through the open woods, discovered they were spruce trees, and two were growing from a nurse log, providing additional visual protection. She retrieved the binoculars from her knapsack, which she nestled behind a third tree, and made herself tiny and nearly invisible to the road.

The noise level increased exponentially. Three ATVs roared down the road, passed by her, and, with a screech of dirty brakes, pulled to the side of the road. The front guy jumped off and examined the road from one edge to the other. "No tracks," he proclaimed. The other two dismounted, and all three removed rifles from cases strapped to the front racks of their ATVs.

The first guy backtracked down the road until he stopped where she had entered the woods. The others soon joined him. All three peered in her direction and engaged in a conversation she couldn't hear. They soon split up, one staying, one returning to the ATVs, and the third walking a hundred feet up the road. After the two signaled they were in place, the first guy, rifle held in the crook of his arm, tracked her path while the other two walked parallel lines.

The tracker was having no difficulty following her trail. If she let the other two, who she labeled Orange and Camo, flank her, they'd have her pinned down. They weren't Feds; they might be Greenwar or something else. Time to find out.

She formed a megaphone with her hands and yelled, "Stay right there. What do you guys want?"

"A girl?" Orange said in a rough, cigarette-damaged voice. He remained standing, his gun held at the ready but not pointed in her direction. The tracker dropped to a knee and brought his rifle to his shoulder. He aimed to the right of her position. Camo had dropped to the ground and blended into the cover.

She gave them a few seconds to answer and yelled, "Lower your weapons. I am a federal agent. I repeat. What do you want?"

What if they didn't answer, but kept advancing? Tracker looked toward

Orange. Was Orange the leader? Her peripheral vision caught movement from Camo's position. "This is your last warning. If you do not lower your weapons right now, you will be violating Title 18 U.S. Code Section 111. That could be a felony, boys, with big fines and prison time. Do I make myself clear?"

"Alan, go ride to a cell signal and call the DNR. Tell 'em we got the poacher."

They thought she was a poacher? In her best command voice she said, "You have me surrounded. I'm not going anywhere, but neither is Alan. Place your rifles on the ground, stand where I can see your hands, and I'll prove I'm a federal agent. If you do not follow my command, I'll drill a bullet through the gas tank of Alan's ATV. I'm not screwing around. Put those guns down. Now!"

"She's right," Orange said. "She'd not going anywhere. Let's see this proof." He laid his rifle down and stretched his arms wide. Tracker followed his lead. Camo did not.

She reached into the knapsack and removed the jacket with FBI in yellow letters on the back. "You in the camouflage. Up on your feet, hands where I can see them or it's your ATV's gas tank I'll drain."

From Camo's direction came his response, "No fucking way are you allowed to do that."

Niki sighted in on Camo's ATV mirror. "I'm counting to three. On two, I'll destroy your ATV's mirror. At three, it's the gas tank. After that, I guarantee you'll be in cuffs and wondering which lawyer to call." No movement from Camo. She said, "One," waited two heart beats, said, "Two," and squeezed the trigger. The side mirror exploded.

Her ear rang from the rifle shot. She should have thought to shove in the earplugs Barton had given her.

"All right!" Camo scrambled to his feet, hands held high.

Keeping her weapon in one hand, she rose and displayed the FBI-lettered jacket. "Take two steps away from your rifles and tell me what the hell is going on. You thought I was a poacher?"

Orange complied with her order. The others followed suit. Orange explained, "Some punk's been poaching deer all summer. Killed one of our neighbor's dogs, too. We spotted your boot prints, grabbed our guns. We planned to make a citizen's arrest and hand him to the DNR. What the hell is the FBI doing here?"

"Let's do this. One at a time, starting with Camo guy, I want you to remove your rifle bolt and stick it in your pocket. Good. Now Tracker— you in the middle. And Orange. Great. Let's all head to your ATVs for a little confab. I'll tell you why I'm here and pick your brains. And then you guys will leave me all your ammo, and I'll let you go with a story to tell. Sound good?"

They complied and a few minutes later they had their rifles in their cases and Niki had their ammunition in a pocket of her knapsack. "You guys know Christine Jorgensen? She has a camp a couple miles in that direction." She pointed down the road.

Alan, the tracker, knew her. "Not unfriendly, but not friendly neither. Big time preppers. I helped pour the concrete for that bunker of theirs. Man, was that a project. We used—"

"Alan," Niki said. "There's a tunnel that runs toward the marsh. Did they say why they wanted it?"

"For a big fan to extract generator fumes and such. Air exchange pipes line its ceiling. But you ask me, they use it to sneak in and out. What did they do?"

"The Bureau believes there's a person of interest at that compound. This road goes in, but it's blocked by trees, right? Is there any other way in other than the normal road?"

"When I was a kid," Orange said, "this two-track used to be open all the way. Went fishin' in the creek and stuff. It's been blocked for years. It's the only approach 'cause the marsh comes up on one side and the swamp on the other. They used to have a little Jon boat that we'd take through that marsh to the creek and beyond to the woods on the other side. That was years ago." He shrugged.

Niki had never considered someone could paddle across that marsh. Something else to keep in mind. "Give me your contact info, and once this is over, I'll return your ammo. And my advice? Next time you think you have that poacher's tracks, call the DNR. They don't like poachers any more than you boys do."

They left following a round robin of brotherly fist bumps. Niki checked for messages from Seamus. Seamus had left several. Barton had met with the head ATF agent on site, who was checking with headquarters for instructions. The ATF had agents blocking the back exit. Niki should wait for Barton before approaching them. Barton was waiting to hear what the plan was before coming to join her. Niki texted acknowledgment and alerted him to the possibility Greenwar might use the Jon boat to escape.

Noting that acknowledgment was not agreement, she continued the last two miles to Christine's camp. This time she stayed in the woods. A tracker might still follow her, but the standard federal agent wouldn't see her footprints on the road.

SIXTY

AT THE BEEP OF A walkie-talkie, she froze. For interminable seconds, the only thing she heard was her heart pounding in her ears. Then she picked up a garbled voice, another beep, and someone pushing through the thicket. "Say again, base."

She eased to the ground without snapping any twigs.

A beep and garbled noise.

"No sign of that agent." The voice clear and strong. The response was too broken for her to understand.

"Roger. I'll take the MOHUV and meet him on the road. What are my orders if he refuses to turn around?"

She automatically translated MOHUV in fed-speak to Multipurpose Off-Highway Utility Vehicle. Through the garble Niki picked out "restrain," "cuffs if necessary," and "sort out later." From that point she understood nothing from base, but her guy remained loud and clear.

"Burt and Tyler have a drone up. Haven't seen a soul. Nothing moving. There's a significant exposed area we'd have to cross with no way for you to provide armored support. Only approach is yours through the front."

"Say again base?"

"Copy that. You want them to know we have them surrounded. Will do after I take care of the agent. Out."

Once she could safely move, she'd confirm with Seamus that she was *persona non grata*. She remained still, even as a creepy-crawly something explored her neck. Several long minutes passed before the MOHUV drove past her position.

She checked messages using Patrick's protocol. Nothing new from Seamus. She let Park's app do its quick download. Nothing there either. Switching back to Patrick's program, which closed Park's app, she asked Seamus to relay to Barton what she had overheard. Could Seamus determine if Barton would be able to join her? Either way, she was proceeding with the mission.

After that sequence, she reminded herself she was in a stressful situation and needed to check twice to make sure she was using the right messaging application for the right person.

She stayed in the woods until she was close enough to use binocs to glass the remaining MOHUV. Two MOHUVs could carry eight people. ATF matériel in the remaining vehicle and on the ground suggested a four-man squad. Two running the drone, one searching for her. That left one at this pinch point. Maybe.

She had to move before the searcher returned.

To avoid the path the poacher hunters had described, she chose the swamp side and skirted the wet area. Less vegetation meant less cover but quicker movement. She gently pushed through the saplings, careful to avoid rustling leaves or twig snaps. Thankfully, the morning rain had left the leaf litter damp and quiet.

Brighter light ahead gave warning the thick growth would soon end. Her nerves tingled. This was where she expected a sentry. Birds were singing. Either no sentry, or he'd been still long enough for them to adjust. Not helpful.

From behind her came the faint sounds of the MOHUV. Time was running out.

She reached the more open woods and dropped into a crouched walk, veering hard right to follow the edge of the swamp and move away from the road. She reoriented herself using OnX and plotted a route to the far edge of the hill that overlooked Christine's camp.

Staying low, she worked from one tree to the next, checking before each move that she could not see any humans. Several minutes later, she reached the group of massive hemlocks beyond the crest of the hill from which she could watch Christine's camp. Immediately behind them was a depression, lush with tall grasses, that provided her protection on three sides. Using the terrain and trees for cover, she glassed the road leading to Christine's camp.

Barton had failed. The FBI's armored vehicle sat at the bridge, agents inside the vehicle or hidden. Greenwar's vehicles clustered by Donnie's truck—deliberate barricade or because they couldn't move it? Either way, anyone crossing that bridge would be exposed to sniper fire.

Nothing stirred in Christine's camp. Were they in the cabin? The bunker? Already escaped? With no sign or smell of a fire, she had reason to hope the evidence still existed.

"Hey, you down there." The voice belonged to the guy who had taken the MOHUV to look for her, albeit magnified through a bullhorn. "This is the ATF. We have you surrounded. Come out with your hands on your heads."

Niki caught a flicker of movement near the firepit. If he hadn't moved and she hadn't had this angle, she never would have spotted a camouflaged Donnie aiming a scoped rifle across the marsh toward the roadblock. Unless the nearby ATF agents had seen him get into place, they'd have no way to know from their position that he was there.

What to do? Contact Seamus to warn them, thereby disclosing her position, or stay silent and risk a body.

The Feds wouldn't move on the camp until dark. She had time to secure the evidence. Then she'd decide.

Sixty-One

AN HOUR LATER, A SECOND armored vehicle pulled behind the first. The Feds tried their come-out-with-your-hands-up message a few more times, then went silent. Soon a robot carrying a communication device made the long trek up the hill and stopped in front of the cabin. The bullhorn announced its presence and invited Christine to open a line of communication.

Nothing happened.

Time to check in with Seamus and get an update—hopefully. This time she found two messages: They planned to attack at 0300 hours. They had stationed a couple of agents in the woods across the river to monitor anyone attempting to escape by boat. The second message said Barton was tied up. Did Niki want Seamus to join her?

Hell no. She'd remain in place until dark and hope Barton could shake himself loose. Truth was, she wasn't confident she could succeed alone but had a better chance without also worrying about keeping Seamus safe. She framed her response more politely, indicating she required him to remain her link to Barton.

She gobbled a thousand-calorie energy bar of fat and protein with minimal carbs, drank a third of her water, and settled in for a nap, setting her watch to wake her by vibrating.

The watch woke Niki to claustrophobic dark. A bank of black clouds blocking the stars had rolled in while she slept. Perfect for stealth, not good for checking her phone. Even with the satellite phone's screen dimmed and covering it and her head with her jacket, any light would give away her position. Had to risk it.

Bad news. Seamus believed ATF had put Barton on ice and again offered to join her. She replied that she needed him to monitor things there and let her know of new developments.

With Barton unavailable, she was the only hope of securing the evidence that proved Greenwar murdered the execs. If Seamus knew what she had in mind, he'd do something stupid to help. She had five hours before the planned attack to reconnoiter, plan, and execute. Remember, she told herself, the evidence was important, but not worth dying for.

She adjusted the night vision gear with thermal overlay on her head and identified three ATF agents. One was prone, resting she assumed, in a tent they had erected below the top of the hill, near the abandoned road. A second, wearing night-vision headgear, held position at the crest of the hill, scanning Christine's camp. Nearby, a tarp covered a puttering generator—charging what? The third agent patrolled an arc with a fifteen-minute cycle that ran past the tent and disappeared from her sight toward the marsh.

Within the chirping of frogs and the bzzt of feeding nighthawks, she noticed the distinctive whir of a drone. Flying at night, it must have thermal capabilities, and *that* could be a problem. Drones had limited battery capacity. If they wanted continuous coverage, they'd have a backup, which might be what the generator was charging. She spotted the blinking red light heading toward her. Shifting her position behind a tree to hide the muzzle flash, she inserted earplugs and sighted on the hovering drone. A smooth trigger squeeze resulted in a drone-killing shot, pieces of it dropping into the marsh with several distinct plops.

A pair of powerful searchlights she hadn't realized the Feds had set up burst on. Shit. Those suckers changed everything. She flattened herself in the depression. The beams swept Christine's camp and the hill she was on behind it. After the first quick passes, the lights made more deliberate passes: one parsing Christine's camp; the other crawling up the hill foot by foot toward her position.

She dared not move nor hardly breathe. From below they wouldn't be able to see her, but that wouldn't help if the agents on top searched on foot. As minutes dragged, and the lights continued probing the dark, she held her position. Her muscles grew tired and threatened to cramp. Her throat itched from dryness. Even if she dared move, she couldn't reach her water.

She couldn't make out the radio chatter but was relieved that it was not getting louder. The lights inched past her. She adjusted her position and froze again as the spotlight returned, heading back down the hill. She allowed herself a mini-stretch, then noticed the radio chatter was becoming louder.

Of course, they wouldn't want agents to search the hill while the spotlights made them an easy target. They'd wait. Would they put up a second drone or decide not to risk another five-figure piece of equipment to the unknown shooter? She couldn't hear one over the generator's noise, but that didn't mean there wasn't a second drone out there.

She'd already lost an hour. The spotlights had finally clicked off, but the radio chatter continued. They were keyed up, nervous, trigger-happy. If she gave them until 0030 to settle down, she still had two and a half hours before the raid. That should be enough time, but nothing had gone perfectly yet.

During her wait, she concocted a plan. Not a great one, as her nervous stomach made clear—but the only one she had. The generator's hum would cover her sneaking up on the ATF guy on the hill watching Christine's camp. She'd take him down with her stun gun, duct tape his mouth, hands, and feet, and skedaddle down the hill and find where the escape tunnel came out.

Her watch told her it was time. Her gut told her it might be suicide.

She ducked under the cover of her jacket to check the satellite phone one last time before moving. A twig snapped twenty yards to her left. She froze, hand on the phone's power button, ready to kill it.

Only the putter of the generator. Fifteen seconds. Thirty. A deer gave a snort and hurried down the hill.

Her relief doubled at seeing Seamus's message. He was on the road with Barton and would drive Barton as close to Christine's camp as possible. Barton would walk in from there. Seamus would wait a mile away for instructions.

Niki released a slow breath. This wouldn't be easy, but with Barton joining her, at least she'd have support. Meeting Barton and returning would take an hour, maybe ninety minutes—assuming she could sneak past the perimeter guy. That left only an hour and a half before the Feds' raid—and nothing had yet gone as planned.

She typed the message to Seamus to say it was too late. And erased it. She had requested Barton for good reason. Two of them and half the time was better than going it alone. She adjusted the pack on her back and, keeping low, moved obliquely down the side of the hill to the swamp. The frogs were calling up a storm. Like birds during the day, the frog trills suggested they weren't worried about anything other than finding a mate.

And two steps later, as if the orchestra director had signaled a full stop, the noise cut off, leaving only the purr of the distant generator. She froze, listening for anything that triggered the frogs. Nothing moved. No sound but her own breathing and the distant generator.

But something was out there. Close enough to spook them. Maybe close enough to hear her. Unless it was her they had reacted to. Remaining in place wasn't an option. She had to either fetch Barton or retreat. The clock was ticking. She waited an agonizing minute and counted off another sixty seconds. The frogs stayed silent. *Get moving, Niki!*

Avoiding the trail the Feds had made, she stayed close to the edge of the swamp and soon exited the thicket near the two MOHUVs. Walking was quiet, but she'd lost more time and saw a way to get some back. The vehicle would be loud as hell, but she'd save twenty minutes if she could get it started before they caught her.

Seamus had told her how a guy stole a neighbor's ATV by jamming a screwdriver into the ignition. Thanks to him, she had the Swiss Army knife with its screwdriver blade. Chances were good that if she stole one, the Feds would chase her with the other. She turned her headlamp to low, found and disconnected one MOHUV's battery, and deposited it in the MOHUV she planned to take.

Holding her breath, she shoved the flat blade into the ignition slot and cranked the ignition. The starter ground. Once. Twice. Nothing.

Come on. Come on!

She pumped the throttle, the engine coughed, sputtered, and died. Shouts erupted from the direction of Christine's camp.

One last try. She whispered a prayer to the patron saint of thieves and fools and twisted the key. The engine caught and she engaged the gear.

AFTER A BONE-JARRING TWO MILES, she found Barton near where she'd had her adventure with the wannabe poacher-nappers. She did a U-turn and pulled up next to him.

"You stole that and disabled another one?" At her questioning look, he tapped an earbud with a cord running into his pocket. "I borrowed one of their comms. I'm listening in."

"Excellent. Hop in and buckle up. Seamus thought they had 'put you on ice.' What happened?"

Over the engine noise he said, "Intramural squabble. ATF is happy to use the FBI's assault vehicles but is not interested in sharing operational control. They were not thrilled to learn of a surprise confidential informant, even with your excellent intel. They heard me out but decided I might interfere with their plans and had someone babysit me. In the excitement after Greenwar shot down their drone, they ignored me. I walked away and summoned Seamus. What's our plan?"

She saw no reason to confess she was the drone killer, instead detailing what she knew of the three ATF agents minding the back door who were undoubtably alert for her return. "We have less than two hours until the assault." She told him her plan.

When she finished, Barton was quiet for a long moment. "That's borderline illegal, tactically insane, and will probably get us both killed."

"We do this, or those files burn, and the killers walk. Remember the President told you to do anything I wanted, unless it was illegal? Your call. I'm going with or without you."

Sixty-Two

ACCESS TO THE ATF'S COMMUNICATIONS allowed them to refine Niki's plan. She drove partway to Christine's and stored the vehicle on an overgrown logging trail. Barton used the comms to contact the ATF and inform them he was approaching their position, which triggered an intense argument. Barton's trump card was that he held the search warrant, and he damn well would be in position to serve it.

"They're not happy," he said to her, "but they know I'm coming." He checked his watch. "0135. We've got eighty-five minutes before the attack. Here are my comms so you can listen in."

She secured the earpiece and retreated to the woods, where she paralleled his approach on the road. Barton hailed the ATF agents, held high his FBI shield, and walked to them.

With their angst and attention concentrated on Barton, Niki sneaked forward until she was out of their sight, then kicked into a jog, knapsack thumping her back with every step. This time she used the direct path through the saplings, veered left toward the marsh, and followed it, skirting the hill. She arrived unseen at the end of her cover, having heard squawks of garbled radio traffic between the ATF guys but never spotting them.

Now came the tricky part, requiring a fifty-yard dash across open land. She'd be exposed to the ATF agent on top of the hill. He didn't have permission to shoot, and it would take him too long to get it. But if he were trigger-happy from the drone incident . . .

She tucked all her gear other than the rifle into the knapsack and cinched it tight. With a mental, "Ready. Set. Go!" she sprinted down the hill. Counting the seconds under her breath, she was at seven when the bullhorn roared, "Stop where you are." With one more step, the curve of the hill shielded her. It took several steps for her to slow to a walk. She replaced the night vision goggles, stuck the comm device into a vest pocket, and screwed the bud into her left ear.

They weren't sure what they had seen and would launch a drone, starting it on the far side of the marsh away from Christine's camp and swinging around to view the area where she hid. Given their reaction, she doubted Barton would conjure a way to join her, and with—she checked her watch—sixty-two minutes before the assault, she had no time to waste. She scampered toward the spot she thought the escape tunnel ended. Her route cut a path, which she followed. If it hadn't been for multiple scuffed prints, Niki might have walked past the camouflaged screen door.

She examined the hinges, determined the door swung towards her and moved past it. The path continued into the dark, and she thought it wise to find out where it led. It curved around a bend and dropped to the marsh, where a Jon boat with oars was secured to a metal post driven into the ground. The boat was an encouraging sign that Greenwar members hadn't slipped across the marsh. The six-million-dollar question was where they were, and whether they were all together.

She searched for the drone across the way. Didn't see or hear it. Yet. Two barred owls engaged in a duet, drowning the softer trills of crickets and buzz of mosquitoes. Her bug dope was working. The only ambient light came from the distant glow of klieg lights marking the ATF command center. She worked her way to the screened door, texted Seamus the coordinates, and made herself one with the hillside. Minutes later, the comm reported the drone was in position but finding nothing. Damned if she could see it. They were two blind parties groping in the dark to learn what the other was doing.

Once she was inside the tunnel, she'd be safe from the drone. But the process of getting in might attract the drone's attention. Unless they had a third drone to provide continuous coverage, they'd be blind when this one's battery drained. Time was short, but she'd allow fifteen minutes for the drone to clear. Twelve minutes later, ATF agents received an order to retrieve the drone.

Her adrenaline load was building. She felt tingling up her spine; her fingers became twitchy; her legs ready to spring. Patience, she counseled herself, let the drone clear the area before you open the screen door and find out—

"Niki," a whispered voice said. "It's Barton."

From distant memories of her mother singing golden oldies, came unwanted the chorus of Jay and the Americans singing "Come a little bit closer." Amazing what stress could produce. She whispered for him to follow the path to find her.

Barton got close enough to whisper. "ATF agents had questions about the search warrant. Took longer than I wanted."

Niki pointed to a faint red glow leaking from where the camouflaged fabric had bunched, creating a gap. She brought her mouth to his ear. "That just appeared. Get ready for company."

She strained to hear the sounds of movement, but the insect racket was too loud. Their plan had called for Barton, because of his strength, to handle the taser and haul away the stunned individual. After he hit the lead person with the juice, Niki was to rifle a flashbang past the downed person to disorient anyone who might be following. But their positions were reversed from the plan, and they had no time to switch places. She readied the taser, and Barton pulled the pin on the flashbang and stuck it between his teeth in case it was a false alarm, and he didn't use the grenade.

The screened gate swung partially open. The red glow outlined a pole pushed against the gate's frame. No sign of the person holding the pole. Worse, the gate stayed at a ninety-degree angle. That wouldn't cause her a problem with the taser, but that meant Barton had to reach around the gate to throw the flashbang.

The pole disappeared, and she willed the person forward. It didn't happen. What were they waiting for? The red light remained steady, making her wonder whether someone wore it on their head or it lay on the floor while the person returned to the bunker. She flexed her hand to keep it from cramping.

Red finger shadows stretched past the gate. As those shadows shortened, the opposite hand's shadows grew. The pattern repeated. The suspect was crawling with empty hands—no weapons and no mirrors to peer around corners. She needed a big patch of flesh for the taser to work. A gloved hand appeared, arm in a leather jacket—it was like they had anticipated her taser. The arm extended past the elbow, followed by a hat-covered head and a bare neck. At her trigger pull, the gun produced a loud crack, followed by the crackle of the five-second electric charge.

Barton yanked the gate open, threw a fastball high onto the opposite wall, and ducked, holding hands to ears. She screwed her eyes shut and covered her ears too, lessening the explosive noise that barreled out the opening. Using both hands, she grabbed the person's wrist and pulled. She noted no sounds coming from the tunnel, suggesting the guy she was dragging was alone. He seemed the right size for Mike, which would eliminate the hostage situation, but he was face down, and her primary concern was clearing the tunnel entrance to provide Barton a clear shot.

She grabbed his second wrist and spun him out of the tunnel. Momentum rolled them past the narrow path and down the hill. They landed at the bottom with him still face down. She zip-tied his wrists behind him and secured his feet. She lifted his head, forced his jaws open, and tied a bandana to prevent him from making any noise.

Damn, it was Zed. Was Mike a hostage or did he still have their confidence? She patted Zed down for weapons, finding only his wallet, which she returned to his pocket.

The confused chatter in her ear from ATF agents was distracting. She pulled the comm from her ear. "I got him controlled, but I need your help to haul his ass up the hill. Let's rope him to a tree until we can tell the ATF folks where to pick him up. Yes?"

They agreed Barton would handle Zed while Niki maintained watch in case anyone else came out. To help Barton avoid ATF entanglement, Niki returned the comm earbud to him. While Niki waited for Barton's return, she detached the gate from the tunnel using the Swiss Army knife screwdriver tool. The louvered slats made the thing heavier than she expected. She dragged it past the tunnel exit and dumped it down the hill.

HER WATCH REPORTED 0225—ONLY thirty-five minutes. Where the hell was Barton? If he'd run into ATF . . .

She had no time to wait. She risked a peek into the tunnel and was surprised to see that the hellish glow from the red light came from a two-finger-wide opening in the double doors at the bunker. The tunnel contained only the pole Zed had used to push open the hinged gate and the grate three feet into the tunnel, which Zed had taken the time to replace.

Niki held her pistol at the ready, scooched in, undid the wing nuts, pushed the bolts through until they tumbled to the floor, and leaned the freed grate against one wall. No shadows. No sounds coming from the bunker.

She ditched her knapsack, strapped the rifle over her back, and entered the tunnel, leading with her gun and holding the pole Zed had left behind.

The gap provided her a pie-slice view of the room. No major surprises. The exhaust fan pushed to one side, table in place, floors clean, three chairs moved away from the table. Where was the fourth chair? No flickering shadows. No sounds. Retreating to the length of the pole, she used it to push the doors completely open. The red light came from the domed ceiling fixture. The room between the doors and the closed entrance door across the room looked clear.

She placed the pole at the edge of the tunnel and dropped to her belly to present a low profile. She crawled far enough to get halfway into the room.

Something felt wrong.

Movement exploded from her left and two hunting boots landed on Niki's left hand, smashing her fingers. White-hot pain screamed up her arm. The missing chair that Donnie had been standing on clattered to the floor. She swung her other hand like a hatchet at his ankle but had no power behind the blow.

"I've got a thirty-eight pointed at your head," Donnie said. "Stop fighting."

She went still, her hand screaming, her mind racing. He'd been like a hunter in a deer stand patiently waiting for his prey to appear. Underestimating him might cost her everything.

Sixty-Three

Niki screamed in pain and frustration—and to give herself time to think. Retreating was futile; he could shoot her like a dog. She went limp.

"Out now. No fast moves." He should have ordered her to pancake on the ground.

Act insulted. "Whoa. Whoa. Whoa. Donnie, it's me, Niki. I'm on your side remember? It took me fucking forever to find a way through those ATF and FBI guys. But as you can see, I made it." She rose gingerly, her injured hand held close to her body.

"What I see is the ATF rat Zed suspected had infiltrated us."

"Donnie, that's nuts. I stole this rifle from one of them and used it to shoot down their drone. You think they did that to their own drone? Smell the rifle. It's been fired."

She read confusion in his eyes. *Build on it. Keep him talking. Tired people make mistakes.* "Donnie, I can get us out of here. They think Greenwar killed one of their agents up at that refinery or whatever in Superior. I know that wasn't you, because you were here, soused to your gills. You made a pass at me and got physical. I ran away into the woods, and by the time I figured it was safe to return, the place was crawling with Feds."

His hand wavered a little. "A federal officer died?"

"They didn't tell you? Huh." She let that question hang for him to chew on. Swelling prevented her from bending her finger much, and it felt like he'd broken her pointer finger. "Here, smell the gun."

She slid the rifle butt toward Donnie, her hand catching on her jacket pocket. The search warrant. Had he seen it? She casually readjusted her jacket, pushing the paper deeper, and eye-checked Donnie. No reaction. Close call.

"Smell," she said.

She tensed her legs, preparing to launch herself at Donnie when he leaned down to pick up the rifle. He shifted his target to her chest, kicked the rifle to the wall next to her pistol. Stepped back.

"Close the doors behind you. You're letting in mosquitoes."

Pissed that she had no choice, she reflexively used both hands to slam the doors shut. Agony shot through her broken finger.

"Now set yourself at the table and pull the chair all the way in and put both your hands where I can see 'em."

She wiggled the chair without moving it more than an inch closer and placed her hands on the table, the injured pointer twice its normal size. Her watch read 0232—twenty-eight minutes to kickoff. If she was still sitting here when ATF attacked, would Donnie panic and shoot her?

Donnie hooked a chair with a foot and dragged it away from the table. He sat and rested his arm on his lap and kept the pistol pointed at her head.

Her legs twitched, and the throbbing in her hand increased—adrenaline abandoning her. *Remember, keep him talking.* "What's Christine's plan?"

"If she wants to tell you, she will."

Which meant he didn't know. The laptop was no longer on the table and not visible from where she sat. Had they already destroyed the papers?

While Donnie stared at her, she cataloged potential weapons. The chair—too heavy for her injured hand. The table—bolted down. Her backup piece was in her ankle holster, but Donnie would shoot her before she could reach it. The vest would stop a chest shot, but it would knock her down and give him an easy headshot.

To keep him talking, she tried a fresh approach. "How did you get involved with Greenwar? You and Olivia are about the same age. Did you meet at college?"

Donnie rubbed his nose. His eyelids briefly drooped before he forced them open. He was exhausted. Good.

"Tell me why you left and came back."

Niki elaborated on what she had already told him, but kept it short, plausible—the fight, fleeing into the woods, returning to find the camp surrounded. 0245 on her watch. Fifteen-minutes before the shit hit the fan.

He closed one eye and squinted the other, like he wasn't buying what she was selling. "How'd you know about that tunnel?"

"I saw someone appear from nowhere. Big like Mike or Zed. Once they left, I went exploring. Was I right? One of them escaped?"

"Zed's not—" Donnie swatted a mosquito on his neck

Almost had him. One more push. She nudged her chair a few inches away from the table. "Who's still—"

"I hunkered down at the firepit," Donnie said, "and saw a flash of light and heard a bang from the other side of the hill. I came down to see if something had happened to—if something had happened. The doors were open and it smelled funny. Then you showed up."

So he hadn't been here when the flashbang went off, but it brought him to the bunker. That's why he had waited in ambush. She needed to play dumb. "Flash and bang? I didn't notice, but you're right about the smell." Get back on the offensive. "Who's still here with us holding the bag? Christine and Mike? Olivia? Timothy had that horrible thing he had to do in D.C., right?"

"Only horrible because he had to testify in court to a brutal assault he witnessed, a domestic dispute that became a violent knifing. Makes him sick thinking about it. Timothy takes after Christine more than his father. Zed's like this big-game hunter. He and Olivia are super aggressive. Nothing much rattles Christine or Timothy. That's why—never mind."

Dang, dang, dang. Twice he'd been close to telling her something about Zed and Olivia. What did he know? Had Donnie figured out they were the killers? She wanted to nudge him over the edge.

The clang of footsteps on the ladder echoed down the shaft. She froze. Donnie sidled to the wall at the side of the door, gun still trained on her.

0248. Too early for the raid—unless Barton's flashbang triggered them to accelerate the start.

"Donnie," Mike called. "Unlock the door. It's Christine and me."

Relief flooded her body. They still trusted Mike. Soon it would be two on two.

Donnie turned his back to Niki, and she edged the chair several inches away from the table. One more jiggle and she'd be able to get up. With a start, Donnie seemed to remember she was there and again covered her with the gun. With his other hand, he opened the door.

Christine preceded Mike into the room. Her face opened in surprise. Mike's glare focused on her FBI jacket, and for a moment something flickered in his expression. Not surprise—something else. Calculation?

Stress was making her paranoid. He was just an undercover agent maintaining his cover.

Donnie waved his gun at her. "Niki showed up through the tunnel wearing that FBI jacket and toting a rifle. She says she got it off one of the guys out there, and that someone got killed around Superior. Claims she found the tunnel after she saw Zed leave."

Niki didn't correct him that she hadn't known it was Zed. While Donnie continued his story, she tracked everyone's positions. Mike walked in front of Donnie and placed himself against the wall. Donnie then eased into the corner, preventing anyone from getting behind him. Seemed he didn't trust Mike. Christine remained at the end of the table. She cocked her head in a gesture of listening, but the death-mask look on her face wasn't giving Niki a good feeling.

Donnie concluded with, "Was someone killed in Superior?"

Christine: "Olivia called and told Mike. That's why we came back early. We're wasting time. Zed didn't signal us, so he must not have made it out. They got helicopters circling the camp. He wants us to burn his files. Olivia and Zed worked down here for the quiet. I prefer the light. I have no idea what he thinks is important. Pick a drawer and empty it. We'll burn them in the tunnel and use the fan to blow away the smoke. We'll surrender after we're done."

She opened the nearest cabinet. "Donnie, put down the gun and help."

0255. Five minutes, but how long until they breached the bunker? Too long. She needed to save those murder files and Mike didn't know they were here.

"There's no time," Niki said. "Those helicopters mean they're about to launch their assault. We start blowing smoke out that tunnel, they'll spot it, blast in, and kill us all."

She pushed away from the table. "There's nothing in those files worth dying for. There's a Jon boat in the marsh. Get out through the tunnel and use that. We need to move now."

Christine stared at her. "How do you know about the boat?"

"I told Donnie, I explored. Right now that's our only way out."

She moved toward the doors to the tunnel.

"Don't—" Donnie started.

Too late. She yanked them open.

Light flooded the tunnel. Shit.

Sixty-Four

"**Did you execute the search** warrant?" Barton's voice called from beyond the spotlight.

The light blinded her. Her heart raced. Her head pounded. Had the others inside heard him? She slammed the doors shut and spun around. "Crap. Zed must have told them about the exit."

The three faced her. Donnie, in the middle five feet away, pointed the gun at her. "Bullshit. You led them."

Christine, standing to his right, looked poleaxed. "You really are FBI, aren't you?"

Mike, a step to Donnie's left and leaning against the wall, looked nonchalant.

Time for *some* truth. "I *am* a Fed." She glared at Donnie. "You can't do anything about whatever happened in the past, but don't make it worse. I have a search warrant in my pocket. That means it's a crime to destroy anything here. We can crawl through the tunnel and surrender or go up top and do it there."

Christine rounded on Mike. "You too?"

Niki answered, "We've had him under surveillance for some time. My assignment was to insinuate myself into his sphere and wrangle an introduction to you." She held out her good hand. "Give me the gun, Donnie. And let's not get anyone hurt."

Donnie's blood vessels throbbed on his forehead and neck. Christine's shoulders slumped, her head bowed. She was licking her lips, and her fingers looked like she was playing a piano on her leg.

"Don't be stupid, Donnie," Niki said. "With a good lawyer, a jury will never find you guilty for our little escapade at the mine site. At least one juror will think I entrapped you. You kill me, and no lawyer can save you."

Mike had been silent through the entire exchange, watching from his position against the wall. He took one step—away from Donnie, away from Christine. In a voice too calm, too controlled he said, "You are a scumbag, lying to me like that."

He wasn't looking at Niki when he said it. He was staring at the floor, shaking his head. He took another step away from them. Still talking to the floor, he said, "I'm sorry, Christine. I never suspected her."

Niki's neck hairs prickled. Something was wrong. To maintain his cover, he should be acting shocked or angry. Why was he edging away from Donnie instead of closer to help disarm him? Why was he looking at the floor, not at her—or even Christine?

"Too many ways crawling out the tunnel can go wrong." He moved toward the ladder. "I'm going up top to turn myself in."

Christine said, "Mike—"

"I suggest you all join me." His boots rang on the metal steps, the top door opened, and he was gone.

Niki stared at the ladder. She had to give it to him: he had an undercover agent's instinct for cutting his losses and saving his ass, but this was the second time the bastard had abandoned her to her own devices. She'd deal with that later, but right now she had a man with a gun pointed at her face.

Niki gave Donnie her full attention. Christine might be the leader, but he had a gun. Her heart was thumping, and with each beat, pain pulsed in her injured hand. She had no idea how Barton had reacted to her slamming the door on him, nor could she know what Mike would do once he reached the top. Sand was pouring through the hourglass of her life. "You're the man with the gun, Donnie. How this turns out is up to you."

"Meaning what?"

"Until you knew I was a federal agent, what could they charge you with? Not much that I can see. A little destruction of property—but I did that—so you can use the entrapment defense. Maybe trespassing. Big whoop. But now, if you don't let me go soon, kidnapping a federal agent drops on the table. Even if you only hold me long enough for you and Christine to destroy whatever evidence is down here, the kidnapping charge will stick—along with destroying evidence. You wait, and leaving here a free man will not be an option."

To Christine, she said, "Zed's already in custody. Greenwar broke the law to stop unchecked environmental abuse. I get that. What will the files show—that you destroyed machines, damaged property? But you didn't intend to hurt people, let alone murder them, did you?"

"Never people. We were always careful."

A lot of heat in her voice. Didn't seem likely Christine had been involved in the killings. "I believe that. But if Donnie kills me, that's all Greenwar will be known for."

Christine's spine straightened. "How did this all go so wrong? This is not what I intended. I don't want her hurt, Donnie." She pressed on Donnie's arm, lowering it a few inches.

Niki moistened her lips. "And I don't want you guys hurt. Anytime guns are involved, accidents can happen. If Donnie gives me his gun, you have my word no one will press charges related to him holding it on me. My partner is out there." She gestured toward the exit tunnel. "Let me get him, and he'll get you out of here safely."

"I'm not going to prison," Donnie's voice crackled with anger. His finger tightened on the trigger.

"Donnie, don't." Christine pressed on his arm.

"No!" Niki yelled.

A punch from Mohammad Ali hit her chest, driving air from her lungs, knocking her to the ground. The room echoed with the sound of the gunshot; the acrid aftermath of the gun firing filled her nose. Niki instinctively rolled to avoid a second shot, came up with her ankle piece drawn as Christine drove an uppercut into Donnie's jaw. He crumpled. Christine collapsed beside him, crying.

Niki grabbed Donnie's weapon, controlled him, and told Christine to open the doors to the tunnel, and then sit with her back to the wall.

Christine complied, and Niki yelled to Barton that she was safe and to come now. Her watch read 0302. The assault had started and she needed to disappear.

Barton arrived with his gun drawn.

"This one, Donald 'Donnie' Franken, shot me. Christine Jorgenson had already surrendered and saved my life and is cooperating. Treat her gently, please. The only other one I know about is Michael 'Mike' Yoncey. He wanted to surrender and went up top where he thought it was safer. Is there anyone else, Christine?"

Tears streamed down Christine's cheeks. She shook her head no.

Barton zip-tied Donnie first and then Christine. He communicated the situation to the ATF, who were stealthily approaching Christine's camp. "Given our information," he said, "they're changing tactics and will soon light this place up like the Super Bowl."

Meaning she had to disappear now, but not if Barton still needed her. "You got this?"

"Go."

With ATF and FBI agents all around, Niki figured the only safe place to wait them out until Seamus gave her the all-clear was hidden in the marsh. Moments after she pushed the Jon boat away from the shore, a helicopter with a searchlight rose from behind the hill, and ground-based banks of portable lights clicked on. Even though the lights were all pointed toward the camp buildings, the area around her was as bright as dawn. Fingers crossed, Mike's "surrender" and Barton's prisoners would hold everyone's attention. She used the paddle to one-handedly pole the Jon boat into a thick bed of reeds.

Nothing she could do for her sore chest, but she stuck her throbbing hand in the cool water to relieve the pain. What would happen at Christine's camp? Would they lawyer up or talk? Did the evidence prove Olivia and Zed were the killers? Or was that Donnie's doing as well—she sure had misread him. And misread Mike, too. His leaving her wasn't right. Saving his cover wasn't more important than supporting a fellow agent in trouble. If it weren't for Christine—Stop! This thinking would drive her crazy.

She told her mind to think about something—anything—else. The bastard Gex sprang to mind. Fine. She focused on how to deal with him and his FBI stooges.

Several hours later, Seamus contacted her by satellite phone. The Feds no longer had men stationed on the back way from Christine's; he'd wait at the highway to pick her up. She poled to shore. To avoid being seen by the Feds swarming Christine's compound, she followed the marsh's edge. Once through the saplings, she jogged up the road, every step bringing a twinge to her ribs and pain shooting through her left hand.

She found the MOHUV where she had left it. Using the screwdriver attachment again, she brought the beast to life and drove it to the highway and found Seamus waiting.

Despite cold from a bag of ice she applied to reduce her hand pain, she fell asleep on the drive to Minneapolis, woke long enough to strip and shower at the hotel and fall into bed. She slept a solid fourteen hours.

SEAMUS INFORMED HER A LOT had happened while she was getting her beauty sleep. The ATF, still maintaining Mike Yoncey's cover, had arrested him at Christine's and were holding him in the same detention facility as Christine, Zed, and Donnie. The FBI had peacefully arrested Timothy Gentle and Olivia Jorgenson together at Timothy's apartment.

Her assignment was over and ADNI Park wanted her reunited with the ankle monitor that afternoon. "I used one of your fake IDs and credit cards and booked a flight. Rick will meet you."

He pointed to the pile of FBI gear and weapons he had brought in from his car. "What do I do with all this stuff? Having those guns around makes me nervous. And I can't exactly leave them for the hotel staff to see."

"Barton will arrange to collect it." She gave him the combination to the gun safe in the basement of Legacy House. "You'll find plenty of room to store them. How long do I have before we leave for the airport?"

"Just long enough to put on a disguise and take a beta blocker."

The ibuprofen she had taken to dull her pain meant it was too soon for her to use a beta blocker. Well, crap.

Sixty-Five

DESPITE THE LACK OF DRUGS or alcohol to dull her plane phobia, Ashley arrived safely at Dulles to find Rick waiting for her at the baggage claim. She slipped up next to him and startled him when she spoke his name.

"I didn't recognize you."

Despite feeling like she was heading for her funeral, she laughed. "That's the idea, Rick. All I have is this roller bag and my knapsack. Let's go."

In an hour, they pulled up to a Trappist Abbey in the country outside Berryville, Virginia. Nice place, but too hot for her comfort, especially wearing a wig and makeup. Her heart felt heavy, like she was approaching Mordor even though only two gray clouds marred the bright blue sky. She had to give it to the monks: the place oozed tranquility. She'd need every bit of it. Once they reattached the tracker, she went from free and unleashed to tethered and controlled. At least she was done with the Greenwar mess. That left Gex.

The receptionist pointed them across the street to the cemetery. Fitting, Ashley thought, a place to bury Niki and all her hopes and dreams. She had expected to meet Park, the woman who had worn her ankle monitor, and a technician to switch the monitor to her own ankle. Seeing Clyde Barton instead of Park chatting with the other two set her heart racing. She stopped Rick. "Did you know Barton was meeting me?"

"I had no clue. Honest. ADNI Park left instructions to drop you here and return to work. After your meeting, someone else will take you wherever you want."

She supposed it made some sense. Park worked best from the shadows, and Barton had responsibility for the Greenwar investigation and needed to debrief her.

Ashley's ankle-bracelet "double" filled her in on life at the monastery and what the various retreats had involved. The tech made the switch, and the two drove away with Rick, leaving her with Barton. They walked the grounds, Ashley getting accustomed to the feel of the ankle monitor.

"How's your hand? Ribs?"

"Swelling's going down. I'm breathing fine. What happened after I left?"

"Yeah, about that. I'll formally interview you inside, but first, I want your take on some things. ATF has not yet released their report, but I learned friendly fire killed and wounded their agents. Each of the groups thought the other one were the bad guys."

Her chest ached. It was a law officer's worse nightmare to kill one of their own. "But after the shooting, Greenwar aborted whatever they planned, right?"

"Mike got a call from Olivia Jorgensen warning them to avoid the pipeline. Olivia must have been close. Nothing actionable there. And we don't think Timothy Gentle ever went near Jim Ford's place. He did, in fact, testify at a trial on Monday. Olivia showed up at Tim's place later that day, and we arrested them both on general terrorism charges, details to be filled in later. Their cars and Timothy's apartment had no evidence. The explosive-sniffer dogs came up empty. The information you found in Christine Jorgensen's cabin concerning Jim Ford had a jumble of prints. We identified Christine's, Olivia's, Donald 'Donnie' Franken's, and an unsub's—yours, I suspect. Not Mike's. Smart move, whoever removed your prints from all databases."

She chose not to offer an explanation.

"We're still processing all the material inside the bunker. It's proving interesting, but nothing related to the murders had prints. The laptop was also print-free. It was password protected with George Gentle's month and day of birth."

She squinted and he stopped. "Sorry," she said. "Took me a moment to make the link. George Gentle is Zed's real name. That's not sophisticated security. And why wipe that stuff clean and leave prints everywhere else?"

"Exactly. The computer contained detailed plans regarding the murders of executives outed by the *Blame and Shame* blog. George Gentle claims the laptop is not his, and he's never seen those folders. He has alibis for only two murders. Olivia Jorgensen makes the same claims about the laptop and folders. She has alibis for the two Gentle does not but doesn't for the others. We found guns registered to Olivia and George Gentle that matched the calibers of the murder weapons. Plenty of ammo, too. Looks like the two of them split the assignments. Ballistics will wrap this in a bow. Preliminary hearing is tomorrow afternoon. None of them will get bail. To keep the ATF agent's cover intact, they plan to keep him incarcerated until Friday morning. At that point, his lawyer will secure bail to release Mike."

Ashley's gut said they were missing something big, and she had a hunch what it was. Barton and the Bureau would process the evidence, which she hoped would prove her suspicions incorrect. While she had Barton to herself, she wanted to pick his brain on her personal problem. "You and Bianca Jenoff both work at Quantico. How well do you know her?"

"She's a crackerjack instructor. Trainees love her. She's tough, but supportive. Rumor has it the director had slotted her to be Gex's number two at Quantico. Why?"

"Meaning she runs in Gex's circle."

"More than that. Wouldn't surprise me if she was the first one he talked to about your role in forcing him from the Bureau. She won't be your biggest fan, but she's much too straight and narrow to go rogue like those guys who beat you up. But I'll repeat what I told you before: trust no one at the Bureau."

Which is why she didn't tell Barton that Jenoff had used Quantico trainees to run surveillance on her. Or that she was done with letting others ineffectually address Gex's harassing her. Starting now, she was on the offensive, and she didn't plan on quitting until Gex was no longer a problem.

She must have given away something of her thoughts because he said, "Forget I asked. I don't want to know what you're thinking. Let's get this damned interview done, and then I'll take you wherever you want."

The only thing Ashley learned from the formal interview was that Christine had been one of the first women to participate in golden gloves competitions in the early 90s.

Afterwards, Barton delivered her to a Metro stop and left. She performed a thorough surveillance detection routine and determined no one was following her—at least not physically. If someone had hacked the ankle-tracker information, they could follow her from the comfort of their favorite easy chair.

At her motel, she tested her hunch against all known facts about who had killed the executives and found no contradictions to her conclusion. If she was right, it was political dynamite.

She raised both of her issues with ADNI Park, who had powers she was coming to appreciate and fear. On the Gex front, he provided her Special

Agent Bianca Jenoff's home address. For Greenwar, he gave her the cellphone numbers of several suspects but turned down her request to use the Bureau to analyze phone data.

"Nope. The FBI knows everything you know. Let them and ATF conduct their own investigations. Until you have proof, I don't want to stir up any more interagency warfare. We have better software you can use. When you do have proof, give everything to the Bureau. If you're wrong, no harm, no foul."

Sixty-Six

THE NEXT MORNING, ASHLEY WAITED in a rental car for a light to come on in Bianca Jenoff's condo, which was close to Quantico. She had one chance to flip Jenoff. If she blew this, Gex would know she was coming after him. She'd figured Jenoff for an early riser, but 0730 arrived with no lights, no movement. She was running out of time to still make the 0830 appointment Park had set up for her.

Approaching the stoop, Ashley triggered a porch light, making it easy to spot the camera. She gave it a wave, rang the doorbell and pounded on the screened door with her healthy hand, raising a fearful racket.

A disembodied voice asked what she wanted.

"Ten minutes of your time. I have video you need to see."

"And if I don't trust you and don't want to see it?"

Ashley leaned into the camera, giving Jenoff a close-up of her face. "Then I'll assume the rumor that you and Gex conspired to kidnap me is true, and that you know who beat me up and have condoned it. I don't believe the rumor, and I want to give you a chance to prove it's malicious nonsense." She paused. "But if you aren't willing to give me ten minutes, the next time we see each other will be in court. Civil for sure. Probably criminal as well."

Silence. Ashley counted her heartbeats. At forty-one, the lock clicked.

THEY SAT OPPOSITE ONE ANOTHER on Jenoff's deck, each recording the conversation with their phones. Ashley said, "I'd been gone from that apartment for weeks. I doubt you kept a squad of trainees waiting around that building prepared to tail me. But I return, and poof, you and your trainees show up."

Jenoff gave nothing away.

"The video comes from cameras hidden inside my apartment in the building where you and your trainees tried following me. A private security firm will testify that the time and date stamps are accurate. Remember, this is long after Gex's retirement from the Bureau. In the video, you'll see Gex enter the apartment and remove four audio recording devices. I can show you zoomed in stills that capture the make and serial number of one device. Another photo shows Gex wearing an FBI badge on his belt and wearing an FBI jacket."

All that was true and Jenoff had not yet interrupted her. Now came a guess that might be dead wrong. "The desk clerk will testify that Gex claimed to be FBI and showed a badge to access the apartment."

Jenoff fluttered her fingers in an impatient gesture. "The video?"

Ashley pressed play and held the phone to allow Jenoff to see and hear the first two minutes. "I don't have to quote to you U.S. Code about impersonating an FBI Special Agent. Or Section 2511 regarding illegal recording of conversations. Not to mention the D.C. laws he broke."

Jenoff looked like she was about to say something. Ashley raised a hand to forestall her. "Section 2 concerns aiding and abetting. Given how the public views the FBI these days, what do you think a jury will do with that?"

Jenoff's feral smile had become a rictus of repulsion. "What the fuck do you want?"

Ashley checked her watch. She needed to leave to make her 0830. "For you to understand Gex is a sleazeball only interested in himself. He leaked my undercover information to sabotage my assignment. Despite whatever he told you, I have no interest in embarrassing the Bureau. It has good people and does important work. Here's a thumb drive with the entire video. Watch it. If you're the person I think you are, together we'll jointly make sure Gex never has an opportunity to harm the Bureau or any of its agents again."

"Let me see it." Jenoff motioned toward Ashley's phone. "Then we'll talk."

Ashley could feel the momentum shifting. Ten minutes more might seal it. Fifteen, max. She checked her watch. She'd pushed her luck trying to squeeze this in before the appointment Park made for her. What would happen if she were late? Probably nothing; this was the government, after all. But if her contact only had a short window, then what?

She could not, would not, screw up her chance to take down the Greenwar killer.

But walking away now, with Jenoff so close to flipping . . .

No. She'd made her pitch, given Jenoff the evidence. Laid out the situation. If Barton was right and Jenoff valued the Bureau more than she valued her relationship with Gex—and the loss of a great promotion, she'd do the right thing.

Ashley rose. "I can't stay. I'll call you at exactly 1145. If you don't answer I talk to my lawyer at noon." She held Jenoff's gaze. "Do what's right."

She walked away before Jenoff could respond, before she could second-guess herself, before she could see whether the gamble had worked.

SIXTY-SEVEN

ASHLEY HIT EVERY DAMN LIGHT between Jenoff's condo and the warehouse district. She was going to be late and gunned it at a yellow—damn near clipped a delivery truck making a right. Her hands were shaking on the wheel.

She arrived at 0835—five minutes late—and she still had to disguise herself. Makeup and costume change, ten minutes minimum. Whatever agency this was, they'd have facial recognition. Park had been explicit: no one was to know she was there.

Ten minutes meant fifteen minutes late. What if they turned her away or her contact had another meeting?

Professional trumps personal. Identifying the killer was what mattered. She parked, checked her face in the mirror. This was her—Ashley Pendergast Prescott, buzz cut, bruises, and all.

Au naturel it is.

A tech, looking like he was still in high school, collected her and brought her to a conference room. "I am not going to ask what happened," the kid said.

Ashley shook his hand. "Good decision. What have we got?"

"Luckily, we only had to deal with two carriers. I've run the data through Sting. What do you want to look at first?"

"Sting?"

The kid released a nervous giggle. "Sorry, my bad. Not to be confused with Stingray. You know that song, 'Every breath you take?' Sting sings it. It's my name for the program I developed that converts cell tower data and maps it with a running timeline allowing us to visualize the cell phone's movement for the period in question. They didn't tell me what you were looking for, so I plotted all six of the cellphones on the same map to make it easier to observe their interactions. Each subject phone number has its own color."

He handed her a one-pager with the color for each phone number. "I only had time for a quick and dirty pass. What we have is CSLI—cell site location information—not the phone's actual GPS. If I had another day or two, I'd triangulate to provide more precision."

Niki was betting on the Blue or Green. "Start with the first day."

"I can enlarge the map to focus on a particular area, but if you want to see them all, you pretty much need half the country."

"Broad's fine. Run it between three and seven p.m." That provided a two-hour window each side of the estimated time of death for the first murdered executive, which had occurred in a Chicago suburb.

The kid chose a sixty-to-one time compression. During the four-minute run-time, Christine's White marker and Zed's Red one were not present. Niki guessed that meant they were at Christine's camp where there was no cell coverage. She'd have to check that assumption. Donnie's Black stayed outside Watersmeet, Michigan for the first two and a half hours before moving twenty-five miles in thirty minutes and remaining in the new location the rest of the time. Olivia's Violet bopped around D.C., making numerous brief stops. Timothy Gentle's Yellow originated in West Virginia and around six p.m. traveled toward D.C. Mike's Blue (personal) and Green (undercover) phones remained stationary in Minneapolis.

"Can we run the program backward to find where and when the White and Red phones last had coverage."

The kid increased the compression ratio, and they found both phones had last pinged a cell tower south of Minong, Wisconsin the day before the targeted time. The phones were likely at Christine's camp, although their owners could be anywhere.

"Terrific. Let's check another time." Her notes said the second assassination had taken place shortly after noon near New Orleans. She gave him that four-hour window, and he played the video.

Again, Mike's Blue and Green stayed in Minneapolis. Zed's Red traveled around the greater Minong area. Christine's White traveled inside Boston's Route 128 belt. Donnie's Black made one round trip within the Watersmeet city limits. Olivia's Violet moved around D.C. as before, but this time, Timothy's Yellow remained in West Virginia.

The third, fourth, and fifth murders showed a similar pattern: Christine, Zed, Olivia, and Timothy—or, she reminded herself, at least their phones—moved around, but never approached anywhere near an assassination. Mike's phones remained static in Minneapolis.

"Can you show me the seven days preceding and following that first date? Just for Blue and Green. And speed it up. I want to see if those phones ever move."

"If I knew what we were looking for, maybe I could make suggestions?"

Niki felt sorry for the guy, but one stray remark in the wrong ear, and, as Park had pointed out, she'd find herself shackled and on the way to jail.

During those two weeks, the Blue and Green phones moved frequently and stayed together—except twice when Blue remained fixed in Minneapolis and Green traveled a half-hour west to Delano and stayed for ten minutes. The first time it returned to Minneapolis; the second time, it continued moving and winked out a few miles south of Minong, reappearing the next day. Christine's camp.

"What's in Delano, Minnesota?" Niki mused out loud. "Can you Google it?"

The kid consulted his cell phone. "Six thousand people. Oldest and largest fourth of July celebration in Minnesota—who knew? Otherwise, just your average white bread manufacturing city turned suburb."

Since neither date was July 4, Mike wasn't there for the fireworks. "I sure wish I knew *exactly* where he was going."

"That's a sparse area. Even if I'd had more time, there aren't enough cell towers for us to triangulate. These two phones are Android. You could send Google a warrant for the GPS if he had it on. Problem is, Google often takes months to respond. What kind of car does your suspect drive? A lot of those new vehicles have GPS software that track location. And to get lower car insurance rates, people let their insurance company put trackers on them. And there are services like OnStar."

Niki considered whether they'd be able to get a judge to expand the search warrant Park had obtained to collect the phone information. Wait, Mike used rentals to travel to Christine's. "How about rental cars?"

"Ah, ask for rental-fleet telematics," the tech replied. "Most majors archive door-open, ignition, and GPS pings. Get an addendum to your warrant, and you should have the info in a day, two at most."

Assuming he used his real name—something she'd never do. She asked if he could run the same two-week analysis for the other four dates.

"It'll take fifteen minutes."

It was 1115, half an hour before she had promised to call Jenoff. She asked the analyst to do it and added on the date of the recent attempt on either her or Ford in Washington, D.C.

The only time Blue and Green did not stay together was when Blue remained in Minneapolis and Green traveled to Delano or Christine's camp.

A 100% correlation.

Ashley leaned back, the conference chair squeaking. Her chest felt tight. Her head ached.

Unless one of the Greenwar suspects had arranged for someone to take their phone and act as they usually did, the only person who was available for each of the murders was Mike—assuming, as she did, that he left both cell phones behind on his assassination trips.

Seamus would remind her, she didn't *know* anything. She had gobs of facts that supported her supposition. And proved nothing. The killer could be some random nut who read the *Blame and Shame* blog.

She pressed her palms against her eyes. She really hated the idea of it being a federal agent, but it wasn't that simple.

No. It was Mike Yoncey. ATF agent. Firearms expert. The man who had introduced her to Greenwar and left her to die at Donnie's hand.

Ice-cold murderer.

Damn, she wished Barton was here seeing this. He could assign an entire team to gather the evidence and chase down the details, build the case that would convince a judge and jury.

Instead, it was on her.

She checked the time: 1140.

She thanked the kid and raced to her car. The moment the clock flipped to 1145, she called Jenoff. Voicemail. "You got fifteen minutes to call me back."

She kept her phone open for a return call. At noon, she called Clyde Barton. "Are they still keeping Mike, the undercover ATF agent, until Friday morning?"

"The new plan is to free him Thursday evening after the others have their bail hearings. They'll let me know if anything changes." Barton paused. "I don't suppose you'd care to fill me in why you're asking."

Two full days. Enough to prove what she already believed.

SIXTY-EIGHT

PARK HAD BEEN SCARY EFFICIENT. In less than two hours she had a new search warrant and a cooperative contact at the national car agency from which Mike had rented the SUV he had last driven to Christine's.

She plotted the GPS data on a map and learned where Mike lived in Minneapolis and that his Delano destination was a storage facility. Minutes before close of court business Tuesday, she received permission from the judge's clerk to travel to Minnesota for "up to a week's time for personal business." The only thing missing were search warrants for Mike's apartment, personal vehicles, and storage facility. Park promised they'd be on her phone tomorrow morning.

She had all day Wednesday and most of Thursday to accomplish everything before Mike got bail. How long her tasks in Minnesota would take depended on what she found and how cooperative various law enforcement agencies and prosecutors were. Two days *should* be enough if she started first thing in the morning.

Still taking the occasional ibuprofen for her hand, she eschewed her beta-blocker and flew to Minneapolis. She rented a car at the airport and checked in at a nearby motel.

The last thing she did that night was check for a message from Jenoff. Nothing—she'd called Ashley's bluff.

THE WARRANTS CAME THROUGH EARLY the next morning, and after an uneventful stop at Legacy House to raid the gun safe for a Kevlar vest and back-up weapons, she presented Mike's apartment super with a warrant. He gave her the key, and she threatened him with ten years in a federal prison if he told anyone about the search. He promised on his wife's first born. She flagged it as an odd vow and moved on.

Gloved up and bodycam on, she cleared the one-bedroom apartment, confirming no one was home, and photographing everything. The space was what she expected from a male single, federal agent. Guy-clean, meaning dust in the corners and a hint of mold tainting the bathroom. Spare furnishings, but humongous TV screens that dominated the living room and bedroom. The bedroom gun safe, big enough for a couple of handguns, was open and empty. Empty made sense if he had his guns with him, but she always locked her safe.

Her exhaustive search exposed no hidden storage areas, long guns, or any evidence of crimes. The LaserJet printer didn't have any stored documents she could force it to reprint.

She checked the fridge: nearly empty except for condiments and beer. Freezer had half-filled ice cube trays and a frozen pizza. Bathroom with generic men's stuff.

No photographs, nothing that you couldn't buy from a box store. Nothing personal. She had more personal stuff in her undercover apartment than Mike had here. It was like he lived here, but didn't *live* here.

Or he was getting ready to disappear.

A keyring holding his car key and apartment key was on the kitchen windowsill. She found his car, an older model Pontiac, parked on the next street. Unlike Mike's apartment, the interior and exterior of his ride looked pristine. Even under the floor mats vacuum marks showed—someone had scrubbed this car. She photographed everything. The glove box contained only his registration, insurance card, and a tire-pressure gauge. The only thing besides a donut spare tire and jack in the trunk was an unopened safety kit. Vacuum marks also decorated the trunk. Why had Mike done that? To remove evidence of the detonators? She'd leave that puzzle for the CSI people.

She pocketed the spare apartment key for future use and returned the keyring with the car key to the windowsill. With much searching, she found a storage unit key drowned in a bottle of dill pickles on the top shelf of the mostly empty refrigerator. She rinsed the storage key, donned a new pair of gloves, and tucked the key in her pocket.

She returned the apartment key to the super. The drive from town was uneventful and by 1330 she had found the storage facility and scouted the area for cameras. She didn't find any, but Mike might have them inside to warn him of intruders—a risk she had to take. She parked her car in a spot hard to see from the highway.

Gloved up and bodycam running, she photographed the outside. The key opened a padlock on the sliding door of an end unit. She pocketed the key, opened the door, and hung the open lock through the hasp. A gun safe big enough for five or six long guns occupied the unit's center. The patina of dust covering its top suggested it had been there for some time. The unit was clear of any cameras or sound-recording equipment. From scrapes and patterns on the floor she concluded Mike had once stored several boxes here, but nothing provided evidence of what they contained. The safe's electronic lock, clean from use, explained why she had not found a safe key with the storage unit key.

She stepped outside to improve her cell coverage and noticed a dark sky in the west. Smelled like rain was coming. A YouTube video showed her how easy it was to bypass the safe's locking mechanism: pry off the keypad, access the solenoid, and trigger it to fire, which would release the lock. The accompanying notes included a list of necessary tools.

FORTY MINUTES LATER SHE RETURNED to Mike's storage unit with her purchases from the local hardware store. In her absence a car had been and gone, leaving a set of tire tracks that cut across hers. No one around now.

She gloved up, restarted the bodycam and set her phone on continuous video and placed it where it could focus on her work. Two minutes and one minor shock later, she had the lock disabled. She repositioned the phone to record what was inside the safe when she opened it. Three rifles and a shotgun filled all but one of the five slots. A gun-cleaning kit in a plastic storage case sat on a shelf above. Multiple boxes contained .260 and .300 ammunition. Her pulse kicked up. Those were the assassination calibers.

On the floor were black contractor bags, each packed with heavy, waxy bricks giving off a sweet, oily scent. The missing C-4—enough to bring down a lot of buildings, bridges, or pipelines. She hadn't thought much about the missing guy with his explosives, but now she suspected Mike caused his death and these were the goods. The missing detonators were the ones she had overheard Mike mention to Zed while she had been listening from the cabin. Without detonators and wires, the stuff was safe.

Her hands were steady, but her mind raced, as she examined the rifles. One was a Savage 11/111 Trophy Hunter XP—the same model Olivia had used at the range. Another rifle was the same Remington Sendero model she'd seen in Christine's bunker.

Duplicate weapons, the last piece he needed to frame Olivia and Zed for the murders.

She read the serial numbers aloud for the video, photographed every angle, documented every piece of evidence.

This, surely, was enough to justify calling in the Bureau's crime scene experts to process the evidence. She'd let Park figure out how to involve them. She downloaded the secure app and typed "Good News! More—"

"Drop the phone and hold your hands away from your body."

The voice behind her was flat, professional.

Mike.

Sixty-Nine

WITH MIKE'S FINGER ALREADY INSIDE the trigger guard of a silenced pistol, Niki did not want to make any quick movements to startle him into pulling the trigger. He wouldn't make the mistake of shooting her in her chest. She eased the phone onto the floor, her objective to survive the next sixty seconds without a headshot.

She evaluated diving to the floor to disrupt his aim and pull her gun. Although she was fast, Mike only had to pull the trigger. No contest, and she'd learn for sure if there was an afterlife.

"Pull out your service pistol with two fingers," he said. "Put it on the floor and kick it to me." He had her do the same thing with her ankle piece. "Now move to the corner away from the safe. Good. How did you figure it out?"

She slid her feet sideways, maintaining balance. A trickle of sweat curled down her back and she was suddenly parched. Her voice sounded raw. "Evidence you left pointed to Zed and/or Olivia as the killers, but I couldn't get my head around them wiping prints from the computer and the files in the bunker. Why would Zed or Olivia do that when their prints were everywhere else? That got me thinking, and I replayed all our interactions. You knew the assassinations had used ammunition with two different calibers. The FBI withheld that information from the ATF, and I didn't tell you. The only way you could know was if you were the shooter. Or at least one of them. I was sure I was right when both your personal and undercover phones remained in Minnesota while you were targeting the executives. Why?"

"They poisoned my mother. The company knew they'd created a cancer hotspot. They buried the report, filled their pockets, and bankrupted the company. Greenwar found the records for me."

He shifted his weight, but the silenced pistol never wavered. "They were happy to deliver psychological punishment—protests, shame, bad press—but made it clear they drew the line at anything physical. No real justice."

His calm voice and smile were as frightening as his words. "I finished what they wouldn't. The first one was hard. The second easier. By the fifth,

I was just doing the world a favor. It was all going so well until you showed up." His smile vanished. "Now, your warrants mean my time's fast running out. You should have listened when I told you to bow out."

He wasn't *crazy* crazy. She could reason with him. *As long as he's talking, you're alive.* "I didn't see any cameras. How did you know I was here?"

"While I was at the bail hearing, the super texted me a video of your 'ten years in prison line.' You should have made a duplicate key and left the original in the pickle jar. I saw it was missing, drove here—you were gone, but I knew you'd be back. If you had brought a team, my only choice would be to run. But since you didn't . . . Well, it'll be your last mistake."

She pointed to the phone. "It's a live connection. They may not hear you, but they can definitely hear me telling them Mike Yoncey has a gun pointed at me."

He reacted like she had slapped him, then quickly recovered. "Good one. Kick that phone to me." His aim remained steady.

She walked to the phone, wondered if in dropping it she had sent the message to Park. Taking careful aim, she booted it across the cement to him. "The search warrants prove other people know where I am. Shooting me will get you the needle."

"If they find me." He kept his eyes on her while he picked up her phone with his free hand, pressed the power button. "Nice bluff. Screen's dark."

"Battery management. Only my fingerprint turns on the screen. We set it up that way so perps don't know we're recording them. ATF doesn't have that?"

The phone sounded a soft double-buzz. He flinched and nearly dropped it. Ironic if that was Jenoff finally reaching out.

He powered off the phone and tossed it outside. "You've got a brass set, I'll give you that. I'd prefer not to kill you in here, but I'll do it if you don't cooperate."

So my blood won't be in this unit. "Your objective is to escape, right? Killing me won't help that. Every second you waste here is a second closer to them showing up. By now the Bureau has contacted the local sheriff's office. If I were them, I'd be coming in silent with a flashing roof rack clearing my way. Take the explosives and the damn guns—without them there's no case—and leave me locked in. They'll waste all kinds of time figuring out if it's safe to open the unit."

"True. Why tell me this?"

While Niki had him talking, she had eased a few inches closer to the gun safe. Because she had the vest on, Mike needed a head shot to kill her. How much closer did she have to be to dive behind the safe and protect her head and neck? Sure, she would die if he severed a femoral artery. But if he rushed her, she'd have time to draw the extra Sig Sauer she had shoved in the back of her pants.

"Like you, I want to stay alive." The wheels in his head were turning; she had to show him an escape hatch. "The C-4's stable and the rifles aren't loaded, right? I'll toss them out. Not the nicest way to treat a rifle, but I'm sure you don't want me anywhere near the door." *Once she removed the C-4, could she pull the safe door closed and lock herself in?* She'd have the guns and ammo. He'd have the C-4 to blow her up.

"Killing scumbags is one thing," she said, "and I get that. Do you want killing me on your conscience? Take the guns, lock me in, and get the hell away from here. You have an escape plan. I can tell." She shifted her weight, like she'd been standing too long, brought her heels together closer to the safe. "False papers to leave the country and some money waiting for you. Your biggest problem is getting enough time before they come looking for you. Lock me in and leave." Two inches closer.

"Well," he said and released a long sigh. "I knew it wouldn't last forever. If you do as I say, I'll let you live. I can't just lock you in. You have enough ammo in there to carve a hole in the door and leave. First thing, toss out every one of your tools. If anything hits me, you're dead. Understand?"

"Sure." Niki shook out her left hand, like it had grown numb and wiped sweat from her forehead, gaining another foot nearer the safe.

"Then you'll close and lock the safe, which solves the weapons problem."

"Anything else?" With two more scooches, she could make her move.

"Stop talking. Move now. Or Die."

Shit. So close. Niki underhanded the tools, scattering them on the gravel away from Mike. She closed the safe door, having no opportunity to duck inside or behind, and spun the dial. The handle pulled up with an audible click.

At his command, she stepped past the safe, taking her farther away from the corner where he would lock the door.

"If you move a muscle before I get this door locked, I'll empty this weapon through the door and you die."

"I got it."

He stepped back and pulled down the screeching metal door. The instant he could not see her, Niki dove behind the gun safe, jammed her injured hand. Pain screamed up her arm, causing her eyes to tear. She crawled to the far side and pulled her second backup Sig, blinked away the pain and the tears.

The lock clicked.

Ashley remembered exactly where the lock was situated. She pictured Mike standing where she'd been when she'd opened it—maybe stepping right since he held a gun in his right hand and would use the left to close the lock. He was taller, he'd crouch. She aimed below the lock, where his gut or legs would be, and fired three rounds in a tight pattern, leaving three rounds left.

His return fire punched through the door at head height, hitting right where she had been standing. At his pause, she poked her weapon out and fired twice, guessing he would have moved to her right. She saved the last round in case he opened the door to finish her.

With the noise from the shots still reverberating in her ears, she had trouble hearing and began trembling. *Burning off the adrenaline.* She remained behind the safe until the shaking stopped, and her ears cleared enough to catch an engine starting. Tires on gravel pulling away.

He was running. For now.

She was locked in. Needed to get out before he returned.

Niki had never worn a smart watch, but right now the ability to send a text or email would have been nice. Useless thoughts.

Her ankle tracker was reporting her position. But since she had permission to be in Minnesota, no one would care unless it stopped moving—or if she tampered with it!

With scissors, she could cut it off. The tech guy had been so careful about keeping the electronic connections. She pulled and twisted. Three minutes later, all she had accomplished was to bruise her lower leg trying to pry the monitor off with her gun.

Next?

Light streamed through seven holes in the rear wall, but all she could see through them was the next row of storage units. Same thing for the one hole in a side wall, a ricochet? The clustered holes she had made in the front provided a wider view. She hoped to find Mike lying dead in front of the door or that a bullet had busted the lock. Nope to both. Mike was executing his escape or getting a bazooka to blow her up, or gasoline to pour under the door and roast her in a conflagration.

Aren't you the creative one? At least she had saved one last round for contingencies.

With the adrenaline drained, her aches and pains reminded her of all the abuse her body had taken the last two weeks. Remembering her beating at Quantico, she wondered if the text had been from Bianca Jenoff. What was happening with the proof of Gex's illegal activities? Was she taking action or helping Gex cover up?

Unable to sit still, she looked through the holes in the front. Her scattered tools and phone remained on the gravel. Her car was still there. Now she wished she had left it visible to the highway. How long before someone came by to check their unit and realized something was wrong? Before Mike returned to terminate her?

She took her pistol by the barrel and hammered the steel around the bullet holes.

SEVENTY

NO ONE CAME THURSDAY AFTERNOON. Or Thursday night. Ashley took comfort that meant Mike was not returning—but, she kept squinting through the bullet holes in the front door, expecting to see him standing there with a gas can.

Friday morning, she convinced herself someone would surely arrive late afternoon or early evening, given it was a weekend late in August with kids heading to college. By supper time—if she'd had something to eat—hope curdled. Her throat had gone from scratchy to raw, each swallow a tiny razor blade cut.

To keep busy, she resumed kicking the door with her heel. When her leg cramped, she switched to hammering with her pistol grip. The dents grew, but nothing broke. Not even a crack, if she was honest. She had never been and never would be a quitter.

She woke Saturday, parched with a headache behind her eyes that wouldn't quit. The rain she'd thought might happen on Thursday arrived in buckets. Thunder rolled all around her; a downpour rattled the roof. *Water, water, everywhere, nor any drop to drink.*

Mrs. Jensen, junior-year English. She laughed, except it came out a croak.

"Random, useless facts," she told the empty unit. "Yay brain!"

All day long, she continued her useless assault on the door. The dents deeper, but still no cracks. By evening, her stomach had moved past hunger to a hollow ache that radiated into her back. She couldn't remember when she had last urinated. Her tongue felt furry. She rubbed her cheeks to generate a little saliva. When she tried to swallow, her throat seized.

Tomorrow—one way or the other—was her come-to-Jesus day.

Night arrived with distant lightning flashes. She sat leaning against the door, weary arms resting in her lap. The rain had lessened to a pleasant drizzle. She tried her trick of finding comfort in a Glacier sunrise—but couldn't hold it. Instead, she kept seeing herself rocking on Seamus's screened porch, listening to the rain on the roof, watching birds at his feeders.

She promised herself that if she lived through this, she would make sure someone always knew where she was and what she was doing—someone who would come looking.

She wasn't afraid of dying, but the process wasn't attractive. In the distance, a lone mourning dove cooed. Such a sad, sad sound.

ASHLEY WOKE TO TIRES CRUNCHING over gravel. For a moment she didn't remember where she was or why every part of her ached. The memory came crashing back—trapped in Mike's storage unit.

She pounded on the metal door, pushed it back and forth while yelling to attract attention. She made such a racket, she didn't register someone was talking to her until she paused to breathe and heard, "Hold on. Hold on. I need to get bolt cutters to remove this lock."

"Don't go away," Ashley yelled. "I can slip a key under the door." She pressed the bottom of the door, creating enough room. A hand grabbed the key from her.

"Step away from the door," the woman's voice commanded. "This will take a minute."

Ashley leaned her ear against the door, heard steps walking away. The idling car revved up. She was leaving, damn it. Ashley kicked the door with all she had left. Then bright light flooded through the bullet holes in the front and under the door.

Putting an eye to the largest hole, Ashley watched a figure approach.

"This is Trooper Maggie Cloud, State Patrol. I'm going to get you out of there, but right now I need you to move away from the door so I can safely unlock it."

Ashley's training kicked in. The officer didn't know if she was armed and dangerous. "Yes, officer. I understand and am complying."

She shuffled back behind the gun safe. The padlock shackle scraped through the metal hasp.

The voice called, "You can open the door. Keep your hands where I can see them."

Ashley left her gun behind the safe—couldn't risk spooking the trooper—and walked to the door on legs that barely supported her. "I'm an undercover U.S. Marshal." She croaked the words out one word at a time. "My badge is in my car. Please stand so your body cam will not capture my face."

"You're what?"

Ashley focused on forming the words and added that this was a crime scene.

"I'll try. No promises. Remember, hands where I can see them."

Good as she could get. Ashley slid the door open partway and crawled through, face turned away, holding arms wide.

The fresh air hit her like a shot of speed.

"Whoa, easy." Trooper Cloud, a young female, took Ashley's arm and helped her to stand. "What's that smell? What the hell happened here?"

Ashley tried to answer, but her throat locked. She gestured weakly at the bullet holes. "Two days."

"You've been in there two days?" Cloud helped her sit with her back against the unit. "Don't talk. I have water."

She returned with a plastic bottle and made Ashley sip, pulling it away after each gulp. After a few minutes and half the bottle, Ashley told Cloud where to find her badge.

Cloud brought it back. "N. Iki? What kind of name is that?"

"Undercover. Call me Niki, but please don't use any name in your reports." Her voice came out jumpy and scratchy, like an old-time record. "My phone—" She pointed to it lying on the ground. "—has search warrants for this storage unit and an apartment in town. This gun safe contains weapons and what I think is C-4. No detonators. We must secure everything and then determine if the perpetrator—an ATF agent—is at his apartment. The nature of my undercover assignment means I can't allow other federal agents to see me."

"Whoa," Trooper Cloud said. "This is a federal case? I need to talk to the sergeant."

Turned out Trooper Maggie Cloud had been returning home from her ten-hour shift, recognized that Niki's rental had not moved all day, and stopped to check.

Niki discovered the phone battery was dead, or the day's rain had destroyed her phone. Trooper Cloud's phone had internet access. Niki accessed her email and showed Trooper Cloud the warrants. The trooper visibly relaxed and contacted the night duty sergeant. No officers were near, but he'd mobilize forces to keep eyes on Mike's apartment and provide support at the storage unit, including bringing energy drinks with electrolytes to prevent Niki from suffering water poisoning as she rehydrated. The bomb squad would take a little longer.

Remembering her promise, Niki received permission to call Seamus. He didn't answer—he wouldn't recognize the number—and she left a message telling him where she was and that she was okay.

During their wait for more officers, Cloud forced Niki to down a protein bar while Niki explained the gist of her involvement with Greenwar and ATF Agent Mike Yoncey.

Niki wasn't waiting for any bomb squad. It was her warrant, and she knew the shit wouldn't explode. While Cloud recorded, Niki used the tools to reopen the safe, this time without shocking herself. Once reinforcements arrived, a six-pack of sports drinks in hand, she transferred the evidence, including her backup piece, to state police custody. She and Trooper Cloud returned to Mike's apartment, where they met two other state troopers who reported they had scanned the apartment with thermal imaging and found it vacant.

Since it was Niki's search warrant, she unlocked the door with the key she had swiped. Despite the thermal imaging, they treated their entry as if Mike was there and cleared the rooms one at a time, recording as they went. Niki found her two pistols sitting on the kitchen counter next to Mike's silenced pistol. A bloody shirt lay in the sink. She followed a trail of blood drips to the bathroom and found Mike, eyes open but unseeing, on the floor. Room temperature, he'd been dead for a while. One of her shots had caught him in the right abdomen. He'd made it home and bled out. The ME would pin down the time of death, but now she knew why he hadn't returned to finish her.

She should feel something—at least sorry that a human had died from her actions. Even if he *had* tried to kill her. Maybe it would come later. Now, all she felt was anger at a federal agent who had betrayed his oath, his badge.

Betraying badges brought Gex to mind, and with him Jenoff. Had that been a text from her? No, she was grasping at straws, and it was late. Oh hell, swallow your damn pride and call. She borrowed Cloud's phone again, retrieved Jenoff's phone number from the cloud, and dialed.

Voicemail.

Seventy-One

ASHLEY SPENT THE REST OF the weekend sleeping and, when awake, dealing with the aftermath of incriminating ATF's Mike Yoncey in the executive murders, his theft of the C-4, and likely responsibility for the death of its previous owner. The first thing Barton did on arrival was to apologize for the screw-up that allowed Mike to catch her at the storage unit. Because the other Greenwar members couldn't afford bail, the ATF had arranged Mike's release earlier than expected, and no one thought to tell Barton.

"Or," Ashley said, "it was ATF payback for you—in their minds, the FBI—having an undercover agent you didn't tell them about screwing with their operation. And then you, not them, arrest the Greenwar people."

"I thought it was just a normal cock-up, the right hand not letting the left hand know what it was doing, but you might be right."

"Maybe if we had some women in charge, the swinging dick bullshit might change."

That at least got him to smile. "When they put me in charge, I'll see what I can do." He had sequestered her away from other federal agents and made sure all the paperwork attributed her actions to an "undercover U.S. Marshal."

Monday morning arrived with Ashley opening her eyes to another anonymous hotel room, momentarily disoriented about which city, which case, which version of herself she was supposed to be. She shuffled to the bathroom, caught sight of Niki's hard face staring back at her. Stripped to inventory the damage. Bruised ribs that hurt with anything more than a half-breath. Left hand still swollen despite the ice and painkillers. Tooth broken, mouth sore.

"Morning, gorgeous," she said to the mirror. "What's on today's agenda?"

Thinking about it, she found herself at sixes and sevens. Jenoff had never responded to her voicemails. Before she poked that bear again, she needed a plan—and a lawyer. Barton had everything on the Greenwar investigation he required from her—at least for now.

Three free days before she and her ankle monitor had to return to the D.C. area meant she could drive a rental and avoid another plane ride.

The brief endorphin rush of avoiding airplane travel crashed as she remembered her personal obligations. She was in the Twin Cities, and there were people here she should see. She should show her face at Pendergast Holdings. Before that, she should talk with Seamus and have him update her. She'd like to see her nephew Jacob. The idea of dealing with Chloe upset her stomach, but Jacob was worth it. She checked the Twins' schedule. They had a game tomorrow night.

Pulling off her plan was worth staying in the Twin Cities for two days and then flying to D.C.

She used the new phone she had bought at Mall of America and called Seamus. Left a message with her new number and a summary of what had happened. He'd worry otherwise, and she'd promised no more radio silence.

She got a dentist referral from her half-brother Garrett Pendergast and explained her wishes for creating a surprise for Jacob at tomorrow night's Twins' game.

"Junior's the one who had the sports contacts."

"Crud. Is there any way . . . ?"

"I'll try, but no guarantees."

Disappointing, but the most she could expect.

Miracle of miracles, the dentist had a morning cancellation. The problem was only a large chip, which he repaired by bonding on a veneer. "It's strong but weaker than a regular tooth." He advised her to avoid using that tooth to eat nuts or even chomp into an apple.

Looked like her luck was improving.

While at the dentist, Seamus had called back. "Tag," his voicemail said. "Call me soonest. It's important."

He answered with, "Are you still tied up with your—" he paused. "—other responsibilities, or can we meet? I didn't want to interfere, but we need to talk. In person, if possible, if you're still around. I'm at Pendergast offices in meetings all day."

Given what she'd gone through, she was surprised Seamus had not asked after her health. Something momentous was weighing on his mind.

He had a brief window at 1520 hours. She'd be there.

* * *

SHE ARRIVED A FEW MINUTES early and found Seamus in Pendergast's executive conference room. Watching him through the window before announcing herself, she decided he seemed worn down. She tapped on the door and walked in. "How bad is it?"

He gave her a hug, then held her at arm's length. "You look better than I expected, but are you sure you shouldn't be resting?"

"I heal by moving. I meant, what's so bad that you had to see me?"

He gestured her toward the chair next to his. "Lots happening you should know about. When Greenwar didn't release the information to expose Pendergast Holdings' bribery, Garrett and I forced the issue with the FBI. Garrett informed them that the company was going public and blaming *them* for the slow progress. After a hissy fit that changed no one's mind, the Bureau agreed to issue a joint statement in which they gave us credit for bringing the information to them and cooperating. The Board is very pleased."

Niki waved her hands to keep him talking.

"Paddy and I have been unraveling how Junior set you up. We can't prove Junior did it, but we can prove the money didn't come from any Pendergast Holdings' accounts. Without that link, I don't think the Feds can prove their case beyond a reasonable doubt. On the civil side, Junior's lawyers have offered a settlement that's not too—"

"Not a penny, Seamus."

"I told my lawyer the same thing. Two more pieces of company information you should know. Both good news."

More good news. Seamus was loading it on. What she wanted was the reason he had to see her. She motioned for Seamus to hurry.

"The board's Compensation Committee discussed your bonus as Interim CEO. They recommended grossing up the cost of the flights you took to and from D.C. in order to do your FBI work."

She rolled her eyes. "In English, please. Grossing-up sounds faintly disgusting."

Seamus rapped his head with his knuckles. Like *he* was the knucklehead? "The bonus will pay for your taxes on both the private flights and the bonus, so you come out even."

"This was your idea, wasn't it?"

He shrugged. Of course it was his idea. He knew she didn't want to take any of the money she had inherited from Robert Pendergast, but that the tax situation was a big problem. "Thank you."

Garrett stuck his head in the doorway. "Ashley, it's all set up. I'll take care of getting everyone else there. Your ticket will be at will call." She gave him a big hug. "See you there."

Excellent. She returned to her seat, and Seamus continued as if there had been no interruption.

"The Comp Committee is also recommending board compensation—cash, options, meeting pay. As non-executive board chairperson, you'll be well paid. And before you yell at me that you don't want it, let me remind you that you're currently homeless."

That landed. She *was* homeless. All her stuff was in storage.

"Given your responsibilities," Seamus said, "you should maintain residences in both the Twin Cities and wherever you want to live."

Wherever I want to live? He didn't say around D.C. Her mouth dried out, like it was day two in Mike's storage unit. What is he leading up to?

He held up a hand to forestall any interruption. "One last Pendergast thing. Chloe started her new job at Pendergast Holdings today. And she's attending AA and Gamblers Anon."

Niki remembered the shoebox with the $3,200 and the notebook with the coded writing she had locked in the gun safe. "She's the gambler? I thought that stuff was Bradlee's."

"They both were. Bradlee and Chloe met playing high stakes poker. The markers she mentioned were hers, not his. That's why Bradlee didn't let Chloe near their finances—not that he was a paragon of virtue. When things went bad for them, Bradlee turned to sex and cheating, Chloe to alcohol and gambling. Bradlee had hidden the shoebox from her and told Jacob where it was. I gave her the money. She didn't want the notebook, which was a record of winners and losers at each game. Said it would tempt her to think about gambling."

"Well, good for her. I wish her luck. You done?" Ashley heard the edge in her voice. "Because that bunch of good—great even—news does not justify needing to talk in person or that you look like someone just burned down your house."

"On Pendergast stuff, yeah."

"What is it?" Her fidgeting fingers now pressed into her thighs. Her chest a hollow gourd. "Are you sick? Something happen to your family?"

He wouldn't look at her, and her heart skipped a beat before thudding in her chest and pulsing in her ears. He'd always been healthy—well, other than the times he got shot or broke some bones. But he'd recovered from those. Cancer? She peered at his face. He hadn't lost weight. Was it grief? His mom was up in years. "Seamus, tell me. What is it?"

He pulled his phone from his pocket, squinted while pecking on its surface, and held it out to her. His hand was steady, but something in his expression made her reluctant to take it.

"What. Is. It?"

"Read."

She took the phone. Her eyes ached and wouldn't focus. She enlarged the text and read the heading "Snitches and Bitches" with the subheading "Truths from within."

The first paragraph was the usual white supremacist conspiracy garbage about how the government was undermining white males. She flicked her finger to skim the article and jammed her thumb down to stop the movement after her academy graduation portrait from Quantico flew past. She scrolled up and devoured the words: a well-placed source within the FBI had provided information about Ashley Prescott, an undercover agent going by the name Niki Foster, who had infiltrated militias in Michigan, Indiana, Virginia, and Maryland. The bitch was responsible for the arrest and false imprisonment of four hundred patriots for freedom.

The phone's screen blurred. She blinked the words back into focus and reread the lines pertaining to her. The court papers had never named her. Now 400 armed, violent felons knew who had put them in jail.

Gex did this to her, giving Jenoff the video. Unless Ambrose? No, this didn't benefit him or the Bureau. It was Gex. He'd leaked her information to a white supremacist website, putting her life at risk. He even sneaked in mention of the militia she had infiltrated, Patriots for Freedom. Most people wouldn't get the reference, but PFF people sure would. And they'd be gunning for her.

Her hands were shaking. She lowered the phone onto the table before she dropped it.

Seamus laid his warm hand on her shoulder and gave it a squeeze. "I have a Google alert for 'Niki Undercover.' This popped up early this morning. I contacted Park to get him to take it down. He said doing that feeds it; he plans to starve it. They have a way of minimizing the SEO— search engine optimization. By now, the only way to find it is to know the URL."

She took his hand and held it between hers. "I thought you were dying."

"No, I'm mourning Niki's death. Park says he wants to meet with you as soon as your work with the Svalinn investigation is over."

Which it was. Well, screw Park. No way she was giving up tomorrow night just so he could fire her a day earlier. She'd reserved tomorrow for Jacob's joy. Wednesday, she'd fly back to D.C. and face the fire.

SEVENTY-TWO

THE NEXT EVENING, ASHLEY SURVEYED Target Field's section fourteen from above and observed the Pendergasts sitting in the first row to the left of the first-base cameras. Chloe sat far left. Next came the two daughters, then Jacob, an empty seat, and finally, their uncle Garrett, who had used the Pendergast name and connections to make this all happen. The empty seat was hers. That was her plan, and she ached to join them and continue her connection with Jacob. Who knew, maybe even form one with the girls.

But in anticipating this moment, she realized it wasn't fair to Chloe. The woman had made great strides in the last weeks. Admitting she had problems with alcohol and gambling and going to meetings. Applying for, interviewing, and getting the job at Pendergast—and Seamus swore it was on her merits. Who knew how Chloe would react upon learning Ashley had been the trigger for this outing? If it went sideways and Chloe backslid, Ashley would be to blame. Garrett could decide whether to reveal Ashley's role. She'd enjoy this next surprise from afar.

The Twins' infield practice ended, accompanied by a blast of organ music to pump the crowd. Ashley watched the Twins' third baseman approach the visitor's dugout and meet with his opposite number. The Twins' bat boy ran to them and handed each third baseman a new baseball and—the part she had been waiting for—the Twins and White Sox third basemen walked together past the TV cameras and stopped in front of Jacob. A broadcast camera panned their section, projecting it on the jumbotron for everyone to see. She hid behind a pillar and watched the giant screen.

The players reached through the railing and each shook Jacob's hand. After some conversation, they borrowed a pen from Garrett and each inscribed a ball, Garrett recording it all with his cellphone. Jacob's smile was bright enough to power the entire city.

Rather than risk any of them spotting her and ruining Jacob's thrill, she moved to the other side of the stadium and watched the game from the nosebleed seats. At the end of the fifth inning, Chloe left with the girls, leaving Jacob and his uncle Garrett. She wanted to join them, be part of the family. She got up and plopped back down.

Chloe would have good reason to think Ashley was going behind her back. She might never get to see Jacob again. Even the Twins' winning in extra innings couldn't pull her from the funk.

On the way to her car, she received a text from Rick. She stepped out of the flow and stood under a streetlight. He, Tiny, a close former co-worker who worked on her Benedict Arnold undercover assignment infiltrating Patriots for Freedom, and Liya, her bestie and former roommate, had received orders to arrive at the Hoover building at 1530 hours on Friday. Did she have any clue why?

A lead weight pressed on her shoulders. Her first thought was it must have something to do with that "Snitches and Bitches" article. Then she realized it might be even worse. Those three had helped her on the assignment that had resulted in her resigning from the FBI. Were they being terminated because of her?

She texted Rick that she had heard nothing and then downloaded Park's secure app and checked for a message from him. Nothing. That made sense; she was supposed to be contacting him. Her phone said she had a new email in her Ashley Prescott personal account.

Deputy Director Ambrose asked her to be in his office on Friday, 1600 hours. He reminded her to arrive early enough to pass through screening.

Her stomach lurched, threatening to upchuck the beer and brat she'd had at the ballgame. He hadn't contacted her through Rick or Seamus. He'd used her personal email. In case the message disappeared from her files, she took a screenshot and texted it to Seamus as proof.

Looked like more revenge. Friday she'd find out.

SEVENTY-THREE

WEDNESDAY, ON THE FLIGHT BACK to D.C., the plane's Wi-Fi took bloody forever to download Park's secure app. Gex and Ambrose were taking all her headspace. She needed this meeting over with.

I'll be in D.C. in two hours. When do you want to meet?

The reply rocketed back: *Not until after Friday. I'll contact you.*

She stiffened reading his reply. The seatbelt contracted across her bruised ribs, each breath reminding her she'd damn near died twice on Svalinn.

She took a deep breath and eased the seatbelt away. Gave the phone the finger and killed it. Ambrose summons her, and now Park meeting her is no longer urgent. She hated this crap, but it sure made her decision to stay and watch Jacob at the game seem righteous.

Settled in a plain-vanilla motel room in suburban Virginia, she used the communication system Patrick had set up for her and Seamus to bring Seamus up to speed. Because the "invitation" was by email—not through Seamus or even Rick—she didn't know for sure it had come from Ambrose. FBI thugs had already spoofed texts to kidnap her once. Following the procedures she and Ambrose had set up for "Boern," she used Seamus, as the cut-out to contact Ambrose and confirm the meeting.

Seamus received no reply.

Rick, Tiny, and Liya reported no news about the Friday 1530 summons.

To test the waters, she contacted Barton and asked about the Greenwar investigation. He was curt, but she gleaned that ballistics had tied Mike's guns to the five murders.

Her undercover work had prepared her for being isolated, working inside the enemy's camp with limited intelligence. Whatever was going down on Friday, she'd be mentally and physically prepared to take what came and show them nothing.

Ashley installed a "find me" app on her phone. Wouldn't do any good inside the Hoover building because they'd take her phone—if she got that far. She also replaced a button on the slacks she'd wear with a tracker used in her FBI undercover work. She gave Seamus access to both. He argued against her going. After she made it clear that was *not* an option, he promised to monitor her all afternoon until she informed him she was safe. Friday after lunch, they spent an hour agreeing on the specifics of which details about her secret agreement with Ambrose and Park Seamus was to leak and to whom—if she disappeared.

ASHLEY ARRIVED EARLY FOR HER 1600 appointment, but late enough that Rick and company had already cleared security before their 1530. After giving up her phone and receiving a visitor's badge, an escort arrived by elevator. The woman wore no badge. No identification. With a blank expression, she gestured toward the elevator.

Ashley fingered the tracker button on her slacks. Seamus would know where they took her.

They exited onto the executive floor, and the woman delivered her to an empty conference room. "Wait here. They'll collect you in a few minutes." The click of the door closing sounded like a trigger pull.

The buzz of the fluorescent lights was as disconcerting as the horde of mosquitoes she'd faced in the woods at Christine's camp. She'd forgotten the executive floor kept the A/C at refrigerator temps. They might have the room under observation, and she refused to rub her arms. She paced, doing laps around the table, pulled out a chair, sat for all of thirty seconds, paced some more.

On the dot of 1600, the door opened. Ashley faced it, hoping to see Ambrose but found herself trading stares with Special Agent Bianca Jenoff.

Of course. Gex and Jenoff had flipped the damn script on her, and they'd co-opted Ambrose. *Remember, show nothing.*

Jenoff closed the door behind her. "Where's your hair?"

Ashley rubbed her buzz cut, buying time to process. Jenoff looked like she hadn't slept in days. Her voice had none of its usual edge. Ashley mirrored that tone. "I'm here as me. I have nothing to hide. What have—"

"He suckered me." Heat entered her voice. "I swear I didn't know what Gex was doing. Please sit." She pointed to the end of the table farthest from the door. "And whatever he says, please don't speak."

She had to know. "My friends—"

"Are fine. Won't be long."

Whatever that meant. Jenoff remained standing. Ashley adjusted the chair to face the door and sat, projecting a picture of calm as spiders crawled inside her. She tried bringing up the image of a favorite spot in Glacier. Nope. Seconds stretched to minutes, and thoughts whirred through her head, none lasting long enough to land an emotional blow.

A quick double tap sounded at the door. It opened, revealing Gex, his eyes on Jenoff, a smile lighting his face. No escort.

Ashley's hand flew to her mouth, her heartbeat redlining.

Gex reached toward Jenoff with both hands, as though to hug her. Jenoff stepped back. "Alexander Gex, I have a warrant for your arrest. Turn around, get down on your knees, and put both hands on your head and interlace your fingers."

The smile froze on Gex's face. He started to comply, eyes wild, spotted Ashley, and bristled. "You!" Not a word. An accusation. "Gloat while you can, Prescott. I promise you and yours will rue this moment until your dying day."

Jenoff repeated her command. Behind Gex, the FBI director stepped into view, and Gex complied while spewing continuous venom, mostly at Ashley, but also at Jenoff, the traitor.

Ashley stood, taking it all in. Feeling everything, feeling nothing, showing nothing.

The director walked to Ashley. "Prescott," he said, "thank you for coming. I wanted you to see this and what happens next. I'll lead us from this room. Special Agent Jenoff will follow with the prisoner. I want you several steps behind her. Keep that distance as we enter the next hallway. I assure you, you're safe. Do not respond to anything anyone says to you. Special Agent Jenoff will then take the prisoner for processing, and I would like you to accompany me.

On leaving the office, she heard a murmur of gathered voices over Gex's rant. The group ahead of her turned into the next corridor, and the murmuring stopped. Rounding the corner, her feet refused to take another step. Lining the hallway was a gauntlet of fifty people, maybe more. All dressed in shades of dark blue with white shirts or blouses. American flags decorated every lapel. She looked down at herself: pressed tan slacks, patterned short-sleeved blouse, flats. Outsider.

Show nothing.

She forced herself forward, keeping the requested distance, and noted familiar faces: Deputy Director Ambrose—expression neutral. Rick gave her a subtle thumbs-up. Tiny and Liya—safe, still employed. The two special agents tricked into kidnapping her to Quantico—miserable. Barton, arms crossed, stern face. The rest a blur.

And there—smirking, was her ex-, Martin Prescott, who they had hauled down from the Boston office. Her left kidney throbbing with phantom pain. *And this is for not screwing Martin.*

She walked by, spine straight, expression blank, refusing to acknowledge his presence or that they shared a last name.

After they passed through the gauntlet, two agents joined Special Agent Jenoff. The three led Gex toward an elevator bank. Had the director chosen late Friday afternoon to deny Gex a bail hearing until Monday? Or had he chosen the time to bury any press coverage during the weekend? The director waved for her to join him. "We're convening in the auditorium. Grab a seat in the back. I want you to hear what I say. After, we'll talk."

She sat in the rear at one side where no one noticed her. The director spoke without notes. He stated they had arrested Gex on a variety of felonies, the exact charges would become known through the court system process. However, he wanted everyone to understand that Gex had left the Agency because he had intentionally sabotaged an undercover assignment he was in charge of, putting the lives of fellow agents in jeopardy, and creating a threat to public safety. He had done this to further his personal career.

The director believed everyone present had either been Gex's victim during his tenure with the FBI or had abetted Gex's post-retirement harassment of those he held responsible for his dismissal. Each of them knew which camp they fell into. To the first group, he apologized for having failed them. To the second, he guaranteed that if he heard of any continuing harassment, he'd quickly and severely punish the perpetrators.

There were no questions.

Niki waited for the director to find her. She rose at Barton's approach. "Pendergast, the director and I want to make you an offer. We want you to return to the Bureau and work at Quantico. Seems we need an arms instructor."

A bribe if there ever was one. Ambrose and the director were still worried she would make public the Agency's dirty linen. They were fighting enough PR fires; they couldn't afford another one. Had today's entire performance been to keep her quiet. There would be no news of Gex's arrest unless she leaked it, or some reporter lucked onto the arrest record. "Are you retiring?"

"The director asked me to take charge of Quantico. I accepted on the condition I could hire the personnel I wanted. I want you. Not only can you shoot, but you and Special Agent Jenoff will be an inspiration for all the women we train. Plus, I know you will disabuse any jerks who think they are superior based on their chromosomes. And I trust the hell out of you. What can I do to convince you?"

She shot back, "I thought you told me to trust no one in the Bureau?"

"I did. But you aren't in the Bureau, and I want to correct that. After which, of course, I won't trust you. I'm sure you'll make my life impossible because you won't follow my rules."

Despite herself, she snorted. What was she feeling? Conflicted? Deep down, she desperately wanted to be an FBI Special Agent. But that might be pride talking—to show the world they couldn't run her off. Could she make a difference? Maybe, but others were better teachers: had the patience, the natural ability to relate. Empathy was the word she was searching for. That wasn't the kernel of her truth, though. She wanted to be on the front line, fighting to keep her country safe. Training future agents was vital, just not *her* vital. To be close to the action and not in it would kill her. She'd shrivel and die of boredom. Or resort to booze to deaden the pain.

"Thank you. And thank the director for me, if he did actually want me back." She waved off Barton's protests. "I may have the skills. I do not have the temperament. Neither one of us would be happy."

He leaned in, invading her space. "Your decision isn't because of how you've been treated, is it? I told the director you were a bigger person than that."

"That's history, and truth is, it's impossible to undo the damage. But you said it yourself. I'm not built to follow rules that don't allow me to get the job done. Despite the setbacks of these last few weeks, they were some of the best of my life because I did what I knew I had to do."

"Swear to me you are not recording this conversation?"

"I surrendered my phone at security."

"Come on, Pendergast. You worked undercover and have access to all kinds of electronic doodads."

True that. She held up her hand. "Swear."

He leaned in, his voice a whisper. "They'll only charge Gex with the crimes he committed after he left the Bureau. Besmirch the man, not the institution. You want the whole truth told, it's on you." Leaning back he continued in a normal voice. "Can I hire you from time to time to run surveillance classes for us?"

Ashley felt a smile warm her face. "That *would* be fun. If we can arrange it, then sure, I'm game. And I want you to know I've taken some of your advice."

His eyebrows quirked. "A first. What advice?"

"Before I forget, thank you for giving me insight into Jenoff's motivations. Without that, this afternoon wouldn't have happened. Seeing my ex- here today crystallized my decision to ditch the Prescott name. Not returning to Pendergast either, too much baggage. I'll let you know what I decide and where I settle. That way, if you want me to teach your charges how to spot and lose surveillance, you can contact me." She offered her hand. "Deal?"

They shook. He gave her a playful tap to her shoulder. "I had to try. Catch you later, Ashley."

Her body reacted like he had punched her in the gut. Barton had called her by her first name. Not Prescott. Not even Pendergast. Ashley, a civilian name. She was officially out of the fold.

Seventy-Four

0300 HOURS FOUND ASHLEY STARING at the motel ceiling, replaying an endless loop of the afternoon—Gex's arrest, Barton's offer, his calling her Ashley, her leaving the Bureau and lying to Seamus, telling him she was fine.

No sooner had she recovered her phone from FBI security than the barrage started—former colleagues crawling out of the woodwork offering congratulations and support. Where had these cockroaches been when she'd needed them? She'd stopped reading at 2100 hours and turned off her phone at 2300 hours—already twenty-seven unread messages.

Saturday afternoon, she struggled to let go of her anger after Ambrose's email arrived. Three fucking lines:

Thanks for handling the Svalinn operation.

And keeping Jim Ford alive.

And not embarrassing the Agency.

He signed it, *All the best, DD Ambrose.*

Barton was right. The director had engineered everything to give the Bureau maximum protection. Ambrose was covering his ass like all the Bureau's so-called leaders. She visualized holding her pillow over Ambrose's face until his legs stopped twitching.

She read it again. *Thanks for handling.* Like she had picked up his dry cleaning. *Keeping Jim Ford alive.* No mention of nearly dying. Twice. *Not embarrassing the Agency.* That was what really mattered to him.

She stabbed her finger on the trashcan symbol, deleting the message.

After that, she stopped reading any more. Her anger drifted away. She'd won, so why did she feel like crap? Because she didn't have a job. Because she wondered how much of the director's fine speech had been to fend off external investigations or a lawsuit by her rather than being heartfelt and real.

What had she accomplished? She'd refuted Gex's lies. In a few years no one would remember or care. Unless someone squealed, no one would ever learn who had arranged her kidnapping or beat her up at Quantico. And even if that happened, she'd bet they'd quietly retire, another sordid Bureau chapter swept under the rug.

No firings, no reassignments—just a warning to the sycophants to be careful. Tiny, Rick, and Liya were still at risk.

When had *she* ever done anything to embarrass the Bureau? The Bureau had done plenty to embarrass itself. If anyone in the FBI broke the implicit agreement, she'd let loose with both barrels. And she wasn't lying to save the Bureau if internal investigations or some congressional committee dug into things.

Sunday afternoon she created a list with two columns: Trust. No Trust. Gex headed the no-trust list. His "You and yours will rue this moment" threat was real. Rick, Tiny, and Liya went in the first column—they'd always had her back. Ambrose fell under Gex on the second list. Barton—she hesitated. He'd been square and right about Bianca Jenoff. Despite his continued insistence that Ashley should trust no one in the Bureau, she wrote him in the first column. Park? He hadn't disappointed. Yet. That "yet" was the problem. If she came between him and his mission, he'd crush her and walk away without a regret.

Feeling that jaded ate at her. Being unemployed sucked. Not that she was *unemployed* unemployed. She had all her Pendergast Holdings duties. If that was all she had to live for, she might have to slit her wealthy wrist.

That got her wondering how Seamus was doing. She added him and his son to her list of trustworthy individuals. Six people in the entire world she found trustworthy after thirteen years in federal law enforcement. How sad.

If each of them made a list, would she be in column one?

Not if they knew. Hell, Seamus belonged at the top of her list in bold capitals, and she was lying to him right now: telling him she was physically and mentally fine. The physical was mostly true. He deserved better. They all did. They'd all paid prices for her choices and she'd let them.

She crumpled the paper. The real question gnawing at her wasn't who to trust. It was whether she was any different from Park. Would she sacrifice the people she cared about over what she thought was right? Were ideals more important to her than the people she was with?

She stared at her phone for ten minutes, wondering how to even start her apology to Seamus. Knowing it was a delaying tactic, she checked Park's secure app. One message left that morning:

10:00 Monday. Trappist Abbey. Come in disguise. Use Uber. Tell no one.

She checked her ankle—the monitor was still there. The circular band had become second nature to her. Another caution that, if you weren't careful, you would adjust to things that should stay foreign.

One more mysterious summons: another test, or a different game? She'd go, of course she would. But she'd tell Seamus and have him track her.

After she apologized.

Seventy-Five

Ashley arrived in a Lyft ride, not Uber. The conversation with Seamus Sunday night had been harder than facing Gex. While pacing the motel room, she'd admitted everything—the lies, the half-truths, the "I'm fine" when she was anything but, the Trust/No Trust lists. He'd listened without interruption until she'd run dry. After asking if she was done, he made an observation.

"If you actually trust a person, you let them under your shell. I'm not saying you tell them everything. Every person has parts of themselves they don't want anyone in the world to know about. But what you do? That's not trust. That's using people—even if they don't mind being used."

She collapsed to the floor, bawled so hard and long, her eyes no longer had tears to shed. Snot covered the back of her arm from wiping her nose so often. Her ribs ached—not from being shot—from understanding the truth: she was at the top of list two.

When she controlled herself enough to speak coherently, she said, "A decade we've known each other. I wish you'd have told me earlier. I could have changed."

"You weren't ready to change. I think you are now. I guess we'll see."

Then he had focused their conversation on her meeting with Park. Of course he'd monitor her apps. He, not she, had pointed out she needed to find a mode of transportation Park couldn't suborn. Old school, he suggested a traditional taxi. She chose Lyft, setting up a new account using one of the fake IDs she had not yet used.

She found Park sitting on a bench overlooking the river-rock stones marking the cemetery graves. He patted the seat beside him and without preamble asked, "What did you learn from these three weeks?"

She placed her knapsack on the ground next to the simple bench and sat, feeling its warmth through her pants. The Assistant Director of National Intelligence wouldn't care squat that she was still a little tired and sore and her thirty-six-year-old body took longer to recover. "That I was damn lucky to survive the Svalinn operation. Ambrose rushed it into existence. I should have never said yes. That doesn't mean it shouldn't have been done or take three months to get going, like the FBI requires. To quote one of my softball coaches, 'You can't get hits if you don't swing.' We can't be a government of chickenshits We have to keep swinging, even if that means we sometimes strike out."

Park waited, hands folded.

"And I let you talk me into tackling Mike Youncey with no backup. That's all fixable, but not for me. My use-by-date has passed."

"Has it?" Park's smile did not reach his eyes. "Or have you just been playing with second stringers?"

No one at the FBI considered themselves second stringers. *Show nothing. Hear him out.*

Like he'd read her mind, he said, "The Bureau is filled with professionals, but Ambrose acted like an incompetent amateur. I agreed to let the FBI director and Barton make their pitch. If that's what you wanted to do, you weren't the person I thought, and I would gladly cut you loose."

Who *did* he think she was?

"Your undercover career at the FBI is deader than dead. Beorn, working independently of any agency can be very much alive if you want her to be. Here's what the first string has already done. We suppressed access to that *Snitch and Bitch* piece that outed you. It generated only five comments and got little traffic. For now it's a zombie. We'll soon kill it. Within a month or two, we'll have all the people involved under surveillance. Based on their website, I'll bet they have illegal guns, are sex offenders, or are pushing fentanyl. They'll be behind bars, the website will vanish. Besides, you're hardly recognizable from that picture from years ago. You're planning to jettison your Prescott last name. Niki Foster won't work in some situations. But from what I heard, you prefer to simply use Niki, anyway. Lots of those around."

She stopped herself from chewing on the inside of her cheek. Was this a resurrection or where he drove the silver stake through her heart. "I sense something more."

"We're experiencing a massive growth in militia movements across the country. Most of them are predictable—routine white supremacist, male-dominated groups following the same old playbook. Not to say they aren't dangerous, but the Bureau is adept at infiltrating them. Patriots For Freedom and a couple of others worry me more. They aren't white supremacists, and we can't discover their funding. Niki is not dead, but soon I fear many *will* die. If you continue this extremely risky work, I can't promise a long life."

"I don't have a death wish, but I have no illusion about the risks. Gex is the one who exposed me to the 'Snitch and Bitch' people. He'll do it again."

"No, he won't. Gex already understands that if he plays ball, he gets a cushy prison. If not, we stick him in with the worst of the worst, where every inmate knows he's a former cop. Barton said it, you can't trust anyone in the Bureau right now. Tons of good people; leadership sucks. No more Bureau. No more Ambrose. That also means no more Rick."

Hearing the finality of his "no more Rick," hit her harder than she anticipated. Rick with his junior-high humor she pretended to hate. Rick who had always had her best interests in mind, even when she thought just the opposite. He'd taken risks, been summoned to the gauntlet because of her, slid her a thumbs up under the watchful eyes of the brass.

"He'd have to leave the Bureau. It's in his blood. He'll understand. It's just you and me."

She nodded. She understood because it had been in her blood.

"I like your Seamus McCree," Park continued. "And I like the idea of someone knowing where you are and what you are doing. If Seamus will do that for you—for us—that's our team."

"Why Seamus? Why not one of your people?"

Park was quiet a long moment. "Because I don't know who my people are anymore." He met her eyes. "The government is under attack from without and from within. I have assets, intelligence officers, analysts—and I can't be certain who is loyal. Seamus McCree is a private citizen with no allegiances to any agency, no career to protect, no supervisor to report to. And he's proven he'll go to the mat for you."

Holy shit. Park didn't know who was loyal? "How do you know I'm loyal?"

He chuckled. "Ashley, no mole would ever join the FBI and do the things you've done."

No normal mole, but a truly excellent mole might. "You've vetted Seamus?"

"Before I agreed to use him as a cutout. He's clean. More importantly, he's loyal. To you, not to any institution. That's what we need. Here is what I propose: Be Ashley until you clear up the criminal charges and that civil suit against you. Could be months. Could be a year. You use that time to recover, train, keep your Mandarin sharp. I'll use that time to airbrush your past. When you're clear, we'll create a backstory to cover the missing months and reintroduce you into Patriots For Freedom. We've learned your old captain is with a new cell. He's a good in for you. My number one objective is to uncover their leaders and their funding. You've already made contact with their arms dealer, Sam. We'll leverage that."

She watched the wind riffle the cemetery grass. There was a problem with his not being sure of anyone's loyalty. "If you can't trust your people, how can you support me?"

"We'll tap any resources we need. They'll never know why or what for or who you are. Never use the same person twice. Nothing written for snoops to find. Encryption only the three of us can read. You'll have all the support you need, but you'll also be on your own in ways you've never experienced."

"Financing? Pay?"

"Dark government pockets. As long as we keep it under eight figures a year, it's not an issue. Contractor rates for you. Six figures plus expenses. I'll negotiate with Seamus."

Thinking about the hassle she'd had trying to get Ambrose to approve cutting a lock and trespassing, she asked, "Rules of engagement?"

"Don't get caught. Don't get killed. Use your judgment."

This was it. Last chance to walk away, be just Ashley Prescott—or whatever name she decided to call herself—board member and trust fund recipient. Safe. Comfortable. Bored out of her mind. A big bird circled overhead. Vulture? That could be a bad omen, not that she believed in signs. Light caught its head. Pure white. Eagle.

"I have conditions."

Park looked amused. "Do you now?"

"Seamus knows everything. Not operational details that could compromise security, but he knows I'm alive and where I am. Always. Non-negotiable."

"Agreed. What else?"

She lifted her knapsack. "You approve my Svalinn expense reimbursements without giving me shit."

"Should I give you shit?"

"They're all good, but that's not the hard part. I want the payment to come out of Ambrose's FBI budget."

He tilted his head back and let loose a long and hearty laugh, the first time she had seen him anything but serious and focused. He tossed her the fob to the Porsche. "I heard you prefer driving, and I have some expense reports to approve."

She settled into the Porsche 911, brought the seat forward so her feet reached the pedals, and ran through the gearbox to make sure she knew its idiosyncrasies. The engine started with a sharp bark that settled into a throaty idle. She pressed the button to retract the soft top and lowered the windows. In first gear, the beast vibrated, straining against the brake like a caged animal.

She ripped off her wig and flipped it onto the micro rear seat. "You, Assistant Director of National Intelligence Park, had better buckle up."

I hope you enjoyed reading this story. To help me reach other readers, I would appreciate your posting a short review of *Niki Unleashed* on your favorite retailer or review website.

Author's Note

This story takes place in 2020, which is when I wrote the first draft. As with the previous novel, *Niki Undercover*, I chose to ignore COVID-19 because including it would cause all sorts of complications for the characters without adding substance to the story.

With the time delay between when the story takes place and its publication, the world has not stayed constant. To stay true to the story, I have ignored any events that occur after the story's timeframe. Sharp-eyed D.C. residents might notice a reference to a trail called the Melvin C. Hazen Trail that no longer exists. In 2021, the National Park Service renamed it to the Reservation 630 Trail. Delta Airlines has changed its flight schedules, so please do not use Niki's itineraries to plan your next trip.

I like to read stories that use actual places and businesses, and I include them in my stories. I also make up things—this is a work of fiction. There is no Greenwar offshoot from Greenpeace. There are many trade organizations and lobbying organizations in Washington, D.C., but American Hydrocarbons Institute is not one of them. Niki's prior work (detailed more fully in *Niki Undercover*) infiltrating militia groups and unmasking foreign arms suppliers also references organizations I made up. You can search a long time in the woods surrounding Minong, Wisconsin, but you won't find Christine's camp, the marsh, swamp, and hill, or the roads and bridge I described in that area.

Some ankle monitors include microphones. Where audio exists, it's generally used for live check-ins/identity confirmation and sometimes to sound an alarm. State laws and law enforcement policies govern their legal use. My paranoia says that anything that *can be* hacked *will be* hacked, and that includes the fictional ankle monitor used in this story.

Many people helped improve this novel. My beta readers. Clinton Bell, Dawn Marks, Denis Parsons, Donnell Bell, and Rita Stull offered suggestions and asked questions that allowed me to make the story tighter and stronger.

I want to give a special shout-out to my ARC readers. They spot typos that tenaciously remain unobserved through multiple drafts, eighty-seven read-throughs, and multiple proofreads, or that snuck in at the last second through an errant finger striking the keyboard or a failed search and replace. Their eagle eyes allow me to correct them before you read this novel. My ARC readers are also invaluable because they give ratings and post reviews so other readers can learn whether the book is something they'd like to read. Thank you, thank you to everyone who takes the time to leave ratings and reviews.

Jan Rubens is always my first, last, and best reader. Any mistakes that remain are mine, and I take full responsibility for them. But I hate mistakes, so if you find a typo or layout error, please let me know so I can correct it for future editions.

My email is jmj@jamesmjackson.com. I love hearing from readers and try to respond to all my email.

James M. Jackson
Amasa, Michigan

James M. Jackson authors the Seamus McCree and Niki Undercover Thriller series.

Jim has also published an acclaimed book on contract bridge, *One Trick at a Time: How to start winning at bridge.*

He calls the deep woods of Michigan's Upper Peninsula home. You can find out more about Jim or sign up for his Readers Group newsletter at his website, https://jamesmjackson.com.